Kaleigh's Protector

Nicole A. Brown

PublishAmerica
Baltimore

© 2006 by Nicole A. Brown.
All rights reserved. No part of this book may be reproduced, stored in a retrieval system or transmitted in any form or by any means without the prior written permission of the publishers, except by a reviewer who may quote brief passages in a review to be printed in a newspaper, magazine or journal.

First printing

All characters appearing in this work are fictitious. Any resemblance to real persons, living or dead, is purely coincidental.

ISBN: 1-4137-9635-4
PUBLISHED BY PUBLISHAMERICA, LLLP
www.publishamerica.com
Baltimore

Printed in the United States of America

This book is dedicated to my husband James and my son Nicolas for all the support they have given me, and to Kristi Collier Thompson who always pushed me to do better.

Prologue

The vast trees spread their taunting leaves through the stale night as a warning that all who enter would die an unmerciful death. Neither humans, nor animals that spoke of a mortal life were allowed entrance through these woods of wicked. One false step and the norms of the human body would burst into internal flames, shouting their cries over the distant town.

To the humans that is.

Not to the soulless immortals created from three sacred animals that impale the world with their magic and strength, destined to destroy the demons created from the depraved human souls. They were known as the guardian, the saviors of humans.

The guardians were allowed to enter the woods, but to prevail, only suffered the great consequences of losing their powers to the highest form of demon that stalked these woods known as a guardian hunter.

Magic and strength were futile against this type of demon for its wisdom in the art of manipulation in deception was greater in power than any has known to the immortals.

The demon was waiting, full of patience, for his mystic woman to arrive to get one last use of her body before he cast her spirit into his. He had waited an eternity to have this opportunity and finally after centuries, he was going to get what he had always dreamed: his place to rule next to his master.

Tonight was going to be that night, and the pure soul he had tricked to love him was going to be his sweet victory.

"You shouldn't go, Lucia," said Mace as he pulled her back from the entrance of the woods and turned her around to face him.

Lucia instantly took a step away from her only friend and courageously smiled. "It'll be all right. I know what I am doing. Can you please trust me?"

Mace's human soul and the wolf's basic instinct inside of him were giving him every indication that Lucia was about to enter the woods that would lead to her death, and for that insight, he must stop her from making a terrible mistake. He knew she and the other six pure souls were the only ones that could destroy a guardian hunter without any repercussion, but they were not supposed to fall in love with them. The guardian hunters were tremendous in their efforts to manipulation, and if he found out that this pure soul was in love with him, he would use it to his advantage in every possible way.

"It's not about trust; it's about your perception of this situation, Lucia! Guardians are never to fall in love because it is our greatest downfall. Sure, you can't lose your powers like us, but you have no defense against him if he ever discovers your secret."

"I want him to know."

"What!" Mace screamed. "You are not serious, are you?"

Lucia nodded. "I am. It's my defense against him—Mace, don't turn around from me," Lucia said as she caught his arm and swung him around to face her. She reached up and stroked his cheek and saw the fire in his eyes dying.

"Listen to me, Mace. This is one of the strongest guardian hunters that we have ever faced. With our connection he's still too powerful for us to defeat, but I have found the solution to our problem if I can get the pure souls connection before he knows my secret."

"And what is that?" Mace asked.

She frowned as she looked over her shoulders to the darkened woods that were brewing with malevolence and torment of the lost souls that would be forever trapped with the demon until she freed them. In all the centuries she has been destroying demons, she never thought she would actually find love in the one thing she was forbidden to ever get involved with. He came to her one night, buying her services for the hour to use her for his release, and wound up falling in love.

She tried dramatically to change her heart's mind, but the heart wanted what it wanted, and that was a guardian hunter.

Over the course of his comings, she promised to refuse him, and use her powers to destroy him for what he was. Each time he came back to her again, she allowed him back in her bed, free of charge, and dwelled in the rapture he gave to her body. Then he would leave, and she would vow to promise the same thing by destroying him the next time he visited her. But something kept her from refusing him every time she saw his face. She didn't know what it was until she discovered it was love.

If she had the courage to stay away from him she wouldn't have to use her love as bait to lure him into his hell. The pure souls said it was the only way to destroy him.

Lucia faced Mace and hid her anxiety that was contradicting with her overwhelming feelings for Leo. "I have to open up to him."

Mace cleared the space between the two of them by grabbing her shoulders and shaking her senseless. "Have you gone mad?" he yelled.

Tighter, he gripped her shoulders and gave her another hard shake. "What are you thinking? Do you realize what will become if he was to get the other pure souls existence?"

"It won't happen, Mace! My love is the only way to defeat him because it will be his weakness once he feels what I feel. The pure souls will be waiting for my connection."

Quickly he said, "It will never work," and then added with a softer voice, "Please don't do this."

"I have to," she whispered.

Mace sighed and nodded as his face became a stone of impassive emotions. The humans were screaming for him to drag her away from her death, but he knew it would be useless as her divine plan to destroy the strongest guardian hunter that had ever graced them with their presence. Lucia would not go with him nor would she be forced to go with him. She would come back another night to achieve the pure souls' triumph, though, he knew this would be a marking of a great error of the guardians.

"Then go, Lucia."

He stepped away from her and vanished into the mystic of the wind. Lucia sucked in her breath and entered the woods.

The guardian hunter had a different view about her. The deities above with their useless powers found a weakness that was a weakness to all demons, and for hundreds of years it has nearly successfully worked, and to triumph they had never managed to destroy him. He was far too powerful, beyond their reach. But what do you expect when the ones that were supposed to destroy him were women?

Women!

They were weak creatures made from the flesh of a man to bring temptation and chaos to the world with their emotions and bodies. They were the reason why men suffered from wars, illness, and weakness. Men had this internal ambition to conquer, control, and rule—all this death and destruction for their mates.

They wanted to be the most powerful, to be the strongest, and to be the richest so women would swoon at their feet, and they would have all men jealous of their great fortune.

They had been doing since the beginning of time and would never stop until the end of time.

Tonight, the guardian hunter was going to ignore the temptation of the blessed woman they had brought forth to him and break her into submission. She would tell him of the others, the other six spiteful little bitches. They weren't in hiding; they still walked among the world, disguised as poor berated whores that led to most of the demons obliteration. They purposely, internally blocked their spirits so they couldn't be found, and chose their wicked profession to lure demons to their deaths.

Stupid, repugnant, unsullied demons thinking more with their cocks than their missions to the demon master. They deserved no immortality. They deserved no powers that the master gave them by the darkness. What they deserved was every pain they received by the guardians and pure souls.

But not him.

He would not give into temptation tonight! If he could destroy her there wouldn't be another to chase him or others of the darkness. He would finish his mission and be by placed by his master's side for the ruling of the world.

A smile flickered on his face.

The pure soul was a fairly young peasant girl that prostituted herself so she could eat for the rest of the week. If that wasn't wicked enough than what was? They should have someone come after her and destroy her for what she represented.

At least his master gave him riches and glory. *Their* master; whoever that may be, only gave them sacrilegious immortal life and enough power to destroy a demon. He was glad he chose the darkness instead of tortured years in a prison chamber.

Lucia was not going to destroy him. She loved him and he was going to use that against her to get her to open up to him and let him into her "pure" spirit soul, which would give him everything that every guardian hunter has long to know: the pure souls' spirits.

She had no leverage that could make him weak. He used the face he created to visit the tavern where she whored herself and seduced her by his charm that she actually gave him no charge; she paid for it all on her own.

This was going to be his victorious night! His master would be so pleased with him.

He summoned her and then she appeared before him. She was covered in dirt, sweat, and grime and she smelled like a variety of mens' come and a wet dog on his worst day. Her clothes were tattered, ripped, and were filthier than her face. He noticed that since he had known her that the girl never changed clothes. She wore the same yellow (that once was white), low-cut dress to expose her full, ripe bosoms.

The girl looked about twelve, but under the ruined dress she was all woman. She had voluptuous curves and full breasts that were high, firm, and responded to any man's touch. Her legs were long and wrapped perfectly around his back. She had soft rounded, hips and a flat stomach that quivered under his touch.

It was her face that brought men weeping. Such beauty couldn't exist in the world, and yet here she was standing in front of him looking like the most beautiful exotic flower that he ever come across in his entire existence. Her face was delicately round, a small chin, a straight, pointed nose, and large, beautiful, emerald, full eyes that made him see the depths of the purest soul. She had long, golden blonde hair that bounced whenever she walked and it was soft as silk.

He was going to love destroying this flower.

"Lucia," he spoke with sweet seduction in his voice.

"Salve, Leo."

Her voice was soft and sensual, making his gut clench.

"Rincrescere, Lucia," he said apologizing in his most inhumane voice.

He had expected her to cry or run, but she stood, looking like she was about to be carried away by her knight and shining armor. She was smiling and he wanted to destroy her quicker. Except he wasn't ready to destroy the beauty yet; he wanted to remain a moment and watch the beauty that dazzled in the purest, blackness of his eyes.

"Rincrescere, Leo," she said, and in one swift bat of her eyelash, he realized that she had saved all her love, her purest thoughts, and deepest emotions for him and she completely opened up for him. For him!

Exactly what he wanted, but not the love to go with it! It was supposed to be the lust!

Leo should have known. Now he was being dragged under her temptation, and he agreeably came forward to her.

But not for long.

She was not going to be the one to destroy him!

Leo cupped her face and kissed her as much as he wanted to, and threw her down and buried his cock in her. He heard her surprised gasp, and laughed. What stupid creatures they were. No one could defeat him, not even this pure soul that loved him with all of her heart.

Lucia felt her spirit being sucked out of her body and into his, making her weak and him stronger. She tried to put all her love into the kiss, into her touch, and into her soul, but it wasn't working with him! He fought back harder until she dropped to her knees and felt her spirit leaving her body.

Help me, my sisters.

No.

It wasn't the voice she was expecting. Her sisters, the pure souls had not heard her call, but their leader of the guardians did. *Your soul is too far gone. Death has come for you.*

Lucia shed her tears as the darkness swallowed her whole, hearing the laugh of her lover. It was the last thing she ever heard as she felt his soul die along with hers.

In a parallel dimension of the true gods of the world, lived a highly intelligent being on the polar side of their sphere. Crset sat in his jewel-crusted throne, fat and slumped, as if nothing could aggravate him enough to arouse his posture. The most beautiful woman he ever saw in his life, that he created for him alone, was so angry with him for letting Lucia die.

It wasn't his choice to let Lucia die; he didn't work in that department. He could only save the ones that Death hadn't taken over yet.

"Why didn't you let us save Lucia?" the leader of the pure souls angrily demanded.

Crset rolled his eyes to the ceiling and yawned. "If she didn't fall in love with the demon, she would have defeated him. Instead, she subconsciously let her heart get carried away and didn't want him to die. She in the end destroyed herself."

"What are we supposed to do without Lucia?"

He lifted his shoulder and sighed. "Like always, Salene—guard the humans and protect the guardians. That's why you were put on this Earth."

"We cannot guard the humans without Lucia. Without her, our powers are defenseless against the guardian hunters. We need seven to connect to destroy one. It was the only way to defeat them. One alone couldn't possibly do it by herself. What will happen to the guardians if we are not seven? You don't have any more souls to take from the other gods. They let you use the dragon, the fairies, and the unicorns. The only souls left to use are the humans, which you forbid to even consider."

Crset knew this. He also knew that the remaining six pure souls couldn't save Lucia if they had come to her aide. Her spirit was beyond redemption that not even he could save her. She would be missed by many, but soon forgotten. The girl should have been wise enough not to let herself get deceived. There was only one thing left to do and he was really going to hate it! Vaeth had used all the humans for his servants until he put a stop to his powers. They were the only ones left to be used.

But the thought of taking a human life without their sanction was an abomination of everything he stood for. He knew what it felt like to have your soul illicitly stripped from your body and tossed aside. Crset couldn't see himself doing the monstrosity that his kind had done to him.

Crset still had a problem. If all the guardians were destroyed and he had to use the humans, they were going to be as useless as the guardians against the hunters. He needed a pure soul, but all the unicorns were gone; he used the last seven to create his ultimate guardians.

If they were all destroyed, the demons would take over, and Vaeth would have all the domination he always wanted. Crset couldn't let that happen. Even if he decided to take the human souls, how was he going to choose which ones to become the guardians?

"Crset," Salene said, breaking his concentration.

"What?"

"What are you going to do? In fifty years time, the guardians will be depleted from the world. The humans are our only choice."

"I know," he sighed. "But they can't make a pure soul, Salene, now can they?"

"You should have saved Lucia and we wouldn't be in this mess!"

"She was too far gone for me to save her," Crset said, bored. "If I could have saved her, I would have, but I couldn't. Her soul passed on to the afterlife."

Maybe it was time for him to leave this planet and find one that had effective more beings. Then again, he only had a few choices, and the water planet was so far, by a long shot, the best to resort to.

"Then what are we going to do? Are you just going to let us die?"

Then where would he be? He had to do something and the only thing that came to mind was cowardly, but would be successful until he could figure out how to bring the pure souls back together.

"You know better than that, Salene. I can't let you all die and I don't want to use the human souls unless I'm desperate."

"What are you planning for us to do?"

Crset yawned again. He should be pacing and acting hysterical like a bleeding widow, but he didn't need all the melodrama when he knew that Vaeth would never have his control.

"My warriors and sorcerers are very strong and skilled to destroy the weaker demons and so they must continue to fight."

"What about us?"

"The guardian hunters can't grow in strength if they can't find your existence and you can't destroy them if they find either of you. I need you and the rest of the pure souls to block yourself from everything and everyone as you protect the guardians from their destruction of the demons until I can find a way to bring in another pure soul."

"You want us to disappear?"

"Yes. I don't even want to know where you are, Salene. When the seventh pure soul is born you will know; it'll be an instant connection."

"What will you do until then? What about the guardian hunters?"

"I thought this day would never come when I would have to ask one of my guardians for their blood, but you cannot fight the guardian hunters; you will be destroyed without the seventh connection. However, I can destroy them with your blood, Salene."

"You're going to fight them alone?" Salene asked, outraged.

Crset shrugged. He had destroyed bigger and badder things than any guardian hunter could compare to. He just didn't want to do it anymore. It was one of the reasons why he was banished from his home. When he and Vaeth came to the water planet, he thought he found a requiem of hope to ease the humiliation and distraught memories *they* forced on him from his "other" home. Then Vaeth betrayed him, and he was stuck in the same situation as before. It was the reason why he created the guardians—so he wouldn't have to concern himself with the evil anymore. He had no choice, but to interfere.

"I'm the only one that can do it," he said to himself, forgetting that Salene was only inches away from him; she was bound to hear what he said.

And she did.

"Then why not connect with us, Crset? With us we make seven," she said, pleased.

"*No*," Crset said too quickly as he fervently shook his head.

Salene willfully took a step forward to him and narrowed her eyes as if to study a new species of life. He couldn't connect with them! The possibility of what they might discover about him would be atrocious. An ominous fear would grip their hearts and shatter their beliefs, for what they believed was evil!

"Why?" Salene asked with keen interest.

"Salene, I know I haven't given you much reason to trust me, but please believe when I say that I cannot be connected with the pure souls or anyone for that matter. Don't ask me anymore."

Salene studied him hard, trying to crawl into his mind, but it was slammed by a rich depth of unadulterated evil that it sent her staggering backwards.

"Don't ever do that again, Salene," Crset said, his voice dripping with a peril of danger. "It isn't safe. Are you willing to give me your blood?"

"Y—yes," she stammered, too afraid to ask any further question about Crset. Never again would she try to force her way into his mind, terrified at what she might find.

Crset produced a small dagger out of thin air as Salene held out her right palm without hesitation. For a second they found themselves looking into each other's eyes for the first time in five thousand years, and the electricity that crackled between them was heart stopping. Neither of them commented on the sexual energy that connected them, as they both looked away.

Salene gasped as the dagger sliced the middle of her hand. The dagger clashed to the ground as Crset grasped her wounded hand, and held his free hand under the dripping blood. When it was filled, he cupped it to his mouth and poured the rich liquid down his throat. His body was filled with the highest ecstasy immortals or mortals could ever feel in their lives.

His body jerked and came alive for the first time in five thousands years, and all he wanted was to bring Salene to the same pleasure that was literally shaking his entire body. He clenched his fist at his sides and breathed in the intoxicated fumes of Salene's womanly scent. He released it with a sensual groan.

Salene's eyes grew wide, her heart trembled, and her insides clenched with the antagonizing lust for the one man she despised more than anything in the world. She had to hurry up get out of here before she made a serious mistake like Lucia.

She took a few steps back as Crset closed his eyes and shook the last tremor from his body. Slowly, his eyes came open, but they weren't looking at her; they were looking down at the marble floor with a gleam of satisfaction. "I have you connected with me, and when the pure soul is born you'll be the first to know. Now leave me and tell the others."

Chapter One
Saturday

The sun broke through the white mini-blinds, showering its golden rays in the bedroom with small particles of dust dancing in the sunlight. Old cobwebs that didn't deserve attention stayed hidden in the hollow corners as the light slowly brightened on the curled, femininely body lying vulnerably on the floor. The sudden penetration of the golden light caused Kaleigh's eyes to stir, awakening her senses.

Kaleigh blinked her eyes until they adjusted to the sun's pouring rays and slowly, oh so slowly, she lazily ran her hand over her eyes and crept it through her tangled, carefree hair. No longer feeling blind, she languidly sat up and pushed her head between her unshaven legs. The microscopic hairs on her knees prickled her chin as her nose twitched from the noticeable awful body order steaming underneath her armpits and flesh. She smelled like she had been in rolling on the floor of some little hole in the wall bar.

"Jesus," she said, pulling back her head and then giving it a little shake as she sat, wobbly on her knees, letting her head hang back away from her disgusting odor. "What the hell happened last night?"

Instinctively, her mind tried to conjure all of last night's lost memories, but they came in blurry, quick flashes for her to snatch one and stake a claim. She knew she hadn't been drinking because she labeled herself as the designated driver, and therefore, she wasn't suffering from this pounding headache, nausea, and sandpaper tongue because of a hangover.

A startling memory came to a full-bloom explosion of vivid colors and deafening music. Kaleigh's head snapped up so quickly that her neck popped and dizziness caused her to sway. She rubbed the nape of her neck, easing the tension that befallen her and groaned in frustration.

What the hell was she doing at the Temptation last night? She'd only been there once before with her friend Susan, and she hated every minute she had to endure with those exhausting, wannabes freaks.

Another memory as clearly cut as the first raptured her thoughts. She was arguing with Susan in her office because Susan wanted to her come with her to the Temptation. Kaleigh repeatedly refused, but Susan promised she wasn't going to be long because she was going to break off a relationship before it became too serious, and she needed her moral support—and a ride.

When she got there, Kaleigh felt out of place in her long, black skirt and white blouse, as the others were wearing provocative attire that made her shrink back and hide behind Susan.

"Do you want something to drink?" asked Susan as they made their way to the bar.

"No," Kaleigh said sternly.

"Oh, come on, Sarah. Lighten up a bit. One drink is not going to kill you," she said with a laugh as they settled on the empty bar stools.

When she still refused, Susan rolled her eyes and ordered a shot of Tequila for herself as Kaleigh order a coke. Susan downed the liquor in one second, making a sour face as it slid down her throat.

"Whoa! That was some good shit! I see him through the crowd," she pointed. "I'm gonna tell him we're through, and then we're outta here. 'K?"

She nodded as she watched her friend jump from her stool and bounce her way through the thick crowd with a happy face. Susan seemed a little too thrilled, and Kaleigh wondered instantly why she was really here.

Kaleigh turned back to her glass of iced Coke and took a sip, and that's when everything went black.

Thinking about it now, Kaleigh imagined someone had put that date rape drug in her drink. What was it called? Rohypnol? Yes, that's what it was called. Then how did she get home?

A fuzzy image came slowly of her staggering in her apartment and then falling into her bed. But she woke up on the…floor.

That didn't make any—

Something had awakened her in the middle of the night. What was it? A dream? She was having a dream about a man. It wasn't any man she had met recently because there hadn't been any. It was a man that was going to enter her life whether she wanted him to or not. But something was awfully special about him; something unique, awkward, powerful, and though she couldn't remember what the man looked like, she could remember that she had this dream before.

It wasn't the dream that had awakened her. It was something frightful, distraught, and cumbersome.

Kaleigh had an instant hard vision of choking.

Then it all came back to her in a flash, and she was choking, she was losing air. She was dying! Dear heavens! But she was alive right now. She wasn't dead.

Whisper of howling words seized her from any further movement. Her hand was in mid-air to clutch her throat when she remembered the demoralizing words of the carrier.

Run, Kaleigh.

A wave of nausea churned her stomach to a tilt-a-world funhouse, and Kaleigh scrambled to her feet and rushed to the aid of the toilet. After several moments, her stomach was at ease, but Kaleigh couldn't shake the remorse feeling that was hurling at her. She had no words; only the feeling of emptiness. It was the same feeling that she was born with and most likely the same feeling she was going to die with.

Susan was dead.

Her emptiness took the blame of Susan's death. Susan had died last night, and she could no longer feel the strength of her friend's beating heart with hers.

Well this is what you get for connecting with humans. Didn't you learn your lesson when you were seven?

Susan had called out to her. She did as she was dying. She did it at her last moment of life. But she couldn't save her because she had blacked out from whatever poison had prepared her to be unreachable while someone murdered her only friend.

Kaleigh felt her pain. Kaleigh felt the air slipping from her body as Susan's slowly came to her death. Kaleigh's connection died with Susan early on Saturday morning, and she awoke to remember all the terrible pain that Susan had felt. She must have been so scared.

Oh, why Susan did you wait so long? I could have come to your rescue. I could have saved you.

It was too late for could haves. Susan was released of Kaleigh's inexplicable psychic ability and could no longer feel the life that transformed from soul to soul.

Susan was dead and Kaleigh could no longer feel the happiness that took part of heartless life and made her complete.

All she could feel was the emptiness splitting her. She didn't want to feel that one emotion anymore. It was the whole reason why she thrived on Susan. Kaleigh didn't have a happy, spirited life that was full of agility and sentiment. All she had was moroseness.

No more would Kaleigh feel the spirits of sunrise flowing through her now tainted blood. She had to feel the emptiness as it ripped through her soul and desolated her heart. She hated herself when she was like that. After she connected with Susan, she never wanted to go back to her lonely concept of her world.

Now she had to carry the burden of the feeling of death and decay; like she did five years ago when Mark and Melissa split from her life. It was the most depressing thing anyone could feel and Kaleigh had felt it all. She was a walking zombie with no remorse and compassion with her soul or the souls of others.

Why was she the only pure soul born without a soul? Why did she have to connect with humans to feel any compassion, happiness, or plain guilt?

Her mother, Gina, had on numerous times tried to get Kaleigh to unblock her spirit to have it opened to the world and let free souls roam in her. Kaleigh couldn't. It was too important not for her to do it. The guardian hunters would find her and destroy her, the rest of the pure souls, and finally the world if she did. Tired of feeling empty, she took a chance on Susan, and she was back where she started from; just like the pure souls wanted her to be.

Though, the dream from last night brought up a lot of question about her near future. If she saw any man that resembled shape, form, or facade, as the man in her dream, she was going to run and never look back. If that was her signal from the pure souls she was going to follow it as a direct order. The man in her dreams was dangerous, exhilarating, and was the one that could break her spirit.

Once again, she had been found by a guardian hunter, which meant she had to block herself from the world again before he found her.

Kaleigh stripped off her clothes in slow motioned as tears were brewing in the creases of her eyes. She hated when she had to commit suicide, but it was the only way to block her spirit from the guardians and the guardian hunters. She would be happier without the tears; she didn't want them or need them. They were a useless commodity and couldn't change anything.

Standing naked, she opened her medicine cabinet above the bathroom sink, and pulled out a new razor blade she bought years ago just in case she needed to block herself from the world again. She pulled back the blue shower curtain, careful not to let the blade graze her skin as she turned on the shower, and slowly dipped her feet in the tub one at a time. Then she lowered her body to the bottom of the tub, and lay on her back.

Tilting her head back, she breathed in the hot steam that rose from the shower as it flushed her body and wetted her hair as she tightly held the edge of the razor blade between her index finger and thumb. Without thinking, she brought her left arm to her chest, and lowered the blade above her wrist and closed her eyes, chanting positive fortification words to quicker her death.

I can do this. I can do this. I can do this, she repeated over and over in her mind while the blade was only a breath away. *All you have to do is press down and you'll be safe.*

What's the point? A soft, sensual voice sang in her ear. *Your protector has already found you.*

The cold, wet metal sliced her skin before the words made any sense to her. What protector? She asked herself as the blood ran over her thighs.

Mary Blanchard's hunch about her cheating husband was true. This man was balling every woman that came within a ten foot diameter around him and then some. Mr. Blanchard didn't have a specific type of woman that served to accommodate him. No, they were all different, from the tips of their nose to the pair of shoes they wore. They were young and beautiful, married and bored, blonde and brunette, or out for a little excitement, and that's what they wanted with the man that had been married for twelve years, two kids, a mortgage, and a ton of bills. The man would wine and dine them, whisper soft promise only his dick could keep, and leave them around ten o'clock at night to go pork his wife.

Jesus, Jack Pierce thought as he took another snapshot through the thick glass window of the Grotto from his twenty-year-old, still-running-like-it's-brand-new red Jeep. How in the hell did this man have the stamina to screw his brains out with two different women each night? It must be Viagra.

He'd been watching Mr. Charles Blanchard for the past three days and nothing had changed, expect for his clothes and a new pack of economy count condoms. He left his home thirty minutes until seven, stopped at a Starbucks for a large nonfat cappuccino, and pulls into First Community Bank in Downtown, Houston where he was the corporate manger banking officer, making seventy-two thousands a year, and then started his day processing loans and collecting on past-due receipts.

He may sound important to the bank, but to Jack he was a sleaze-ball with too much self-esteem. This man thought he was God's gift to women that melted at his feet. Wrong was he! He may get a lot of chicks, all different, but they shared one unique quality; they were as brainless as a kitten playing with a rabid pit bull.

Mr. Blanchard met them always at the Galleria during lunch time, just looking for someone to sink their claws in and usually deciding if they should go for the thousand-dollar pink dress or the white. That's when Charles approached with his Platinum Discover as a pick up line, and he decided for them. The woman agreed to meet him for dinner (wearing the dress he bought for them) or a drink and follow him to a hotel room because they believed that he made six figures a year as the CEO of First Community Bank and he lived in a fancy house with fancy cars and unlimited power. If anyone didn't know about style this man could play the part of the CEO of First Community Bank, but Jack knew his style and any woman with a half of brain cell could see through his cheap suit and used Lexus that Mr. Blanchard was anything but a sex god or rich. He was the everyday, average Joe looking for something better than what he had: a loving, caring wife, two great children, and a place to call home.

Of course, once he showed the pictures to Mrs. Blanchard he wouldn't have that American Dream anymore. It was going to be lost during the divorce settlement.

Damn, why do men think more with their dicks than with their heads? Jack couldn't understand it. He never played the woman for a fool. Then again, he wasn't looking for any relationship. If they wanted to know he gave them honesty. He would tell them about his career, the low-five figures he made a year, and the shit-hole apartment he called home. Even though he hadn't been with a woman what seemed like years—shit it had been years—he could never lie to a woman. It was as simple as that.

There was a lie to be kept from the human females, and they could never know what he was.

Mr. Blanchard kissed the hand of the giggling woman who could be no older than twenty-one, and paid for the check. He led her out to the parking lot where he pushed her against the passenger door and kissed her like an amateur.

Man, this guy was awful! Jack could tell easily that this woman was squirming beneath his touch. His tongue was going everywhere but her mouth and she was taking the abuse. Why? Jack asked himself. Oh, yes, that's right—he was supposedly rich, unmarried, and harvested a lot of future for a bright girl like her. Mr. Blanchard gave her one quick kiss on the mouth and then pulled out of the parking lot. Jack followed two cars behind him as this guy had no idea that he was being followed.

Because he was so horny and couldn't wait much longer, he pulled into an Express Holiday Inn and rented a room for the evening. Jack checked his watch: it was a quarter after four, and in one hour he was going to leave her and promise to call as soon as possible, which was a bold-faced lie. Of course the naïve woman would believe him. It was his scheme.

As Jack studied the adulterer's physique and appearance, he could only think of "Where's Waldo." He was tall, lanky, with no muscles structure and had a long neck that led to an oval, pale face. He wore wire-framed glasses that fit perfect to his pointed nose and around his large, brown eyes that said he was full of shit.

He steadily took snapshots. He never actually got picture on the inside of the hotel room, but let's face it, he knew that they weren't up they discussing if she qualified for a student loan. Mrs. Blanchard wanted hard cold evidence that he was a no-good, lying, cheating son of a bitch.

Well, Jack was just the man to provide her with that. Two nights of hard work and without sleep for weeks because of those damn dreams were not going to slow him down one bit. He was ready this time and tonight there would be no fuck-ups. Mrs. Blanchard wanted hard, cold evidence; well she was going to get hard, cold evidence.

Charles Blanchard took his key card from cheerful clerk and wrapped one skinny arm tightly around the girl's waist and then pinched her ass. She gave out a shriek (and who wouldn't with a creep like him), and faked a humble laugh. Some women were too pathetic.

Thirty-six was his room number and it was on the second floor. Jack took the stairs to avoid any conformation while they were in the elevators.

When the elevator dinged Jack opened the stair's door to watch them make-out the entire time as they fought to get the key card into its slot. Jack reached into his pocket and pulled out what look like ball-point pen, which was actually a mini-size camera he bought off eBay for half the price it would have been at an electronic store, and tucked it the breast of his pocket of his cotton T-shirt. The mini-camera had a lot of range that could at least cover ten feet of circumferences space (which would hit the feet of the bed and any clothes tossed off), and had audio. It recorded five minutes of conversation, and man, did this man like to talk during sex. Jack believed he got more pleasure out of hearing himself than with the actual intercourse.

When the lights were off, he slipped the "pen" underneath the door and flashed himself in the next bedroom for the next forty-five minutes; listening to all the grotesque words that were shouted and the fake orgasm scream of the woman that penetrated through the thin walls.

"Oh, Charles," she screamed. "That was magnificent!" This woman could win best actress of the year. And was this man was dumb enough to use his real name! Fortunately for him it was true. Unfortunately, for Mr. Blanchard, he was an idiot. He had good thing going and than he thought he was Mr. Cool and fucked it all up. What a shit-head. If Jack wasn't so prone to non-violence he would have beat the living hell out of him.

While they were still huffing, Jack flashed himself out of the room and quickly wedged his fingers through the crack of the door and snatched his "pen," and then got the hell out of Dodge. He had the hard, cold evidence resting against his beating heart, and thanks to Mr. Cool, he had more money in his bank account to afford more little gadgets such as this. That's what he lived for, little gadgets that made his work easier and they were a lot more fun to play with then a tape recorder.

He hopped into his jeep and called Mrs. Blanchard from his cell phone and told her that he had the evidence that she wanted and told her to meet him at his office in forty-five minutes. He would be at his office in twenty, but he had to have time to record the evidence on a video tape and grab what little food he had in his refrigerator to stop the rumbling in his stomach.

Jack hadn't always been a private investigator; he used to be one of the finest cops in Houston. He was awarded with metals of bravery and honor, handshakes of gratitude from the finest of Houstonians, and once featured in *Time* magazine as one of the best detectives this country had seen in a long time.

Within the last decade, Jack Pierce had exploited some of the largest crime developments in the Southeast; ranging from capturing Robert Berner, the notorious drug lord that provided half of the Southeast with drugs, guns, and street crime, to the small merchant in Dayton, Texas who was running a mechanic shop and an illegal cathouse.

He couldn't say that it was his fine detective skills that made him notorious to thugs on the street. He would have to say that it was his inborn sixth sense—gift as he would like to call it, blessed by whatever unnatural entity gave it to him and his parents of so many past generation that made his headway in the criminal justice department.

It was the greatest gift of all and yet at times it was a ragged curse. He loved it because it brought a lot of criminals off the street and he hated it because it raised too many eyebrows in the police force about his impeccable information. And he hated it because there was no way to live a normal life among the humans.

Jack loved being a P.I. He could work when he wanted to, while working in incognito to destroy the darkness that roamed the back alleys of the most grueling places of Houston.

Who would have thought Houston a nice necessity for the demons? But they were everywhere! It didn't matter if they were in a small, inbred town or a large city such as Houston. Where the humans lived did not matter to the demons. They were here to take control of their souls and see to that their strength was gain.

It was up to the sorcerers and the warriors to keep the balance of the world. These two groups weren't your average, everyday medieval servants to the gods. No, no, no. They didn't practice black or white magic or fight for any man or war. They had their own dealings with the demons so mankind could continued to create disaster and chaos for themselves.

The guardians used their crafts and weapons for the demons that haunted every aspect of the planet to protect mankind. In fact, no human even knew they existed. The guardians walked around with the humans, worked besides them, and even develop some close relationship ties, but beyond that, the humans didn't have a clue that such two-legged creature with magnificent powers to bring down lightening bolts with their fingertips or enough strength to bring down forty armed men with one sword could be their next door neighbor.

Yes, many humans believed in the old legends of vampires, warlocks, witches, and so forth, but what they had was an idea of these legendary creatures. Some humans even claimed to be warlocks and witches, and Jack had always laughed. The humans might have their version of witches and Hercules, but they were nothing compared to the guardians with their supreme powers. What they had was a small fraction from their god or gods.

Their beautiful and magical powers came from the blood of the dragons and the fairies. The sorcerers could see, smell, and feel the demons. They could bring a demon out of a possessed body and destroy the demon within with their rich and divine powers of the elemental magic of Earth to eradicate they soul. They also acquired a gift to save a human life from a lifetime of hellacious torment resulting from becoming a human servant; a human soul that got manipulated by a demon and only worked to bring him souls.

If a human was in danger of succumbing to a demon's whim, a sorcerer would destroy the prying demon and save the human. The sorcerers could also guard the souls of warriors and humans by shielding their souls from the demons that roamed the streets, looking for souls to possess.

They were very powerful; more powerful than warriors, but they didn't have the agility to fight them off with a weapon or fighting proficiencies. They were capable of holding their own when face-to-face in a situation that required them to fight, but if a situation like that ever arose, a warrior would be a good back-up.

The warriors were the extreme opposite of a sorcerer, except they could sense a demon's presence. They couldn't bring a demon out of possessed body; all they could do was destroy the demon that was inside of the human.

Warriors were the great shape-shifter hunters from the entity of the chosen animal their blood came from, ranging from wolves to tigers. They were very fast-paced, quick to act, and always ready for action by carrying a concealed, sacred weapon, blessed by their blood, tainted to defeat the demon for when the moment might arise. No holy water or crucifix was going to destroy these types of demons, but a blood of a warrior would do the trick. Between their swift sword actions and creative fighting techniques, they could destroy a demon in seconds.

There was another type of guardian in this crazed-inhuman world, and they were called the pure souls. There were seven of them; all female, and no one knew if they were sorcerers or warriors or a combination of both.

Doubtfully though, no one in over two thousands years had ever encountered one, and if they had, they would never know if it were a pure soul because what he had seen through is vision, they were very guarded individuals. Even from legends that had been passed down through the elderly guardians, they weren't really out in the open. They hid only to come out when the moment arrived to destroy a guardian hunter, the most powerful demons of all, and then they poof back to their hole.

Such legends had been whispered through the ears of the guardians that a pure soul could change a demon to the purest form of life itself. With just a touch of her soul, she could destroy a demon and bring it innocence, pureness.

But they were no longer out in the world helping to destroy demons. Since that fateful night when one of the pure souls fell in love with a demon, they cursed their maker that until they had been given their justice from the flawless error of one pure soul's heart, they would never help again.

Many of the guardians believed that the pure souls completely vanished from the world. If they had, they would have seen the decline of guardians. And it was true. If they cared an ounce for what was happening to them, wouldn't they have come to aide them in their time of crisis?

Jack knew they existed; he'd known al his life and up until five years ago he had one in his hands. If one of the guardians should ever write about the many failures of their missions, he would have been above them all.

Because of pure souls, the guardian hunters had become stronger and took as many guardian souls as they possibly could. Most of the sorcerers had guarded their souls from the others as they shielded the warriors to continue their nightly rituals of destroying demons.

Jack was a supreme guardian of souls; he was a dragon, the most lethal and magical of sorcerers, and the only guardian ever to be born by two guardians that turned human after they fell in love. From his parents' strong bloodline he was given the greatest challenge to ever face a sorcerer or warrior. He was to protect the born-again pure soul and reunite them.

It was his mission to help her open up, but he failed, miserably. He royally fucked-up their only chance for survival because he let the light of his heart rule his ego instead of understanding the woman.

For the past five years, he'd been drivingly searching to find her, his Kaleigh, the only one that had ever made him feel alive than all the souls he could carry in his tiny beating heart. Guardians aren't supposed to fall in love, for their longevity and powers were stripped, making them human. Once they became human they never returned as guardians and never bore children.

Jack didn't know how his parents managed to conceive him, nor did they. Both of them had many children before they met and fell in love, and as guardians-turned-humans it was impossible to do so. All the many guardians that succumbed to love to feel their own emotions instead of the others they had to carry had never been able to conceive any children.

Why his parents? It was one of those questions he was never going to find an answer to. Whatever the question for his birth, he was glad that he was born to fine parents.

And because of Jack's anomalous birth, he was known through the guardians as a leader. And because he was much stronger than warriors and more vital in the contents of his magic, they sought him out for advice, help, and protection.

Jack fell in love with Kaleigh from the first time those green eyes held his captive and for some strange reasons his powers were never stripped. He'd been through hell and back and yet he lived and kept his powers. He didn't know why at the time until that long-ago night botched at the end.

He had to find Kaleigh. The guardians were becoming extinct as they did almost two thousands years ago.

With only a few thousands left in the world and the demons overcrowding their population, there wouldn't be any left to protect mankind from the world of destruction. When he found her again—and he would—he was going to do his mission that weighed upon his chest, and force it to bring the pure souls back into the humans' salvation.

For now it was time to see Mrs. Blanchard and she wasn't going to be too happy. Why did he have to be the bearer of bad news?

Something caught his senses; a quick feel of steaming water, tears, and a rustic smell that could be only one thing. A glimpse of blood spattered on the bottom of the shower and drained down the silver pipe. A woman was smiling at the unbearable pain as her tears flowed happily down her face.

Jack saw her face again and nearly ran his jeep into a passing car. He pulled to the shoulder and sucked in his breath as he saw another flash of another woman who was in total darkness. He didn't know the one buried six feet under, but he knew the woman killing herself.

A soft seductive voice touched his heart and showed him a vision that brought a tear running down his unshaven cheek.

After five long years, he had finally found her.

Kaleigh slid down the damp tiles of the small shower stall, smiling the entire time as she slipped into delirium. The hatred of a demon's black face and red eyes flashed before her, and she laughed chaotically. They couldn't harm or interfere with her anymore. Her connection was lost to them. If she had the strength she would have laughed harder, but she didn't because the blade had already enter her other wrist.

Closing her eyes and letting the darkness follow her, the last thing she saw besides the demon was the man in her dreams taunting her with a devious smile and then said, *"You can't hide from me anymore."*

Chapter Two

Kaleigh awoke with the sudden decisiveness to grab her immensely beating heart and grasp for the oxygen that was quickly evading her lungs. Clutching for air, she staggered off the bed hitting her right knee on the jagged corner of her cheap wooden night stand and fell to the cold hard floor with an exploding thump. Loud, howling words echoed through her bedroom like a slow seductive drug as Kaleigh repeatedly tried to clutch the floral, peach-colored bedspread to pull her upright. The bedspread steadfastly beat her back to the ground. Kaleigh rolled to her sides, her knees huddled to her waist, chest pumping like a marathon runner, and arms still clutching the pain of her wildly beating heart.

Breathe, Kaleigh. Just breathe.

She couldn't breathe. All the air in her lungs betrayed her rightful place to live on the valley of the earth as she was rolled in a fetal position to contemplate on the rash decision to die or keep fighting for the air that was left to sustain her surroundings.

Breathe, Kaleigh. Just breathe.

Trying to make sense of the fraught words in her air-deprived brain, Kaleigh intentionally let them falter through her brain waves and slip past reason of sanity as she fought desperately to save her life.

Just breathe.

The whispered words bit back in her face like a rapid hunter sneaking on its prey. Kaleigh closed her eyes and avoided the words that endangered her life.

She could already feel the quickening of her breath losing the battle of the airless room as her heart slowed to the rhythmic pace of dying person. She let the world claim its own. She was prepared to die. She had expected to die one of these days: just not tonight. She hadn't accomplished what was set out for her and hadn't lived the normal life that she had destined for herself.

The whispered words were no longer whispering; they were shouting at the top of his lungs.

His?

Kaleigh's eyes snapped open.

What in the hell? Why was there a strange man in her bedroom? Why was she naked and why in the hell were her wrists burning and bandages.

Out in the shadows the man tried to grab for her. She screamed at the top of her lungs and tightly held herself in her fetal position. There was a man in her house and he knew her real name. She didn't remember bringing a guy home with her tonight. She didn't remember anything at expect for all the blood as she blocked herself.

A man's face shadowed her vision.

Kaleigh didn't know who he was or what he was doing in her room, but she was going to get him out of here as fast as her lungs would allow her to scream.

She felt a callous hand touch her shoulders. She jerked back, her teeth chattering like it was below zero.

"Kaleigh, I need you to breathe. Breathe in…breathe out." The man's voice was rough, deep, and just a pinch of accent that instantly told her he wasn't from Texas.

She obeyed because frankly she didn't want to die twice in one night. Or did she even die at all? If she were breathing then she must be alive. She had to think! She had to come to an understanding of all of this.

Kaleigh took in a calm, controlled breath, closed her eyes to the darkness and blocked everything from her mind except for where she was. She didn't loosen her fetal position, and the scream was ready. She did, however, reopen her eyes, and saw from the dimness of the room, the stranger was kneeling beside her.

She screamed at the top of her lungs and suddenly a hard hand was slapped across her mouth.

"I'm Jack Pierce," he said harshly. "I was sent here to help you."

Unaware of his words, Kaleigh acted out of pure instinct: she bit down hard and stopped before the blood could flow in her mouth.

"Ow!" he yelped, yanking his hand away from her mouth.

Kaleigh didn't think twice, she sprang up, not caring about her nudity and ran for her dear life. She barely made it past him when his hand wrapped her wrist in a vise-like grip, and yanked her against a hard chest. She cried out from the stark fear and dangerous pressure of her induced injuries. She could have sworn she saw him wince, but he didn't let up on her wrist that was dying with pain.

She pushed at him and with her free hand and tried to slap every bit of his free skin she could connect with. Her hand was quickly seized and she was utterly under his power.

"Will you stop and look at me!" He all but shouted in her face, gripping her wrist so tightly that they began to bleed from their wounds.

Shaking her head, she hid her pain. She didn't want this man to think that she was totally at his disposal, and she wasn't going to look at him either. Fearing for her fate, she lowered her head to the floor and saw that he wore a plain pair of white sneakers. Her feet were bare and small compared to his. She couldn't inflict much damage with her feet, but her knee could.

To catch him off guard, she looked up and gasped. Her heart slammed against her ribcage, her breasts swelled and tingled, and an unwanted ache pulled in her lower abdomen He had the bluest eyes she ever seen in her life! There were such a shade of violet that she could almost drown in those pools and be satisfied for the rest of her life. They weren't the gentlest eyes; they were cold, as if she had caused him to be brutal.

The stranger's eyes never wavered off her face, thank God! Or else he would have seen how her body responded just by looking at his eyes. Then she quickly remembered this man was a total stranger and an intruder.

Kaleigh only hesitated a moment before her knee rammed in his groin. He shouted a curse as he went down like a sack of potatoes, holding his most sensitive area.

The intruder freed her from his clutches as she bolted out the bedroom. She stopped suddenly, half way to her freedom and her bedroom when she suddenly realized that she didn't have a stitch of clothing on. She looked down at herself and blush a crimson red. She couldn't go outside naked! What would the neighbors think?

A noise coming from her bedroom caught her attention. She jumped and looked over her shoulder to see the stranger coming towards her at full speed. Kaleigh raced for the door, no longer caring if she was buck-naked, but she barely made it to the door knob when his arms circled around her waist. He picked her up and threw her over his shoulders.

Kaleigh screamed as loud as she could as she beat at his back with her fist and kicked at his knees with her feet, which wasn't causing any damages. This man was built like a tank and it was going to take a lot more than her puny fists and small feet to hurt him.

He threw her on the bed and slapped his hand over her mouth again, silencing her before she could let out another ear-splitting scream, while his other hand circled her wrists and held them above her head. He straddled her body, captivated her legs with his thick thighs as his hard butt pressured her upper thighs against the mattress so she couldn't move.

"Don't even think about biting me again," he said with a menacing glare. "I let you have your fun and now…" he trailed off with a whisper.

Kaleigh couldn't believe this was happening. She had never been as scared in her life as she was right now. The demons that came out of the shadows when she was a little girl did not scare her as badly as this man did. Even now when they still came for her, she was not afraid. She could hold them off; defeat them.

Though, with this man, this strong beast of a male; it was nearly impossible to defeat him and she didn't know how either. The pure souls didn't teach her much about her mystical abilities to defeat the darkness that rose from the underworld. They basically gave her a quick run-down about what she was, what she was do about her soul, and was destined to do in life. The rest about herself and the guardians, she had to learn by observing her mother

She closed her eyes to shield what was about to take of her virtue, and she lay perfectly still. She had heard that rapist get off on fear and struggles, and it was best to lie like the dead. She let the tears fall down from her lashes.

The man above her deeply sighed. He relaxed the grip on her wrists that were burning and bleeding.

"I'm not here to hurt you. If I take my hand away from your mouth, will you promise not to scream?" he asked in an almost concerned voice.

She nodded, too scared to do anything else.

He released his hand from her mouth cautiously. "I need you to look at me, Kaleigh."

Kaleigh's eyes came open at hearing her name. The cold look in his eyes was gone, filled with an unexpected tenderness and guilt. She averted her eyes to look at the ceiling. She wasn't going to blow-up her guard because he was feeling remorse about hurting her. He was the enemy.

"What do you want?" she whispered.

"Not to hurt you. I could never do that. And as soon as we get an understanding between us, I'm going to bandage your wrists." He paused. "I'm going to let go of your wrists now, so don't do anything stupid. They're bleeding pretty badly and you don't want to lose any more blood than you have because I need you conscious to understand."

He brought her wrist to his eyes and studied them. She heard his indrawn breath. He should feel guilty; he was the one that made them bleed again!

"How do you know my name?" she asked as he continued to turn her wrist to both sides.

The stranger frowned. "Let's just say a little birdie told me and leave at that until you understand a little more about your purpose in life. I need your promise that you'll trust me and believe me in what I'm about to say."

"I don't think I can make you that promise," she said lowering her lashes.

Kaleigh wanted to hear what he had to say before she made any promises. No one knew about her existence but the pure souls, and to have this man find her by her real name and blocked from all the guardians was incomprehensible! The only way he could have found her if he was connected with her, which he wasn't, or if he came into contact with a pure soul. If that was the case then why did they send him to her? She was to be kept hidden from all others to protect the pure souls' existence. Yet here he was, claiming to know her!

Why did the pure souls compromise the situation of her existence?

Kaleigh was going to listen and see how much he knew about her, and when the right time came decide if she could trust him.

Quickly, Kaleigh glanced at him and mentally sighed as her heart did a back-flip.

He truly was a gorgeous, sexy man and if she wasn't so scared, she would have let him do anything he wanted to her.

Where had that thought come from?

It was hard to keep her eyes off him, though. If he stood he would surely be over six feet tall. His body frame was like a linebacker of a professional football team, and he had jet black hair that would feel like silk if she ran her fingers through it. His blue eyes that made her body respond so rapidly sank deep under his bushy eyebrows and appeared to have waves swirling in them. She blinked. He had long, thick lashes that shaded his wondrous eyes. He had a straight, arrogant nose, thin and very kissable lips, high cheek bones, wide forehead, an angular jaw, and his cheeks were covered in a five o'clock shadow. When she looked at him she thought of the Marlboro Man with his rugged, dangerous, outdoorsman looks. She mentally smacked herself in the head as she remembered she was supposed to be scared, not in a dreamy, teenage girl trance.

But darn it! There was something about him that was familiar in a déjà vu sort of way that made her want to trust him, reach out and stroke his fine sculpted face to see if it was real. And something about him made her body ache in places that had been dormant for years.

"You're going to have to believe me, Kaleigh, because everything I'm about to say to you is true and before you say anything, I am a guardian, so you can trust me. Do you remember anything before you blocked yourself?"

"Can we please discuss this with you off of me?" It was really hard to concentrate with his invigorating body pressing down on hers.

He stared down at her mouth and without any decorum, lowered his eyes to her breasts that were vulnerably displayed for his view, and then slowly lifted his eyes back at her face. He looked content. She wanted to slap that look at his face. What was he trying to intimidate her? Well, it wasn't going to work anymore. He confessed he was a guardian and like he said, he wasn't going to hurt her.

"You promise me you're not going to run or attack me again?"

Attack him! Of all the nerve this man had. He was the one that had intruded in *her* home! And it wasn't as if she hurt him badly, she was the one bleeding, for crying out loud! She had every reason to attack.

But she wasn't going to run or attack him because she hadn't simplified her powers nor would use her powers if she had, and that was his advantage for why she wasn't going to do anything stupid. She was going to listen to him, see what he wanted, and then throw him out of her life. She was forbidden by the pure souls to interact with any guardians.

"I promise that I won't run or attack you again," she said.

"Good."

Jack got off her slowly and turned his back as she quickly jumped from the bed and then began shuffling around the floor for the sheet that was stripped from her body and then opened her closet door.

It was hard to concentrate on anything when there was a naked woman behind him and his cock straining against his fly. It took a lot of mental control to squelch his hard-on when he was on top of her, but his control snapped and his jeans blossomed. If it had been any other woman, his cock wouldn't have given a flying fuck, but this wasn't any woman; it was Kaleigh. Other women came and went through his life, but it was the way of a guardian to never get attached; they were just a pastime, a hobby to get his mind off of her.

Since puberty he'd been dreaming about her, connecting with her to protect her from the night shadows that pranced around her room while her mother was too busy intervening with other lives than hers.

Jack couldn't understand why he was connected to her or why he was the one to be dealt the responsibility of watching her. He told his parents about the woman in his dreams and they told him it was a sign from their god that the woman was very special and to find her as soon as he could.

When he graduated high school, he announced to his parents he was going to find the woman, and he left his small town of Brothertown, Wisconsin and headed for a small town on the outskirts of Houston. He knew she lived there because of the signs he gotten from his dreams—the places of the stores she visited and the Astros jersey she occasional wore to bed.

As he touched down in Houston, he felt her connection stronger than anything possible. It was like she was a part of his soul, an unbreakable bond that nothing could destroy. And once he found her in a small town called Crosby, it was his nightly ritual to protect her without her ever knowing.

He watched her confused when she faced the demons at night. He watched her as she cried at night for a normal life. He watched her grow from young, scrawny girl to a beautiful angel only the humans' heavens could make. He watched and watched and in the background as he with each passing day fell more in love with her, as impossible as it seemed, since a guardian wasn't allowed to fall in love; doing so would make them human with no powers to destroy the demons.

Jack was able to overcome the flaw in their designed system. He got lucky because of what she was.

Then one day, he lost her connection. He didn't dream about her anymore. He couldn't smell her scent or see her beautiful soul. She blocked everything from him and the world and the demons or he would have found her.

But to his dismay, she *came* to him, and then that terrible night, which he couldn't remember so well, occurred and he lost her again.

Something had found her again, bringing him back to her, and the guardian hunters were just getting started.

Jack wanted to peek over his shoulder to see if he could catch a glimpse of her naked skin and knew better than to think that; she had already been through so much tonight he didn't want to cause anymore damage to her emotions or be accused of voyeurism.

He cleared his throat and asked, "Do you need help?"

She didn't answer him for several minutes and then finally she said, "No. I can do it myself. Just be quick to say what you have to say when I get back," she snapped.

Kaleigh walked passed him, dressed in tight jeans that cupped her ass splendidly and a black tank top that curved the outline of her breast and her hardened nipples. Dear lord! She wasn't wearing a bra! And the tank showed a hint of smooth skin just below her navel. Jack's body tightened and his mouth went dry. He had to squeeze his fist at his sides to keep from reaching for her.

Jack knew he could trust her to leave the room because she wasn't familiar enough with her powers to do anything to save herself yet. It was something he planned to teach her so when the end came, she would be prepared.

She left the room, leaving him standing, watching the quick sway of her ass. He blew out his breath that he didn't realize he was holding, and when she came back several minutes later with clean bandages, he had to remain in his spot from doing something stupid.

"What is that you have to tell me?"

"You know what you are?"

"What do you mean?" she said looking up and when their eyes collided, Kaleigh felt sparks. No. She felt explosions! Her heart drummed a thousand beats per minute and her blood boiled. She wanted so much to reach out and touch the stubble on running down his neck to see if his pulse was beating as errantly as hers.

She folded her arms across her chest and glanced away from his face.

Finally he spoke after he cleared his throat. "Do you know you what you are? Let me rephrase that. Do you still believe in the monster in you closet?"

Kaleigh gasped. No one knew that! Not even her own mother knew about the demons that visited her nightly as a child.

"How in the hell do you know that?" she yelled.

"I told you. I know everything about you. I know when and where you were born. I know about your mother. I even know," he stopped to slant his eyes at her, "about Mark."

She sucked in her breath, her mouth dropped as her eyes grew wide. Slowly, she shook her head. "This is impossible! No one knows about him. Just who the hell are you?" she shouted.

"I'm Jack Pierce. I'm your protector, Kaleigh."

Jack watched her expression change from anger to pure shock. Her jaw dropped, her eyes were as large as saucers, and he could see the vein pulsating to a thunderous beat on her neck.

Trying to make her believe that she was born a pure soul—the only one in the world that could destroy a guardian hunter would be a struggle. Her love and emotions and her divine sense of her immortal soul that could bring evil to goodness were her powers. She thought she was seeing a boogie man in her closet…well…she was seeing something much worse.

Kaleigh had no idea what she was coming across when they haunted her bedroom at night. They were trying to end her life so the demon master could rule his day when he knew of the six pure souls' existence.

The first time he actually saw her she was nineteen and he was twenty-five and she was gorgeous as ever. Except for now, she had grown up. Her body filled out to nice, voluptuous curves. She wasn't hard or rigid in any place and that's the way he preferred her. She had long legs that reached to her well-rounded hips and slim waist, and they wrapped perfectly around his waist. Her stomach was soft just like her high, rounded breasts that fit perfectly in his hands. She had the most beautiful, greenest eyes he ever saw. They sparkled whenever they moved along her long, black lashes. Her mouth was so full and exotic that he was fighting every urge to bend down and taste her sweetness. She had milky, white skin and golden blonde hair that reached to the middle of her back. No doubt about it, it shone in the sunlight.

A memory of her hair spread across his chest as she kissed around his navel and further down to…

When their eyes connected he felt the same explosion she had. It took his breath away looking into the depths of her emerald eyes. If he wasn't restraining himself he would have crushed her body with his and kissed her until neither one could breathe.

He couldn't think about that now; he had to tell her who she was.

"Kaleigh, all those nights you spent with the demon they weren't trying to be your friend; they were trying to slaughter you."

"Yeah, I figured that one out," she said mumbling.

"If it wasn't for me, you may have never survived."

"You? I never saw you before in my life? What were you doing? Sneaking around my bedroom?"

"Not exactly." This was going to be harder than he thought. He expected her retaliation, but not the sass.

"Do you know what the guardians are?"

She hesitantly nodded her head. "I know about them, but nothing about them, if you know what I mean."

If she didn't exactly know what they were, then there was so much to tell her that he didn't know what order to begin with or how to fully tell her everything.

"Okay. There are sorcerers, what I am, and warriors. The sorceries protect the warriors and the humans from having a demon take control of their souls. For example, if a human decides to commit a crucial, heinous act of violence there's usually a demon berating on his subconscious and our intention to foresee that he doesn't become one."

Jack sounded like the imitation of the pure souls when they came to her as a young child, enlightening the true nature of her anomalous existence in the world. They didn't give her much familiarity with the guardians for the reason that she wasn't to have any contact with them. She was going to give him the benefit of the doubt to listen him because she was curious of the guardians' nature and he *did* know about her. Jack wouldn't be here unless the pure souls sent him to her.

"And if he does?"

"Then it's my job to kill the demon inside the human."

"How do you do that?"

Maybe he should have taken her with him first before he began talking about the guardians. Her apartment was unsacred, and at any moment a demon could burst through here now. They had to leave as quickly as he could make her come with him.

"I extract the demon from the human body and destroy it from the world."

"So you're something like a guardian angel," she asked in bewilderment.

Jack didn't know what kind of game she was playing by prolonging him with questions that could just wait! He needed to hurry and get her out of here.

Frustrated, Jack shook his head and quickly answered her question. "It's a little more than about your self-conscious, Kaleigh and believe me, I'm no angel. I'm a dragon sorcerer and I am to guide the demon away from a human before it can possess a human soul and destroy it.

"A demon's mind is weak; it can be controlled by someone like me easily. But if that human had strong intention on the evil act of life and if the demon had already possessed some of his soul then it's too late for the human and that's when it's time to call in us to implement the demon out of the human body."

"What do warriors do?"

Jack was ready to grab that long hair of hers like a caveman and drag her away. He could already feel the tension rise in the room. Couldn't she feel it, too?

"They are all about combat and weapons as the sorcerers use elemental magic."

"You said you are a dragon sorcerer. What is your magic?"

"I use anything that conducts heat or gives heat."

"So what do I have to do with this? I haven't seen any demons in several years before tonight."

"I'm getting ready to tell you," he said calmly. "For thousands of years as long as there have been humans, there have been guardians of mankind, and there have been demons so powerful that they can destroy us.

"They began as very weak demons and to gain their strength they started by taking the souls of the humans until they are strong enough to take over the souls of us. They called them the guardian hunters or as the Christians like to call them, the angel executioner because that was their ambition; gaining as many souls to make them more powerful and bring forth their strength to their master demon for control of the world.

"Sorcerers and warriors were unable to stop them. They couldn't even get close enough *to* stop them, and therefore, the guardians over mankind initially began to decline until they were almost annihilated from Earth. Only a handful remained compared to the thousands of executioners that were literally taking over the world until finally a light of hope was shed.

"They were called the pure souls. They sent seven spirits—all females—with the strength of a warrior and the senses of a sorcerer. They were the only ones that could get close enough to destroy the guardian hunters or any demon for that matter with just her touch.

"But something went terribly wrong two thousand years ago. The pure souls came across a guardian hunter that was so powerful he couldn't be destroyed, but they found a way. Lucia, the seventh pure soul fell in love with him, and they got her.

"What they didn't know was the hunter knew. At the end when she came to destroy him, she cast her poisonous love and he was destroyed and so was the pure soul; her punishment for falling in love with a demon."

"I already know that story and it's terrible! She did what she had to do! People can't help who they fall in love with."

"I know, but so many guardians were killed because she let love instead of her promise to the world rule her heart."

Kaleigh shook her head. "I still don't understand. What does this have to do with me and why are you here?" Jack was grateful she let the subject drop so easily, but he feared that the topic would be discussed in the near future.

"When the pure soul died, the remaining six were enraged by our maker's choice of decision. They made an oath that they would never help mankind again unless he righted what it did wrong. Meanwhile, they broke their connection to the world and have been hiding since then, waiting for their justice. Now the guardians are almost depleted once again and there is no one to stop the hunters, but you."

"I knew this was going to happen!" she raged as she paced around her room. "What did I ever do to deserve this bane of life? I've never asked to be granted this responsibility!"

Jack looked upon her face and sighed. "You are the seventh pure soul. You have the strength that will bring together the others and help us save our race…and mankind."

"Listen to me, Jack. I may be a pure soul, but I have no strength to do anything!"

"You do, but you have to find your strength to defeat them. Let's face it; we both know you don't have any knowledge about your powers, but that's what I'm here for."

Why didn't the pure souls warn her of his comings? Wait a minute. There were the dreams about his coming, and about the protector the pure souls warned she couldn't be blocked from. Jack Pierce was the man from her dreams and he had come just like the pure souls said he would. She didn't understand why they were sending him now when all her life they told her to never get involved with a guardian. Why now after all these years had they sent him to her? Was this some type of test? Or was he even a guardian? He could be anything proclaiming to be her protector.

"How do I know that you're not making all this up so you can kill me yourself? How do I know that you're not a demon, sent here to confuse me?" she said, looking panicky.

Jack had a moment of conflicting spirits pulling him opposite directions. She was a curious woman—always had been—that always gotten herself in trouble, but she had every reason to ask and he decided to go with the side that was losing.

"I'm not here to kill you and if you want proof, then I'll show you."

Jack took off his shirt and Kaleigh sucked in her breath. She thought he heard her, but made no signs to acknowledge it. She was expecting a hard body, but what she wasn't expecting was a perfect body…yes she was; she just wasn't prepared for the fine, sculptured body.

He was all sinewy, hard and muscled. He had broad shoulders, powerfully built pectorals and that contour to his lean, tapered waist. His biceps and triceps bulged with each movement he made, making her loins clench and her face burn. Her eyes trailed down his body to long, muscular legs, and big feet…

Well if the rest of him is so endowed then that part must be the same…Right?

She cleared her mind and looked back to find him looking at her. Did he realize that she was drooling from the mouth? Of course, she was looking at him like he was an exotic animal, and her tongue was practically hanging out.

Kaleigh felt her cheeks flush more when he smiled cockily and turned around. Seeing the middle of his back is what caused Kaleigh really to catch her breath. It was hard not to want to touch the smooth contour of his back, but it was even harder to resist the strange tattoo that was marked in the middle of his back.

The tattoo didn't look anything like a tattoo one would get from a parlor. It looked real, but too impossible for a tattoo artist to generate with a needle. It looked to be scarred into his skin; ridged and harsh. It was a black circle about the size of a homemade pie and when she looked closer, she realized that the circle was written in small scriptures. The language was nothing she had seen before, but all seem too familiar to her. In the middle of the scripture was an eyelid at half mast with the blue eye burning into her soul, and on the lid was some sort of reptile.

She leaned closer, wanting to touch him, resisted, and realized that it dragon with its wings spread.

As his back was still turned she asked, "What language is this?"

"Latin," he said over his shoulder.

"What does it mean?"

Jack turned around and Kaleigh couldn't help but noticed the dark patch of hair that dusted lightly over his chest and arrowed down to the waist of his jeans. Her eyes quickly shot up and saw him looking handsomely smug.

Oh, lord, she hoped his ego wasn't as big as his grin. Jack didn't say anything; he dismissed her wondering eyes, put his shirt back on, and continued.

"Adduco prosperitas fortis ab draco. It means that I bring prosperity and power of the dragon. The dragon—it's a symbol for me being the highest type of sorcerer, supreme in greatness and integrity. I provide protection to all of those that are human. Basically, it means that I'm the best on the Earth to protect mankind from succumbing to a demon's will."

"And you believe this?"

"I not just believe it, I know it. If you would have been brought up by the pure souls as you were meant to be, then you wouldn't find what I'm saying ludicrous. But since you are still listening, that means you believe me just a little."

"So what? Call it curiosity."

"Curiosity about a total stranger that you think wants to kill you. I don't buy it, Kaleigh. Maybe it's because you do believe me."

"No! Yes!" Kaleigh couldn't act more like an idiot if she tried. What was wrong with her? She was never this dimwitted or rude around anyone, but something about Jack brought the worst out in her.

"Well," she said slowly. "The thing is I was never to interact with guardians and vice versa for them and so I don't know anything about them. They wanted me completely hidden as well as they are, but then they started showing me visions of you, calling you my protector and I don't know if I should run or stay or do anything. My entire life I was supposed to be nonexistent, and they brought you to me and I guess what I'm saying is why now?"

Curious to the very end, Jack thought. She couldn't know the truth now; it was too early in their game for her to know anything about him and her destiny. First, she must gain some courage, then learn some of her powers, and then maybe…maybe, tell her the truth. For reasons that are meant for her protection, he was going give her the short cock and bull story.

"The pure souls don't trust you to be on your own anymore."

"What?" Kaleigh shouted.

"It's true. In the past you have had more than one attempt on your life and they don't want you to be at risk anymore."

"But I bl—"

"Doesn't matter what you did," Jack interrupted. "Or what you do anymore. They sent me to protect you and I will not let them down."

They would have done better if they didn't send him, Kaleigh thought. How was supposed to live her life with this outrageously good-looking man hovering around like her personnel shadow until…god knows when? Thinking about him being near to her, would drive her crazy. She felt brazen enough almost to touch him when he was the enemy and now she knew he was the good guy, how in the world was she going to resist him?

This was certainly a test from the pure souls to see how well she could resist the temptation of Jack Pierce. And if she kept him at arm's length, everything would be fine. She would pass their ridiculous test. She'd managed to resist everything so far, including letting Mark in her spirit. Kaleigh could definitely, without a doubt in her mind ignore Jack, hopefully. No—she would.

Sighing, Kaleigh said, "I don't know why I believe you, but I don't think the pure souls would have sent you to me if said wasn't true. I have made some mistakes in my life, but there won't be anymore. Once they see that I am capable of protecting myself, you won't be needed anymore."

Jack nodded only to agree. The humans say the truth will set you free, but under his condition it would only make matters worse. His will was stripped from him five years ago and there was no turning back. Lying and half-truths were all he had until she could be trusted enough with the truth.

"You spoke of others? What are they?"

Ah, shit. Another round of questions. He needed to her out of here as soon as possible. Just wait until he told her she wasn't staying here in her own apartment, but his.

"I told you there are dragon sorcerers and then they are the fairy sorcerers. The dragons use heat or anything that conducts heat as the fairies use the elements that Mother Nature uses to shape the world."

"That's fascinating," Kaleigh said with a laugh. "So what about the warriors? Let me guess, gnomes and gargoyles?"

Jack scowled at her with a piercing look, dismissed her sarcasm, and said very seriously, "No they have the magnetism and hunter ability of the animals they were born with—"

"Whoa, whoa, whoa, Hold on a just a second. What the hell are you talking about?"

Come on! Shape shifters? Fairies? Dragons? She was either trapped in a very realistic fairy tale book or Jack was serious. She could feel the bubble of laughter begging to be released, but Jack was serious. That kind of stuff only existed in movies. Then again, she should be in movies, too.

Jack let out an exasperating sigh. "Changing from—"

"I know what they are," she said cutting him off again. "But call me a realist; I thought they were just in movies and books."

"As we are made of legends," he retorted. "Look, how about I make you a deal. You should have a similar marking somewhere on your body. We all do. Do you have one?"

"I don't know. My head doesn't bend all the way around like an owl, so I wouldn't know." Kaleigh didn't know if she did. Her mother never said anything about her having deformity on her back and the one man that had seen her naked never said anything about it.

But if Kaleigh did, she wasn't going to find it while she was standing in front of this man.

"Have you ever checked? The markings usually don't appear until you reached puberty. That's when I got mine," he said.

What Jack said made sense to her. After she started to mature, her mother never saw her naked. Only one other man had seen her naked, and he never said anything about a tattoo on her back; no one had in the past five years.

She cleared her throat. "Well, I haven't seen it on any body parts that I can see. Do you think it may be on my back?"

"If there's one on your back, then I'll leave and you'll never have to see me again. But if there is one, then there must be some truth to me, right?"

Before she could say anything, Jack was behind her, touching her shoulders with his large, calloused hands. The heat of him went straight through her skin and burned her. The temperature rose in her body and her knees felt weak to his touch. She almost lost her balance when she felt Jack's breath stir her hair. Never before had she felt his way about a man. No other had made her heart race or made her feel like she was on fire; not even Mark of what she could remember.

Her breath caught when an ache woke between her thighs. It began to quiver and melt when his large hands slowly grabbed the hem of the shirt and pulled it below her breasts. She felt the flush of the cold air rush against her bare skin and shivered.

"Are you all right?" His warm breath breathed in her ear.

Kaleigh dumbfounded, nodded. Jack Pierce was so close to her that his heat dissipated the cold and if she lifted her head she could kiss him. His touching her back was the most sensual, sexual experience in the past five years of life. It was all she could do to stand on her own two feet.

He touched the middle of her back and Kaleigh's knees nearly buckled. The throbbing in her wrist had totally vanished and the feeling of gloom suddenly seemed overrated. All she could focus on was his hands over her back, the male, spicy sense that invoked her sanity, and the warmth of his body that surrounded her like a blanket. She wondered if he could feel her heart race or the trembling in her legs.

"You have a marking," he said in deeper voice. "But it's not like mine or a warrior. It's about the size of a quarter on your upper right shoulder with a unicorn and the scripture says ab cor, evenire castimonia. From the heart, comes purity. Hence for what you are: a pure soul. Do you want me to get you a mirror or something so you can see?"

As he said the words, she repeated them back in her mind and a warm glow began to rise in the pit of her belly as the darkness in her didn't seem so melancholic. The pure souls never said a word about the tattoo on her back, and why would they? They didn't want her to know anything about herself.

"I wouldn't repeat those words," Jack said in a low voice. "They are your key for when you face the demons."

"I'll take your word," she breathlessly said.

Jack gently pulled down her shirt and stepped away. Kaleigh immediately missed his warmth and the smell of his skin. She turned around and caught him looking fervently up and down her body. She blushed and lowered her head. She wasn't used to men looking at her and if they did, she didn't notice.

For the past five years, she lived much like a recluse. So when this drop-dead gorgeous man was eyeing her like she was a piece of forbidden fruit, she wanted to bury herself underneath the coverers. She felt exposed and wished that she chosen a more modest shirt to wear. It was too late to change now.

Jack asked if he wanted to get her a mirror. For right now she was going to take his word. She didn't know why, but she believed him. From the first she saw him she had this kindled trust towards him and it hadn't changed when he told her about who she was or about him. Still something seemed familiar about him.

"How do you know this about me?"

"I already told you that I know everything about you, and of course the legends of the pure souls have been spread far and wide, giving the guardians intellect on your beings. We all knew someday that a seventh pure soul will be born; we just didn't know who or when."

"Do they all know about me?"

"No," Jack said, shaking his head. "I'm the only one, but the guardians are waiting for her arrival because they are all counting on her."

She had believed him that she was sent upon this earth to destroy the demons known as the guardian hunters, but it was highly unlikely for her to do that. The six pure souls spoke to her often about her promise and she would never break it.

Whoever was the higher existence of their souls could have found someone stronger than her and more determined to take on such a great responsibility because her soul was weak. Even for a pure soul. Right now she was having a hard time dealing with this most dangerous man, the sexiest man she ever seen in her life.

As if he knew what she was thinking, he smiled. He looked from her legs and ran his scorching eyes all the way up to meet her eyes, burning her with his touch. He looked at her with lust blazing. His smile descended to a faint frown. He was all serious now. "You're going to pack and then I'm taking you to my apartment for safe keeping."

Kaleigh raised her right eyebrow. "Excuse me? I don't even know who you are. I gather you're not here to kill me, but do you really expect me to go with a total stranger? I figure you were just going to watch over me."

Frustrated, he ran his hands through his hair. "Yeah, in my apartment so I can have you close and in my sights at all time. That's what the pure souls wanted." *Laying it a bit thick, aren't you, Jack.*

Shut up, he said to the voice.

He stood there like a statue, and when Kaleigh didn't move, he folded his arms across his chest, glared down at her, and tapped his foot patiently. Kaleigh saw that he was stern about her leaving with him. Was this man out of his mind? She'd barely known him for twenty minutes and he wanted her to race off with him! Well, he could just forget it because that wasn't going happen.

"You know, I can make you do anything I want you to," he said.

"I already know that you won't hurt me," she said lifting her shoulder with a smile. "So really you can't make me do anything. Actually, I should call the police and say I have an intruder in my house that's trying to kidnap me."

He closed his eyes and laughed. "Go ahead. By the time they get here, you and I will be long gone."

"You really believe that I'm going with you?"

He smiled and her heart melted. She had to look away or else she was going to beg him to take her away. Oh, she really couldn't go with him.

"I believe it. In fact, I'll even give you five seconds head start to try."

"I'm not going anywhere with you!" she yelled.

"Kaleigh." He said her name like as father scowling at his child. "I can't leave here without you and we are not safe here. I was sent here to protect you and I will do everything in my power to keep you alive until the pure souls join the world again.

"I can already feel them coming for you. Now I can give you your five seconds of hassle or you can come with me freely. Either way, you're not staying here."

Kaleigh stared at him and knew that he was speaking the truth. She wasn't frightened of him because she knew he wouldn't hurt her physically, but emotionally this man could rip her apart and that was the biggest part of her not to go with him.

What was she going to do?

If she stayed would more of those demons come for her? She looked at Jack and felt his protectiveness like a blast of cold air. If she stayed or if she went with him, she wasn't going to be safe. Either her body or her heart would get damaged.

From what her dreams had shown and from what the other pure souls told her a man was coming to help her. He was a man that would die protecting her and a man that would end them all if she let temptation rule her heart. The seriousness of the situation told her to choose the latter, but what about the consequences that should follow?

In the past, she had loved deeply once and that loved betrayed her. In the future, she could only see the same thing happening. In the present though…

She was going to have to keep herself extremely guarded from the outcome her dreams had predicted.

"All right," Kaleigh said with a nod. "I'll stay with you until I'm safe."

Chapter Three

"The time has begun," Crset said as he lightly tapped his fingers on the arms of his jeweled throne. "The seventh pure soul has taken the shelter of her protector that *we* have sent for her."

"Do you think she'll remember?"

Crset shook his head. "When the time comes, she'll remember most of everything."

Salene folded her hands behind her back and paced with her head lowered. Her long mane of black hair was held high in a ponytail as a few tendrils had slipped free around her ears. Crset's body tightened and he had to look away from the gorgeous pure soul to not submit to his creation again.

"What is on your mind, Salene?"

She stopped before him and frowned. "I believe what we are doing is wrong. We shouldn't have lied to her or to them. The pure souls need to be rejoined with the guardians before anything else can go wrong."

"No," he said urgently. "We must be patient. She'll do everything right this time."

"How can you be so sure?" Salene asked as she lowered her brows. "She totally screwed up the last time after you said that she was going to do everything right. Well, Crset, she completely did the exact opposite."

Crset smiled. "She wasn't strong enough; she didn't trust herself to do the right thing. Just be glad I was able to capture his soul before Death took over him."

The leader of the pure souls straightened her back, threw her long mane of black hair over her shoulder, and shook her head. "I hate lying to the guardians. I really do, Crset. They all hate us now, blaming us for their diminution. I still don't understand why we told her that lie. Why couldn't we just tell her in the beginning?"

"I looked at both sides of the passage that I had destined for her. If we didn't lie to her, she would have gone down like Lucia because she wasn't strong enough with her responsibility in the world to defeat the guardian hunter. The other path shows her building her strength, believing in herself, and in the end will do the right thing."

"I hope you are not lying to me, Crset!"

Crset smiled and shook his head. "I have no reason to lie to you, Salene."

There was a long stretch of silence as the atmosphere became heavy with tension and sizzled with sexual attraction. For thousands and thousands of years, Salene and Crset had been the weirdest paired couple of their outer-world dimension. They were not related, lovers, or even from the same species. "Friends" was about the closet thing they even considered themselves, and they never overstepped that boundary to conclude in their relationship.

Salene was too repulsed by his selfish character, his unattractive face, and the imperfect proportions of his body to even further their relationship. His head was too big, with cow eyes and long greasy hair, his stomach large and round, and his legs were the type you see on a leprechaun; short and skinny. But now, seeing him actually care for something other than himself or the humans was quite overwhelming.

She knew how Crset felt about her, but he never would tell her because he knew how she felt about him. For that, she was grateful. Their relationship should be strictly platonic. If anything more should come between them it might be the end of their so-called friendship.

"We lost two more guardians to be human," Salene said as she drifted away from her intruding thoughts about them.

"Well isn't this great! How many more am I going to lose? My guardians are not to fall in love. That's why I created them with no souls! Love does dangerous things to a person's mind and I won't tolerate the distraction. Love is for humans, and by God, if that's what they want than they shall be humans!"

Love was always a touchy subject for Crset. He never liked to discuss it or deal with the corrupt emotion because it made people do and speak unfathomable comprehension to themselves and the world.

Yet, the one emotion he tried to banish from his guardians wound up being one of their weakest faults.

"Why then are the pure souls able to fall in love, and if a guardian falls in love with them, our powers are kept? It's what destroyed Lucia! Why is that, Crset?"

Crset was silent. He made a sorry judgment call in creating his seven pure souls. Why seven? Because there were only seven unicorns left. The only way to kill a guardian hunter is by the touch of purity and the unicorns were the purest, living creatures that ever graced mankind with their presence. He had to give his new creation the fortitude of emotions, though he shouldn't have given them the blood of his first guardian that had a real soul. He should have found some lost human with too many scars to care, feel, or love. That was his mistake and he couldn't undo it and he couldn't do anything stop them from falling in love. And whoever the lucky guardian was get to keep their powers intact.

Just another flaw in the system, he told himself.

Or could it be that the true God of the Earth had a little sense of humor.
Well, I'm not laughing.

Luckily, the dragons and fairies weren't born with souls, and the warriors' blood of the chosen animals the god let him disperse from gave them basic animalistic natural behaviors for survival, or he might have an uprising. That he didn't want. He loved this water planet and would hate to leave or see his guardians wiped out because of the emotional turbulence that would have those raising questions about his existence. His pure souls were the only ones who knew about him, except for Kaleigh, but she would learn soon enough. They took an oath straight to the heart that they would never reveal who their creator was.

Two of his pure souls had already surrendered to the ill temptation of love. One had died and the other was living under the guardianship of her panther warrior husband.

"Look, Salene. This is Kaleigh's final chance to get it right. There won't be a next time because I don't have any more souls left."

That and he couldn't make a repeat of how he got Kaleigh in the first place. It was malicious and a burden that had been on his mind for the past twenty-eight years.

"Speaking of Kaleigh, tell me Crset, if you don't mind shedding some light on this dark time we are in, how did Kaleigh become a pure soul when you used the last of the unicorns on us, and Gina is a fairy sorceress?"

He was silent for a long time with an impassive face and bored eyes. "Not your business," he said flatly and then added with the same bland tone, "Kaleigh is your concern as far as the pure souls. Other than that, she is my responsibility. So tell me how the human child is doing?"

Salene snorted at his quick decision to change the subject. He was holding back something (something he had never done before) and come hell or high water she was going to get to the bottom of it. "She is no more a child; she's a woman. But the human is doing fine as far as crazy goes. She can sleep on her own now without waking up every five minutes screaming."

"I don't care if she's sleeping or not. How is she taking her responsibility of a guardian?"

He truly was a heartless bastard, Salene thought. Just when she thought she could care for him, he did something that made her hate him more.

Why did he care so much about the damn humans and not enough about them? Why was he letting the guardians die? What did the humans have that they didn't? The guardians were the ones protecting the balance of the world and sacrificing their lives for these mortals so they wouldn't have to be a slave for Vaeth.

Didn't he care what happens to them once they were all gone? Didn't he care that if they died, he would no longer be of this world either? Maybe he didn't. He had the choice from hopping to one galaxy to the next.

"She's still alive, isn't she?" she said callously.

"Don't be a bitch, Salene. I know how you feel and I could care less if you feel unworthy." Actually he did, but she could never know that. "Leave me and if you still want to remain on this planet, you'll see to it that Kaleigh destroys the guardian hunter. He's a nasty one."

As Salene was leaving in his room, Crset felt Salene seething with loathing for him. He shouldn't care, but he did. He jumped from his seat and rushed to her side, capturing her elbow and swinging her around to face him. She had to look down at him because he only came to her chin.

"What do you want?" Salene asked hurting inside.

Crset winced and then took a step back, shielding his face. He planted his chubby fingers on his hips. "I have seen all the signs of Kaleigh's future, and I know that she will do the right thing. If she doesn't, it's imperative that you all breed. I can only defend them for so long before I grow weak staying in the human world too long."

"I know all of this," Salene strained. "I bore countless of children, praying one of them would be a pure soul. So have the rest of the pure souls, but all we can get is warriors or sorcerers. We love our children as much as the next one, but it all seems pointless and heartbreaking to continue breeding when it causes us to be disappointed."

"You know the males are dominated. You have to try harder," Crset said and then words that had been swimming around in his thoughts came out. "How about trying with me next?"

Crset didn't miss the cringe that distorted her face. She made it very clear that she had no interest in him whatsoever. Damn him for caring.

"Then you better give them all the guidance that is needed, Salene. Kaleigh is your only hope."

On the polar side paced the soft-spoken demon master, the most powerful demon of all, the leader of all demons and guardian hunters. His plans were going well. All he needed to do was wait, and his nights of plotting would all be over.

Vaeth was just as powerful as Crset with free range of the world, but had an advantage that made him more able to force his will on the world. He had unlimited souls that he could extract from the humans that chose to follow the dark path of life instead of the gracious one. He didn't give a shit for the humans' souls as long as he could get them for his own purpose.

Crset couldn't seem to get that concept through his thick skull that he had the mercy of the humans at the touch of his finger and could make them his puppets. Yet, he wouldn't allow himself to use the humans. He would not take their souls.

When Vaeth first learn to use his powers, he showed Crset the glory of the power and what they could have in a matter of minutes if they combined their strength. They could have the world in the palm of their hands and no one could stop them. Crset refused to take the human souls because he had this fanciful idea that it wasn't their planet to take control. It belonged to others and he didn't want to be the cause of a war being waged. Also, he didn't want the worship that went with the power.

But Vaeth did. He wanted it all—power, control, domination. He got a taste of what the gods lived for and couldn't live without it. It was better than the sweetest high or woman underneath him. The power was his drug and his sex.

Of course, Crset found out his little secret and ordered him to never take another human life or there would be consequences. Vaeth didn't listen, and when Crset found out, the consequences were heavy, severe.

No longer could he live in the heaven of Crset's palace. No longer could he watch the sun rise without it burning his skin. His beautiful face turned into a hideous beast that not even he could stand to see in the mirror. Crset stripped him of his powers as the souls he carried in his spirit were burned by the sunrise. Vaeth was left with nothing!

He begged for Crset's forgiveness, but his master looked down at him with his cold eyes and said, "I brought you here with me to start anew and you betrayed me like so many others. I can never forgive you for that, Vaeth. Live with the sins you made for yourself." Then he turned his back to him and walked away. It was the last time he saw his Crset.

But Vaeth kept his eyes and ears open until that one day came when Crset made his gravest mistake of all.

And for thousands of years, Vaeth had been in control of his own paradise, and soon would be control of this planet if the pure soul fell into his trap. The sorcerer was her failure and his future.

They drove in heavy silence on their way to Jack's apartment. The radio was low, on a classic rock station, and Jack could care less what was playing. He had Kaleigh sitting beside him and was the greatest feeling.

He stole a quick glance at Kaleigh. She was looking out of the passenger window, dwelling in her own little thoughts. She had been silent since they left her apartment and hadn't said any more than quick mono sentences to him. Jack would pay money just to hear what she was thinking.

He turned his attention back to highway, concentrating on the light traffic of the hours of darkness. It was late in the evening. Most of the stars were covered by thick, low clouds and it looked like rain was going to be on their way from the smell of the humidity in the air. There wasn't going to be any rain for several days now. And when it came, it was going to be one hell of a storm.

"So tell me a little more about us."

Jack tensed. Did she remember him after all? He looked at her, cocked an eyebrow, and asked just enough just in case she was talking about something else. "Us?"

Kaleigh stared at him with a blank expression. "Um...what do you call us?"

"Guardians."

"Yes, that's it. Tell me more about us. Where did we start? How did we get our name? Where did we come from? How many are they? You know that kind of stuff."

"Oh," Jack said relieved. He was glad she wasn't talking about what happened to them five years ago. He was still a little vague on those memories.

Jack cleared his throat. "No one really knows how we started or where we came from. We were just here one day. We got our names from the elders and as far as I can tell, it doesn't matter about our belief system because some of the elders that I know still worship Apollo or Zeus. As to how many guardians of the world, I really don't have a number. Let's just say there used to be tens of thousands of us all over the world and now we are down to a few thousands. More reside in American than anywhere else, as you know Americans are the most susceptible to demons."

"How old are you?" Kaleigh asked.

"Thirty-two," he said with a laugh. "Thought I was older?"

Kaleigh shrugged. "From the way you act, you make yourself appear ancient."

"I guess that comes from my parents. Since the crib, they have been feeding my responsibilities of the world. My father was a warrior and my mother was a dragon sorceress."

"Was?"

"Uh...I guess I should tell you whenever a guardian falls in love, he or she loses powers and immortality."

Kaleigh heard of this by the pure souls, but they never gave her an explanation for the cruel judgment on the guardians.

"Why?"

Jack shrugged. "To tell you the truth I really don't know why. Some of the elders—ones that are thousands of years old—say it's because it makes us lose sight of our first responsibility to mankind and makes us weak. My parents were both over thousand years old before they fell in love with each other and I've never seen two people happier than them."

"Yet, you weren't a born human?"

"That's right," Jack said with a nod. "I inherited my mother's bloodline of the dragon and my father's good looks of warriors."

Kaleigh laughed and Jack felt his boil and his cock harden. "I should point out," Jack continued. "That I'm not normal."

"You didn't have to clarify that for me," she said without the laugher.

Jack should have been hurt by her comment, but what she said was true. He was extremely different from the rest of the guardians, and soon she would see how different he was. But she was talking about his character, while he was talking about his birth.

"I didn't mean that," he said solemnly.

"Then what are you talking about?"

"Even though we can't fall in love, it doesn't mean we can't reproduce. We breed so we can bring more guardians to the world. And before you ask, they aren't any little Jacks running around, but once we turn human, we are no longer to have children."

Kaleigh raised her eyebrows and rolled her eyes towards him. This was just getting weirder and weirder by the minute. "Then how—"

"No one knows for sure how my parents were able to conceive me, but I was the only one. I was born just like all the guardians, but I possess a certain power that only the warriors do, and that is I am the only sorcerer that can shape-shift."

"Into what?" Kaleigh asked a little frightened.

Jack sucked in his breath as he slanted a curious look to her and then back to the road. "A dragon," he said quickly.

"Are you serious?" He couldn't have sounded more serious if he had just said, "It's dark outside." So far everything he had told her had been serious, why would he start playing with her mind now? "For shits and giggles," as Susan used to say? Jack didn't appear to have a sense of humor about the guardians' history.

"As a heart attack," he said.

Kaleigh bit down on her lower lip, wanting rather to bite down on her thumbnail. She shook her head and coughed out a light laugh. This was getting to unbelievable. She'd heard of werewolves, but changing into a dragon? *Please!* Seeing is believing right? Well, Kaleigh couldn't see a lot of things and she believed and she was going to take his word until she saw with her very own eyes.

Jack seemed distracted by the light traffic on the winding highway and that was her signal to drop the conversation when she really wanted to ask a dozen more questions about his "dragon side." Instead she decided to ask some question about the guardians.

"Why did you say breed? It's not like we're animals."

Jack exited the ramp and drove on the feeder until he stopped at a red light. "Jack," Kaleigh questioned him when he went silent. The light turned green and Jack stepped on the accelerator.

"Are you going to answer me? Why did you say breed?"

"Kaleigh I don't know how much the pure souls told you about us, but the guardians are totally different from the humans. We are born without souls and don't get attach emotionally to anything. The ones that take human souls into their spirit can only feel the humans emotions, not their own."

"I know that, Jack."

Kaleigh didn't to tell him that she was a rare oddity of the pure that was born without a soul. She had to obtain emotions from the humans as well. Though, since meeting Jack, she realized that she was gaining emotions—her own emotions. She didn't know how or where they came from or why she was getting these feelings, and she didn't particularly care either. Anything was better than feeling the emptiness.

"The females of the guardians know it's their duty to reproduce. The more we have, the better. They get pregnant; meanwhile the father protects them until the child is born."

"And then what?" Kaleigh asked amused.

"If the child is born of the mother's bloodline, then the child will stay with her until the child is capable enough to live on his own. If the child is born of the father's bloodline, the child stays with its mother until puberty, when his father comes to teach him of his responsibility."

"Does the mother ever get to see her child again?"

"That's the child's decision if he chooses to go back home."

"But what if the child wants to see its father?"

Jack made a sharp right and drove down a narrow road with several apartment complexes. "The child is connected to both parents. So if it wants to see his father than all he has to do is call him and he'll be there."

Kaleigh got quiet and Jack looked at her with worry. She wore a low frown and even in the dark, he could see that her eyes were deeply troubled. He wanted to reach for her and comfort her, but he held onto the steering wheel.

Was she thinking about her father? Jack knew that her father died before she was born. It was a tidbit she told him five years ago. Whether or not her father was a human or guardian was his question, and the only person that could answer that question for him was Gina, Kaleigh's mother.

"So we are descendants from some unknown source, we can't fall in love, and we can never die unless a demon takes our soul or turn human." She paused briefly. "Anything else?"

Jack turned into a large complex and parked in his space that was in front of his building. He switched off the ignition and the overhead light came on. He looked at Kaleigh and quickly back at the window.

Gina didn't teach her anything. She made her an outcast of the humans, the guardians, and in her own home. What Gina did was wrong, and she should have been stripped of her powers, but in a way he knew that she was just trying to protect her daughter from her destiny.

If his child was to be responsible for thousands of lives…well…he wouldn't know what to do. He did know that he wouldn't treat his child like he or she was an unworthy piece of specimen.

"There's so much, Kaleigh, I don't even no where to begin. How about you get settled first?"

Kaleigh nodded and opened her door before Jack could come around and help her out. *Woman's lib.* He rolled his eyes. He may have been born a guardian, but his mother taught him human mannerism because of his father's barbaric behavior.

Warriors were like that: the most dominant alpha males you could ever meet. They were ten times more dominant than the regular egotistical, arrogant human males. His father wasn't a brute toward him or his mother; he loved his wife and son like they were the only ones on Earth, but he had very caveman like tendencies that drove Mother crazy.

And because of his father, his mother wanted another male around the family that wasn't malodorous with testosterone.

He grabbed the two suitcases from the back of the cab and led Kaleigh into his building as he thought of his parents.

He wished they were alive.

The moment Kaleigh was led into Jack's apartment she fell a stirring of comfort, a surreal since of belonging. He had everything that a home should have but the family, and at any moment, Kaleigh expected them materialize out of thin air.

Jack showed her to the guest room that was blandly decorated with a full-sized bed, night stand, and a dresser that sat across from the only window of the small bedroom. He set her suitcase next to the night stand and turned on the bedside lamp.

"There's a bathroom right across from you and at the end of the hallway is my bedroom if you need anything."

If you need anything.

There were so many meanings to that one little phrase that Kaleigh found herself blushing. If she needed to curl up next to his body and feel his warmth, would he give her that? Tempting to ask, but no, she wasn't going to. From the way he was looking at her earlier, he probably wouldn't turn her down. She wasn't going to find out tonight or any other night. She had to keep Jack at arms length until she was able to get back to her pathetic, lonely life.

"Thank you," Kaleigh said.

Jack lingered as if he wanted to say something to her, but not wanting to overstep his boundary. He looked at her face and frowned. He licked his lips and Kaleigh felt her blood heating. What would it feel like to have his—?

"Are you hungry?"

Depending on what I'm hungry for, Kaleigh wanted to say. "Not really. I do have a question that's been bugging me."

Jack sat at the foot of the bed and spread his hands over his thighs. "I'm waiting."

Kaleigh wondered if she should join on him on the bed or just stand where she was. Instead she moved away from the night stand and came around to stand in front of him. She folded her arms under her breasts and tried not to look into his eyes. "Do you know how we are chosen?"

"It shouldn't mattered why we chosen. We were born as *guardians* over mankind's soul; we are here to protect and save the humans."

"But why us?"

More questions she had to know that he didn't know or care to know. "Do you always ask this many questions?"

She glared at him and tapped her foot impatiently at his humorless and dry attitude. This man's personality changed every five seconds. First he could be sweet, and then there was that nasty person that sprang out of nowhere. "I only ask question when I have a right to know."

Jack rolled his eyes. Fine, if she wanted answers then he would provide them. She did have the right to know about them since the pure souls failed to her that option. "Like I said, no one really knows where we came from. It's been a big mystery since the time of man, when we all got started and what created us. Each civilization had their own meaning for us and the demons that hunt. The Christians believe we are some form of God's mercenaries, angels sent to maintain the balance of good and evil. They started calling themselves angel mercenaries, and the dominant demons, angel executioners. The universal name for us is Guardians Saviors, which is what I call us. And the universal name for these types of demon is guardian hunters."

"Which you go by as well," Kaleigh said.

"Yes. I don't really follow religious beliefs and it would be wrong of me to say we are something we are not. I just go by the faith to save mankind from the destruction of the evil. If I keep my faith in that then there is no need for me to search of our creator."

"Yeah," Kaleigh said, lifting her shoulders. "But some may not see your point of view. Some may need that constant guidance to keep their faith. Rather it is Zeus, God, or Buddha. They need that reassurance to follow through with their destination in life."

She would be in that category that wanted guidance and something to answer to.

"I know what you are saying, Kaleigh, and I don't disagree with you. I think it's great that they believe in a possibility of our creator. I just believe whoever is our creator is not going to smite us for the chosen god we fixate on. If it did, then I wouldn't be here and neither would the other thousands of guardians."

"Have there been any that have tried to find our maker? I mean, there has to be some clues from where we came from. Why would a deity of some sort create us with such extraordinary powers and just leave us here? Wouldn't he be afraid of some kind of uprising or one of turning rogue?"

Jack scratched his stubbly chin, getting more irritated by the second. "Apparently not, because there has never been one. Remember we are born with no souls, with one agenda planted in our mind: to guard the humans. We don't crave power; we crave justice. Demons are made from human souls—bad human souls—and they care about power."

Kaleigh went mute. She got most of the answers she was seeking from psychoanalysts of their race. She was also dead tired and her wrists burned badly, but knew that by the time the sun rose, they would be completely healed.

"Well, do you have any more questions that pertain to our little mystical dimension of our world or any question in general?" Jack asked mockingly.

Kaleigh chewed on her bottom lip, shooting him another glare, resisting the disgusting habit of chewing on her thumbnail, as nothing came to mind. Well…there was one question, but she was sure that she wouldn't get a definite answer or if he was going to be more annoyed by her questioning. It was a small question. "How long am I staying here?"

Jack ran his hand through his hair and slumped. "Until you can be safe on your own."

"I thought you might say that," she softly said. Feeling disappointed, Kaleigh turned her back to Jack and brought her right thumb to rest on her lower lip. She didn't chew, but oh how badly she wanted to.

A slight sting of her left wrist made her wince and she was glad that she had turned away. She hated to have people see her pain.

"Do you want anything for the pain?"

Kaleigh jerked her head around and quickly shook her head. "No, I'll be fine. Come morning, I'll be completely healed."

"Aaahh, so you do know some things about yourself," Jack said with amusement.

She fully turned to him and planted her hands on her hips. To hide the surprise on her face, she frowned and narrowed her eyes at him. "It's kind of hard to miss that fact when you break your leg at seven to have it completely healed in less than forty-eight hours."

"Have many cuts and bruises in your life, Kaleigh?" he said drawing out her name.

The way he said her name woke a deep, yearning emotion that had been dead for five years. She fingered her hair as she looked away from him. "I didn't go see if I could fly from a two-story house with an umbrella if that's what you meant. I mostly stayed inside, avoiding everyone as much as possible."

"And why was that?"

It was Jack's turned to ask some of his questions to see how much she would tell him. She told Mark everything except for the major emphasizes of her not being human.

Kaleigh couldn't understand why she was telling him all of this. She had only spoken to one other person about her oppressive childhood, and he was dead. Somehow or other, Jack reminded her a little of Mark with his cool confidence and laid-back attitude when he wasn't annoyed with her. She just hoped that Jack was for real and wouldn't betray her like Mark.

"Kids don't like you too much when you know their deaths," she whispered.

"Excuse me?" Jack said, straightening. "What did you say?"

Kaleigh hugged herself and lightly shook her head. "Betcha didn't know that about me, did you?"

"I'm not exactly sure what you are talking about. Care to explain?" Jack asked as he folded his arms across his chest.

"When I was kid, I used to let anyone that was nice to me inside even though it went against the pure souls' judgment. When I started taking them in, I felt their every emotion, and it was so rewarding from…nothing." She didn't want to talk about her childhood growing up with Gina. He probably already knew, but it was depressing to talk about.

"I kept getting these visions of these adults. Some were young and some were old, but they all had one thing in common."

"And what is that?"

Kaleigh hesitated. "It was all about their deaths. I could actually feel their deaths as if it was happening to me. At first I didn't know that they were my classmates until I saw a tombstone with this boy's name on it that recognized in my class. He was twenty-one when he died."

"How?" Jack asked curiously.

"He drank too much one night, wasn't wearing his seatbelt, and when he crashed into an eighteen wheeler, he couldn't be saved. I told Toby about it the next day and he called me a freak and spread rumors that I was witch and devil worshipper. Teachers and parents got concerned and I became an outcast. No one wanted to be my friend anymore."

Then softly she said, "It was awful. I cut all connections that were tied with me and didn't let anyone in for a long time. Junior high was the worst. I couldn't even walk down the hallway without someone screaming "Freak" at me. I hid in the girl's restroom to eat my lunch, and in high school I skipped lunch all together."

"I can relate to that. I, too, made mistakes by showing my attributes to the world. Luckily, my father taught me how to fight and they didn't bother me when I finally pushed back."

Kaleigh noticed a grim glaze that quickly passed over his eyes. Something had troubled him and she had this need to wrap her arms around him and hold him.

Stupid, she thought. She shouldn't be caring about him.

"I wonder if all pure souls can see the death of humans. I've never heard of a thing as you are saying. Creepy to feel and see that, but I guess I can understand why you broke all connection and blocked yourself. Who would want that?"

Kaleigh didn't want to talk about herself anymore. She wanted to crawl underneath the covers and sleep for two days, wake up to discover this was all a bad dream. Yet, she found herself enjoying Jack's company. He was an easy person to talk to and she felt awfully safe and comforted around. It was like she wasn't ready for him to leave…yet.

"So where are you from? You don't sound like you're from Texas. You sound like you're from the North somewhere," she said, hoping to lighten the mood and instead only darkened it.

Jack licked his lips and smiled, which didn't quite reach his eyes. "Brothertown, Wisconsin."

"Small town?"

Jack laughed. "Very. My parents decided to move there after they became human to be far away from people as much as they could."

"What are they doing now, now they can no longer save the world?"

"Hopefully, looking down on us with our maker."

"Oh, Jack! I'm sorry. I didn't mean to—"

He threw his hand up and stopped her. "Don't worry about. They died about eight years ago."

"How?" Kaleigh asked before she could stop herself and then quickly added, "It's none of my business. I shouldn't have asked and you don't have to answer me."

"Car accident," he said solemnly.

Kaleigh lowered her head. "Oh, Jack. I'm so sorry."

"Thanks. How about we turn in for the night?"

He stood and his tall frame immediately crowded her. Kaleigh stiffened when the heat of his body smothered her. She came to his chest and so much she wanted to lean against him and console him. She looked up and saw the fiery look in his eyes. Was he thinking what she was thinking?

Jack's hand reached up and softly stroked her cheek with his finger, sending fire straight through her belly. It was a gentle caress, but nonetheless, it was powerful. It was a touch that lay bare so much emotions that it made Kaleigh dizzy with sensation.

He bent his head and she surly that he was going to kiss her. Instead his head bent to her ear and whispered. "Good night, Kaleigh."

He left firmly shutting the door behind him, and Kaleigh dropped to her knees and ran her hands through her hair. She had to learn some control or she was going to lose it big time.

Chapter Four
Sunday

Jack lay awake in bed and thought how wonderful it was to get a full night's sleep. He needed it badly from the hours he lost this month and last month. If he had his ways he would have slept through Monday just to be greedy. But he couldn't have it his way because the blaring sun wouldn't let him go back to sleep and he had this constant nagging feeling that he had to get up.

He vaulted out of bed and remembered that he had beautiful woman sleeping down the hall from him and she needed his protection.

When they came back to his place last night, he made it quite clear that she was going to have her own room and if she "needed" him for "anything" he was just down the hall. He sat in bed for a long time hoping there would be a small knock at the door and it would creak open and she would say something like she was to afraid to sleep alone and then she crawl in his bed and he would hold her for the rest of the night.

There wasn't a knock and he was disappointed.

Touching Kaleigh was like touching live ignition, hot, wild, and explosive. He wanted to kiss her soft lips and ease all her suffering from the years of torment that caused her grief of what she was, but he refrained because it wasn't the right time. Jack wanted her to get more comfortable around him, and then hopefully fuck her until she fully trusted him enough to open up, take his blood, and tell him of the others. It was a mission; he wasn't going to fail—this time.

He stepped out of his king-sized bed that accommodated his large size and well physique body, and padded barefoot with only his black jockey shorts to shield his nudity to go take a shower. Normally, he slept in the nude, but since Kaleigh was here, he was going to keep it casual and decent while she was under his roof.

When he walked towards the connected bathroom, he felt energized, restored, and completely famished. *Damn*, he thought, when was the last time he'd eaten? It's been awhile. Since he was taking some time off to help Kaleigh, he could eat respectable food at a respectable time. This week was no time for fast food or quick energy bars or cat naps.

He needed and wanted coffee. He rarely drank the stuff unless he needed a jolt of caffeine and this morning was that morning. He drank it once and it never could satisfy his taste buds, but he noticed that Kaleigh had a coffee pot and would be looking forward to a hot cup of coffee. He bought one because his friend, Sebastian, came over quite frequently and he drank the coffee like it was going out of style.

First a shower.

After he took a very cold shower, shaved, and dressed in a pair faded loose jeans, a grey cotton T-shirt, and a pair of white-ankle socks, he made himself two slices of toast with grape jelly and three scramble eggs, lightly salted. He finished the meal in two minutes, and made a second helping of toast with grape jelly. He never thought he was going to get full, but after the second helpings his appetite was somewhat satisfied and now that he was taking off from his job permanently, would have time to eat, shower, sleep, and hopefully save the world from a bad faith.

As the coffee began dripping, he made a quick phone call to Adrian Walker to discuss the recent invents in the guardian world. Then another phone call to Mrs. Blanchard about his unexpected departure yesterday. She understood about his family emergency and would be sending him a check as soon as the pictures and tapes arrived in her hands. Then he slipped on his Nikes that were by the foot of the couch and walked quietly down the hall to Kaleigh's bedroom. He knocked lightly. No answer. He knocked a little harder the next time. Still no answer. He breathed in as turned the door knob.

He walked in and the first thing he saw was Kaleigh's long blonde hair spread across the pillow. The soft, yellow blanket covered from her feet to her soft, delicate chin. She was breathing slowly, softly that it made Jack's heart clench and his cock throb. He took two strides to the bed and saw her stir. The blanket slipped off her, exposing the thin, sleeveless, white nightgown she wore. A little pink bow laid crooked above two white buttons that centered her chest. If he could only touch that bow…

Shaking his head, he gently pushed her shoulder and she stirred under his touch. Jack wondered how many more degrees it would take to have the air conditioner crank on. His palms were damp and a bead of sweat moisture above his left eyebrow. He couldn't believe he was sweating over a woman. He hadn't felt this reaction from a woman since the last time he was sweating over her and that was five years ago!

Jack remembered those days as it was yesterday. The days they first met over her missing friend, Melissa. His first reaction to her was *mine*. Jack never felt any of his own emotions until that day she walked into the police station, back into his life. He had to have her and keep her locked away from the world. That all changed when the pure soul told him of his mission.

Which they both failed.

He wished that he could remember what happened that long ago night, but it was like pulling teeth to remember.

Jack just knew that when he awoke in that cold hotel room, he failed. He lost her.

This time around, he would not fail. He had taken her blood while she was still unconscious on the bottom of her bathtub to always know where she was at or in danger.

Her eyes blinked open and Jack couldn't help but smile. The smile quickly faded to a frown when he sensed her confusion.

Kaleigh took her time letting her eyes adjust to the sheer-blinding sun that raped the bedroom. She saw Jack hovering over her and for a brief moment she almost reached up and touched his cheek. She stopped herself and rubbed the cobwebs from her eyes and noticed that the covers passed her breasts. She wondered what he thought of her nightgown.

Let him wonder.

The strong scent of coffee filled her nostrils and she did everything but jump out of the bed and attacked the hot brew. "Where's the coffee?"

"No 'Good morning' or 'Hello Jack'?"

"I'm sorry," she said laughing. "I'm not really a morning person until I have my first cup of coffee."

Jack moved by the door and propped one shoulder against the frame. "I know what you mean. I have a friend that drinks about eight pots of coffee a day."

"That's a lot of coffee," she said stepping out of the bed and pulling on her robe.

"Yeah, the work he does he has to stay awake," Jack said as he tried not looking at her breasts moving up and down.

Kaleigh could have sworn that he looked disappointed when she covered herself. At first he was drinking her expose skin like a man dying for the thirst of water, and now he was looking everywhere else besides her.

She was also slightly disappointed.

"You hungry? I can make you something to eat."

"What time is it?"

Jack checked his watch and glanced back at her. "It's a quarter to ten."

"Oh, my God! You let me sleep that long?"

He shrugged his shoulders and laughed. "Hey it's not like your going anywhere. Get dressed and I'll have breakfast ready for you."

He walked out and Kaleigh suddenly remembered that she was supposed to be a work this morning at seven-thirty. This is just perfect. How was she going to explain why she wasn't coming in and why she was calling so late!

She quickly threw open her suitcase and found no apparel that was suitable for work. When she was packing, her job was the last thing on her mind. All she had were blue jeans, T-shirts, and tank tops. She couldn't wear that to work. Well, she was going to have to call Walker Security and make up some kind of lie.

Man, did she hate lying.

It wasn't in her nature to lie and she wasn't any good at it either. Whenever she lied, her left eyelid twitched and she stammered like it was in her nature. That's why she refrained from lying all together. It was a waste of time and too much that went along with it.

But she couldn't tell her supervisor the truth! How would she sound? "Hi, Mrs. Dell, yeah I can't come into work today or the rest of the week or ever, I might add, because I have to go save the world from these horrible demons that want my soul. Don't worry about me. I'll be all right. Just look for fire in the sky."

She jumped in the shower and quickly washed her hair and skin and used the moisturizer on her face she brought with her from her apartment. Jack didn't own a hair dryer (typical of a male) and so she ran a brush through her hair and then jumped in a pair of jeans and a black, nylon shirt that had large, pink daisy across the chest.

When she reached the kitchen, the smell of coffee and cooked maple bacon hit her nose and that stopped her from rushing. Her mouth watered and her stomach growled. Darn it! She didn't have time to eat.

Jack was just finishing pouring her a cup of coffee. She looked frazzled and on the margin of losing her cool.

"What's up?"

"I have to go to work and I'm already late. I also need you to take me to my house so I can change into something more appropriate."

"There's nothing wrong with what you're wearing, considering its Sunday."

They stopped her dead in her tracks. It was Sunday? How did she let the days pass by her? Oh, she was losing it. She ran her fingers through her and thought back to the last two days. Something was wrong. Something terrible had happened.

She looked at Jack, hoping to find the answer on him, and just gave her a questionable look with a frown. "You okay?"

"You keep asking me that and I'm going to keep telling you the same thing. I—Am—Fine," she said more rudely than she intended.

Jack shrugged his shoulders and turned back to his coffee. He was brooding about something and Kaleigh for some reason wanted to know what was troubling him. Not that she cared or anything, but the saddened curiosity was alarming.

Kaleigh saw the plate of scrambled eggs, bacon, and toast waiting for on the table and wondered how he knew she liked scrambled. Didn't everyone? Wasn't it the preferable choice when cooking breakfast for someone when you didn't know what the other person ate?

Well, she wasn't hungry anyway. She had this annoying nagging feeling biting her in the back of the head and for the life of her she couldn't remember what it was. Something awful had happened over the weekend.

She turned her head away from the food, hoping the nagging would spark to a memory and focused on the manly décor of his moderate apartment. It was spacious. He had black leather sectional sitting few feet away from his big screen television. A matching recliner was catty-cornered in between the sofa and love seat that held imprints of uses in the cushion. Delicate, glass end tables were wedged on each end of the couches and state of the art electronics filtered around the television, ranging from a DVD player to a microscopic camcorder plugged in behind the television. She vaguely wondered what was on the camcorder and then the thought turned into what he did for a living.

His apartment wasn't exactly in the projects, but more like middle class. She could tell by his leather furniture and name brand electronics that he wasn't exactly living on the borderline of being evicted.

Then that thought brought up what was itching in the back of her mind. Susan!

How could she have ever forgotten about Susan! She died. She was dead. But why? Why would anyone want to hurt Susan? She was one of the nicest person she ever met and truly a good friend.

Kaleigh's known Susan for almost two years when she began working at Walker Security and not once out of those two years had she known Susan to ever disgrace another human being.

It was because of Susan that they found her again. How though? Who could have Susan known that would connect them two together?

Someone had to have found out about her other than Jack.

Kaleigh wanted to scream and cry. She wanted to punch a hole in a hole or drop herself from a building. She couldn't stand this anymore. She never asked to be born and she certainly didn't ask to be a pure soul of all things!

God, why wouldn't they leave her alone? Why couldn't they go torture one of the other six? Why her?

Kaleigh chewed on her thumbnail, a disgusting habit her mother tried years for her to break.

"Something on your mind?" Jack asked, interrupting her thoughts.

She pulled her nail from her mouth and turned to face Jack. "I need to go home."

Jack stood from his seat and stood in front of her. "You are not going anywhere," he said pointing his index finger at her.

Kaleigh wanted to take his finger and shove in a very awkward place.

"I already told you that you are not to leave my side for any reason. You are my responsibility!"

"You don't understand! I can't stay here!" And she meant that as a warning.

She may not want to be who she was, but she did have a large connection to the other six pure souls and she wouldn't betray their whereabouts for anything in the world. She promised to never tell and she never broke a promise.

Jack was her protector, a dragon sorcerer and he knew about the demons and could protect himself. What he couldn't do was protect her if the guardian hunters began to come after her, which they wouldn't because she was blocked from them. She and the other six were the only ones to destroy them. Jack could possibly get killed trying to protect her from one of them and she didn't want anymore deaths in her life and she didn't want to be responsible for his death. The guardian hunters could crush him with just a stirring of their breaths.

"I can't leave you, Kaleigh," he said stubbornly.

"Why Jack? Why can't you leave me? I've been on my own for so long, fighting them off without any help. Why now? Why are you here with me? You know something that I don't?"

He went silent and very still. His lids fluttered at half-mass and his muscles strained against his cotton T-shirt. "What?" Kaleigh asked, taking a step closer to him.

"You know the guardian hunters have found you, right?"

Kaleigh's breathing stopped and she feared her heart was going to burst through her chest. This wasn't something she was eager to hear. How did the guardian hunters found her if she was blocked?

The demon she saw as she was disconnecting herself from the world again. It must have kept her connection with her as she died and told the others. No wonder Jack said it wouldn't do any good for her to save herself.

This was worse than she thought.

"I guess I do now," she said slowly.

"Then you know that you are the only one to stop them?"

"And I keep telling you that I can't."

He spread his hands in the air and asked, "You want to tell me why?"

She gave him a sheepish look and lowered her head. She couldn't tell him. She wasn't going to betray them.

"Kaleigh," he growled as his eyes glowed a devilish purple and quickly changing back to his normal shade of blue. "Can you please trust me and tell me why? They are destroying us left and right and yet you're standing there like a fucking eunuch as if you don't give a damn about your duty in the world!"

"How dare you speak to me like that?" Kaleigh screamed. "You don't know a god damn thing about me, Jack! You think I like being what I am? You think I asked for this?"

"None of us did, but you don't see us running with our tails between our legs, do you? We stand up and fight every day and night so the humans can be safe. What have you ever done, Kaleigh besides take up space? Not a god damned thing. Do you realize how many guardians have died over the years because of the pure souls won't aid us? Do you realize how many humans have turned demons in the last decade alone? You came to us as a savior and we need your help or all will be lost for the world. Please tell me why you won't help us? Can't you trust me a little and tell me why?"

Strangely, Jack had her convinced to trust him. Kaleigh wanted to tell him so badly and couldn't. She didn't know where he got the idea that she didn't trust him. She did go with him last night without any force or cajoling. It wasn't a matter of trusting him with her life, but with her heart. She just didn't trust it to get taken by his heroic demeanor and his gorgeous self. Him just standing there was a deadly temptation to throw her arms around his neck and kiss him senseless.

The temptation was great, but forbidden. Opening up to Jack would be her greatest mistake of all and the hardest thing not to do.

She cared. Kaleigh cared more than she should about their dying race, but she promised the pure souls.

Kaleigh twisted her hands together and shook her head. "I'm sorry, Jack, but I can't."

Jack took a step closer to her and she realized that only a foot separated them. The heat from his body threading through the short distant space, making Kaleigh want to hurl herself at him, seeking his comfort and warmth that was sure to make her forget all her problems for just a short time.

"The guardian hunters are coming for you whether you want them to or not. There won't be any escaping them this time. You'll either have to destroy them or die and it's up to me to make sure you don't because we need you too badly. I told you what you had to do to destroy a demon and your powers are the same to destroy a hunter."

She knew that and yet it still made her feel more threatened than before. "You don't seem to understand whether or not what I do against the demons I can't do anything until the pure souls tell me to." she shouted.

He looked at her sharply and narrowed his eyes. "So if it comes down to it, you are going to let yourself be destroyed and in the process, the world?"

How was she going to tell him without giving too much away? The other six trusted her to be sacred with their secrets, and it was abundantly clear if she should say anything about their existence then the guardian hunters would find them and that couldn't happen. The guardian hunters fed off the pure souls strengths and it would be an abomination to the world if she were tell where the others where hiding because they wouldn't do anything to protect themselves. They'll let the guardian hunters take their souls.

Truthfully, Jack was here to protect her from something he couldn't destroy himself and she had to tell him the truth before he died from something she could prevent.

"Jack, I'm going to tell you something that would hopefully make you understand why I can't do anything. Together we are seven and we all have to be connected with each other to destroy one guardian hunter. We can't do it alone."

"Why?"

"Because it's the way we were made. So even if I try to do it alone, I wouldn't stand a chance; I have to have their connection."

"And they won't give it to you if come face-to-face with one?"

Kaleigh blinked and then looked into his eyes. "No they won't connect with me until—"

"—until they have been amended by our maker."

"Right," she breathed.

Jack smacked his lips as he nodded his head. "You think you would be safer on your own?"

"I don't know," Kaleigh said honestly. "But if I leave, I won't be putting your life in danger and you won't even have to worry about me anymore."

He frowned and then eerily chuckled, sending chills down Kaleigh's spine. His voice became rough and commandingly hazardous. "Listen, Kaleigh. You are not going to be putting my life in danger and don't ever say I won't have to worry about you! My entire life I did nothing but worry about you and its not going to change if you leave me this minute. I was sent to you by the pure souls for a reason and I will not compromise another failure mission because you are not doing your part in the world!"

"What are talking about?" Kaleigh shouted as she threw up her hands.

Jack blew out an exasperated breath and ran his hands through his hair. The next time he spoke it was more gentle and at ease.

"How about we sit down?" Jack sat down in his recliner as she sat down on the love seat, in the seat closet to him.

He spread his hands over his thighs and leaned comfortably back in his chair. "I already told you that I have been watching you for some time until I lost you. Before that, I was getting dreams about you as you are now. I didn't know why at the time; except that I knew I was to watch over you, protect you from them. And I did until you decided to block out the world from your connection with us—with me. I was suppose to protect you that night five years ago when the first guardian hunter tried to come after you, but I got there too late, and everything went to shit and I lost you.

"Afterwards, I went a little crazy trying to search for you my every waking moment and always came up against dead ends. And I was a detective for Pete's sake! Yet, I couldn't find you."

"You were a detective?" Kaleigh screeched.

Jack looked at her warily. "Yes."

Oh this was just great! Kaleigh wanted to scream. What was with her and cops? She was drawn to them like moths to fire. She just couldn't stay away from them! Her first real date out with a real man was a patrol officer. Then she met Mark, a detective for Houston Police Department. He was smart, cocky, and...wonderful.

But for the life of her, she couldn't remember what Mark looked like. She knew that he was gorgeous—much like Jack—a very virile man—also like Jack, and gentle—not so much like Jack.

God, he was a cop! *Was* being the key word, but it remained that he used to be a cop and had all the cop's propensities; protectiveness, saving the streets for the good sake of man, and that arrogant streak of pride.

Was this a coincidence or what? She hoped this wasn't a repeat of five years ago.

Kaleigh met Mark from her friend's disappearances. She went to the police department to fill out a missing report form, and saw Mark for the first time. It was instant attraction; chemistry so potent that after two days of knowing him, she gave her virginity to him. He made it so painless for her that it was beautiful.

And like Jack said, *everything went to shit that night.*

After Mark, she made a promise to herself that she would never date another cop as long as she lived. She wasn't dating Jack, but she sure was involved with him.

She prayed that Jack would not betray her as Mark did. Her heart couldn't take anymore grief.

Still, why didn't the pure souls tell her about Jack? Certainly they would have given her some kind of heads-up that he was coming to her rescue when she needed someone desperately that night.

"How come the pure souls didn't tell me about you?" she asked after she got her emotions under control.

"I was to never have any contact with you."

"Why?"

"They simply didn't want you to know about me because they feared the guardian hunter would get to me so I would come after you."

"And now?" Kaleigh asked in near hysterics.

"Because you need my help more now than your entire life. You can't save yourself from the guardian hunters or protect yourself anymore even though you can block yourself."

"I can't block myself from then anymore?" Kaleigh asked.

Go ahead, Jack and tell her the real reason why it doesn't make a difference if she blocked herself or not. Tell her what your plans are for her. I dare you.

Jack quickly shut his eyes and squelched the voice before his alter ego could come out to play. Kaleigh'd already seen him several times changing and it was getting hard not to bring him out until the pure souls told him it was his time.

"Whoever the guardian hunter is who is after you is playing for keeps. He's very strong and is having his demons watching you. It's very imperative that you do not leave without me and stay with me at all times."

"Anyway," he said so quickly Kaleigh didn't have a chance to voice her opinion.

There were so many questions she had brewing that she was ready to explode.

"I became obsessed with you."

"Me," she said pointing at her chest, getting her to quickly be side-tracked from the earlier topic, and, boy, was this man sounding more and more like a stalker.

"Yes, you. They gave me the responsibility to protect you and I felt like I failed you and them. All my visions and dreams of you were dead and I thought they saw me as waste to them."

They were the reference to the ones of the higher plane that gave the guardians the supernatural powers to destroy the demons.

"I realized that you changed your name, otherwise I would have found you," he said quickly.

"Y—yes," she stuttered. "I changed it." She didn't expand on any more details than that. The vivid memory was too calloused to recollect on the past, and she rather not even remembered it.

"Well what did you change it to?"

"Uh…Sarah Smith," she hesitated.

"How common," Jack replied.

An uncomfortable silence filtered between them and they both squirmed in their seats. The ticking of the wall clock that hung above the television was the only noise that vibrated their eardrums.

Kaleigh had enough and asked. "How did you find me?"

"I told you the pure souls sent me to you," Jack said with a smirk. "I got another vision of you, but it was strange. While they were showing me visions of you, they showed me something about another woman who was being buried alive."

Kaleigh's head snapped up. She knew who it was without asking, but she had to be sure. "Who?"

"I think you know who, Kaleigh. It was someone you were connected to and that's how the demon's found you again."

"Why would Susan have anything to do with me? I mean, I was connected with her, but what's the probability that they would know about her unless…"

"She knew a human servant," Jack said finishing for her.

"What in the hell is that?"

She truly did not know what they were.

Jack sighed. "They are humans that work for demons under their own intention to bring them souls, and if Susan was involved with a human servant than it's a great possibility that they found you through her."

Kaleigh jumped to her feet and paced around the living room. She steadily ran her hands through her hair, looking everywhere besides the one man in the chair that was forbidden as the fruit in the garden of Eden.

She didn't want any of this to be real. She wanted it to be a really bad nightmare and at any moment was she going to wake up. The trouble was, she had already awakened this morning and staring her right in the face was the bold truth of reality.

What in the hell was Susan doing behind her back? Susan was a bit bold and assertive, but she wouldn't get mixed up with…in a human servant if not she did not know about him or it. She had to been deceived by whoever had control over her. And Kaleigh was going to find that person responsible for her death if is the last thing she does in this world!

Susan deserved that much. She was a good person—more of a good person than she and it was only fair to give her a proper burial and bring the human servant to justice.

Kaleigh stopped and turned her eyes to Jack. He was watching her closely as if she was ready to bolt for the door. He stood from his recliner and fisted his hands at his hips and the cold look was back in his eyes.

Kaleigh stared back him and wickedly smiled. Jack came to her with a purpose: to protect her. She sensed there were other reasons why he was sent to her, but she wasn't going to explore his reasons for now. Right now, she had a godsend; her personnel protector, sorcerer, and warrior all in one.

If she was going to find Susan's body and the one responsible she was going to get help and Jack was just that person to help her. He used to be detective and he had links that could possibly discover who was behind Susan's death. Not only that, he was the only person she could trust at his point.

"What are you thinking about?" Jack asked with a raised eyebrow.

Kaleigh tightly folded her hands together, sucked in her gut, and quickly said, "We need to find out who killed Susan."

Jack shook his head. "That's a very bad idea."

She threw her arms up in the air and then marched right up and his face. "Why?" she demanded.

"For one, I'm supposed to keep you out of harm's way, not throw you directly into danger!" he yelled. "If we get involved with Susan's death, it could tie us to a human servant and bring the guardian hunter right to you!"

"Susan was my friend and she didn't deserve what happen to her. We have to find out who killed her and I'm asking you to help me!"

"No," he said as his hand diced the air.

Kaleigh's nostrils flared, her eyes narrowed, and her mouth pinched. "If you won't help me than I'll find out on my own," she said in cool temper.

"The hell you will," he yelled as he gripped her shoulders and pulled her off her feet, bringing her directly meeting her eyes. He gave her a hard shake and said through clenched teeth, "Do you realize they are looking for you? Do you realize that if the first hunter finds you, it will deliver to tell them where the others are hiding?"

"Isn't that what they wanted? Isn't that what you want? To bring the other six out of hiding, right? You all need us together and what better way than to bring them directly to me?"

"What good will that do?" he stressed. "Yes we need the other six, but if they are not going to do anything to save us, then who in the hell cares if they are found. My duty is to protect you at all costs from the demons before they get to you because if they do, we are screwed one way or another."

"Then how are you supposed to save them from me when you have no means of protecting me?"

Jack you are going to have to tell her on this one. You can't keep this part a secret.

I know, he answered himself back.

"There's a way that I can," he said.

Kaleigh was about to say something and paused to study his face. Guilt filtered in his eyes and she wished that she did have a two-by-four handy. She tightly closed her eyes and muttered an unladylike curse under her breath. "Why did you do that?"

Jack slowly and gently set her back on her feet. He took a step away from her and turned his back to her. "I couldn't resist, Kaleigh. I've lost you twice so far, I can't lose you again. You are our future and my means is your blood."

"But connecting with me? Is that your best protection for me, Jack? Jesus!" Kaleigh shouted. "What if they come after you?"

Tell her, Jack.

I can't.

He shook his head and she could tell that his impassive stance, he was thinking. "I can't undo what has been done, Kaleigh. You are too important to lose and just trust me on this, that as long as I am connected with you, they will never harm you," he said coldly.

"Are you going to elaborate on that?"

Jack looked over his shoulder and emphatically said, "No."

Kaleigh was abashed by his total lack of concern for her safety. Some protector he was.

What was he hiding from her? What was he keeping locked-up that he couldn't reveal his ingenious protector plan? He was connected with her by her blood. It couldn't be any different from taking blood of another guardian.

If a guardian took the blood of anyone, he could be connected to their whereabouts and emphatic to their feelings. That should have been a clue to her when he looked at her as if he knew what she was feeling and thinking. For the connection to break, a human or guardian had to die or the guardian had to commit suicide.

But by opening your spirit and letting a person in, you were totally connected by body, mind, and soul; you could see the subconscious; hence the need for Kaleigh to open up and feed that knowledge of the pure souls situation. Something she would not do and something Jack had not done yet.

If a demon got that openness from a guardian or human he could use that connection against you. For a human, the demon used that person's greatest love, undying devotion to end the soul they want and spare the other. For the guardian saviors it was quite the same, and yet different. Guardians were not to fall in love because it made them lack in their conviction of hunting demons, their number one priority. So, the demons took the human souls they were connected to.

Kaleigh first took blood from Susan when she accidentally slit her finger on a paper cut. Some of the blood spilled on her desk, and when Susan wasn't looking, Kaleigh swiped the blood on her finger and drank it before Susan could turn around, and connected with her on the physical level like Jack did with her. Then feeling more comfortable with her friend, she let Susan into her spirit, the only person she ever allowed after a long abstinent period of rejecting others, and if she were strong enough—if she could have controlled her mind more—Kaleigh would have been able to save her.

Was that Jack's great plan? To know her every moment? But could he stop the guardian hunter before he reached her?

Whoever had killed her must have been one of those servants and found the connection between them from Susan's death by handing the soul over to the demon before Kaleigh could apprehend what was happening. They realized the only pure soul in the world was a hand stretch away.

It wouldn't have been hard to figure out that she was a pure soul. Radella told her that if a demon ever found her soul, it would be like toxin to their brain, driving them mad until they couldn't take anymore and killed themselves.

Obviously, the demon passed on this information to another demon before he died.

The demons weren't strong enough to take her soul, but the guardian hunters were much more powerful to do so. The only problem was: she never would be prepared for them because she never knew when they were coming. Her ability to sense them was momentarily blocked until she could build her strength by destroying demons. The more she would destroy the better her powers would be at an advantage. Unless she walked into a room that was so constricted with malevolent emotions, then she could feel if a demon is there or had been there.

The demons would use every tactic to take her soul from her. From what the six pure souls foretold her in her dreams the guardian hunter wouldn't waste time finding her weakness. He would toy with her, bring up her guards, keep her prepared, and then use her strength against her to bring her down to her knees.

And Susan died for this. She had let Susan get killed by not protecting the way she should have done. The pure souls warned her not to let anyone into her spirit, but she was tired of feeling nothing!

They say pure souls could feel emotions without the use of a human. Then why was she born with no emotions?

Kaleigh may not be strong like the rest, but she was going to make it right. She was going to bring them to justice. Even if that meant battling her way through hell! It wasn't right for Susan to die for something that was not her fault. And if the guardian hunters come, she would do her best to slay them without jeopardizing her and the other pure souls' position of the world.

No one could destroy them but the pure souls. When were they going to get over their grudge and help aide mankind?

One step at a time, Kaleigh. You don't have to know all the answer right now.

"Jack," she whispered. "I need to find Susan. It may not be worth the risk to you, but to me it is. She was the closest person I had to a family or friend and I let her down by not protecting her the way I should have."

Jack threw his head back and groaned. "Let me see what I can do."

Sebastian Ames stood on the thirtieth story building in downtown Chicago, overseeing the early twilight of the night. His black leather jacket flapped in the wind as his blonde hair whipped around his face.

He breathed in the air and spread out his arms, embracing the cool night air to separate the evil from the good. His head cocked to the right and he sniffed. He found a very strong smell of a demon working in a dark alley about five miles from the building. Sebastian dropped to one knee with his hands braced on either side of him and jumped straight in the air with a fist high above his head and landed on the building across from him like a graceful cat. The ground shook under him and made him shiver with the power of his ability. His black Raybans fell lopsided and he straightened them to fit firmly over the bridge of his nose.

The scent got stronger as he jumped from building to building. With his final jump he gracefully landed behind an old warehouse that had busted windows and trash rolling with the wind. A rotten smell hit him that almost knocked him off his feet. He waved his hands in front of his face and choked as tears blurred his vision.

Turning towards the smell, Sebastian found two beady, red eyes glowing from the dumpster's shadow.

Sebastian smiled. The demon growled.

"What do we have here?" Sebastian asked as he pulled his sword from the back of the inside of his leather jacket and held it like a samurai warrior. "A scared little demon?"

Sebastian made a tsking sound that only infuriated the demon. "Why don't you come to play?"

The demon snarled and hissed.

Razor-sharp, daggered claws stretched from the shadow and scraped the hard concrete. The piercing sound made Sebastian cringe. It was like hearing finger nails scraping across a chalkboard.

Its other arm stretched out and did the same thing.

"That's enough, demon. Stop wasting my time and get the hell out here so I can home."

The demon hissed before he obeyed the warrior's command. Its slimy, vein-full brown head came out of the shadows as his pointed, long ears twitched with the moving of the cool breeze. It turned its red eyes on Sebastian and exposed its stained, yellow fangs with a growl as the rest of its skeletal, slime-covered body slithered like a worm from the dumpster. Sebastian growled back and rolled his eyes.

"Come on demon, I don't have all fucking night!"

The demon stood on its clawed hind legs and growled loud enough to shake the broken windows of the warehouse as its thin wings expanded on either side of his body to the length Sebastian height.

"You think that scares me, demon?"

The demon hissed louder and then jumped towards Sebastian with one fluid motion. Sebastian raised his sword above his head and pierced his sword in the demon's left shoulder. The demon retreated back and growled. It came after him again and stupidly made the same mistake, Sebastian pulled back his arm and stabbed straight through the demons' stomach, sending the sword thrusting all the way to the hilt through the demon's body.

He pulled out his sword, turned in a quick full circle, gathering the wind as his strength and slammed the sword through the demon's neck. The demon barely audible a sound as its head sliced off and rolled several feet away from him. Seconds later the demon burst into a million dust particles—along with its head.

Sebastian wiped the dirt off his leather pants and put the sword back inside of his jacket. He popped his neck from side to side and smiled. Damn, it felt good to kill a demon, he thought.

As he started to leave, his cell phone vibrated against his hip. He unclipped it from his belt buckle and looked at the caller I.D. "Holy shit," Sebastian shouted with a quirky laugh.

He answered the phone. "Jack! What in the hell are you calling me? Don't you know that I'm a very busy man?"

Jack chuckled on the other end.

Sebastian liked to hear from his only friend, Jack; he was the only person he could tolerate long enough without punching him in the face.

"I was wondering if you're free for a few days."

He shrugged his shoulders, knowing Jack couldn't see over the phone. "It all depends on what you want."

"I'm in some deep shit, Sebastian and I need your help."

Jack needing my help? Sebastian wanted to say. That was very unusual. Jack was the strongest guardian ever known to them, and it was usually them calling him for help, not the other way around.

Then if Jack was calling him for help, then that must mean he really is in some deep shit. And Jack was his only friend and he felt obligated to help. "What's going on?"

"I don't want to talk about it over the phone. I need you in Houston with your cowboy hat on and spurs jiggling."

"How about some chaps to complete the outfit?" Sebastian sarcastically suggested.

"Why do I picture you as the cowboy from the Village People," Jack said with a laugh.

"Go fuck yourself, Jack. You won't ever catch me singing "Macho Man," and if you do, I'm giving you special permission to bring my soul on a platter to a demon."

"You still remember where I live," Jack said all serious.

"Yep. Just give a couple days to find someone to replace me. You know how hard it is today with these goddamn guardian hunters every corner you turn."

"I know what you mean," Jack said in a deep voice that wasn't too sure. "Just get here as soon as you can." Then he hung up on the phone without giving Sebastian time to reply.

Sebastian looked at the phone for several seconds and replaced it back on his belt loop. Jack was acting skittish, which was so unlike him. First he was calling for help then he was acting like he was hiding something from him. Shit, maybe he was.

Whatever it was, Jack had good reason and he soon was going to find out.

"I called a friend of mine to help us out," Jack said after he hung up the phone. "He's a wolf-warrior and he's damn good at what he does."

They were sitting in the kitchen, munching on turkey sandwiches and potato chips and drinking ice tea. Kaleigh sat across from him, silently in her own thoughts. Jack wondered what she was thinking. He hated what he had done, but he couldn't help it. He saw her and let her in his spirit for all his protection. She would have to get over it because there was nothing he could do to change it. He was her protector and he was going to do everything in his powers to keep her safe and alive from the guardian hunter that was patiently waiting for her to come to him.

Kaleigh wiped her fingers on the napkin and then picked her plate up, rinsed it in the sink, and then placed it in the dishwasher.

"What's his name?" she asked as she shut the dishwasher door.

"Sebastian Ames. He'll be here in a couple days so don't freak out when you see him."

She turned to his back and he twisted around the chair to look at her. "Why would I freak out?"

"He's a scary looking man. He's much bigger than me and one mean son of a bitch, but he's safe. He's just looks like a psycho killer from the dark ages. He carries his sword everywhere he goes. So don't scream when you see it."

Kaleigh laughed. "Thanks for giving me the heads up."

She washed and toweled off her hands and sat back down across from Jack. She acted like she wanted to say something, but leaned back in her chair and chewed on her thumbnail. Jack wasn't disgusted by it. In fact he ignored it and asked, "What is that you want to tell me?"

She lowered her hand to the table and sighed. "How long do I have to stay here? I have to go to work tomorrow," she blurted. "I can't stay in your apartment for the rest of my life, waiting for these things to come after me. I do have another life that doesn't revolve around them."

Jack shook his head. "You stay as long until they tell it's time for you to go. Where you go, I go. Besides, I can take care of you."

"That's not what I want!" Kaleigh jumped from the chair and slammed a fist on the table. "I do need your help for other reason, but please, Jack, don't make me rely on you for everything else and make feel like a prisoner."

"You still don't understand that I can't and won't leave you."

"Then what are you going to do about your employment? Surely you're not going to retire to watch me around the clock. You have responsibilities of your own that do not involve me."

Jack had no problems with his business; he wasn't going to be around long enough to see it prosper for a chain. He already referred his clients to another investigator that was quite good and had more time on his hands than him.

Yet, he couldn't see himself sitting idling around his apartment with a beautiful woman two feet away from him, while waiting for the pure souls' signal. It was hard enough being in the same room with her without wanting to touch her.

Reluctantly, he agreed to help Kaleigh find her missing friend—again, and the first place he would check, besides her apartment, would be her office for any incriminating evidence that she may have left behind.

Kaleigh may believe she was a good person, but Jack believed that middle-aged woman with nothing to win had to do something terribly wrong to be buried six feet underground. This didn't smell like a random serial killer act of violence. He saw the vision clearly. Susan was in that coffin for a very good reason.

Sebastian would stick out like a sore thumb if he sent him to Kaleigh's place of employment and Adrian did know him and would give access to Susan's things at work. Jack would have to spend a day at Walker Security to snoop around Susan's desk.

Kaleigh was in for a surprise though. Her vacation was going to come a little early. Tomorrow would be the only day she was going to work this week because hopefully that's all he needed.

"Okay," he said roughly. "Tomorrow you will go to work. You're not leaving a building without me. If you happen to be in any kind of trouble, I'll know right away. Got it?"

Kaleigh nodded and smiled. Jack felt someone socked him in the gut and he had to look away. "Great. Now sit back down and tell me everything you know about Susan."

"What do you want to know?"

Jack lifted his right shoulder. "Who did she hang out with? Where did she hang out? Was she married? Did she have a boyfriend? When was the last time you saw her?"

"Uh...I really don't know who she hung out with. I think she's was married once, but I thought it wasn't my business to dwell in that part of her life because every time I ask, she sort of side-step the question. There were a few men she went home with from the club she took me to call the Temptation."

"The Temptation? Isn't that the club on Westimer with all the freaks and weirdos?"

"We're freaks and weirdos, Jack," she snidely said. "We just hide it better than most."

Kaleigh had a point there.

"Actually, that's the last time I saw her. She went to meet her boyfriend to break things off with him that had all these tattoos and piercing, and then I don't remember anything after that."

"Come again," Jack said.

Kaleigh scratched the back of her head and rolled her eyes to the ceiling. How was she going to explain to him something she didn't remember? After Susan left her, everything went black.

"Stop avoiding me and look at me," he said.

She shot him a fierce look and said, "I wasn't avoiding you because I really don't know myself. One minute I watched Susan get lost in the crowd and the next, I woke lying on my bedroom floor. That's never happened to me before."

"*Shit*," Jack cursed under his breath. Someone had found her before Susan's death and all his fingers were pointing at the problem they were trying to solve. Susan was undeniably involved with a human servant, and he believed without a doubt in his mind that Susan knew who Kaleigh was.

How? He couldn't answer that yet, but he would find out. The human servant's master was not going to get Kaleigh. None of them would. Kaleigh was his and his alone and no guardian hunter was going to take what he sold his body for.

"Do you remember what the man's name was?"

"I really can't remember. His name didn't exactly go with his character. I think it was like Hank or Harold or something like that."

"So if you saw him again, you could spot him?"

"I thought you didn't me to get involved," she said folding her arms across her chest, pushing her breasts together, giving Jack just a glimpse of how her breasts would feel filling his hands.

Jack looked at her face and cleared his throat. He played with a corner of his napkin to busy hands from reaching out for her. "I know what I said, but no one knows what he looks like but you. So I guess you do get involved after all. Though, all you're doing is going to point him out and then we're outta there. We'll let Sebastian take care of the rest when he comes."

"You're no fun," she said teasingly. "So when are we going?"

"What?"

"When are we going to the Temptation? From what Susan told me, he's usually there almost every night of the week."

Jack didn't answer her immediately. There was something strange between Kaleigh and Susan's relationship and it bothered him that she didn't know much about her friend as she should have. A total connection with a human or a guardian would have Kaleigh knowing everything about Susan.

"Why is it that you don't know much about your friend? You said you were connected with her, but you act as if you don't know her at all. I know everything about the humans that I've taken in."

Jack saw Kaleigh blush. She was silent for a moment and then answered him with a shrug. "I'm not trying to make you feel guilty, but the ones I let inside, I know their dreams, when they're having a bad day, and if they're about to do something against their good judgment. You act like you don't have that kind of connection with Susan."

"I do…I did, but I didn't want to know who she really was."

"Why?"

"Because I wanted to get to know her like humans do, okay?" she said angrily. "I let her in, I connected with her, but I blocked those visions from me."

"Did you ever see her death?" Jack asked.

Kaleigh shook her head. "It was odd with her. I didn't see her actual death or else I would have never left her alone, but I did know she was going to die soon."

Jack figured it was enough about this conversation. It obviously pained her to talk about it.

"I had planned for us to go out tonight to test your powers against a demon, but I guess it can wait until tomorrow night. What time do you have to be at work tomorrow?"

The plan was to let Kaleigh enter first scope out the club and find the man Susan left with Friday night, and about ten to fifteen minutes later, Jack would enter asking her to dance and they would leave together.

Kaleigh saw a few guys and a few familiar faces that had asked her to dance and she respectively declined their offer. Her body didn't have the energy to dance. She just wanted to go home and watch a late show wake up in the morning with the life she had before meeting Jack.

She wasn't the type to drink alcohol of any kind, but this time she wanted to blend in with the crowd and an order a Bailey's on the rocks and was even dressed casual. She wore a pair of denim faded jeans that fit snuggly against her hips, a pink glittered tank, and a pair of pink flat sandals. The drink's burning sensation traveled down her throat, to her lungs, and led straight to the pit of her belly as the toffee flavor filled her senses to an erotic pleasure. She had to hide her choked tears and the urge to cough.

The bartender noticed her discomfort and laughed. "Not much a drinker, are ya? You want another?"

She wanted to refuse, yet she found herself nodding. Once her second glass was placed in front of her, the burning sensation had passed, replaced by an overpowering feeling of relaxation. Kaleigh downed the next of Bailey's like it was ice water and it wasn't as bad as the first.

A man in his early twenties, pierced in every hole on his face, and dressed like a biker asked Kaleigh if she wanted to dance. It took her moment to register that he was asking her and not the girl sitting next to her with tattoos and piercing and pink hair.

She was going to say no, but then she really got a look at him and saw that it was the man Susan was going to meet. She shrugged her shoulders and thought, Why not? What better way to pry some information out of him.

She paid the bartender and Mr. Biker Man led her on the dance floor by the hand.

The white and red strobe lights danced to the beat of the grinding music as Kaleigh and her new friend made their way through the tight crowd and found a space in the middle of the dance floor. For a Sunday it was very crowded in this dark and dreary atmosphere of the Temptation as it was every night. The Temptation was known for its great music, semi-beautiful people, and cheap alcohol to the women. Where the women go to find a nameless fuck for the night, the men were sure to follow and the Temptation managed to get their name of the bar patted down to a T. One could barely dance without bumping elbows and getting a drink spilt on them.

Mr. Biker Man wasn't such a bad dancer. He dipped her, turned her at all the right beats, and swayed his body with hers to the rhythm of the music.

Kaleigh was having a great time. She never felt so free or loose in her life than she was now dancing with this stranger. It would have been much better if this were Jack.

The only annoyance she found in him was his silver crucifix that dangled from his third hole of his left earlobe; it constantly tickled her cheeked and she wanted to rip it right out of his ear along with the rest of the piercing and throw them in his face.

"Aren't you a friend of Susan?"

"Not really. I just know her through work."

"That's too bad," he said whispering in her ear. "I would really like to get to know you better."

Kaleigh was going to retort, but she got this tingling sensation that Jack had just walked through the door. She turned and saw him pushing his way through the crowd. He changed from his normal jean and cotton T-shirt to a silk, long-sleeve white, button down shirt, black trousers, and black shoes. He was contented with himself and at the same time she could detect a hint of jealousy by the narrowness of his eyes. Maybe because he just found her dancing with another man. Oh, well. She had no papers saying that she belonged to him or rings on her fingers. They just met yesterday and he had no claim on her!

Though, Kaleigh was lying to herself. She wanted him to claim her in the worst possible way.

Jack had pushed his way through the crowd and was standing right behind her when the music ended and turned into another upbeat song. Mr. Biker Man asked for another dance and Jack rudely cleared his throat.

"Sorry, man, I got this one."

Before Kaleigh could respond, the young man was gone and replaced with Jack's strong arms, wrapping firmly around her slim waist and a well-physique body. His thick, hard thighs meshed with hers as his broad, smooth chest smashed against her full, firm breasts. Kaleigh drowned in his spicy cologne and male intoxicated scent; it drove her senses to the boundaries of insanity. She had this quick impulse to rip off his shirt and feel the ridged muscles straining pressed against her skin.

Kaleigh was of average height for a woman and he was about a head taller than her, making him about six-two or six three. Her head would fit perfectly against his shoulder if she ever needed it.

"You're early," Kaleigh said to get her mind of that impulse.

Jack laughed. She was surprised he heard her; the music was blaring in all four corners of the bar and it was foolish to think that anyone could hold a normal conversation without shouting.

"I'm only five minutes early, but I can see you were doing fine." Kaleigh wanted to respond and before she could do so, he press his hands to her lower back and pushed her firmly against his groin, letting her feel the length of his desire. Kaleigh stiffened and her breath caught in her throat. Jolts of electricity sprinted through her veins as her legs became Jell-O and her heart was trying to break through her chest. She wanted to feel more, more, more!

Kaleigh relaxed against his body and felt his heart beating against her chest. His arms tightened around her as he moved her with the beat of the music, turning her on so badly that she had to squeeze her thighs together to repress the urge to rub herself against him. But what she wasn't doing for herself, Jack was doing it for her.

His hands moved lower to cup her ass, rolling his hips with hers, letting her feel the rigid bugle that was done by her. Having his erection against her sex was sheer torture and exciting at the same time. Kaleigh moaned and gripped the back of his T-shirt and didn't realize that she was rubbing herself against him on her own.

"Tell me what you want, Kaleigh?" Jack asked in a deep whisper in her ear as he stroked the length of her spine with his finger and then traced it around to her waist right below her navel. Kaleigh's mind turned to mush and her knees wanted to give. A hard, deep ache pulled to her loins, heating between her thighs, moistening in her panties as her breast tightened and perked through her flimsily bra and tank. She crushed her throbbing nipples to his hard chest and her thighs surrounded his.

They became one in an instant.

Kaleigh had never felt this reckless and shameless in her life before. She was never the one to display her affection, but the ache in her belly couldn't see fault. She wanted to throw down Jack in the middle of a crowd, strip him naked, and make love to him until they were both sweaty and exhausted.

With Mark, she was young and didn't know exactly what he was doing with him or what she was supposed to do with him. He took her virginity with gentleness and made loved to her the first time with restraint, giving her pleasure first and then his release. Mark didn't sexually provoke her inner bounds to make her feel this abandoned with wanton needs. He treated her like a fragile doll that had to be stored away in the dark for safe keeping; very unlike Jack. He wanted to protect her, keep her safe, but in that dark closet she knew he wanted to ravish her unrestrained.

Jack asked what she wanted and she damn well knew what he was talking about.

Kaleigh looked up in his eyes and saw the waves for a second just before they were gone and replaced by a heated, feral gaze.

He bent his head to hers, his mouth a breath away from her lips. "Tell me what you want," he repeated in that same whispered voice.

To have the word freely flow from her lips sounded so easy and yet so freaking hard. She wanted to, but couldn't. He was her protector, sent here by the six pure souls to guard her. She wasn't to fall in love with him and she wasn't supposed to open up to him. And if she made love to Jack, she would definitely lose her heart, which means she had to end this lunacy before it got out of control.

Kaleigh pushed away from his chest, giving about three inches of space between their bodies and concentrated on how well he danced. He never missed a beat or a pause. He was always there to guide her with each tempo and pulse.

She found no fault with him. He was perfect in every way. He had no annoying jewelry to tickle her. He always said the right words at the right time. His aura was beautiful and delicious as the pink glow of a warm sun setting over the horizon of a perfect spring day. He showed no signs of violence when he was provoked. He shows no signs that would make him deceive another person into liking him or avoiding the truth. He was upfront and honest man and an all around man's man. He was very good with people; he showed no judgment—even with these bottom feeders. He was the type of man that no woman would be ashamed to bring home to Mama.

"What are you thinking about, Kaleigh?"

Kaleigh didn't respond. If she told him what she was thinking he would laugh at her and tell her that she had a very vivid imagination.

"Are you thinking about me?"

"What makes you say that?"

He shrugged and then ran his fingers through her hair. "Maybe it's the silence your body is giving me. Maybe it's the way your eyes are swaying with interest. Maybe it's the way you're smiling or maybe it's the way you're touching me. Either way, I'm glad you're thinking about me."

"You can be very conceited," she said blushing.

"I know, but am I wrong?"

"No, you're not wrong. For some reason, I feel…safe with you. It's the first time I felt this way in a long time, but I don't trust myself around you."

"Why?"

"I have my reasons and I don't feel like talking about them."

Jack shrugged his shoulders as the music stopped and for a pregnant pause they stood locked together like two people in a fight to save each other's souls. Neither wanted to let go as for this sacred moment their world came to a stop, the strobe lights descended in the background as white light glowered around them as if they were the only two remaining on the dance floor. Kaleigh and Jack never felt more alive then this moment and they never wanted it to end. The ways of the dark world could not interfere with cherish moment or break them apart to embellish their world with the demons of hell.

Then the next song sprang into life.

Slowly and reluctantly, their arms came apart and their eyes locked and they saw the realms of heaven grasping out for them. Kaleigh's eyes widened as Jack raped through her soul asking for all the love and attention that he so desired from her. Kaleigh wanted to give it him. She desperately wanted to opened her heart up and let him take all, but just couldn't do it. She felt ashamed of herself. She wanted to trust him with her heart more than he could know and she knew by asking him to do so may end up costing his life.

Why could she never feel the happiness or the heartache in a human? All she could feel was their forthcoming deaths. That's why she cut all connections and never took another single soul into her spirit. Even when she met Mark, her first love, she couldn't risk the dark emotion to trample her spirit.

Kaleigh was tired of feeling remorse and bitter and that's why she opened her spirit to Susan and let her inside.

It was different with Susan; she felt the conviction of happiness for once. It was the first time she experienced the joyous emotions from another human being and it terrified her that the illusion would slip away.

And slowly it did.

After several thrills of roller coaster emotions, they began to slip away and turn into a havoc of despair. Yet, she could not save her. Perhaps a warning would have been sufficient, but Kaleigh couldn't tell her what she was. She knew it was forbidden to ever speak to a human about the guardian's extreme powers. If she could have said something—anything—that would have stopped Susan from that fateful night.

"Sometimes, Kaleigh I think you worry too much," Jack said as he led her to an empty table near the exit signs of the club and they sat across from each other. A waitress with blue wig, wearing a leather halter and leather pants asked if they wanted anything to drink. Jack ordered them both Heinekens.

When the waitress was out of ear range, Jack scooted his chair closer to Kaleigh's and asked, "Did you see him?"

"Who do you think I was dancing with?"

Jack looked over her shoulder and cringed. He turned to look back at her and his jaw was set and his lids heavy as if something had upset him. "Did you catch his name?"

Kaleigh shook her head, wondering at the same time if it was her that he was upset with her because she didn't grab the man's name. "From what I gather of our short conversation, he wasn't too interested in name-swapping if you know what I mean. He did know that I was a friend of Susan."

"Shit," Jack said as he gnashed his teeth. "Maybe I shouldn't have let you come here."

"Are you getting a feeling? Because since I blocked myself, I really can't feel anyone or anything unless it's very enraged."

"Yes," he said confidently. "I think it was him—almost positive—that it was him that tampered with you the last time you were here. I think he or someone else that he's associated with wanted you out of the way to…" Jack trailed off as he noticed the shadows of sadness dimming her face.

His heart ached for her. She had just lost the only friend in the world to her and probably the person responsible for present troubles. He didn't feel any pity for the woman that was lying stiff in a coffin underground somewhere. There was something about Susan that wasn't quite right with this picture and he blamed her.

Then again, if it wasn't for Susan, he may have never found Kaleigh again. He'd erase one of the strikes off Susan's side of the scoreboard.

He cleared his throat as he watched her face through his lashes. She looked so small sitting there and he wanted hold her, tell her everything was going to be all right, but he knew from both sides that were constantly pulling on him that everything was far from all right.

"What are you going to do about it?" Kaleigh asked in a deep, heavy voice. It sounded like she was trying hard not to cry and Jack wouldn't mind a bit if she cried on his shoulders. He'll let those tears soak his shirts.

"I'll get somebody to watch him."

The waitress brought their drinks back and Jack pulled out a bill and told her to keep the change. When the waitress was gone, the dark, brooding mood lifted around them. Kaleigh had conceded the grief for her friend and Jack found he could breathe easier.

"How come you're not a cop anymore?" Kaleigh couldn't believe she blurted that out. The question had been on her mind all day because she had this feeling that he was leaving something out that he didn't want to tell her.

"Too many questions rose when I couldn't provide proof of my information. They began suspecting me of playing a dirty cop."

"They didn't!" Kaleigh shouted and a few people looked their way.

Jack laughed. "It's true. They became very suspicious, following me around, keeping tabs on me, and so I figure it was best to call it quits. It wasn't one of my proudest moments to turn in my badge, but I was tired of the stipulation circulating about my resources."

Kaleigh took a sip of her beer, cringing as she set the bottle down hard. "I'm ashamed of you, Jack. You don't sound like a quitter."

"Well, I didn't want to be known as a dirty cop either. When I turned in my badge, I started my own private investigation business. I like it better being my own boss. I don't have to answer to anyone and I can work freely without the invasion in my life. What about you?" he asked and then taking a quick drink from his bottle, blatantly changed the topic of the conversation.

Where could Kaleigh begin? Starting from her deranged childhood or starting from Mark's death? She thought about it and knocked the two choices down.

"I grew up near Houston, earned a degree in business administration, first job was in the mailing room of Walker Security. I worked hard, earned my promotion, and now I'm head of Human Resources."

He finished his beer and crossed his arms over his chest as he studied her for a moment. He could see straight through the holes that were missing from her story. Kaleigh knew it and she really didn't care. She didn't have to tell this man anything! Her life ended five years ago and he didn't need to know anything about it.

"You're being evasive," Jack said. "I think your boyfriend found another dance partner."

Kaleigh startled by his quick turn in conversation, and curiously looked over her shoulder to see Mr. Biker Man dancing with a woman that looked seventeen that had a sour face like she was about to spill her guts.

"My loss," she said turning her head back to Jack. Well, I guess we should be leaving now." She must have stood up too quickly from the red vinyl chair because her feet stumbled over each other and Jack was there by her side helping her lean on him.

"How much have you had to drink?" he said with a laugh.

"Not much."

"I think you had one to many," he said worried.

"No I've only had two drinks and this," she said with slurred speech as she pointed a lazy finger at her bottle.

"Come on, Kaleigh. You can barely walk. Was your drink near you the whole time?"

Kaleigh couldn't remember, but she knew he was right about her barely walking. Kaleigh felt the club spinning around her and her legs felt like they weighed a hundred pounds. There was no way she would be able to reach Jack's jeep on her own. She leaned on him for support and found him very comforting.

She sighed heavily and wrapped her around his waist. "You feel so good to touch, Jack," she said purring as she rubbed her head against his chest.

Jack said something to her, but it was hard to concentrate when the world was spinning. She nodded her head at everything he said. He could have asked her to strip her clothes off in the parking lot and she would have agreed. Then she became very heavy and droopy. She tried to force herself awake and the last thing she remembered was the rundown parking lot.

Kaleigh never saw so many trees in her life. They were everywhere! The late night sky and the hidden moon almost made it impossible to see where she was going! The trees steadily popped out in front of her, smacking her in the face with their loose branches.

Her feet were tired as if they had been running hundred-mile marathon and she still had a hundred miles to go. She wanted to stop and take a breather, but someone was after her. He wasn't that far away and if Kaleigh's feet could keep their balance and avoid those ghastly trees she might outrun him.

"Kaleigh! Kaleigh!"

The man screamed her name from behind, but it sounded like he was calling her from the entire perimeter of the woods. His voice was deep, husky, and dripping with satisfaction of her difficulty.

She stumbled over a thick tree root and quickly regained her balance. He was getting closer to her. The stumble had set her back to the possibility that she could get caught. Her breathing was tired and sweat poured over her face like she was caught in an unexpected summer storm.

Another tree branch whacked her in the face and this time the greenery smacked her eyes and she was blinded temporarily by the stinging tears in a place too dark for her to see where she was going. All she could do was run and try her best to escape the clutches of whoever was chasing her.

"Kaleigh!" The man called out to her again. His voice was louder and not so distant. He was coming up close and any minute the man was going to tackle her down and kill her with all the force and strength he had left.

That could not happen! She had to live. She picked up her pace in a flash she was tumbling down on the center of the earth. She clawed, kicked, and screamed for the mercy of her life. The man wouldn't budge. He fought her with every inch of his strength.

Her arms were pinned down above her head. Her thighs were trapped underneath him. She couldn't move a muscle. Before her, death came, and she wanted to see the man who was going to kill her.

The tears blurred her vision, and she could see a small sample of his face. It was black as the night. Her eyes crept further and she wished they hadn't. She saw the face of her killer. She saw the man that was going to kill her. His red eyes told her future.

"You belong to me, Kaleigh."

She tried to scream, but her breath was trapped with his mouth took possession of hers.

"Kaleigh, wake up!"

A hard hand forced Kaleigh to uplift from her dream. She didn't need to open her eyes to know whose hand it was. Then the dream came back in focus and Kaleigh shot up. She inched her whole body against the bedpost and wrapped the covers around her shoulders. Her body shook violently like a leaf caught in a tornado as the sweat dripped from her body and ran onto the canary yellow bedspread.

"Are you all right?" Jack asked with concern.

She couldn't speak. All words that she learned were lost. She opened her mouth, hoping something would come out and failed. She felt an intense arm wrap around her, pulling her against a calmly beating chest. He smothered her body with simplicity and whispered soothing words.

Her body instantaneously calmed down with his powerful caressing hand strokes and she felt safe and protected. The man in her dreams became a cavernous past as this man's calming-effected words gave comfort.

Kaleigh sucked in her breath, and took her time releasing her exhaustion. She was controlled, calm.

"Feel better?" She nodded.

"Want to talk about it?" She shook her head.

She was thankful Jack was here. If he hadn't awakened, she feared she might have been dead. Just that thought brought her body snuggling against him, wrapping her arms around his solid chest.

Jack was her protector. She felt so safe around him that she wondered how she ever survived without him. His chest hair tickled her neck. She had the urge to run her fingers through his crisp golden curls. He smelled like the remains of the cologne he wore to the club and a pure vibrant man.

Kaleigh pushed the bedspread to her chest and she noticed something peculiar about her surroundings. She didn't own any yellow bedspreads. Hers were daisy and sunflowers. There were no landscapes pictures hanging anywhere in the vicinity of her bedroom. The harvest gold lamp with the pearl white shade that sat on the bedside night stand was unfamiliar to her. The apple cinnamon potpourri wasn't filling her nose; instead a manly spice smell filled the room. The clothes she wore to the club were still on except for her sandals; they were off.

Her body tensed. His arms tightened. Kaleigh couldn't break free.

"Let me go!"

"What is your problem, Kaleigh?" He spoke gently.

"Let me go!"

Jack released her.

Kaleigh scrambled out of the unknown bed and hit the floor. Jack came around the bed and acted like he was going to grab her. Kaleigh quickly scooted against the night stand and threw her arms up. Jack was only a foot away from her when he stopped and knelt in front of her.

The front of his short-cut hair was tousled, his chest was bare and he wore the same loose-fitting jeans he wore earlier in the day. She looked down at his naked feet. They were nice huge feet; something Kaleigh wouldn't mind touching. Not at this moment! She wanted to know why she was at his apartment.

"What the hell am I'm doing here?" She didn't look him directly in the eyes. She was afraid if she did that she might fall under his spell and forgave him for whatever he had to say. Then an intense pain ricocheted in her head. She had to bite her tongue from groaning and bury the tears threatening to spill.

"Have you forgotten that you are staying at my place?"

"What?" Her head was pounding so badly it felt like nails were driving into her brain.

"Did you forget that you are staying at my place?" he asked more softly and Kaleigh was grateful. The thought of him screaming gave her the urge to close her eyes and cover her ears.

Then everything came back in an instant.

"Oh, yeah, that's right." She rubbed her head and tried not to look at Jack's chest, but it was unbearably hard.

"Nothing happened, did it?"

"Nothing happened. I brought you in, took your shoes off, and put you in bed. I'm not that much of a dick to take advantage of a drunken woman."

"I got drunk?" It seemed impossible because she was never the one to get drunk. Yet, twice she had gotten so mind-numbingly oblivious to her surroundings that it felt like she was deliberately being sabotage. Someone had to have done something to her drink when she wasn't looking. The coincidence that Mr. Biker Man was there both times she lost consciousness pretty much said it all. He must have slipped something into her drink while she wasn't looking. It was the logical explanation for happened to her.

"Not much of a drinker, huh?"

Kaleigh agreed with a nod because it was less painful than talking. Of course, she wanted to know what Jack was doing in her room.

"Why are you in here?"

"You were screaming."

"I was screaming?" she asked in disbelief.

"Like a banshee. I just hope the neighbors didn't think I was beating you or we were having wild monkey sex." It was meant as humor, but she didn't feel much like laughing. She was tired and her head felt like a boulder smashed it. She rubbed her temples and groaned.

"Head hurt?" Kaleigh nodded. "What's some aspirin?" She nodded again.

Jack left the room. Kaleigh slumped against the night stand which was a mistake; any contact with her head intensified the ache. Damn, even the soft sound of the running water made her head split in two.

She heard Jack's footsteps approaching her and then he was kneeling beside her. He grabbed her hand, and dropped two white pills in the center of her palms and then handed her glass of water.

"Thank you, Jack."

"You're welcome." He stood back up as she popped the pills in her mouth and drowned them with the tap water. She gave back his glass and he placed it on the night stand.

"Feel like going back to bed?"

"Yes."

Jack bent over and enfolded one arm around her waist and the other underneath her buttocks. She didn't mean to shriek, but the unexpected lift in the air caught her off guard and before she knew her arms were deadlocked around his neck.

"I'm not going to drop you," he said softly laughing.

"I know." She felt foolish. She was acting like it was her first time around a man. It had been a while since she'd been with a man and she remembered that she normally didn't act this childish. It was probably due to the alcohol and the induced pain in her head. Or could be Jack.

She was carefully placed in his bed. It was still warm from her heat. The yellow covers came over her and tucked beneath her chin. He was treating her like a victim, which she was victim—from the alcohol, but it was no reason to treat her like she was fragile, beaten little girl.

"You don't have to do all this."

He smiled. Kaleigh regretted what she said. "I know I don't have to. I want to. Next time go easy on the Bailey's."

"How did you...."

"I could smell it on your breath," he said with another warm smile and so close to her lips that it would be so easy to lift her chin and taste his delectable mouth. She could lift as if adjusting her pillow and her lips would be on his. The pain in her head vibrated and she wasn't going to get a good night kiss. She sighed and lay motionless, waiting for him to move.

"Good-night, Kaleigh. Sweet dreams." His mouth brushed hers and Kaleigh's insides melted to liquid heat. A spark of desire quivered inside of her most intimate part. Her body was hot and flushed and she wanted to taste him over and over. The headache perished to a calming wave of delight and sensation.

Jack removed his lips and Kaleigh's judgment blew away like her headache as her hands captured his wrists. "Don't go, Jack. Please stay with me."

He fell silent as he looked down on her with skepticism. She didn't want him to think that she was begging for sex; she wanted him to stay for the night while she slept. To sleep with her in the same bed—nothing more. She wanted to feel the security he had to offer and to capture his warmth that made her place in the world a possibility.

Here she was burning for him and she didn't want the sex; she only wanted the comfort that he was going to be there when she woke up.

What she saying? She couldn't be doing this. Getting close to Jack was the last thing she needed, but the dream frightened her badly and she didn't feel like being alone tonight. She was always alone when she was scared and just for tonight she wanted to have someone with her. Jack was here; he was the handiest.

"Please, Jack. Don't leave me. Just lay next to me until I fall asleep. That's all I'm asking." She sounded desperate because she was desperate. She didn't want to have another dream like she did earlier and have to wake up alone.

"You sure?"

"Yes," she whispered.

He crossed to the other side of the bed as Kaleigh lay facing the mini blinds, frantically wanting to turn over and watch him slide in next to her. She blushed as she heard the unsnapped of his jeans and his zipper filling the room. Her heart pounding against her chest and suddenly it was too hot for the covers and too embarrassed to push them off of her. She wanted to see the rest of him, but couldn't conjure the motive to turn around and watch him.

Jack's body weighed down the bed as he lifted the covers and slid next to her. She could tell that he lay flat on his back with his arms to his side, wishing he would move just a little bit closer and hold her so she could fall asleep.

With the short distance he put between them she could feel his body heat, and that added extra wanton desire to her feeble, scorching lions and the excruciating scent of his male body made her heart throb, breasts perk, and a warm dampness fill between her thighs. A moan came half way out. She closed her eyes and swallowed it. She wanted his hands to relinquish the burning ache of her loins and breasts, and to fill her with the passion that her body desired for.

Kaleigh'd been without a man for five years and hadn't suffered an uncontrollable desire until Jack exploded in her life. And what a bang it was! Laying next to him in the stormy silence with the desolate light peeking through the mini blinds and the overwhelming sentiment of an irrepressible yearning, Kaleigh found that maybe five years had been too long. Or maybe her irrepressible yearning was waiting for him. Night after night she had dreams of his coming. He was always standing all hard and powerful and naked silhouetted from the glow of the moon that every time she woke up, it felt like she was in the after glows of a dramatic climax as the tremors shook her body fiercely. She never envisioned that she would actually be in the presence of the man in her dreams and begging him to stay with her.

Never had she thought that she felt so lost without him. Jack was everything she needed and everything she wanted out of a person. But it wasn't possible when she had the worst demon after her and she was forbidden to even have him.

Damn her bad luck!

Kaleigh stared at the motionless mini blinds while her body fought to turn over. Why couldn't she just let her guard down for a second and see what happened? At the club, she knew what would happen if she told Jack what she really wanted.

They wouldn't be lying silently in the bed.

"Kaleigh." She jumped at the sound of his deep, ripe voice. She didn't turn around when she responded.

"Yes?"

"I'm going to hold you," he said softly, penetrating the core of her spirit with his sensual, rugged voice.

Yes, yes, yes! Her body screamed.

"Okay," she said softly.

He turned to his side and pulled her against the hard plane of his chest and had her curved to the contour of his middle and thighs. One arm lay above her head as the other wrapped around her waist, placing his hand on the middle of her belly, igniting the fire again. Kaleigh felt something hard and thick centered on her buttocks and wanted to rub her ass up and down length of him. His body was so hot and hard and comforting that at the moment, Kaleigh wanted him to take her with the wild abandonment that was bursting to come out.

As if he knew what she was thinking, he pressed closer to her body, sensually moving his lower half with hers and his hand moving underneath her shirt. Her stomach quivered under his touch and Kaleigh felt the rise of her heat spread through her body. His hard, calloused hand whispered with soft strokes across her flesh. Her body tightened, her breathing became deep, her body ached in places that were on fire to be touched, and she found herself caressing the back of her head against his chest.

Then Jack kissed her earlobe as his hand deftly slid to the button of her jeans. Anticipation was the goose bumps covering her flesh and she wasn't going to stop him. Thinking was beyond anything that was left on her mind and she wanted this as if she needed this to survive.

Jack's breathing was slow and deep as his heart was thumping hurriedly against her back.

Swiftly, he unbuttoned her jeans as if he to do it before he could change his mind and slowly oh so slowly, slid the zipper down. His hand slid up and splayed across her waist and then slowly dipped back down until his fingertips were scarcely underneath the elastic band of her panties.

"Spread your thighs for me," he whispered huskily in her ear as his hand began to graze further down her.

Kaleigh blew caution to the wind and waited with her eyes closed, her body drumming wildly to their hearts. Oh, how she wanted this. She was not going to stop him this time or maybe…not even the next time.

Then his hand was cupping her heat, his middle finger lightly stroking the slick folds of her sex. Kaleigh moaned and her heart leaped. In all her life she never felt this heated by a man's touch and this ready for a man's touch. She was swollen with need and so wet that Jack's finger slipped into her without his need to push. Then Jack kissed the sensitive flesh between her neck and shoulder and she shuddered, unconsciously opening her thighs further for his access. He lips trailed fire up her jaw and to her cheek and then going to her mouth.

Kaleigh moved her head to meet his lips and when they touched hers, they were hot and resilient and skilled. This kiss started out slow and sweet and soon turned ravenous and fierce. His mouth covered hers all hard and demanding and blissfully burning, as his tongue parted her lips. Her mouth opened for him and she let him claim her, control her with his commanding kiss.

Then as he was kissing her, his middle finger thrust all the way inside to the hilt. Kaleigh moaned in his mouth and he kissed her deeper, more hungrily as another finger slipped inside and she moved with magic of his fingers that were bringing her closer and closer to the edge of the cliff.

Then she fell off and exploded. Her nails dug in the sheets and her cries were swallowed by the kiss he wouldn't let up. Tremors ransacked her entire body and finally after the last one was gone, she realized that Jack had stopped kissing her and his fingers that played havoc with her libido and caused her to have an intense, climatic orgasm were zipping and then buttoning her jeans.

Kaleigh's headache was gone for sure, but Jack's enormous problem wasn't. He was strung tighter than a bowstring, and she wondered what he wanted her to do to him.

"Jack," she said softly, almost embarrassed to say anything. "I—"

"Shh," he said interrupting her. "Just sleep, Kaleigh.

His voice sounded strained and she felt she had to do something to ease his tension. But at the sound of his words, Kaleigh became drowsy. Her lids got heavy and then shut to the comfort of his arms wrapped around her like a blanket.

"Good night, Kaleigh," he sang like a love song.

"Good night," she lazily sang back. Then she fell asleep.

Chapter Five

Kaleigh's body was excitingly warm. Funny, she thought. Lately every morning she'd been waking up shivering with cold chills that she had to start wearing a flannel night gown to keep her body from going under hypothermia. She adjusted the thermostat to keep her apartment at a normal seventy-eight degree, but when morning came around, it always felt twenty degrees cooler. She put a maintenance request to the manager on Friday of last week and she probably won't see him until Friday of this week. She could handle the cold; it was her toes that were cold as a Popsicle! Not on this morning. Her toes were buttery warm. Her body was affectionately warm.

She snuggled closer to the glorified warmth and something tickled her nose that caused her hand to automatically come up and bump the heating system that lay next to her. No. Under her.

Kaleigh froze. She was sprawled on top of a warm, hard body and she didn't have a clue of who he was! Then the familiar scent of Jack engulfed her nose and she slightly relaxed, yet feeling embarrassed.

With her eyes closed, she quietly, carefully and as stiffly as possible trying not to wake up Jack, slid off his broad, hard chest and moved to the empty side of the bed that was cold as her own. He didn't move and his breathing was deep and regular as if he were in a dream. She sigh a relief to herself for the gratitude that Jack didn't wake up. All she had to do now was to get out of this bed and act like nothing happened last night.

Yeah right, her inner voice said. *This man gave you the best orgasm you ever had in your life and you're just going to act like nothing happened?* In other words, she was going to have to face Jack after he woke up.

Stupid! What was she thinking to let him do that to her? It wasn't twenty four hours ago, she was commanding herself that nothing could happen between Jack and her. Their relationship was to be strictly platonic like good old friends in the past, and yet her body couldn't fathom any reason to stop him.

There she was denying she wanted him to touch her and kiss her and…oh god, everything else. But she shouldn't have let it happen. She didn't want Jack any closer to her, and nothing, she vowed, would ever happen again!

Satisfied with her oath, she opened her eyes and the morning sunlight filled the room. Squinting, she slanted her eyes to Jack. The covers had slipped down below his navel and Kaleigh took the time to study his body.

It was magnificent!

She wanted to run her hands all over him, lick every inch of his mouth-watering body, and see if his kisses were as powerful as he.

Kaleigh's body came to life.

You're doing it again!

She could not be thinking about this! Jack was too much of a risk. Oh, but a what a risk worth taking if she could find that nerve of steel and let it unleash! She could be wild, wanton, desirable, and have Jack completely at her mercy. The things she would love to want to do with him were mind-disturbing and wickedly bad.

It was fantasy for the books and the daunting nights of a cold bed alone.

When this was all over…when she was safe to be on her own again, it would be a fantasy that she would embellish.

She closed her eyes, forgetting the fantasies and vaguely wondered what time it was. She knew today was Monday and guessed by the traffic noise outside and the morning light trying to fortify her lids to open that it was around seven. Her alarm at her apartment was always set for six-thirty, giving her approximately one hour to get dress and twenty minutes to get to work, thus, leaving her ten minutes to find a parking space, get into the elevator, and start her day in the office.

Well, she wasn't at her apartment; she was in Jack's, and she was going to be late. Then she remembered that she didn't have any appropriate clothes to wear for work.

She was going to be real late.

What was she going to do?

Out of almost six years she'd been working at Walker's Security she had never been late and had never called in. She only took her two weeks of indispensable vacation time out of the year, which was mid-April, and she wasn't due for her vacation until the last week of May. She planned to go to Hawaii because she heard it was beautiful there from a co-worker, and she wanted to let her mind relax with the ocean waves. Kaleigh could have done that in Galveston, but she wanted to be away from the States.

Kaleigh decided to wait to call her assistant when she felt like getting up. Not to worry, Jack knew Mr. Adrian Walker; therefore, she couldn't get in trouble, could she? Either way she was going to be late and she would deal with the consequences when she got there. Kaleigh wanted to lie next to Jack for a few minutes longer to add a special memory that would replace one of the bad ones that she had too many of.

It was really quite sad now that she thought about it. In her entire life, she could only remember a handful of times that she had genially smiled. It depressed her more as she realized that most of those smiles were from her childhood—before her life became a total factor for the world.

She knew in the past five years she had never smiled. Even when she was with Susan, she never smiled, except to please the person that was talking to her. With Mark it was a few times and as a teenager, never.

Gawd! She was pathetic! Why did she make her life so dark and orderly when there was a world of opportunities waiting—figuratively and literally speaking—for her to open up? Kaleigh especially had a very special offer lying right next her and she knew that Jack wouldn't turn her down.

Could one night of tenuous passion break the mold she spent years of perfecting or lead her straight to the path that she had been avoiding her entire life?

Thinking about the consequences gave Kaleigh chill bumps up her arms and down her legs and she felt her nipples become erect. Thanks to her great tank it revealed everything!

If Jack woke up right now he would think that she had something else on her besides getting those damn covers off—

"How long are you planning to lie there and freeze to death?"

Jack was awake. The real question was: how long had he been awake and watching her? She didn't want to know. She was mortified!

Kaleigh opened her eyes as if she was thinking nothing at all and the first thing she forgot how bright the room was. She had to hurry and shut her eyes before she was blinded by the strength of the sun's rays. Typical man living on bachelorhood, she thought. Only a single man wouldn't have the decency to put up some kind of cloth over the mini blinds to block out some of that morning sun.

Kaleigh's eyes finally adjusted to brightness after several times of blinking and readjusting them. Now she had to face reality and talk to Jack about last night. Just thinking about it made her face hot.

No need for the covers anymore, her face was doing a pretty good job of warming her all over the place.

Jack sat against the headboard about the same time as she did. She tucked her heels under her rear and glanced at Jack who was still covered from the waist down, baring his golden, crisp chest hair and the smooth texture of his ridged abdomen, and strong build of his arms.

His hair was tousled from last nights sleep. His sapphire molten eyes were vivid as the brightness of the room. He looked content and rested with a smirk on his face like he had wet dream, while she must look like she had a serious case of a bad hangover. Her hair was all over the place and the remainder of last night's sand was still embedded in her eyelashes and around the corner of her eyes.

"The proper the thing to do in the morning is to say, good morning," Jack said with a lazy smile.

"G—good morning," she said. Urgh! She must sound like a damn fool! Probably looked like one too. She didn't realize that she had been staring! Nonchalantly, she looked away to perceive the dusty, off-white mini blinds.

"You want some coffee?"

"Yes." Then she suddenly remembered that Jack took off his pants last night. One sight of him in his underwear and...she'll just keep staring at the mini blinds.

Jack got out of bed and put the same faded jeans on he wore all day yesterday. When Kaleigh heard the zipper come up and the faint snap of the button, she turned her head and saw the most delicious back she ever seen in her life. It was broad, darkly tanned as the rest of him, and every time he moved he rippled with muscles. His butt filled out the loose-fitting jeans and she imagined grabbing a hold of that firm ass and squeezing it for all that it was worth. She had to restrain herself not to wrap her arms around him and stay put.

His tattoo appeared to have become more ridged from the last time she had seen it, like it was coming it to life. The eye followed her, the dragon's wings looked liked they were on the approached of flapping, and she waited to see if they were about to.

"Can I change?" Kaleigh asked before she could stop herself.

Jack turned around with a screwed up look on his face and asked, "What?"

"I'm meant…you said warriors were the shape-shifters, do you know if the pure souls are?" she asked looking down at the bed then back up to meet his eyes.

Much better conversation to discuss then the one she had on her mind.

"No, the warriors are the only ones that can change and me of course. Your power exceeds ours by far, Kaleigh. The pure souls are the only ones that can touch a demon without getting infected and can destroy a guardian hunter."

"They didn't really teach much, Jack, but how to hide myself away from the rest of the world. They just told really what I was about and there were others that were like us."

"They should have told you everything about us and you," he said with a frown. "If I so happen not to be with you when a demon comes after you, you just believe in yourself like Peter Pan, and you will see how assertive your powers are."

Kaleigh laughed even though he meant every positive word. It was the way he associated her with Peter Pan. It was the first time she'd laughed in what seemed like months. Scratch that. Years. It had been years since she laughed out loud and thoroughly enjoyed it and wanted to do it over and over again.

"When can we find out?"

"Hopefully never," Jack said with a chuckle.

"Thank you, Jack," Kaleigh said with a timid smile.

Jack looked at her warily and narrowed his eyes in suspicion, and then asked. "For what?"

Kaleigh shrugged, truly not knowing why she was thanking him. It could be because he made her smile, laugh, or for his generous behavior that made her felt something besides the aloneness. Or what he did to her last night. Pretty much—everything in general.

"For helping me before…when I didn't know you and now," she said quietly.

Jack hesitated before he bent to her ear as he softly caressed her cheek with his knuckles. Kaleigh's heart slammed against her chest. "You don't ever have to thank me, Kaleigh. It's my honor to protect you. Why don't you take a shower, we'll stop by your place to get some of your clothes, and then I'll take you to work," he whispered to her in that soft, gentle voice she'd only heard a few times from him that made her like she couldn't breathe.

"Okay," Kaleigh said, barely breathing.

Jack straightened and as he was about to leave her to privacy, he stopped in front of the door and said with the husky voice he used last night, "I immensely enjoyed last night." Then he left.

Kaleigh sank against the hard bedpost and groaned and pounded her head a few times before she got the nerve to get out of bed to take a shower and face Jack again.

Jack took another cold shower in the hallway bathroom, shaved, and dressed in a in his usual jeans and cotton T-shirt. Today was hunter green. It wasn't like he was going anywhere specials; he was going to see Adrian Walker about his fake job, which he had a pretty good assumption of what he might me doing. He wasn't going to like it, but what the hell could he do? He had to stay close to Kaleigh.

After his shower, Jack snatched up the Monday edition of the *Houston Chronicle* outside of his front door, sat down at the kitchen table, flipped to the sports section, and tried to read as his mind wandered to Kaleigh.

Last night was like a dream come true. For five years he had been dreaming about her, wondering if she still felt the same, smelt the same, and if her skin was still the soft touch of velvet. Jack discovered all three while he was holding her, trying to fall asleep with the largest hard-on he ever had in his life.

It was so hard—no pun intended—to sleep next to his once lover and not be able to take her the way he wanted to. All night his thoughts kept coming back to how she responded to his touch and how wet and tight she was and thought how blissfully painfully it would to have his cock buried in her.

He could feel it now. Her tight, wetness surrounding him, taking all of him as he went in and out with slow deep strokes and then taking her hard and fast as she moved and cried beneath him.

Jack had to put a stop to his before his erection burst through his jeans.

He knew how Kaleigh felt about him; he was after all emphatic to her feelings. She was at a constant battle with herself to take the first step with him or not. Well, he took the initiative last night to step over her safety boundaries.

But he had to have her soon. He was tired of walking around in a constant state of arousal, as he'd been for the past five years; he couldn't take it anymore! He could have had her last night; she would have complied to his every whim, but he didn't because his good conscience said to earn some more of her trust as his other side was laughing devious for chicken-shit he was.

Kaleigh doesn't make up her mind soon then be damn with her inner conflicts! If she only knew how much he wanted to be bury deep inside of her.

Last night he came close to taking advantage of her while she was sleeping. Her skin was soft, smooth as velvet. Her breasts were firm and fit perfectly in the palm of his hands, and he so badly wanted to lift up her shirt to sample her rosy, perky nipples. He also wanted to sample some other places that weren't on her northern regions, but he didn't want to do anything unscrupulous that would compromise her trust in him.

But, her invigorating feminine scent made him wanted to take her unscrupulously, like a wild man, and be damn with her trust.

With all his control, he refrained from attacking her during the night, and finally hours later he fell asleep only to have a wet-dream about her. Jesus! He hadn't had a wet dream since he was a teenager! When he woke up to find her lying on top of him, it took an act of congress not to take her.

He gripped the sides of the newspaper to dampen down the hardness that was burning a hole in his jeans now. It only relieved the tension for a second as the dramatic dream from last night invaded his mind. It was erotic and full of promises that were meant to be carried out. She was lying on her back with those big sparkling emerald eyes clenched shut as ecstasy heated her body in a way she never felt before.

Jack was kneeling between her legs, caressing the inside of her thighs with his scorching, powerful tongue. He tasted and licked and kissed the pure wholeness of her slick folds.

Kaleigh moaned. She begged for him to be inside her. She wanted him hot, hard and throbbing, taking her fast without restraint. But Jack wanted to taste her first.

Sliding his tongue up, he stopped at the first signs of the soft curls as he became drunk by the infatuation of her womanly scent. As the only means to control his sanity, he ravenously gripped her thighs and plunged his tongue into her wet, wet folds. Kaleigh's scream of pleasure almost sent him over the edge. He had to dig his fingers into her flesh to keep him from spilling his seed on the dampness of the sheets.

Each stroked he thrust into her made her come closer to her own release. Her knees were trembling, quivering to unleash the power of the climax, but Jack made sure as he nipped at her engorged bud that she didn't come without him being inside her.

Jack felt her breathing quicken, her moans becoming progressively higher, her juice flowing like the Nile River, and her climax on the verge of exploding, and then Jack lifted from her thighs and drove into her hard, pulsing, and ready to end her misery.

Then he woke up at the best part so hard that Kaleigh's disturbing movements almost sent him flying.

"I'm ready if you are." Kaleigh's voice startled him that he nearly ripped the newspaper in half.

Jack realized that the newspaper was on the brink to becoming confetti. His grip was so tight that the paper was no longer decipherable. He loosened his grip and tossed the newspaper aside. He also realized that he had a hard-on larger than his pants could cover-up. Hopefully, she was too much in a rush to notice.

"Do you want any coffee?" he asked out of politeness.

Shit! He forgot to make the coffee.

"Very much, but I'll just pick some at work. I'm late as it is."

She looked so sexy standing there with her arms crossed and her tousled hair spilling over her face. He wanted to jump up and kiss her good morning. He knew better, though. He also knew that he had to get himself under control before he lost it. What did she think about last night? She hadn't said anything, but both of them knew what was on each other's mind.

"You don't have time for a cup of coffee?"

"I'm already late as it is. I do have to go to work," she said.

"Why don't you call and tell them you're coming in late."

"I can't do that! That will show poorly on my part! I am the head of personnel. What would the other employees think?"

Jack waved his hand for her to sit. "I have some things I want to say to you."

She looked at him warily and her shoulders slumped. "Fine, but hurry up. I don't have all day."

"You sure are bossy this morning." Kaleigh rolled her eyes and stared everywhere but at him. Jack got up to make some coffee.

"Oh, by the way," Jack said as he filled the filter with coffee grain. "You might as well know that I cancelled all my appointments for the rest of the week."

"Why?"

"Because of this morning, I'm a new employee of Walker Security."

"You're what?" Kaleigh shouted.

"Stop shouting," he said as he pulled a coffee mug from the cabinet and set it under the drip. "These walls are paper thin. What will the neighbors think?"

"You are not funny, Jack" she said fuming. "First my life gets invaded and now my job, too? When will this end?"

"I told you I can't I leave you unprotected, Kaleigh and I meant it. Sorry if you feel smothered, but I really don't give a damn. Your life is in *my* hands, and I'm going to do everything in my powers to keep you alive!"

"This is crazy, Jack! I'll be perfectly safe—"

"And I say you won't," Jack interrupted. "This is one argument you are not going to win, so don't even try to fight with me."

Kaleigh wanted to slap that smug look at his face. It wasn't bad enough that she had to live with him, now she had work with him too! God, this was just getting better and better.

Let's be honest, Kaleigh. You don't mind be smothered by this man; you're just afraid that you might do something stupid like fall in love with him, which you are already half-way there.

Jack couldn't know that.

"How in the hell did you acquire a job at Walker Security in such a short time?"

He shrugged his shoulder as he lifted the coffee cup from the burner and handed it to her. "I know Adrian," and then sat down as if he just told her it was warm outside.

"How do you know Mr. Walker?" Kaleigh asked unbelievingly.

"We are old friends, Adrian and I. Did you know that he's a panther warrior?" Jack said arrogantly.

After Kaleigh's initial shock, she looked Jack up and down and glared at him when she met his eyes. "I was astonished myself, too. While, you were sleeping in yesterday—don't interrupt me, Kaleigh. I took it upon myself to give Adrian a called, your boss. Apparently he had no idea that a pure soul was working directly under his roof. And Adrian is quite good at what he does."

"Talking about putting me in harm's way," Kaleigh said sarcastically. "I thought I was supposed to be this great secret."

"You are, but it wouldn't hurt to have a couple of more looking after you. Sebastian would have to know too. Anyway, he knows about Susan and is going to let me check her desk while you are working. It shouldn't take me too long, but he doesn't want his employers to get suspicious that something bad happened to one of their co-workers. It's best anyway to go incognito."

"You're not going to be interviewing the rest of the employees are you? Because I'll have you know none of them knew Susan the way I did."

Jack had a thought about that; Kaleigh didn't really know her friend at all. "If I don't find anything, I may have to. By the way, you should let Gina know that you are no longer living in your residence for the time being. She's a fairy sorcerer and they often get dreams about the world and she will find out about you. It's a wonder she hadn't already."

Kaleigh wondered how to respond to that. She never knew what type of guardian her mother was and if wasn't for Jack—again—she would have never known at all.

Her mother isn't the easiest person to get along with. All those lonely days she spent as a child, wishing for her mother to acknowledge her instead focusing on other people lives that only withdrew her further away from her daughter's life. She wished so much that her mother would forget about her duties for one second and see that she needed guidance more than any of them.

Thinking of her mother, she would have to call her and let her know what had happened in the past few days. She may not care what happened to her daughter, but Kaleigh, despite her mother's neglect and faults, loved her dearly and had to warn her for what may be to come.

"Just leave my mother to me, Jack. I'll talk to her."

Kaleigh wasn't late to work; thanks to Jack driving eighty miles an hour while whizzing his way in and out of traffic during Monday morning rush hour. They, of course, didn't have a problem with traffic jams because Jack magically spread the exhaust fumes' motors clear of them.

He first stop was at her apartment, where she quickly changed from her T-shirt and jeans to a pair of soft black slacks and beige short-sleeved blouse. Next, he sped his way to Walker Security. It was the first time she had ever gotten carsick and she said a few choice word to Jack when he dropped her off in front of the building. She said them loud enough for him hear and he heard them all right, laughing as he pulled away from her.

Monday mornings were also especially quiet at Walker's Security. Most of the employees were between their late twenties to the age of retirement. Kaleigh got lucky when Mr. Walker decided to take a chance on a young twenty-two year, and Kaleigh proved she could be a prominent employee for advancement. She started working in the mail room and kept on pushing herself until she landed as the administrative assistant of the former head of personnel and when she retired, Mr. Walker thought Kaleigh was just the right employee to take on the position.

It was strange knowing all these years she worked for Adrian Walker that he knew Jack and yet neither one had any idea that she was right under their noses all along. That brought a smile to her face and it quickly turned into a frown when she realized everything she was doing was not going according to the other six pure souls.

They forbade her to get involved with another guardian and they forbade her to ever show herself to the world. Now, before this day was over, three more people were going to find out about her, making her accessible to the demons and the guardian saviors.

What was she doing?

She remembered the last time she encountered a demon and…

Oh, Mark. She had never felt so betrayed and so stupid in her life. There for a while, she considered herself fancy in love with him. Who was she kidding? She loved him like a fool.

God! She was so stupid!

She blocked herself at nineteen when she was tired of the demons haunting her every move! Then she met Mark and he turned out be the very same thing she tried to block.

Shaking her head, Kaleigh had checked over her daily planner. She had two interviews in the early morning for a mail clerk position and several applications to look over for opened position as a customer specialist relation. She also had to see a couple of employees that were ready for their six-month evaluation.

Walker Security was a fairly large corporation that installed state-of-the-art security system for homes and businesses in and outside of the Houston area. Adrian Walker Senior built it from ground up when he was barely a year over twenty, providing first for business and then twenty years ago made his security system available to homes. He retired the year before Kaleigh was hired on, leaving his legacy to his son, Adrian Walker Jr. She never met him, but from what she heard, his son was the spitting image of him.

Kaleigh worked all the way until lunch and wondered what Mr. Walker had Jack employed as. She was going to have to worry about that later. She needed to make a phone call her to her mother.

After three rings, she heard her mother's brightly lit voice. "Hello, Kaleigh. It's nice that you are you finally calling. How are you doing?"

Her mother sounded very chipper about her call, for it had been years since she last spoke to her.

"I'm fine, Mom. How are you?"

"I'm worried about you."

That was a first. Not once in all of Kaleigh's twenty-seven years of life had her mother worried about her. It almost sounded like her mother really cared; therefore, this wasn't her mother or she was on something besides the souls that lived in her spirit.

Gina made sure that the day Kaleigh could walk and talk at the same time, she was on her own. Kaleigh was on the only girl in the first grade that could make her lunch, pick out her own clothes to wear, and walk home unescorted. She really hated those days it rained. At least the school was only five short block away from her house.

"You're worried about me, Mom? Care to tell me why or did I just get you on a good day?"

"Don't be a smart-ass, Kaleigh." *Now that sounded like Mom.* "I've been having some strange dreams lately that have me concerned."

"What kind of dreams?" Kaleigh picked up a pen and began tapping it on her desk. Her mother was a fairy sorceress just as Jack said. She should have known from all the "guests" she consulted during her childhood.

"They're weird and confusing. They don't make any sense." Then her mother paused and slowly said, "Kaleigh, you are a sorceress, right?"

"Uh...."

"Because, in my dreams, you're not. All the symbols are saying that you are a pure soul. But I don't see how that is plausible when I'm a fairy and your father is...anyway. It just doesn't make sense."

Kaleigh stopped tapping her pen and then crossed her legs and settled back in her executive chair. She wanted to scream.

Whenever her mother started talking about her father, she would stop or change the subject. She knew her mother wasn't in love with the man, for

Pete's sake, or like Jack said, she would lose her powers and her powers, from what the pure souls showed her, were quite extreme.

Kaleigh wanted to run away from all her problems like she when she was nineteen and like she did with Mark. Why was all of this coming out now? Why couldn't this have happened to her a year ago or five years ago when she learned that Mark was nothing what he appeared to be?

She inhaled long and deep and released it all in a gush. "Yes, Mom. But please don't try to connect with me."

Kaleigh broke her mother's connection along with the other children she had let in a young child. She was probably the only seven-year-old in the world that committed suicide by drinking an entire gallon of bleach.

"Don't worry, I won't let it happen," Gina said a bit too enthusiastically.

Really, Mom, can you at least think about it? She wanted her mother to show her love that the humans showed towards their children, and yet now, she wondered if her mother put her at a distance on purpose.

Jack said that the guardians were detached, unemotional species, but Kaleigh specifically remembered that all guardians taught their children about their responsibility. Gina never did. She only told her that she wasn't human and to be prepared for the coming of the demons.

If that didn't scare a four-year-old what would?

Was there a reason for her callousness? Or was Gina just plain cruel?

There was a long stretch of silence and Kaleigh thought maybe her mother had forgotten she was on the phone. Finally after several minutes, her mother spoke and Kaleigh wanted to cry. She only allowed herself a few private moments to grieve for her lost friend and now her mother was asking about it and she didn't know if she could keep the tears from unleashing.

"Who died, Kaleigh?"

A jolt of pain hit Kaleigh's heart. She wasn't going to break down yet. She wasn't going cry and whimper to her mother of all people and tell her anything about Susan's death or guardian hunter and the meeting of her protector. She had to block it out as far out of her mind as she could so her mother wouldn't ask any more questions.

Though Kaleigh really needed a shoulder to cry on, she couldn't let her defenses down and regress back into a sniveling, naïve girl that was feeble and full of repentance. She had to stay stronger than what she was capable of and stay strong to stay alive. If she left her defenses down the guardian hunter would come and seize her at once.

Denying would be pointless. Gina knew there was all to know about her life. Just like Susan's death; her mother knew who died.

"It was Susan, Mom..."

"Who's Susan?"

"A friend I work with," Kaleigh choked.

There was another long stretch of silence. "Something terrible is coming, isn't it, Kaleigh?"

She nodded over the phone even though her mother couldn't see her. Her lips had thinned, her eyes were tightly shut. She would not cry. She would cry.

"Kaleigh?"

"Yes!" Kaleigh shouted to stop the flow of the tears. "Something terrible is coming and it's all my fault!" Screaming was so much better than crying.

"Who's the man you met?"

"No one."

"Bullshit! He's your protector, isn't he?"

"If you know than why are you asking me?" Kaleigh asked through tight lips.

"Kaleigh," Gina said, drawing out her name.

"Yes, he is and I don't want it to be him, Mom. I can't go through heartbreak again like I did with Mark." Kaleigh couldn't understand why she was telling her mother all of this. She never confided to her mother, but for some strange reason, she really wanted to talk to somebody and anyone would do, even her mother.

"Honey, who is Mark?"

"Mom, don't play dumb with me," Kaleigh said sardonically. "I told you about him."

Gina gave her another one of those long cold silences. "Something is going on, Kaleigh, and the only advice I can give you is to be careful and watch for any signs of danger. Something bad is going to happen. I can feel it."

"Don't worry, Mom," Kaleigh said as she brushed her hair out of her eyes, "I'll be careful. Remember I have my own special protector."

"Kaleigh?"

"What?"

There was a slight pause then her mother said, "How long are you planning to keep your barriers up?"

Kaleigh had no answer. She would keep them up as long it kept others like her out of harms way; breaking them down meant havoc and the end of their race. She promised the pure souls she wouldn't open for anything or anyone and she was on the verge of just opening to give her justification for a little peace right before she died.

As for her mother's question, she didn't want to answer it and she didn't want to explain why. She simply said, "I have to go, Mom," and slammed down the phone.

She sighed, keeping the tears under the rims of her eyes. Once she was safe to walk the streets again, she was going to give a whole day to grieve for her friend.

Since Saturday night, her life had turned completely upside down and she was thrown into a loop of perplexity that only God could understand. She wished she knew the outcome of her life. She wanted to see where she was going to be in fifty years.

Jack's face appeared before her eyes. It was only natural. She had been living with him for the past couple of days and had slept next to him last night, among other things that her body could and would never forget. It was the only reason his face popped up first.

Kaleigh hadn't had a date in five years and it was the first man that she couldn't deny that made her heart spin out of control. Truthfully, it was the only man that had ever made her heart feel like a young teenager in love. She couldn't stop thinking about him!

When he left her at the front entrance of the building, it was all she could do not to grab and kiss him. He had an arrogant pride that inflated his self-esteem and boosted his male ego up about ten degrees. He was charming, nice, and who was she kidding? sexy as hell.

Kaleigh's breath deepened when she remember his hard, masculine body against hers. They were like two souls fitted for each other. And the way he made her body spin out of control with his fingers! Oh, God. How was she going be able to resist him if she thought about him constantly? It was an irrefutable annoyance that she knew what this man was trying to take over her life. Once again—who was she kidding? The man had already taken over her life and she wasn't safe, she was going to fall in love with him.

He was her protector and he was the man that was going to steal her heart and love her forever. She couldn't let that happen! She mustn't let that happen. Mark was her proof and so was Susan.

Thinking about Mark, Kaleigh's heart felt nothing. He was completely out of her system and she was thankful. All those nights her heart bled for the man who betrayed her and how she could have been so blind to the obvious.

Gina actually did give her advice once as she was growing into a woman. She warned her about the confusion of their hearts.

"Whatever you do, Kaleigh, don't fall victim to the hesitation of the heart."

Kaleigh did. Oh, how she did!

She knew from the moment of the short quiet pause that her heart turned brutal and without any comprehension. She was a victim of the hesitation. Mark said so right before he tried to suck the life out of her.

Strange, she thought. It was strange that she couldn't remember how she got herself out of that predicament. One moment he was sucking the life out of her and the next moment she was waking up in her apartment feeling her life being suspended into the turmoil of chaos and destruction. Her life was gone and the only thing she had left was the cold, emptiness of death.

Why did she always feel like death won? She wanted to feel free and alive; like how she felt with Susan. She had to make it right to get her life past this unwelcome stage and forego the knowledge of the future.

The first place to look for Susan's murderer was at her apartment. If she could go there, she may find out what happened to Susan.

Jack was going to be very angry if he found her gone, but let him get mad. She needed some space between them. And didn't he say if any trouble rose, that he would right there for?

She was going to find out.

Chapter Six

The elevator reached the sixth floor and the large, metal frame door slid opened quiet as a rebellious teenager.

Then everything happened so fast that Kaleigh was utterly stuck in her own demented world.

She was struck with a wave of panic and hysteria that slapped hard in her face. Her breathing stopped, her heart pounded against her chest, and her stomach clenched into a tight, closed fist.

Instantly, her mind blocked out all the right reasons to proceed with the investigation of Susan's death. Blood chilled her veins as the cold dissatisfaction of wrongness that paraded like tornado on the path of destruction frostily nipped at her.

Kaleigh had only felt this sensation once before; in the penthouse the night she came so close to death. Everything from the dimming lights of the elevator to the deranged hollow face of the bellhop told her to flee the other way and never look back. But she ignored those signs.

She ignored those taunts of harsh certainty. She ignored those voices that clouded her mind's judgment. She ignored the blood bleeding through the shag of the carpet. She ignored the flash vision of the demonic blackness of her destroyer.

When everything was pleading for her to turn around and run, she could only judge with her opened, naïve heart that Mark loved her and would never hurt her.

How wrong she was.

She ignored every vision of her murder and it nearly cost her life.

Yet here she was huddled in a corner, arms spread opened, nails digging into the cold hard rails, her two-inch high heels fastening into the carpet, and the reflection of her looking like death warmed over, and she wasn't running! Not because she wouldn't, but she couldn't! She had to see what was on the other side. She had to find out who murdered Susan and had to find out why her life was in danger. They say curiosity killed the cat; just call Kaleigh the cat.

Kaleigh came to grips with her cold reality and shook off the dread that was coming from the closing mouth of the elevator. Swiftly, she threw her body between the sliding doors and slipped out before the mouth closed.

The doors shut and Kaleigh stopped breathing. Her knees buckled to the bitter granite floor, instantly shattering her capability to move. Her nails shrieked across hard surface of the floor, echoing in the hallway with a stabbing wound of affliction. Her eyes, the shade of emeralds, changed to pure, black marbles of malevolence. Her mouth opened to scream out for help, but the only word that rolled off her tongue was, "Susan."

It was just like Saturday morning when Susan died. Only there was a difference; Kaleigh wasn't feeling Susan…she was feeling herself die.

Then her whole body collapsed from the total loss of oxygen. Her eyes rolled backwards, her lids fluttered shut, and that's when the pure soul's words that took their toil.

The first rule was to always ignore the demons taunt's. The second, if you should have failed rule one, always remember to breathe. If you lose that, then they have taken your life; your very spirit.

Breathe, Kaleigh. Don't let guardian hunter get you. They are out there. They are always waiting for you. They know when you are scared. If they catch you, just remember to breathe; it's your only way to survive against him. Breathe. Just breathe.

Slowly Kaleigh tilted her head until her forehead was visible to the fluorescent light above, and like a gush of wind; she slammed her head against the cold, granite floor. Kaleigh's eyes snapped open, her heart began to pump blood, and the darkness that crowed the narrow hallway vanished.

Silence surrounded her as the blood flowed like a rich wine from the middle of her forehead down to her pointed nose and over her lips.

Kaleigh licked the blood with her tongue, and tasted the bitter sweet victory. She had beaten them, but for how long? She knew they were always out there always waiting for her to slip up. They almost got her once and they nearly got her again. She had to be strong like her sisters. They could smell weakness like a ripe virgin guardian.

She never asked to be born with it and she never wanted to use her ability, but it happen like the changing of the days; it was unavoidable and she couldn't run from her gift. No matter how hard she tried not to focus on her gift, it always had a way to make her use it. Just like now. Breathing.

When she was a small child, she wanted nothing more than to experience the great mystery of her life, but as she went through puberty and adulthood, she only wanted it to stop. She hated feeling the loss of Mark. She hated feeling Susan die and hated feeling that she couldn't turn her back now and run away. If the voice screamed louder, she was going to push harder. She was going to find out who murdered her best friend even if it killed her.

She grabbed a tissue from the pack in her purse and wiped the spilt blood away from her face. It still managed to trickle down, and then got it to stop where only a drop was unfolding from the deep gash. She stuck the tissue back in her purse and proceeded down the hallway that was screaming with anxiety and immorality of all things not good to the world. She couldn't let the anxiety overcome her; it would suck her into the complex world of Susan's after life, and then how would she save the ones who help to keep the balance of world?

The guardian hunters were ambushing her again and she wasn't even aware that she was being played. But something felt different about this attack. Something was a lot differently played than when she stepped out of the elevator. She wasn't losing air, but gaining strength and duration. She was being warned.

As the walls screamed for her to retreat, Kaleigh focused on the six doors that were painted puke green with bronze door knobs and dime-shape peepholes.

The gushing of the screams continued to taunt Kaleigh's mind. Who do they belong to? Were they Susan's? Or were they done by the manipulation of the demons?

Kaleigh stopped between two doors and inhaled a large gulp of air and briefly shut her eyes.

Since she got off the elevator she only felt the completion of hell. Now she seem safe and in control of her surroundings. The walls stopped screaming, the immortality of death had vanished, and the cries that pounded her to run were distant howl of a bad memory.

A smile hinted at the corners of her mouth. She relaxed her stomach, exhaled her long-standing breath, and breathed opened her eyes.

Susan's blue vicious eyes were boldly staring into her frightened meek ones. Kaleigh's mouth dropped opened. A yelp tried to escape, her lids tried to shut, but the ability to do so was unavailable! She remained fixated on Susan pale, discolored face, the smell that emancipated from ground she was buried in, and the slimy black worms that tangled around in locks of her black stringy hair.

For an instant, Kaleigh wondered if she was dreaming. She was going to wake up and Susan was going to be in her apartment. It wasn't happening, though. This wasn't a dream; this was real as the worm sliding down the curve of Susan's left cheek.

Kaleigh's eyes moved from the deathly worm to her lower body that was covered in dirt. It looked as if she had broken the seal to the under world, and she climbed her way out just to meet her here in the present state.

Susan had deep, purple bruises that were the shapes of large fingerprints around the curves of her breasts. Bite marks were encrypted on her torso, on the base of her neck, on her shapely curved hips, and inner thighs.

"*Kaleigh*," her voice echoed through the hall and shattered Kaleigh out of the twilight zone.

Kaleigh snapped her head up. Susan was pointing, but not at her—behind her.

"*Run*," her sweet voice that could make the devil himself smile, whispered to her like a death chant from the demons of hell.

Without hesitation, Kaleigh slightly turned her head and saw the top of the elevator button's spring its orange work color from floor four to five.

Kaleigh turned her head back to Susan, and found her gone. The ding of the elevator going to floor six jolted her blood as the voices of the pure souls sang in her ears.

Run!
And go where?
Run!
There's no place to go.
Run!

Kaleigh picked up her feet even though she had no idea where she was going. She was locked in between two doors that had no chance of being unlocked. Susan's apartment was the next door up. The men coming off the elevator were coming to her apartment; she wouldn't be safe there. She had to go somewhere! Where?!

A warm draft shifted through her hair as prickles of goose bumps descended upon her arms and wrapped slowly around her neck.

Run!

She felt a close presence behind her. The men were getting off the elevator. They would see her and they would bring her to the master as they did to Susan. She turned around and didn't have the time to scream for a hard powerful hand was plastered across her mouth and she was smothered against a hard body and pulled inside of Susan's apartment.

"Damn you, Kaleigh. I should lock you up," Jack whispered harshly in her ear. Kaleigh felt Jack's free hand circle her neck and squeeze just enough to put the fear of god in her. His hard body pushed against her and she could feel every tense muscle in his stomach as his thick dominant thighs made it impossible for her to escape. She should have listened to the voices. She should have turned around and run for her dear life. Now she was being held captive by a very large and angry man that must have outweighed her by eighty pounds and there was no escaping this mighty brute.

Though she knew Jack would never hurt her. He wasn't the man she was supposed to be running away from. She got the distinct impression that his arms were supposed to be wrapped around her, protecting her from the bad things in this merciless world. He was powerful, full of agility, and strong as the barrier gates of heavens.

Jack held tight like a man that couldn't be persuaded to let go. He held like a man dying to protect what was his. Kaleigh knew that she shouldn't be afraid of him, but she couldn't shake the uncontrollable feeling that she wanted to run a hundred miles away from him and yet his sole purpose right now was to protect her from the men that were soon going to cross them. She needed his protections. She thrived on the protection. Anything was better than what she was feeling in the hallway and remembering how grotesque Susan had looked.

Then the walls started to die. The high pitch of the wallpaper stripping away from the walls sent shivers down her spine. The landscape pictures of unknown artists, crashed to the floor, spraying glass everywhere. Rich, deep blood seeped in lines of a drill sergeant discipline, cascaded down the unpainted wall, over the cheap red leather sofa, and ran past the glass coffee table and made a puddle around her high heels.

Kaleigh tightly shut her eyes and grabbed handfuls of Jack's cotton T-shirt and held on for her dear life.

Run Kaleigh. Run Kaleigh. Run Kaleigh. Run Kaleigh.

Susan voice bounced through the small apartment and vibrated through her ears and hit the core of her heart. Kaleigh's delusion of not breaking down was coming unglued. A small tear slid down her puffy cheeks and hit her ghostly hand. Her breathing was stopping. The guardian hunters were here. They were sucking the life energy right out of her!

She couldn't breathe and the man holding her for protection didn't have a clue that she was dying under his hand.

Someone or something was touching her shoulders. It wasn't Jack because now he was dragging her across the living room.

Kaleigh opened her eyes, and saw Susan was covered from head to toe in a viscosity of blood. Her eyes burned black through her matted hair. She was touching her shoulder as her eyes scowled her with pure disappointment. "*Breathe!*"

Susan voice chilled her blood, but it was just the kick to make her gasp and catch the air that was aimlessly floating around.

Her emotions shot high and tears screamed down her face like a lost lonely virgin on prom night. Susan faded out and then she was gone. Kaleigh had lost control.

She was crying.

At least she was breathing!

She was breathing like there was no tomorrow and crying as if were tomorrow.

The sound of footsteps carried its way to Susan's door. The man protecting her with all the possession of a warrior and bent on saving her from destruction that lay in their way, turned his head to the noise. Before she knew it, she was pushed inside of a dark empty space that could have only been a closet. Even though she didn't feel any cloth draping around her shoulders she knew by the tiny space they were enclosed in that she was in a closet.

Jack had switched her position from her facing him to her back enfolded with his lean torso and her legs brushing against him.

Susan's scream pierced her ears that she had to clap her hands over her ears so tight that her blood pounded like a jackhammer in her head. Jack felt her unrestrained body fighting its way to the norm of reality and pulled her further into his embrace. His hand was still clamped over her mouth, drowning out her cries when the intruders fumbled with the lock.

The door creaked open and the room was immediately filled with one unfamiliar voice and the other she heard before.

Both of their voices sent icicles through her veins.

"She said it was left on her night stand."

"Well go fucking get it. I'm going to wait here. Don't touch anything! We don't want to leave any prints."

"You think I'm an idiot?"

"Sometimes you make me wonder."

The footsteps began to move around in the apartment. Kaleigh tensed when one of the intruders stomped passed the closet door that she forgot to breathe.

Jack held her tighter and his strength gained her breathing. It calmed her only to the point that she felt safer with him than by herself with two men.

The footsteps came back from the bedroom and move past the closet again.

"Hey, Howard, it's not there!"

Howard! That's what his name was! The man she was dancing with at the club and the man that was the last person to see Susan alive.

"Whatda ya mean it's not there?"

"I mean it's not fucking there. It's not on her night stand. Are you sure she said the night stand?"

"That's what the bitch said."

"Let's go then. We'll come back later when it's dark outside. I don't want to get caught by a fucking neighbor."

They walked quietly out of the door and Jack didn't release her until he heard the door shut and their footsteps were not audible.

He let out a sigh and cracked the door opened to peek outside the room.

"Okay, let's get out of here." He grabbed her hand pulled her out with a mighty thrust.

Kaleigh staggered and nearly fell against Jack, who had just saved her life.

The blood had stopped flowing, the walls were printed back, and the screams were no more. She felt herself become one to the reality of existence and she could breathe, stand, and for god's sake had stopped crying. She felt herself being made into completeness again and she knew she was going to be all right until the next traumatic moment.

Kaleigh wiped the tears away on her silk sleeve and patted her cheeks dry. She knew looking into a mirror would show her red, puffing cheeks, blood-stained, disoriented eyes, and face so pale one would have believed that she actually saw a ghost.

"Are you okay?" he asked as his eyes looked her up and down.

She composed herself before she could justify her unnatural behavior. She looked him up and down and studied him from behind her green emerald eyes. He was all man and then some. She was a tall woman but he towered over her by at least six inches. None of his muscles were hidden beneath the surface of his clothes as they bulged from the flimsy green cotton T-shirt he wore and his denim jeans were screaming to come apart by the thickness of his thighs. She searched his face and found it very stubborn and cold.

Jack was very angry.

Hard lines cornered around his sapphire-filled, narrowed eyes and pinched mouth. If he wasn't looking like he could kill her right now, she would have to say Jack was a fantasy made real, and he was here for her.

"I'm fine, Jack. Could we just go?" She tried to walk past him, but he quickly snatched her wrist and pulled her hard against his chest.

"You little idiot," he shouted.

Then before she could move, his head bent, and his lips crashed down on hers.

Kaleigh's first instinct was to pull back and slap his face, but when his hard, warm lips touched hers roughly, and the explosion ignited her heart, she submitted to his unruly kiss. It wasn't a secret that she had wanted to kiss him ever since she first dreamed about him and she doubted indulging in a little fantasy was going to hurt her even though she knew what she was doing was forbidden.

Her hands came to his shoulders and she opened her mouth for him when she felt the pressure of his hot tongue stroking her bottom lip. His mouth softened.

Jack's tongue was exotic, wild, and he tasted of man. A little moan escaped as he experimented, licking the inside of her mouth, stroking her tongue with his, and devouring her as if he were a dying man.

Kaleigh ran her hand up his neck to the thickness of his black hair, pushing him closer to her body. Jack groaned and wrapped an arm around her waist and the other cupping her ass. He pulled her closer to the desire of his hard length, and it pressed against her sex. Instinctively, she arched up into him. Kaleigh's head fell back and Jack took the opportunity to attack her neck. He licked, nipped, and suckled on the pulsated vein of her throat as her toes curled and knees went weak. She had to dig her fingernails into his skin to keep from buckling.

Jack knew her dilemma; he pushed her against a wall without breaking his hold on her neck and positioned himself between her thighs. His cock seemed to grow thicker and hotter and Kaleigh groaned as she cupped the back of his head in her hands and kissed his neck.

His heart was beating rapidly through his chest and his muscles straining to burst through his clothes. Jack was deliciously harder than he'd ever been in his life, and it was almost worth being what he was to have this magnificent moment!

The feel of her feminine heat aroused him more, making him more restrictive in his jeans and closer to breaching his sanity. She felt right in his arms as she always had. This woman was made especially for him and it was so hard not to take her right now.

He rubbed his hips shamelessly against her. Jack wanted her to know what madness she caused him. His lips moved from her neck, up to her chin where he laid a gentle kiss, and back to her mouth. He tongue plunged deep inside as his right hand lifted from her rear and cupped her breast. Kaleigh gasped and slid a little down the wall. He found the hardened nipple peeking from her blouse and pulled and twisted it between his fingers.

She cried out and then began imitating Jack's brazen behavior, rubbing herself wantonly against him.

"Jesus!" Jack moaned and kissed her savagely again.

Her body was on fire. Never before had a man made her felt this out of control or this wild before. With Mark it was simple, gentle, and automatic. She never got this ache dwelling in the pit of her belly and she never felt hotter between her thighs or hot all over than with Jack. She could never get the emotion from Mark that Jack was awakening deep inside of her. It wasn't wild and passionate like it was with Jack. With Jack it was like the rage of a thunder storm threatening to wipe out the city lights with its explosive lightening and high winds.

And she loved it.

She loved the feeling of the wildness, the threat if she were to lose her head and let him make wild, adulterated love to her.

Jack filled both of breasts in the palm of his hands and ran his thumbs back and forth over the pebbled-hard nipples with his thumb.

Kaleigh's knees bent and she slid further down the wall. Jack gripped under her thighs, scooted her up the wall, and wrapped her legs around his waist. She could feel every inch of him firmly pressed against her and then suddenly he stiffened and set her back to her feet.

"What is it?" Kaleigh asked in a voice she didn't recognized. It was thicker and more sensual. She cleared her throat and watched as he stepped away from her.

She was quite disappointed and embarrassed that Jack just stopped and left her almost at the peak of her climax.

"We need to get out of here." Jack's voice sounded as thick as hers.

He grabbed her hand and yanked her out of Susan's apartment and ran down the hallway. The elevator opened and Jack, being the gentleman, let her step inside first as he followed her. The doors closed and Jack pressed the ground floor button. The silence that swept between them was as deadly as the kiss that turned animalistic.

Jack made sure not to touch her and Kaleigh was grimly disappointed. How could a man kiss her like he was starving then ignore like her she didn't exist? She could see from his jeans that he was still excited and looked as hard as it was just pressed against her.

She sighed heavily, knowing she caused that reaction from him and then felt Jack glaring at her.

Kaleigh glanced at him and saw the same heated look in his eyes as when he first kissed her. His eyes were storming, brewing with emotions as his iris were on a rampage of changing back and forth, and Kaleigh could only stare, wondering why they did that. It occurred to her they only changed when he was angry or passionate. It was probably the unnatural side of his birth coming out. He did say he wasn't normal and the constant change of his eyes proved it.

The elevator door opened and they walked out of the building as if nothing had ever happened. When they reached outside and the afternoon hot air stifle them, Jack asked. "How did you get here?"

"The Metro," she said.

He nodded and then grabbed her hand again and led her to his jeep. He opened the passenger door for her and slammed it behind him. He came around the other side and hopped in the driver's seat. "Buckle up," he said coldly.

They left the apartment complex and back to Walker Security in total silence.

When they pulled into the parking garage and settled on the fourth floor near a darkened corner that was close the elevator of the building, Jack put the gear in park and then sat motionless. Without looking at Kaleigh, he spoke. His voice was severely menacing and oozed with consequence that made Kaleigh want to run far, far away. "Just what in the hell were you thinking? I gave you specific orders not to leave without me! And what do you do? You fucking leave without me. I told you weren't safe on your own, but you can't seem to get that through your head!"

"I'm sorry," Kaleigh said softly.

"Sorry!" he said slamming his fist against the steering wheel. "Jesus Christ, do you have any idea what could have happened to you?"

He was glaring at her and Kaleigh looked out of the passenger window. She closed her eyes and folded her hands so tightly in her lap that her knuckles turned white. Her face was flushed, but it wasn't from the warm April weather. It was from anger and humiliation. All she wanted to do was to get away from Jack and think on her own, which had resulted terribly. She couldn't think with someone dogging her every step. Instead of having a protector, she had an ill-tempered stalker.

Kaleigh swallowed her anger and unclenched her hands. "If I haven't had gone, then we would have never found out that my dance partner was the very same person that broke into her apartment, and the name of last person to be seen with Susan is Howard!"

Jack's head snapped up. "I told you I was going to put someone to watch him!"

"And you can thank me now that we know his name."

"I shouldn't have to thank you, Kaleigh. I would have eventually found out on my own, but you're too impatient and stubborn to wait or listen to me," he shouted.

Kaleigh twisted around her seat and pointed her finger at his chest. "You know, I don't have to take this abuse from you!"

Jack snatched her wrist in a death grip and glared at her with all the venom of a snake's bite. She saw his eyes change from blue to a deep violent purple again and it was truly staring to frighten her.

"Don't push me, Kaleigh. I'm at the point of losing control with you. It's either your way or no way and I'm tired of it. I'm telling you from now on, it's my way. No more sneaking off and leaving without me."

He threw her wrist at her and immediately Kaleigh threw opened the passenger door and stalked away with tears in her eyes. Her arms swung stiffly to her sides as her breathing became labored and rushed.

Damn him! And she was really starting to like him, but he just proved that he was capable of being an asshole just like the rest of the world. There was no reason to use force to get his point across. She would have understood him perfectly it he just yelled, instead of that cold, demeaning voice and the manhandling.

She heard a car door slam and looked over her shoulder. She gasped when saw Jack running to her. She whipped her head around and quickened her space, but she wasn't fast enough. Jack caught her around the waist. Kaleigh squeaked when Jack lifted her up and swung her around to his face. He gripped her shoulders and pulled her against his chest and tucked her head between his shoulder and neck.

Kaleigh tried to push back and walk away from him, but Jack was determined for her to stay and listen to him. She didn't want to hear his excuses. She understood why he was mad at her, but she couldn't understand how he could change from a gentle person to harsh one so quick.

She relented. All her effort was pointless.

"I'm sorry, Kaleigh," he whispered in her ear. "I'm shouldn't have handled you that way. I'm a bastard." He squeezed her tight as if he would never let go.

Kaleigh let her arms fall to the side and let him hold her. She wasn't ready to forgive yet. Then she realized that Jack had said sorry. It was probably the first time for him and probably would the last time she heard those two significant words coming from his lips. Jack wouldn't have said it if he didn't mean it.

She relaxed and inhaled the scent of his spicy cologne. He smelled so good that Kaleigh became drowsy with his scent and his hard body flushed against hers. She wanted to feel more of this comfort. She needed it. She wrapped her arms around his waist and sighed.

Jack rubbed he hands up and down her back and apologized over and over. "You made me so crazy when I realize that you were trouble. It nearly took a hundred years off my life. I wanted to tear down the walls to get to you. Never do that to me again. Please don't."

That's why he was angry. He was worried about her. What he said was true then: if she was in trouble, he would come. He came. He truly was her protector.

Kaleigh wanted to lose her heart to him and never look back, but no, she couldn't. It was illicit for her to fall in love and for guardian saviors to fall in love. How were they able to spend the next hundreds and hundreds of years without a companionship? It didn't make any sense. They were only human—sort of.

Kaleigh thought of Jack as her forbidden fruit. More like her forbidden angel because he was certainly more tempting than fruit. He was the most tempting species that ever was present on Earth. He may not believe in angels, but she did. And this man was the most tempting and forbidden of them all.

While he held her and soothed her with comforting words, Kaleigh felt herself softening and leaning into him. Their heartbeats joined and beat together. It was the sweetest thing she ever felt.

After several more minutes of holding each other, they broke apart. Jack's coldness had diminished and showed her emotions in those blue pools that he was feeling what she was feeling. Why would they put them together if they couldn't be together? It didn't make any sense.

They stared into each other's eyes and smiled. The ultimate sin was to fall in love with each other. The greatest virtue would be the essence to share their time together before everything fell apart.

Kaleigh discovered that for however long she had left with Jack, she was going to spend it wisely.

Jack cupped her face and kissed her tenderly on her forehead and then planted a soft kiss on her lips. Kaleigh felt the heat of his mouth and kissed him back.

He pulled back and smiled. "Before I began acting like an ass, I have something to tell you."

"Yes?"

Jack pulled her to his side and threaded his fingers with hers as they made their way to the elevator. His hand were doubled the size of hers, rough, calloused, and yet he held her tenderly.

"Adrian let me check out Susan's desk and guess what I found?" He paused, waiting for Kaleigh to answer. She gave him an affirmative nod. "A phone number."

"Who is it?"

"I don't know. I had to play hero before I could find out," he said with a smile and then entered the elevator.

It was easy for Jack to get through all of Susan's things once he explained the whole horrid story to Adrian. He wasn't the least bit comforted by the blow of the news. But Adrian understood the dilemma and gave Jack a spare key to Susan's desk.

Jack quickly looked through the several stacks of documents on top of Susan's organized desk while the other employees were out to lunch. He found nothing major. Then he checked the unlocked doors and still came up short. He inserted the key to the pulled out drawer and opened it when he heard the small sounded click.

Susan's desk was filled with memo pads, cosmetics, pens, pencils, and other small office equipment. He pulled the drawer out further and still nothing caught his eye. Susan was obviously not hiding anything here. He didn't find a strap of evidence that she was in...

Then something had caught his eye. It winked at him and told him all the evidence was there. He had ten minutes left before the employees started coming back from lunch. When it came to a commitment on a job, he was there one hundred percent (even if it was a phony job).

Playing as a custodian was more difficult than he thought. Mrs. Wells, his supervisor made it very clear to him that she didn't tolerate the least bit of disorderly work. He perfectly understood Mrs. Wells's rules and would strictly obey them. He didn't want to get caught screwing around on his fake job.

He pulled out the compact powder and snapped it open. There was his evidence. There was a missing part of the puzzle to Susan's murder. A memo loose-leaf folded small enough to fit in the circumference of the circle mirror was gleaming with crime. He plucked out the paper and quickly scanned the letter. It didn't make much sense to him and it wouldn't take him ten minutes to find out what it meant, but he didn't have ten minutes; he had five minutes.

He stuffed the paper into his pocket, locked the drawer, and retraced his step back to the men's restroom and finished cleaning the disgusting filth of the toilets when he felt Kaleigh leave the building.

He threw down the mop, vanished into thin air, hopped in his jeep, and then he was there with her. Luckily, no one had seen him.

Damn those guardian hunters. Didn't they know she belong to him?

Riding in the elevator in silence, holding Kaleigh's hand was the most peace he'd been given in five long years. Since she disappeared on him from a disturbing misunderstanding, his life had been hell, literally.

What would it take to get her to get her opened up to him? All he needed was her to fall in love with him and his hell would be over.

He almost blew it in the jeep. He should have never screamed at her like that, but sometimes a little of Mark just came out.

"You okay?" Kaleigh asked, eyeing him. "You look a little distant."

Jack smiled. "I'm fine. Just thinking who the phone number belongs to."

After the elevator doors opened, they went their separate ways.

Kaleigh was sitting at her desk, going through the employees' files for evaluation when the phone rang. Icy, chills ran down her arms and she knew she shouldn't pick up the phone, but something was pulling her to do.

She hesitantly picked up the phone with a shaky hand. "Personnel, Miss Floyd speaking, how may I help you?"

"Tell me something, Kaleigh, why didn't you fuck him last night?"

Kaleigh nearly dropped the phone. Her heart pounded and she felt the life being sucked right out of her.

Breathe, Kaleigh.

"You should have fucked him. I think you would have quite enjoyed it."

Hang up the phone, Kaleigh!

"No response? That's okay. If it had been me in that bed you would have felt more than my fist." *Breathe!* "You would have felt every inch of my fire burning through your skin as you begged for more."

"Goddammit, hang up the phone!" Jack screamed.

"Can you imagine me stroking your hot, wet skin? Can you feel me touching your breasts, the insides of your thighs, and tasting your tongue as I dig deeper and deeper? You can. I can feel it, too Kaleigh. I can feel your thighs shaking, they're ready to come. They are waiting for your release. You would have loved it my dear, Kaleigh. What's the matter dear, Kaleigh? Can't breathe?"

Suddenly, Kaleigh felt a great rush of bitter, cold wind sweeping through her body. It threw her against the wall, slammed the breath back into her, and her blood began to pump again. The phone never left her hand; it dangled insecurely around her damp finger tips, the receiver standing still next to her weak thighs.

A hideous, evil laugh played on the other end of the phone line.

"Talk to you later, Kaleigh."

Her knees could no longer handle the pressure and they buckled beneath her. She slid down the wall until her buttocks hit red and blue mesh carpet.

She drew her knees to the tip of her chin and wrapped her arms firmly around them, shaking with fear. The guardian hunters were everywhere. They could find her anywhere. She was never going to be rid of them. She was going to play a lifetime role with the devil himself if she couldn't find a way to stop them.

Out of the blue she thought, where was Jack when she needed him? Then something in the back of her mind revitalized as she played the phone call over. He was there. He was there in the back of her mind. He was there and Susan was here. They both tried to stop her from doing what could possibly kill her. She was so stupid to pick up that phone! She ignored what the people in her life were telling her and did what her curiosity wanted.

She practically let the guardian hunter seduce her and take her soul. Stupid! Stupid! Stupid!

God, she could literally feel his tongue stroking her. She could feel those deadly, vile kisses and she loved it! She couldn't get enough of it! She had grown damp, perspired with need by his seduction and she nearly got herself killed! She couldn't have him invading her job; he was already invading her personal life and she couldn't have him disrupt the one thing that meant something to her. Jack.

Kaleigh promised she wouldn't leave him, but for his safety she had to.

Chapter Seven

After everything he just told her not to do, and she did it anyway. He really was going to lock her up somewhere. He couldn't believe she picked up that phone after he and Susan warned her not to. It had something to do with her nature. She had walked out of that elevator on the same impulse and gotten herself into trouble.

He didn't understand why she did this to herself. Did this woman have some kind of death wish? Or was she looking for adrenaline rush? If that was the case he could give her plenty. He was a man and he liked to face danger just as much as the next macho guy, but he wasn't going to face danger if that meant the entire population of the world!

A guardian hunter had already come after her in twice in one day and he was sure his day wasn't over. How was he able to do his job if he kept butting in every hour? Couldn't he be patient like the rest of the world that was thriving on him? He knew she belonged to him and no other, and when he found out who the guardian hunter was, he was going to be destroyed.

Then Susan got involved after he specifically told her to stay the hell out of the way when she joined Kaleigh in her office. She had no right to be there! He could handle things just fine on his own.

However, Jack did learn that Susan was not a very good person and he was going to expose to Kaleigh what kind of friend Susan really was. That woman's soul was black, riding with evil in the lead. Funny, how Kaleigh couldn't see that.

Though, he didn't have much time left before he left to go after Kaleigh again, he had to find out who the anonymous number belonged to.

He played it cool when he called the ten digit number from a pay phone outside of a McDonalds's. He didn't want any numbers traced back to him or Walker's Security's and a pay phone was the safest way to go. He first tried to use Adrian's computers to find the number, but it was an unlisted number and he went to plan B by using a pay phone and acting like he dialed the wrong number.

"McChandey's residence," said a soft ethnic womanly voice.

McChandey? As in Mayor Devin McChandey of Houston? Why was Susan involved with the mayor? "Is Devin there?" Jack asked in his best southern jaw.

"I'm sorry, Mr. McChandey's at the office. May I take a message?"

"No that's all right. I just call him at a later time. Thank you," Jack said as he hung up.

Now it was time for him to tell Adrian that he was leaving and wouldn't be returning.

His original plan was to get Kaleigh, but how he could he do that now when the mayor was involved? He hated that conniving little bastard, but Kaleigh had to be protected. And yet, the quicker he was through with Susan, the sooner he would be able to help save the world from the guardian hunters.

His mind was feeling weary with exhaustion. He hadn't used this much brain power since Sebastian Ames was nearly destroyed in Paris because of a demon disguised itself as woman and used that against his friend. Jack and another sorcerer had to fly to France to stop Sebastian from doing the unthinkable. If he had let her—it—in, his soul would have been theirs and he would never be able to turn or enter the great gates of their heaven. It took the energy out of him that night, but it was nothing compared to Kaleigh.

Sebastian threw a temper tantrum like all the warriors do, and they had to get him soused out of his mind to screw the next available woman.

Kaleigh would be all right for a few hours by herself as long as he was totally connected with her and didn't lose track of her. It was literally going to render him weak. She literally suffocated the life out of him. But she was worth every last heartbeat and every last breath that she stolen from him. He would give her all and give up everything for her.

Susan had to be dealt with as quickly as possible and he didn't have time for Sebastian to appear.

He just wished that Kaleigh would let down her guard and let him inside. He was her protector and he was going to play his role to the very end.

She needed to start playing hers.

"You need to let your guard down, Kaleigh," Gina said over the rim of her coffee cup.

"You know I can't do that," Kaleigh cried.

Kaleigh had taken a cab to her mother's house, and as soon as she walked on Gina's door step, her mother was frowning with disappointment in her eyes. Kaleigh hated that look; it made her feel like she was six-year-old all over again bringing in stray animals of all sorts. Birds, cats, dogs, squirrels, and sometimes, possums.

She wasn't a child anymore. She was a grown woman, capable of taking care of herself and she didn't need her mother disapproving look to let her know what she did wrong.

"You need to open up, Kaleigh. We need you and the others."

"I can't do it, Mother! I just can't."

She was getting fed-up with her mother's pointing things out to her that she already knew! Why did she come here? That's right: she needed answers.

Kaleigh took a deep breath and calmed her nerves. She was being unfair. Her mother was looking out for her for her best interests. She had three guardians protecting her and what good did it do to her? Nada. Zilch. The guardian hunters still came after her. If she hadn't picked up that phone he would have showed himself in his true form and haunted her anyway. It didn't matter. They were only keeping her alive for a few more minutes on this great place they called Earth.

He was going to get her with or without their protection. It was an inevitable that whoever was protecting her, the guardian hunters was going to get her and there was no way to stop them.

Thinking back five years ago…No she wasn't going to torture herself with the past. It was useless and it depressed her. Poor Mark, though. He never stood a chance against her.

"Stop thinking about it, Kaleigh. It doesn't do any good," her mother scowled.

"I hate when you do that." Kaleigh slumped against the daisy-patterned couch and blew her hair out of her face.

The couch was uncomfortable because of the plastic sheeting that protected the cushion. On hot summer days they were really uncomfortable if her mother didn't have the air conditioner running. She learned her lesson when she was young that when her mother was saving money on the electric bill, wear long shorts or pants; it was the only way not to melt with the plastic.

Her mother lived on the outskirts of Houston in a small rural town of Crosby were the population was only a fifth of Houston. She lived in a subdivision, Crosby Terrace, for the middle-income families, in a cozy one-story brick house that indicated that was she was over the age of fifty.

Gina sprouted the pink flamingos in the middle of her well-trimmed yard, plastic lawn chairs, an American flag displayed proudly from the front left window, and her flower garden that was exhibited pompously like it was an award. The inside of her house was no better; displaying every cat nicknack and floral object from her china dishes in the hutch to the pattern of her furniture.

If people were to stop by her house or look inside, they may believe to find a woman that was in her sixties, not a woman that was over five hundred years old that looked like she was thirty and beautiful.

Kaleigh looked nothing like her mother. Gina had fiery, long red hair that reached to her buttocks, large breasts that she was proud to flaunt, and freckles over her cheeks and nose. She was shorter than Kaleigh and slimmer around the waist. The only similarity these two women shared was their green eyes that sparkled on the cloudiest day.

"How long are you planning to stay here?" her mother asked in a tone that made Kaleigh want hop in her car and drive back work.

"Am I that much of a burden?"

"Do you think that is what you are? A burden?" she said scowling her again.

Kaleigh shrugged her shoulders. All her life she felt like a burden to her mother. She accidentally got pregnant by a man she met once and wham! Nine months later, here was Kaleigh, a gift to her mom; if only she treated her like one.

"Sometimes, I feel like I am. I was an accident. It's not like you asked for me."

Her mother looked at her with those disappointed eyes again. Kaleigh felt two inches tall.

"You were and never will be a burden to me, Kaleigh. Never! I know that I wasn't the best mother in the world—let me finish. I know I treated you like an unwanted stepchild and I do regret it. But I am a part of your guardian, and when I give you advice about who you are and what you are suppose to do for the world, I expect you to listen. I know it may not always sound pleasant or what you want to hear, but that's who we are, Kaleigh.

"You were hurt in the past and it left scars. I have scars, too, but that doesn't keep me from doing what is right or my responsibilities for the world.

"I can tell you what to do and what you are supposed to do and you may not always want to be at the recipient end to take upon my advice, but Kaleigh, you have to let those scars heal. When they come after you, I can't do anything to stop them. We have no powers to do so. You were the one chosen because of your strength and your strong heart. It's up to you to defeat them, but if you won't let your guard down how will you defeat them?"

For once in her life, Kaleigh didn't bother with the fact that Gina had neglected her in the past. She listened to every word as if she were her mentor and paid attention. Every blasted word she said was right. She failed her responsibilities for the world because of the turmoil she encountered five years ago. It was time to let those scars heal and be done with Mark.

Thinking of Mark, she wished she could remember his face. She desperately tried to recapture his face from her memories and Jack was the only thing that steadily popped in her mind. He was there, powerful, withholding, and waiting for her to surrender. Her lips curved down at the corners just thinking about him.

Sweet, breathtaking Jack was what she needed to put her back to her responsibilities and to be happy again. She terribly missed being happy. When he held her last night it was the sweetest thing that anyone had ever done for her. She never met a man quite like him. But it was impossible for her to be happy because what she wanted, she couldn't have forever.

"Mother?"

"What is it?" Gina said with a sad flicker in her eye.

"I wish I could tell you why I can't open up to the world. I wish I could help with the guardians and give them what they need from me, but I can't. I can't do it. If I did then we will all be in serious trouble. The others won't come out to help."

Gina sighed and took her daughter's hands and tucked them in between hers. "He's found you, hasn't he?"

Kaleigh shook her head lightly. She didn't know who her mother was talking about Mr. Walker or Jack Pierce or the guardian hunter. "Who has found me?"

Her mother lowered her eyes and frowned. "*The* guardian hunter."

Kaleigh pushed out of her mother's hands and licked her dry lips as she gazed over the orange clock to look at the time. They both were avoiding each other's question and both were acting like children. She put a stop to it an answered her mother honesty.

"They all have found me," Kaleigh said dryly. "I really can't hide from them anymore.

Her eyes were still fixed on the clock as Gina cupped her face and smiled, "He's found you and he won't let any other guardian hunters get to you."

Her head snapped up and it nearly collided with her mother's chin. "What the hell are you talking about?"

Gina's smile blossomed. "He's found you, Kaleigh, but don't worry; it's for the best."

Jack followed the direction he got from internet from Walker's Security to Mr. Devin McChandey's home address. It was late in the evening, the sun had descended for the day, and the quarter moon hung high in the clear, dark sky as the few stars that were throughout, twinkled to the slow music of the wind.

It was a peaceful night. Most of the traffic had cleared by the time he finished his shift and he rushed down the highway, weaving in and out of traffic, listening to the classic hits, while drumming his finger against the steering wheel to the beat of the music. He wasn't in a hurry per se, but he had an obligation to seek Kaleigh and tell her of his findings.

The song ended and he was left with commercials and more commercials on the rest the radio stations. He turned the radio off and made a left when the light turned green.

Mayor Devin McChandey lived in a high-class neighborhood with country clubs, sports complexes, and owning a Mercedes Benz was like owing a Ford. Every yard was perfectly mowed, bushes were well-maintained, there were perfect lighted streets, and houses that were spacious in between and large enough to hold a conference for the White House.

Jack didn't envy them, though. He had a lot of clients out on these streets and most of them were unhappy, paranoid people, putting on a show for the rest of the city to see that they were quite the sophisticated citizens that had no troubles to worry about.

Yeah, right.

Most of these people that lived in this area had more problems than a welfare mother taking care of four children, waiting for the first of the month to make ends meet. Just because people had money didn't mean they were always happy.

Jack parked his jeep next to a dumpster behind Exxon. He then walked to a white van that advertised in blue, bold letters, "Remy's Cable" that was loaned to him by a personal friend that worked at impound lot, and climbed in. He drove and parked the van in front of a restored Victorian, white, two-story mansion with blue shutters and a "for sale" sign sticking next to it's bricked mail box, four houses down from McChandey's. He reached into the glove compartment and grabbed microscopic mini camera.

From his back seat he grabbed a black baseball cap that advertised "Remy's Cable" and leather tool belt with all the instruments he needed. It went along with the rest of his uniform. He had actually forty-five minutes before patrol came sporting about which meant that he thirty-five minutes to do what he had to do and ten to get there and get the hell out.

McChandey's property wasn't set for security. Jack did a thorough back ground check and got inside and outside information from a guardian that worked for the force. He didn't explain the whole truth to Jed about his reason for Mr. McChandey; just the bare essential that he needed; like a client had suspicion that he was hanging around a new lady. Jed came back that McChandey just recently moved in a week ago and hadn't got all his security set-up, which was great for Jack. Bad for Mr. McChandey.

From the house he parked at, he walked behind a large wooden privacy fence, to the back yard, praying that there wasn't a dog on the other side. It wasn't like he was scared of dogs, but it made his job a lot easier without them.

There weren't dogs, just like at the next two houses. He reached behind McChandey's house and it was like walking into a lagoon. Exotic plants, flowers, a waterfall silently spilling in a pool (could fit his living room and kitchen) that was surrounded by large unlit tiki lamps. The strong scent of the flowers and all the pollen circling around in the air stung his nose and if he couldn't keep it together he was going to sneeze and rouse someone. He rubbed his nostrils together and held back the sneeze.

The curtains were drawn on the sliding glass door and Jack maneuvered himself against the side of the house and was hidden by the dark shadows of the ivy poking at him. He pulled from his tool belt a pair of small red-handled lock cutters and found the silver box planted a foot over his head on a post. He carefully took a hold of the silver Master lock and snipped it. He removed the lock and pulled the cable from it transmitter and then replaced the box with a new lock.

By the time he reached the van, he was sweating from head to toe and he smelled and looked like he rolled in the dirt. He grabbed the baseball cap and wiped the sweat from his forehead with the side of his hand. Reaching into his front pocket, he pulled out a stick of chewing gum and popped it into his mouth. He put the cap back on and hopped inside of the van to drive down three houses. He stepped out and pulled open the sliding van's door and grabbed a tool box by the handle and walked up to Mr. McChandey's door and rang the doorbell.

The door was opened by a short, plump ethnic woman that had streaks of silver through her black widow's peak, wearing the standard gray uniform for a maid that fitted down to her knee caps with the white laced apron. Her hands were clamped together as she smiled to welcome the stranger.

"Hello, may I help you?"

Jack put on his smile for his best role ever, and greeted the woman with his best accent of an incompetent worker as he chewed his gum annoyingly. "Yeah, there have been calls out here tonight about the cable going out. Is the cable out?"

The woman stood frowning for what seem hours and then nodded her head.

You're going to let me in this house no matter what. Jack said to her mind.

He could have flashed himself in the mansion, but he didn't know where he would end up at. The last time he decided to that trick, he bumped into the man's mistress while she was using the toilet. Boy, talking about embarrassing for him and frighteningly shocking for her.

"Oh, man," he said disappointed. "I was hoping Ms. Fisher house would be the last one. Looks like I'm going to be out here all night!" he said smacking his gum. "Can you show me to the box?"

"I need identification," the ethnic woman demanded.

"No, sweat!" He reached in the back of his pocket and pulled out a beat-up nylon wallet and opened the Velcro as he was saying, "I don't blame you for asking for I.D. The world is filled with wackos!" He showed her the I.D and she studied it like it was a new breed of dog. She gave her approval and step aside.

"Where is the main box?" Jack said looking around.

The little, plump ethnic woman waved her hand and Jack followed.

He had to hand it to Mr. McChandey that it was good to be the Mayor. Expensive, fragile African antiquities sat in displayed shelves that covered from one corner of the house to the other. They blended well with the decor of the mansion; dark, mosaic colors of Africa spread throughout from the topping of the tables to the color of oriental rugs. If he didn't know any better, he thought he was in Africa. Chandeliers of crystals hung beautifully over his head and it almost made him feel like he was being watched.

He shook that eerie feeling off his shoulders and concentrated on the job. If he was being watched the man of the house had good reasons; Jack was an intruder about to invade the privacy of a man's home.

The maid led him to a family room; filled with lots more of African antiquities and of course a dimly lit chandelier that made him feel like he was being watched again.

She pointed at the television where the cable box rested. He didn't know the first thing about the transformation of cable, but he could buy his way out of anything. That was what made him such a good private investigator and cop.

He flipped on the television and a bunch of noise static bounced off and filled the room to capacity. Jack turned down the volume and pulled the cable box ajar from the wall all while the maid was watching him.

He messed with of wires and pretended like he knew what he was doing. He scratched his head and looked dumbfounded. "It must be the outside line. Is there a way I can get there from here?"

The maid led him to the sliding glass door and pulled the maroon velvety curtains aside and unlocked the door. She slid it opened and once again stepped aside. Jack hastily chewed on his gum and popped a bubble without realizing what he had done.

"Which way?" he asked glancing around.

The maid shrugged her shoulders. "I don't know."

"That's all right. I'm sure I can find it." He did after a fake failed attempt on the left side of the house. The maid steadily followed him. He didn't blame her. After all, this was the mayor's house and she had to be suspicious of any strangers going in and out. Jack could make her feel at ease in the mayor's home, but he liked to keep it natural.

He found the silver box and reached into his pocket and pulled two small silver keys that dangled from a silver key loop. He unlocked the Master lock and acted totally surprised. "Whoa, here's your problem! The cable wire had come lose! That sucks. I'll have this fixed in a jiffy." And he did. He followed the maid back inside and tried the television was set on a C-SPAN network.

"We'll I'm all done here." Except for all the snooping.

"Thank you, sir."

"No problem, I'm just doing my job. Pardon me ma'am, but I hate to ask you this," he said still smacking his gum. "Will it be all right if I used your bathroom? I've been out here for three hours and I haven't time to take a le— to use the bathroom."

The maid studied him hard that it made Jack a little tense. If she said no, then he would back later on tonight. He knew how to get in and out of the house like a shadow now that he got a tour of the place. For an expensive house, the place had cheap locks on the windows and a deadbolt that could be unlocked with a credit card, and the security system won't be set until next Monday. This was going to be like taking candy from a baby. No one would ever know that he had been here.

Though, he didn't want to come back, he had to get to Kaleigh. She was his first priority and she needed him whether she thought so or not. Mayor McChandey could wait until tomorrow night. He didn't know how Susan would feel about that, but Susan had to wait, too. Just as he thought that a cold gust of air filtered through his hair and he immediately regretted what he said. Susan was ready to go to the other side, and he couldn't blame her. She was locked in between worlds for something more than likely she put herself in.

Jack eased her mind for her and the maid smiled warmly at him and showed him the bathroom upstairs two doors to his left. This time she didn't follow him.

As he headed up the stairs he wondered where Mr. Mayor was at tonight. Didn't city hall close down at five? No, that was to the public. Anyway, it was still late for the mayor to be out on a Monday night. What held his undivided attention?

Jack shut the bathroom door behind and quickly opened it and shut it without making a sound. He silently walked down the hall and stopped at a door. His every instinct told him that Mr. Mayor's office was the last door on the right. He jiggled the knob and found it locked. Jack flashed himself into the office.

The room was unusually small for an office. The man was lucky if he could get another piece of African antique in here. With one large stride he was standing next to a very organized desk that only held a white cordless telephone, a black marble paper-weight, and an open appointment book. He quickly took a snapshot of all of his next week appointments. As he was taking snapshots, something caught his eye for this Saturday night at nine. It held no names of the actual meeting place or numbers, just a city name—Creegan, Texas.

When nothing else of importance caught his eye, he put his camera back in his pocket and checked his watch. He had been gone for four minutes and fifteen seconds. He had time to flush the toilet and head downstairs.

Then as he was leaving, a message was calling him. An overpowering sense in the third drawer of the desk. He didn't have time to check, but damn, it was calling him like he was Joan of Arc!

With no more hesitation, he opened the drawer and evil from all vicinity of the four corners of the world engulfed his mind. Jack had to steady himself on the desk to keep from losing his balance. Before the evil took over his senses, he took a snapshot of the documents and pictures, flashed out of the room to the bedroom, and almost passed out from the sovereign pull of the darkness.

This is what he needed. He was getting weaker by the day and it wasn't helping that he was using more powers lately. What he needed was a soul. Mr. McChandey was going to be just fine for him.

The maid was waiting impatiently at the bottom of the stairs. Her hands were clamped together and she looked like she was on the verge of climbing up those stairs and dragging him by the ear all the way out of the house. Jack was feeling awfully tired and weak. He'd done too much today and if he was lucky he would keep it together for the next five minutes.

"Sorry it took me so long." What else could he say?

He reached in his pocket and pulled out a business card. "If you have anymore problems, just give us a call twenty-four hours-seven days a week and we'll be here. I'm sorry for the inconvenience."

Chapter Eight

"Are you talking about Jack?" Kaleigh asked again when her mother didn't respond the first time.

"You can't be serious, are you?"

Kaleigh blew an exasperated breath. "Why would I ask if I weren't serious? Tell me who he is!"

Gina shifted uncomfortable in her rocker that she had since Kaleigh could remember. She folded her hands and pressed them against her heart as to say she felt sorry for Kaleigh. She licked her dry thin lips and shook her head with doubt. Her eyes gleamed with pure dissatisfaction for her only daughter.

"I'm afraid that it's time for you to do your responsibilities. Have you ever saved someone, Kaleigh?"

Kaleigh directed her attention to the crinkled foiled window that silhouette behind Gina. Her mother always had ways to save every penny. She went to keeping her house at warm eighty-degrees to foiled windows, to keeping the heater off during the coldest part of Houston weather. She was the most cost-efficient woman Kaleigh had ever known. She never bought name brand items at the grocery store—they all tasted the same to her—and saved any container (butter bowls, bread bags, or peanut butter jars) to find a use for. Kaleigh didn't believe her mother owned any dishes that were a set.

Yes, she was prolonging the question. She didn't want to answer because she never saved a soul in her life except for hers. She blocked all those who tried to find her and all those he needed her. The last person she changed for the morale of the world was a rapid dog and that had been well over ten years ago. The last person she let in was Susan...and she was dead.

She felt disgraced in the eyes of her mother. Her mother was a fairy sorceress and saved people from the death grip hold of evil every day. Her mother cared. Kaleigh couldn't feel the compassion anymore for the morbid sense of how people decided their fate. If they chose the path to wrongness was she to save everyone? Impossible! They chose their fate. She didn't get to choose hers. She didn't get to choose the darkness. She didn't get to choose the love of her life or who she wanted to be with. It was decided for her at the beginning of conception and she couldn't change her fate! These mortal existences could. They had a choice whether to choose the side of evil or fight against it. She didn't. She never asked to be born a pure soul for Earth; it was all chosen for her and she couldn't do a damn thing about it but ignore it and block them out.

"Never, huh?" Gina said when Kaleigh never answered.

"Well, you can't block or ignore Jack. He'll find you no matter where you are, Kaleigh. He'll found you and you won't be able to get rid of him. He's found you once, he'll find you again."

"Who is he?"

"I can't give you all the answers, Kaleigh. You have to found out some of them on your own."

"Oh, don't give me this, Mother! Just tell what or who he is!"

There was brief pause that stilled the air. Kaleigh heard the birds chirping outside, the low humming of the air conditioner unit running though the house, and Gina's eyes blinking for several seconds as the noisy of the background intensified. Then slowly her mother's mouth opened and Kaleigh was prepared to listen.

"If I tell you Kaleigh then you'll go mad trying to fit the pieces together. This is something you have to figure out on your own. I can't help you."

"You can by telling me what's going on in that brain of yours. Please, Mother, just tell me what's going on. I need some answers which you have; you are deliberately avoiding my questions!"

She bit down on her bottom lip and shook her head. "Like I said, you have to find this out on your own."

Kaleigh threw her hands in the air. "This is lunacy, Mom! You have a chance to help me and you're not! What this secrecy? Why not just tell me? You know I can handle anything."

"Not this," she said catching her daughter's flying hands and looked directly into her daughter's darken emerald eyes. "When you do find out, keep the memories close and don't lose them. They will save your life and his and…"

"What?" Kaleigh was spellbound. She was hanging on to her mother's every last word.

"It will help keep your sanity."

Gina sighed and turned her back to her daughter. "They're giving you a second chance to destroy him." Her voice was a whisper, but Kaleigh heard every word her mother said.

"This doesn't make sense."

Her back was still turned to her when she spoke, "Five years ago you destroyed a demon. He felt a trace of purity and you destroyed him, but not completely. He has come back for you and they are giving you a second chance to destroy him again. Jack is going to help you."

Kaleigh stomped her feet on the floor and threw her hands up in the air. She paced around the small living room, shaking with anger. "Why? Why do they think I deserve a second chance? This isn't fair, Mother! Why can't I have choices like everyone else on this free world! Why can't I decide what to do what to do with my life? Why can't I find my own repentance?"

She never saw her daughter lose her temper at the gods. She knew that her daughter was feeling sorry for herself because of who she was and she understood. When she lost Kaleigh's father, and felt his death, she screamed and begged them to make her normal. They didn't. They all have a purpose in life that must be fulfilled and Kaleigh was questioning hers.

This wasn't bizarre to hear Kaleigh questioning her fate, but to hear her like she loathed them was something much more stranger than met the eye. She had never seen behavior like Kaleigh's or heard behavior like Kaleigh's. When the guardians found themselves unworthy to the world it was up to the sorcerers to bring them back from the brink of disaster and show them what made them worthy. She was afraid that she was going to be unable to make Kaleigh believe that her purpose was very special and very important.

"You have choices, Kaleigh. It all depends on whether or not you want to act on them. You have a choice not to let anybody in and you have a choice to play your responsibility. We all do. And you're not the first who felt this way about what you are and nor will you be the last."

"I heard this all before. Don't tell me that I don't have a choice, Mother! I know I don't. I know I can't let evil win; that's my problem, right? Nobody else's. Then I have the others pulling at me not to do anything, but watch the guardians die. Talking about choices!

"Let's see which I can pick, door number one or door number two. Either way, the outcome is going to be my fault.

"But I don't want this responsibility anymore! I don't want to have these choices. I never asked for it! It was given to me because of who you were. Why is up to me to destroy them? Why couldn't I have taken Dad's blood?'

This time, Gina stomped her feet and turned around so fast that Kaleigh felt heated wind whip across her face. She grabbed Kaleigh's shoulders and shook them with all the energy she had in her body. The house trembled under her feet, the windows shook, and an ominous howl roared through the house.

"You leave your father out of this!"

Then everything stopped and went silent, but their harsh breathing.

Both were shaking with anger as their blood rose to their faces and hearts sped like blue lightening. They stared into each other's eyes and felt the hurt words that filtered between them. Kaleigh didn't mean to blurt out what had been hiding for years, but she was so mad that she couldn't hold back anymore. She felt remorseful. They pushed her to say hurtful words and make her mother feel like the loss of Dad all over again. Her father was a weak spot to her mother and she never like talking about him.

Kaleigh lowered her eyes as she covered her face with her hands. She didn't want her mother to see her frustration or the pain she suffered for the both of them.

"I'm sorry, Mother," she whispered behind her sweating palms. "I didn't mean to bring him into this."

"I want you to leave, Kaleigh."

She was shocked. This was the first time her mother had ever thrown her out and she just looked at her mother with a puzzled face, her eyes questioning her reasons. "Mother all I want is some answers. Why won't you tell me anything?"

"Please, leave," Gina said in an icy, cold voice.

Without further ado, Kaleigh snatched her purse from the plastic-covered couch and slammed the door behind her, rattling the windows as she walked down the steps and found she had no way back to her apartment. The only transportation she could use was her mother's beat-up station wagon.

It had grown twilight outside. Most of the sky was painted in a pinkish canvas that had dark, puffy clouds swelling around the descending sun. If she didn't get a move on, she was going to be stuck walking home in the night.

Walking alone didn't terrify her; the demons did.

Taking the opportunity and knew for sure that Gina was going to mad at her, she decided to use the station wagon.

Kaleigh found the door unlocked with no keys in the car. *Crap!* What's the point of having a car without any keys? She didn't know how to hotwire a car…but she didn't have something better than the average, variety criminal.

She gripped the peeling steering wheel with her left hand and with the other she touched the key ignition and concentrated on the car starting, believing like Peter Pan.

Five seconds later, the car came to life, and she was on her way.

Ignoring the speed limit for the first time in her life, Kaleigh sped down the highway as if she were Jack. She was upset; more than upset, she was anger. How could her own mother kick her out when she needed her so badly? She didn't understand it! Yes, she did. She understood it fully. She hit her mother's tender spot and stomped all over it. She knew how Gina felt about her dad. She didn't love because she wouldn't have any powers, but she cared deeply from the human souls' part. She didn't understand why. He did leave her mother high and dry when she got pregnant! He never called, wrote, or stopped by to say hello. He used her and left her with a baby she never asked for in the first place. And then he died before she was born.

She sped down the jam packed highway until she saw the traffic up ahead slowing down. She hit her foot on the gas pedal and nearly collided with a red Porsche that said "ICUKALEIGH" on the license plate.

Kaleigh gasped. She gripped the steering wheel so tight her knuckles lost all their blood and turned white. She closed her eyes and shook her head. She reopened her eyes. This time the license plate said. "HAHAHA," and an eerie laugh whispered in her head.

She blocked out the laugh.

Her lips trembled, her heart beating rapidly against her chest as the words scrambled before and spelled, "Kaleigh."

A blasted horn honked behind her. Her head snapped back and some jerk in a Lincoln was slamming his fist on his steering wheel and more than likely screaming obscenities to her as well. She turned her back to the attention of the forward traffic and she realized something was not right. Something was missing from this packed highway that could easily make her go insane. Then it hit her; the red Porsche was not there. It had vanished like a mouse on a hunt. An old Buick with a rusted trunk and a broken taillight was now moving in front of her.

The man behind her steadily honked his horn as she tried to find the red Porsche among the other cars. It was nowhere in sight. The guardian hunters were playing another one of their silly games and she was really beginning to get pissed. She pushed on the accelerator and headed for her home.

She needed some time alone away from everyone. If she were to get in trouble, Jack would help her. Or would he? Her mother had said some pretty crazy things to her and she kept wondering who Jack was really.

It was getting late as Jack drove the barren, dark highway. The temperature had dropped from its scorching heat to a warm breeze of tranquility. It was a night to sit back and relaxed when he wasn't saving the world.

He was so exhausted that he was afraid if he turned the radio off he would fall asleep at the wheel. He spent several disgusting hours cleaning men's urinals, sweeping floors, and washing endless amount of widows. Then on top of that, he drove an hour to the other side of Houston, used most of his energy guarding Kaleigh from the hunters, and hadn't had anything to eat since one o'clock this afternoon. He would give anything for a slice of dry toast. Anything to stop his stomach from growling.

Hopefully, the clue he found would lead them to all answer he needed about Susan. After all that work he put in today better be worth something!

As he headed off the Waco Road exit; Jack thought about what Kaleigh would say when he showed up on her door step.

Jack felt the stinging pain of danger. Once again he couldn't be there for her, but he used the rest of his energy to shield the hunter away from her.

When Kaleigh arrived home, she made her a quick T.V. dinner that consisted of a small piece of grilled chicken with a tangy sauce, peas and mash potatoes and a small glass of water and then decided to take a nice hot shower to release some of the tension that had built since this morning with Jack.

She was still angry at herself for bringing her mother grief and the suffering pain of her unknown father. Hopefully her mother would forgive her soon and everything would be back as it once was.

She turned the sprayer on and stripped off her clothes and then dumped them in the country blue laundry basket. She let the water hit her face and then ducked her head, letting the full pressure of the water hit her neck. Her hands were propped on both sides of the knobs as her eyes were closed and she felt her whole body relax. She stayed like that for what seemed an eternity. She was tired, and nothing would do her justice until she was lying in her comfy bed with a full night's rest.

The steamed filled the small shower stall to the capacity and then overflowed to the rest of the perimeter of her bathroom. She scrubbed her face, washed her body, and then her hair. After feeling refreshed and thinking that bed wasn't going to wait around forever, Kaleigh turned the shower off and step out. She pulled a white towel from the hook of the door and wrapped it around her head. She took the other towel off the hook and quickly dried herself from head to toe. Her white, terry-cloth robe was on a hook next to where the towels hung, snatched it off as she threw the towels in the basket, and wrapped her body in the oversize robe.

Then she had this urgent feeling of dread and shook the insensible feeling away. Slowly, she stepped to the fogged mirror and wiped the condensation off with one hand. Kaleigh jumped back, nearly toppling into the bathtub. She clung to her robe like it was her only means of survival and stared at the picture in the mirror.

It was Susan.

She was smiling as if she was taunting her. Her face was pale and the shade under her lids was blacker than the ace of spades. Her eyes were different, too; they weren't the shade of innocence like they were today. Tonight, they burned black like the wicked and made Kaleigh's skin crawl.

Kaleigh slowly stood up and looked at the woman that was once so beautiful that it was unimaginable to see her as Kaleigh's worst fears.

The bathroom door slammed shut with a thunderous roar as the mirror turned black with Susan's pale face as the only picture to desire. Kaleigh's eyes never wavered from the mirror when the door slammed or when the howling noise whistled a demonic tune to the lights flickering off and on with every racing heartbeat. Kaleigh stood frozen like a statue. She didn't want to move even if she had the ability.

Susan's face hypnotized her like the whirlwind of a magical spell. Everything around Kaleigh appeared immobilized and of no use to her. Susan was only person to tell Kaleigh who murdered her. Her soul was a link to the past and Kaleigh would do anything to get into the depths of the nightmare that would novel her soul into blissful freedom.

Kaleigh reached for Susan and opened her mouth but before any words came out, a deep moan of hate filled the tiny bathroom with terror and the lights flickered out to darkness. Kaleigh stood paralyzed, clutching her bath robe so tightly she didn't realize that her nails had dug deep into her palm and that she was bleeding from her wrists again. Her teeth chattered as her eyes fixed on the mirror that was no longer anything at all, just a rectangle reflection that served no purpose. The whistling stopped, the moaning stopped. There was complete silence like the calm of the storm and it was her breathing that kept her from running into insanity.

God, if you can get me out of this, I'll be the most loyal servant!

God wasn't listening.

The darkness remained. The cold, heartless silence grew by the seconds.

Something warm and wet swamped over her feet. She blinked. The lights shouted on and an orange, scrawny demon with scarlet eyes, thick throbbing veins pulsating on top of his slimy head, and long pointed fangs appeared in the mirror and screamed a high-pitch growl, piercing Kaleigh's ears.

Before Kaleigh could move away, the demon shot outside of the mirror and reached and yanked Kaleigh by the wrists, pulling her towards him.

She screamed, fought back with all the strength she had, but the demon was resilient and would not give her an inch to work with. Kaleigh should have gone back to Jack. He said she wasn't safe on her own and now she knew why.

She slipped on the wetness that was too thick to be water, but the demon held steadfastly to her and pushed her further to the mirror.

Where in the hell was Jack?

Out of the corner of her eye she saw darkly, rich blood that looked black and literally covered her entire bathroom floor. Kaleigh grew hysterical as the blood flooded her feet and as the demon steadily pulled her towards the mirror.

The more Kaleigh tried to pull away the more the demon mangled his razor claws into her wrists. Kaleigh groaned as it opened its mouth and screamed another high-pitch growl. It showed its fangs. They were stained black with the mossy glow of slobber drooling all over the flesh of its face.

They warned her of the future that was going to be bestowed upon her and Kaleigh saw what might happen to her if she let this demon take her soul.

Kaleigh tried to look away, but the demon had her deadlocked with the guardian hunter's poisonous affection. Its eyes glowed green and Kaleigh felt herself drowning in the pool of his eyes as he dragged her into the mirror.

Sebastian had been restless all day. After a three hour flight with a layover, getting rental car, and traveling to find the closest hotel to Jack's apartment should have left him tired. But he wasn't.

He tossed the key card on the small, round kitchen table, providing by Motel Six, and carefully laid his jacket and sword against the lounge chair they also provided for him, and then immediately jumped on the bed as he waited for Jack's signal. He turned on the television and was just in time to see the second quarter of the basketball game. The Bulls were playing the Spurs and were losing by twelve points. He didn't get upset; the second quarter just started and they still had plenty of time to win the game.

His cell phone started to ring. He let the voice mail pick it up because during a basketball game he didn't like to be disturbed. His gut feeling told him it was Jenny Hollister, a woman he met a week ago at an AA meeting when he was looking for Shawn, a demon disguised as man, murdering young boys no older than ten.

When he read the front page of the morning edition of the *Chicago Tribune,* and saw the victim, Tommy Plank, a seven-year-old that was dirt poor and a casualty of welfare, Sebastian knew immediately that it wasn't a normal man that could commit such a heinous crime. He visited the crime scene late after work and felt the intense infliction of a demon. He picked up his scent and progressively read the morning the paper for any more victims and there were. In a two-week period there were six victims; all boys under the age of ten; all were raped, beaten, their penises cut off, and finally a blow to the head that caused their deaths.

The cops had no clue or evidence of the person responsible for these extreme acts of violence. Sebastian did. After the second victim, he was only one step behind him and the step wasn't too far.

Sebastian chased the demon responsible for the murders to a man by the name of Shawn Macaulay, a janitor that worked for the Children Memorial Hospital. He followed him after work and wound up at a Methodist church in the beginning of an AA meeting. Shawn was nervous the whole time he was there and that's the way Sebastian wanted it.

When the meeting ended, Jenny Hollister, an ex-alcoholic that had been sober for eleven months, came on to him. She was sexy, sophisticated, and had a beautiful smile that took his mind off Shawn for a second. They exchanged numbers and he quickly left to send Shawn straight to whatever hell he came from.

He cornered Shawn in an old warehouse on the outskirts of Chicago and it only took him one swing with his sword to send the demon back to the place where he belonged. The next morning, he anonymously called the detectives to the murdered of the young boys, and they found Shawn, decapitated.

The fine authorities of Chicago were now looking for him as a suspect in the murder of Shawn Macaulay—not that they really wanted to, but murder of any kind was against the law. Sebastian knew they would never find him and so he had no need to worry.

He let them take the victory as Sebastian called Jenny for his own victory prize. She was good and it made him feel slightly alive, but not enough to make him vibrant or make him forget what happened in France.

Damn! He practically lost his life over a demon. Never again would he misplace lust for the reason to feel the unnecessary emotions of comfort.

Jenny Hollister was a one-night stand and smiled as he remembered the words she shouted during her climax. "Thank God for AA!" It was the first time in almost five years that a woman didn't have to pay him for sex.

Sebastian started tapping his foot rhythmically on the floor as he drummed his thumbs on his thighs. "Damn," he shouted as he jumped up and paced the living area. "What the hell is wrong with me?"

For the past two and half weeks he'd been chasing a demon on zero sleep, while screwing his brains out with every woman that offered him the right amount of money for his services. He should be exhausted. He shouldn't even be watching this game; he should be going to Jack's apartment.

He was shaken up like he was prepare to go to war and automatically reached for his sword that was hidden underneath his leather jacket, hanging. He caught himself and threw his hands to his sides. There was no reason for him to grab the sword. No reason at all. He had no mission as of yet, and so there was no reason to go out and play warrior. But his hands took control and threw the jacket to the side and Sebastian vanished out of his house with his mission.

Jack almost drove straight into an eighteen-wheeler when a horn blasted from behind him. He opened his eyes and saw the large silver cylinder truck two inches away from him. He slammed on his brakes as the car behind raced beside him. A man with a red hat, who was twenty years older than him, stuck out his middle finger and mouthed two words that were unmistakable to Jack. He pulled to the shoulder and put the Jeep in park. He rubbed his face and then ran his fingers through his hair. He had to stay awake for Kaleigh's sake. She was in danger, but his lids grew heavy and sleep sounded so wonderful.

He popped his eyes open as another loud horn blasted. He let out a frustrated cry and hit the leather steering wheel with a balled-up fist. He was so damn tired. Another ten minutes and he would be at Kaleigh apartment, but it felt more like ten hours. Jack plastered his hands on the steering wheel, leaned his head against the back of his seat, and closed his lids.

They snapped open.

Damn, he couldn't do this. He had to be there for Kaleigh. The exhaustion hit him at the mayor's house and he prayed that his senses hadn't let him be in harm's way. They were low, but he never got the distinct impression that he was being followed. Now they were lower than ever and he couldn't tell if Sebastian got to her or not. He didn't know if she was still in danger or she was sleeping soundly in her bed.

Sebastian had to get there before the guardian hunter got to her.

He realized at this instant he used too much of his energy trying to protect Kaleigh. He was in a losing battle with sleep and he couldn't protect her anymore until he had regained his strength. He had to regain his strength by sleeping or getting a soul. He needed to sleep too badly to grab the first available person. He wanted to sleep and to hell with the rest of the world. No, he couldn't think like that. He had to go to Kaleigh if it stripped away all of his energy.

Jack hoped that Sebastian got his vague message. He was disoriented at the time and he knew he sent the message, just not too very clearly where he could understand it fully.

He cried out one last time to Sebastian and let the blackness claim him.

"Kaleigh," the demon called out to her. "Where is your faith?"

She pulled back, but his razor sharp claws dug purposely in her arms. She didn't scream; she wasn't going to let this demon know that she was terrified of him. Oh, how she was! She was more scared of him than any monster lurking in her closet. Mayhap, that is because she had never seen the guardian hunter except for in Mark's form and not in his true form. She shuddered when she remembered the redness of Mark's eyes.

She almost had it. She almost had an incredible thought of something that fit the puzzle to this confounded horror she had fallen to. It had something to do with Mark. She couldn't picture his face, his hair, his built, but it was just those red cold eyes of the guardian hunter. What did Mark have to do with this? He served no purpose in her dilemma. He was dead; gone to the world.

The sensation hit her again.

The demon had asked her a question. Had she lost her faith? No. She hadn't lost her faith; she just lost her way down the yellow brick road and didn't know how to point her sanity in the right direction.

Her mother warned her to be careful, but she never got a signal that she was in danger. Her mother told her she had to open up, but she could not do that! That was what the guardian hunter was waiting for and she wasn't going to give in to him.

Were these the reasons why the attempted deaths? Were the reasons why he tried numerous of times to come after her? He wanted her to open up to get to her and the others.

Yes, it was the reason, she thought to herself as the demon growled. He wasn't going to kill her yet. Killing her would serve no purpose. He had to get her to open up so he could get to the rest of them. She wasn't going to play the fool anymore. She wasn't going to let the guardian hunter terrorize her anymore.

Without thinking, her hands wrapped around the demon's thin, slimy arms as she repeated the chant that Jack made her embed in her mind to destroy the small demons that came after her.

"*Ab cor, evenire castimonia.*" From the heart, comes purity.

She chanted this over and over in her mind and from her mouth as she felt her body shine with an instant warmth of comfort and a white, fuzzy light filled the small bathroom. Her heart cried for the evil in the demon's soul and her spirit demanded the hate to be abolished.

The demon howled in pain as she squeezed with every muscle in her body. Kaleigh thought her ear drums were going to burst with his death cry; it was so shrill and abortive that it made Kaleigh scream for him.

The demon dispersed into dust before her very eyes. He vanished out of her mirror and out of her life. She dropped to her knees in the puddle of blood and covered her face with her hands. She peeked through her fingers and looked down at her robe. It was ruin. Her bathroom was going to take hours to clean and she was going to have to take another bath because she was covered from head to toe in blood.

Was she safe, though? Were they going to leave her alone for the rest of the night or were they just getting started?

She chanted the words and didn't give away the pure souls' position. It worked just like Jack said. All she had to do was believe in herself.

Then the pain in her wrist hit her. She turned them over and saw the gigantic claw marks reaching from her elbow all the way down to the tips of her fingers as her blood gashed out of her wounds onto the floor,

She blew out a sigh and managed to mangle out a laugh.

The bathroom door slammed against the wall as two dogs that looked as if they had been ripped inside came under the threshold. Blood and veins ran the length of their bodies as green pus popped and splattered on the floor. Thick, white saliva foamed over their sharp teeth. Their growling was louder than the demon that was in her mirror. And their bleeding, red eyes stabbed her with the hypnotic wickedness.

This was another attempt for Kaleigh to open up, and she wasn't going to submit to him.

She wished she could scream. Why she had chosen to lock herself out of the world and block them out? Why did this have to her choice? Why was she the one to get picked to destroy the guardian hunters and protect the others from them? She wasn't a guardian; she was a pure soul. This wasn't her job, but they wanted her to have it because of strength. Whoever gave them that idea?

The pair of demon dogs stayed under the bathroom threshold. They were crouching low, ears tilted to their slimy, dripping heads, growling profusely. If they had hair it would be standing straight up in the air.

Kaleigh didn't make any sudden movements, terrified if any might cause them to attack. She had to reach them, though. She had to send them back.

"*Call them, Kaleigh,*" a guardian hunter whispered in her ear.

She could feel him moving through her body like a drug for comfort. He was caressing her face and soothing her with his breath.

"*All you have to do is open up.*"

That's what she needed to do.

Her head cocked to the side and her eyes closed as the guardian hunter ran a seductive hand down her smooth cheek.

"*Give me what I want.*"

Yes, give him what he wants.

She didn't hear the footstep in her living room. She didn't hear the dogs' growls. All she could hear was the soothing voice of the guardian hunter, chanting for her to open up for them.

He was touching all over her face, making her feel like the one man she wanted so desperately was making to love her. She titled her head backwards, wanting to feel more of the sensation he brought forth to the pit of her belly.

"Open up for me, Kaleigh."

Yes!

"Kaleigh!"

The voice boomed like the antidote to his voice. Kaleigh's mind was in a battle now with the faith of the guardian hunters and the faith of her own. She wanted his hands to touch her again. She wanted to hear his soothing voice drowning out all her fears. Though, the voice called her name again and his faith was disappearing quickly. What was she to do when she was longing for the touch from the most inhumane species that could take her soul in the blink of an eye when she had the fate of the world resting in her palm?

Immediately, Jack's face overrode the guardian hunter's. She did not know who the guardian hunter was. All she knew was that Jack needed her and so did the rest of the world.

"Don't listen to him, Kaleigh," the guardian hunter said to her. *"He will betray you!"*

"No!" Kaleigh screamed.

Her eyes opened wildly. The guardian hunter was gone, but the pair of demons dogs was still here in her presence along with a stranger holding a gleaming, bronze sword, wearing a three piece business outfit and looking scarier than the Terminator.

The dogs turned to the stranger, showing their blood-stained teeth and glaring their cold, vicious eyes.

"Come and get me," the stranger said smiling as he swung his sword like a kilted warrior.

Kaleigh watched, kneeling in the puddle of blood, as the stranger took two swings and cast their detatched heads in the middle of the living room and their whimpering bodies dissolved into a pool of acid goop.

Kaleigh couldn't register who the stranger was or why he was sent to her. Her head felt like the largest part of her body. It slumped forward and for the first time in her life she blacked out and could care less that who standing in front of her bathroom.

Sebastian cleaned the bathroom to the best of his ability. He was never the one to get down on his hands and knees and scrub a tile bathroom floor, but after seeing the woman with jagged marks on her arms and then passed out, well he had an attack of conscience to do the dirty work for her.

To make sure he didn't ruin his five-thousand-dollar Armani suit, he stripped down to his white undershirt and blue, silk boxers. If Carly, his adoptive parents' real daughter, could see him now, she'll be taking pictures and sending them as a holiday greeting card for the rest of the family just out of pure spite. He could see the headline now, "MR. MONEY AND TOO GOOD FOR US SCRUBS FLOOR IN UNDIES." If only they knew how he got his money they would be shunned. What the hell did he care? They were already ashamed of him.

Sebastian wasn't really apart of the Ames family. His mother, a wolf warrior, died soon after she birthed him. A demon found her and destroyed her at her weakest moment. His father died during his mother's pregnancy, and if wasn't for the nurse that was a fairy sorceress, he would have been dead, too.

She took him into her heart and home, but only for a short while. Danae, her guardian name, fell in love with a human when he turned five and he was soon out of the picture because she had this concept about living a "human life" and didn't want her past life to haunt her new one. What a joke!

She dropped him off at the nearest orphanage without a good-bye or kiss and he hadn't seen her since.

Two years later, he was adopted by the Ames because they couldn't have any children of their own. They treated him like a normal son until the Ames indeed got pregnant and had Carly. Then they soon learned he was "different" in a scary way and did the unthinkable to him! It was his fault. He knew he was different and he should have kept his fat mouth shut.

If it wasn't for Carly, he would have run away long before the age of sixteen. She was the only one that treated him with any decency and kindness. Of course, she was only eight before he ran away, but what the hell did kids know at that age?

She was always latched onto him, making him feel weak and inferior about his duties to the world, and he hated the thought of leaving her behind.

The guardians were supposed to be these detached creatures that couldn't feel unless they took a soul into their life and felt their emotions. He never connected with Carly, and yet, he felt this weird disturbance beating in his heart whenever he was around her or thought about her.

He didn't like it.

The last time he saw Carly, she was sixteen. He, like all the guardians, knows how to fuck up something up when it's good. He shouldn't have touched her, but she was such a temptation holding him like she cared for him and it drove him crazy.

Then all that shit happened in Paris and there was no way he was ever getting close to another person again.

He wondered what the Ameses were doing now. Most of all, he wondered about Carly.

Sebastian was with the Ameses until he couldn't take anymore of their bullshit about his "out-of-control behavior" and there decided to seek his destiny in his world. So what if he didn't fit in with Polite Society? He wasn't a fucking human and never would be.

It was the thought of Carly turning out to be like them that burned his stomach. He wanted to stay and show her there was a world out there that was forbidden for the humans to ever know about. He wanted to, but knew it was seriously wrong for him to do so. Carly could never know him or where he came from. Shit, he didn't know where he came from. Nonetheless, she or any other humans could never find out.

Even if he could tell her, he would never get that chance because Sebastian didn't belong in the Ames' world and Carly belonged with them.

He rinsed out the blood-soaked rag in the sink and started wiping around the white, porcelain toilet. After seconds of cleaning, the rag was completely filled with blood.

Jesus, he thought as he wrung the rag out with all his strength. Whoever is after her must want to be destroyed pretty badly to conduct evil in this fashion.

Out of his thirty years of life, he had never had a run-in this bad with any demon or demonic plague. Yes, he had run-ins that nearly cost him his life because he was so blinded by what he thought was the human emotions he wanted that he nearly gotten himself killed. He had *never* seen anything in his life as this.

Why did this thing want her so badly? Why did Jack call upon him? A bigger question: who the hell was she in the first place? When Jack sent the message, it was unclear, though clear enough to be transported. When the message was sent, Jack never told him her name or what she was about. The message had been urgent and weak and Sebastian knew that Jack used all his strength, and that he couldn't get out any more than the location. Even when he called a couple of days ago, Jack was evasive.

He finished the cleaning the bathroom and put back on his clothes. His muscles were tired and taut and he could really use a beer. He never knew that cleaning could leave a person so exhausted that it baffled him that people went into this profession.

The rag was beyond repair that he had to throw it away so it wouldn't be kept as constant reminder of what happened to her tonight. After seeing what she had to see tonight, he was going to throw away his clothes as soon as he got to his hotel. He just couldn't believe there was so much blood! There had to be at least three gallons that covered the entire bathroom floor.

Giving the bathroom one quick glance he figured the bathroom was clean enough to his specifications that he didn't have to worry about mopping. He checked on the woman that he put away in her bed. She was sleeping.

When she fainted, he rushed to her and jerked a towel down from one of the hooks that hung on the backside of her bathroom door and wrapped it tightly around her wrists. By the time he got to her, the bleeding had stopped, only for a few minutes because as he began cleaning the blood and applying pressure they began to bleed again. Once he got the bleeding to stop that time he found a first aid kit under the kitchen sink then applied ointment and bandaged them.

If this woman was a human, she would need stitches. From his gathering strength, he knew that she was guardian and would heal in time with rest.

From the loss of blood, she was going to be out for awhile which was great because it gave him plenty of time to clean her bathroom and go get Jack.

"What the hell?" Jack said as he jerked up and gripped the steering wheel when he felt a hard jab punch his shoulder.

"You must have some big balls to stay out in the open like this!"

It was Sebastian. He had gotten the message after all, which meant that Kaleigh was safe and well. He was still feeling like the life was sucked out of him, but it was nothing a good ten hours of sleep couldn't cure.

"Huh?" he asked, feeling disoriented and clearly like he had drunk a whole bottle of rum.

"You passed out with the car running on a major highway, I may add. There's no telling how much longer you would have lasted if I haven't stopped by."

Sebastian was standing on the driver's side with the door opened behind him. His hands were resting on the top of the hood as his body was leaning against the driver's side seat. He was smiling but it was to convey the fact everything had been taking care of to the best of his knowledge. Jack was grateful that his friend had come to help him. He would be indebted to him always. If he hadn't come…he didn't want to think about it. He couldn't think about it because it would scare the life out of him.

"Trust me," Jack said with a weak smile. "They wouldn't have gotten my car without a fight."

Sebastian shrugged. "That doesn't matter. You know you are unsafe out in the opened like this," he said referring to all the loose demons.

"Are you going to bitch me out all night?" Sebastian shrugged again. "I need you to drive me to Kaleigh's apartment.

"I thought you wanted me to bitch you out all night."

Jack managed to smile, but it was an effort to do so. He was so damn tired that when Sebastian tried to scoot him over it was like trying to move a ton of bricks.

"You think you can actually try moving your big ass over?"

"Go to hell."

They didn't get off the interstate before Jack passed out again. His eyes opened for a moment when Sebastian basically had to carry him up the stairs and then for a brief second when he laid him down next to Kaleigh.

Chapter Nine

Kaleigh woke feeling like a piece of mud pie stomped considerably in the dirt. Her wrists were on fire and her body ached in places she thought she never had. She didn't know whether if she was lying in her bed or Jack's bed. She was warm like she was when she woke up in with him, but the atmosphere was familiar.

Nope, not in his bed, in her bed and Jack was with her.

She opened her eyes and conveyed the familiar atmosphere of her bedroom: red and oranges of the Arizona desert, landscapes of the ocean hitting the surface of the white sand, and the dimness of her sixty watt light bulb bringing a touch of melodrama. The familiar springs of her polyester mattress gave it away that she or someone had put her and Jack in bed.

Kaleigh was about a half of foot away from him and she wanted to be nearer. She didn't know what he was doing in her bed and she didn't care. He was here with her and she needed him to be hold close to her.

She enclosed her body on the emptiness and feathered his cheek with her fingers. His breathing was deep and so sedated that it almost pained her to touch him. She didn't want to wake him and question him. She wanted to watch him sleep and have this moment of peace while she still had the chance.

Kaleigh gave his cheek a final stoke. Then she realized that her arms had been bandaged and she was completely naked. The pain instantly vanished from her body as the haunting memories of last night flashed back. She pushed them back. She didn't want to deal with them right now; she wanted to think about Jack and how he saved her life tonight.

It was the only explanation for the stranger in her apartment; Jack had sent him for her. Kaleigh couldn't remember his name, though. She knew that the man in her apartment was a warrior; the sword distinguishably said so.

Kaleigh took this rare opportunity to study Jack. He looked as if he'd been through the wringer. His eyes were puffy, he dreadfully needed to shave (not that she minded), but he looked peaceful. Contented. Unrestricted. As if as all his barbaric attributes vanished to from his face and left him a sincere gentle man. Like Mark.

Once again, the inevitable gnawing on her brain was telling her that this had something to do with Mark.

It couldn't be. Mark was dead.

She softly kissed Jack on his mouth. His lips were dry and warm. She began to feel guilty for what happen tonight. She had rendered Jack into a coma-state sleep because he risked all his energy to save her from trouble and she completely ignored him. Why was the guardian hunter more effective than Jack? Why did she listen better to him? She knew the answer but she was terrified to say it aloud.

It was the soothing and mimicking voice he used as Jack for his own. He purified it, made it more sexual that she just couldn't ignore it. She had to respond to him or else she felt like she was letting down Jack and it was so confusing when the real Jack was screaming in his rough voice for her to come with him.

Damn confusing!

She snuggled closer to Jack, smothering his warmth. She heard his heartbeat as the night played harmonic music of the cars breezing and fireflies buzzing around the street lamp. She smiled to herself and briefly closed her eyes to think how life would be if she wasn't what she was. She could fall in love with this man and not have to worry about bringing down thousands of guardians. She could open her heart and mind to him and let the rest of the world rot as far as she was concerned. But this was her life and she had to deal with it just like everyone else who was like them.

Another thought provoked her until she responded. She blocked herself out right after Mark died. No other species such as them could find her unless she opened up to them. Yet, Jack was sent to her and she thanked the pure souls for once in her life.

Kaleigh opened her eyes and she saw that Jack was looking at her. Hard lines of exhaustion circled around his eyes as his face was relaxed and smiling.

She didn't move. She looked at him with the same expression. It was going to be hard not to open to this man. He was the one for her and she knew it the day she found him, but she couldn't love him. She couldn't let her heart overcome her capability to save them from the guardian hunter.

Jack was the first to speak first. His voice was hoarse and deep. "How are you feeling?"

"No better than you look," she said with a chuckle.

He laughed and then took a deep breath. "Thanks, I think."

His hand moved through her hair and she remembered that she had nothing on underneath. She was completely naked and he was still fully clothed. She almost wished he wasn't either.

"Why are you here?" She didn't intend for it to come out rude, but had to know why.

His fingers tangled in her hair and then loosely fell to cup her cheek as electric sparks were shooting in her veins. He could barely touch her and she went flying in the clouds. She wanted him tonight, but that wasn't going to happen because she couldn't have him. Holding each other was the only satisfaction she was going to get.

"Sorry, I wasn't here to help you. I had some problems on my way over here. I guess I'm not doing my part of being your protector, am I? That's my only explanation. The rest I don't know until Sebastian or you tell me."

"Sebastian was the man in my living room last night?"

His fingers slid down to her chin and tilted her head up to meet his eyes. He was so handsome that she couldn't pry her eyes away from him. Even dead tired and a full day's growth of beard he was sexy.

"Scary, isn't he?"

It was her turn to stop and think. "Yes," she said and then added. "I destroyed a demon tonight just the way you said."

He smiled warmly at her. She sounded like a kid that just discovered the answer to a very complicated math problem. He was proud of her.

"That's good, Kaleigh. I wish I could have been here to see it," he whispered.

She reached out and stroked his cheek. "I shouldn't have left, but I felt trapped and wanted some time to think some things over. I won't leave you again; I realized that I'm in more danger than I thought. I need you too badly to let you go."

He caught her hand with his own and raised it to his lips and kissed her knuckles. Fire shot to through her belly as her heart beat wildly. "I'm glad to have some use. I need you too. From the first time I saw you I knew that you were special. Too damn special for me to let go. I lost you once, there was no way in hell I was going to lose you a second time."

Kaleigh jackknifed up; minding the covers to stay put around her breasts, and sat against her headboard. "Why do you keep saying 'I lost you'?"

Jack gave her a tired look and then sat up on the edge of the bed and almost took the covers right from over her. She didn't want him to see her naked and so she clung to those covers as she watched his reaction grow so cold.

His back was turned to her as it rippled with muscles. "You really can't remember, can you?"

Shaking her head, Kaleigh said, "No."

Jack let out a long sigh and turned his body around to her. He didn't reach out to touch or even look at. His eyes were shamefully gazing all her body instead of her face. The guilt in his eyes caused Kaleigh alarm and the tone he used to speak was detached.

"I told you how I lost you five years ago, but I left some parts out."

Kaleigh wasn't exactly sure if she wanted to hear this or not.

"I woke up one night when this sudden ache of emptiness. I lost something and for the life of me, I couldn't figure it out what it was. I was lethargic to my responsibilities as a guardian and I was apprehensive to find the missing connection that was once a part of my life. I avoided everyone and everything. My work suffered greatly."

"Is that the reason why you are no longer a detective?"

Jack nodded, still not meeting her eyes. "Yes. I was close to having a nervous breakdown and decided to resign before I completely fell apart." He paused as if recollecting his thoughts.

"If it weren't for Sebastian, I wouldn't have been here right now. He saved me from a fate far worse than any guardian hunter. He told me what I was missing." He stopped and finally looked into her eyes. His face was so filled with inner turmoil that Kaleigh almost reached out to touch him. But she held back, wanting to hear the rest of the story. And she had this awful feeling that she knew what he was about to say next.

"He told me the missing connection was you and everything fell into place. I remembered everything about you except for that night when the demon took over my soul."

Kaleigh gasped. Her hand fisted to her mouth as the tears threatened once more to spill. Actually hearing it was worse than thinking of it. Oh god, she thought. What in the hell is happening? She never met Jack Pierce until a few days ago. There was no way that he had ever been connected to her. Jack was still virtually a stranger, but he had a face no one in their right mind could forget!

"How can that be, Jack? We never even met before."

Jack shook his head as he briefly closed his eyes. "I've known since you were born. The first time I saw you were twelve. I was there with you when you were nineteen and blocked yourself to the demons. I got tired of being your shadow and decided to introduce myself a few weeks after your twenty-first birthday. I—"

"No," Kaleigh said shaking her head. "This isn't possible! This can't be. I would have remembered you! I would have recognized the day you showed up in my apartment."

"I'm Mark," Jack quickly blurted.

Kaleigh shook her head and laughed. "Yeah? And I'm the Queen of England. What are you trying to pull, Jack? Mark is dead. I killed him."

"No you didn't. You're a pure soul, Kaleigh. You just destroyed the demon inside of me. You saved my soul from an eternal damnation."

Kaleigh licked her quivering lips as a single tear dripped from her eye. "I don't believe what I'm hearing! You have lost your mind! Do you expect me to believe that you are Mark? Get real, Jack. Mark was a kind decent man that would have treated me as primitive the way you have treated me! I believe that I would have remember you thank you very much."

Jack tried to reach for her, but Kaleigh threw her hands up and stopped him. "Don't touch me. Don't ever touch me again," she whispered. "Please tell me why I can't remember you?"

Silence seemed to stretch into annoyance. Jack sighed and dropped his hands over his thighs. "I am Mark, Kaleigh. They didn't want you to remember because they don't want you to know that you failed."

"Who? Why can't any of you people ever be straight with me?"

"I don't know who!" Jack shouted. "The somebody that's responsible for everything that we are. Your guess is as good as mine."

"But why would they do that to me?"

"Because they need you to get it right this time," he said more calmly.

Kaleigh screwed her eyes at him and threw him a vicious glare. "I swear Jack if you don't give me a straight answer I'm going to fucking scream!"

They were both surprised at her use of language and it made Jack want to laugh, but he didn't. She was already pissed at him enough and she had every right to be.

He ran his hands through his hair and breathed. "Okay, I'll give you a straight answer, but you may not like it."

"Everything I heard so far from you and the pure souls and my mother I haven't liked. What's one more tale? I can handle it. I'll survive. I just want the truth for once. Can you please just give me that?"

Jack slowly nodded even though he wasn't about to give her the entire truth. What she would soon have to face, she would have to discover for herself. He couldn't tell her the end; it could possibly ruin the surprise.

"That night you were supposed to connect with the pure souls and destroy the hunter inside of me and you didn't. Underneath your subconscious, you didn't want to destroy me and so you just made the guardian hunter disappear for a while." That was the truth. If he hadn't pushed so hard when the demon ransacked his body and pushed through his soul, he would have been able to control him, but he was gloried in the profound powers of a demon. Then she wouldn't destroy him. In her heart and in her mind, she had to destroy Jack for everything that he represented.

And she refused to allow her love to destroy him. The same way as Lucia.

"He has found you again and will destroy you. You've witnessed the strength of his power and he's only begun. There's no more evading him or blocking him out anymore. He's playing for keeps this time and will do everything in his powers to bring you under his mercy. If you don't get that connection with the pure souls, we will all die."

"How am I supposed to do that when they won't connect with me?"

He was compelled to keep his distance from her, but he took a step closer to her anyway because he had to feel her near. Badly, he wanted to pull her into his arms but he refrained from doing so until she let down her defenses just a little to snag the opportunity to bring her back to him.

"That is something you have to find out before the guardian hunter demands your spirit."

She was silent, withdrawn from him in her own cumbersome world of her complex, curious mind. Her eyes were saddened with uncertainty as her face was drawn into a gloomy frown.

A phenomenal light passed through the depths of her burdensome query and she looked at him with big, startled eyes. He knew what she was thinking; he could feel her response travel from her soul to his.

"Jack…you are not a…" she couldn't even say the word. If Jack was like Mark, she was going hide for the rest of her life.

"A demon?" he finished for her. "No. When he disappeared, he left my body. You would have known instantly if I were."

"But five years ago I couldn't tell the difference. I didn't know until it was almost too late for me."

"Kaleigh," he strained. "I was only a demon that night. If I were a demon, Sebastian would have killed me on the spot."

Well, he had her there. Pure souls were known to kill only demons, leaving the human soul intact as pure as the day it was born. Still, something didn't add up. Why had she remembered Mark's name and not Jack's? Why would they leave that little piece of information for her memory to repudiate her to open her soul for the other six?

"This is so strange. I have to see for myself."

Kaleigh had jumped out the bed, taking the covers with her. She was pacing around the room naked as the day she was born with only a flimsy cover to hide her nakedness.

Trying to think about Mark's face was onerous. They could take away her memory of faces, but they couldn't take away hard evidence.

She raced to her closet and pulled out a Nike shoe box from the back of her closet, hidden under boxes of clothes she didn't wear anymore. She dropped to the floor, folding her legs underneath her, and ripped off the lid. She grabbed handful papers and scattered them in front of her.

"What are you doing?" Jack asked as he came behind her.

She looked through a newspaper clipping dated five years earlier with the headline "LOCAL COP SAVES WOMAN HOSTAGE." She scanned through the newspaper not once, but three times seeing the name that repeatedly showed up on the black and white. *How can this be*? she asked herself. This was suppose to be Mark Stewart not Jack Pierce. It had to be Mark Stewart.

But on the newspaper clipping it proudly said Detective Jack Pierce with Jack's picture next to the column. This couldn't be. Mark could not be Jack. Mark was dead. He died five years ago along with her soul. She felt him die. He was friggin' dead, but here he was standing in her bedroom like a ghost in the night.

"Kaleigh," he said as he reached out for her.

"Don't," it was all she could say as she skimmed through the pile of newspaper clippings and pictures she and Mark took. Not she and Mark. She and Jack.

Her mother was right: she was going insane.

"How can this be? Mark died. I could have sworn I killed him five years ago," she said so low that it was like she was talking to herself.

"I never died," he said kneeling beside her. "To tell you the truth I don't even remember anything. I woke up in the hotel room and you were gone from my life and my soul. I couldn't remember your face or anything about you until Sebastian told me."

"This can't be. I saw him die. It took over his body. Something must have gone wrong, because he vanished and he was left lying on the ground. There was pulse, no heartbeat. I felt him drain from my body. He died," she said turning to face him. "Who the hell are you?"

He stood up quickly and seethed through his biting teeth, "My name was never Mark, Kaleigh. I don't know who put that name in there for you, but my name has always been Jack. Whatever happened that night put a delusion in your head that told you I was Mark. Tell me something, can you tell me how Mark looks?" Kaleigh shook her head.

"Can you tell me how he acted? How did he dress? Anything about him at all?"

"Yes. He wasn't an asshole."

Jack snorted. "Well they left me with the memories of you. I had no idea what had happened to you until your friend Susan died and the pure souls showed you to me again. I was born to protect you and I will to the very end. They can never erase your memories from me."

Kaleigh's hands fisted the clippings so tightly that her knuckles turned white. She stared off into space and remembered the last time she was with Mark. No not Mark. Jack.

"Kaleigh?"

"I don't remember much. A lot of it's just a blur..."

"But..."

"But I can remember the night you died like it just happened. I can remember every word we spoke, every color of the room, and yet I can't remember your face; it's just a blur."

He studied her expression and she could feel that he was trying to get the whole truth out of her. She stopped him immediately.

Jack sighed. "Just stay where you are," she said. "If you want to ask me something just come out and ask me."

"Can you remember how we met?"

"My friend Melissa came up missing. I couldn't find her anywhere. I spent days trying to search her, but I clearly knew she was dead. Just like how I knew Susan was dead. Though I wasn't connected to her, I just knew in my mind that she was dead. I went to the police station and filed a missing persons report. Melissa didn't have any family and I was basically the closet thing she had to one. I wanted her to have a proper burial because I couldn't stand the thought that she was lying dead in the woods somewhere. She didn't deserve that kind of treatment and I wasn't using any powers to find her, fearing the demons would find me again. I had no choice but go to the cops. The person who was supposed to work on my case was Ronald Fisher, but Mark Stewart somehow took it over."

He lowered his eyes and shook his head. "No, it was me."

"That's how we met. My best friend came up missing and I wanted her found. Then Mark or rather you helped me."

"Isn't this strange that we met again over another one of your friends?" She could only agree. This was the strangest damn coincidence she ever encountered in her life. This is what had been nagging her in the back of her mind all night. Melissa had died the same way as Susan. She met Mark/Jack from Melissa's death and then Jack from Susan's death. There was no way this could be happening, and yet it was.

"The same way as Susan," Kaleigh whispered.

"Go on," he urged her.

"Another memory I have is of you and I." She didn't want to continue the rest of the memory; it was about their first time they made love to each other.

Kaleigh looked up and saw that Jack was thinking about the same thing as she was. "It was our first time. You didn't want to because of some moral law you had about getting involved with civilians, which I now understand because our kind can't get involved. If I had known what you were then, I would have prevented it from ever happening."

"I think it would have been unavoidable, Kaleigh."

She ignored him. "You stayed, though, and it was so…" she paused. "It fades in and out until that night you died."

Jack was speechless. He sat like a statue in front of her with this bewildered expression on his face as if he was disappointed that she didn't go into great details about their past love life.

"What happened the night you thought I died? Tell me everything. Everything! I want to know every little detail. That is the only thing I can't remember."

Kaleigh took in large gulp of air and released it slowly. She pulled the covers around her tight as the thought of her walking down that hallway gave her chills. "I-I don't know why we chose to be at the hotel room, but I was coming to see you because tonight was the night I was going to find out what happen to Melissa. Everything I touched burned. Everything I saw was demonic and evil. All the signs screamed for me to run away. I couldn't. I couldn't leave you. You were in trouble and yet the voices in my head were telling me to go the other way! I just couldn't do it. You needed my help and I...I needed you."

She thought back to that night.

She rushed inside of the elevator ignoring the bellboy that gave her alarming stare. Mark had just paged her in the banquet room, telling her that he had found Melissa's body and needed to talk to her before they went to the morgue so she could identify it. She had been waiting for his call all night and finally, after long hours of waiting, he called.

She had no plans to attend the Walker Security company birthday party, but due to too much deliberation, she couldn't sit idle in her apartment waiting for Mark to call her. She got dressed in the only evening dress she had hanging in her closet; a spaghetti-strapped, slinky black dress that went down to her ankles and threw on matching high heels. She clipped her hair in a french twist, leaving a few tendrils loose and added a light touch of make-up. Then she left a quick message on Mark's cell phone explaining that she decided to go to the party after all and left him the number of the banquet room.

The elevator doors closed and a new soft, mellow music began to play. "Floor thirteen," Kaleigh announced to the bellboy that was standing squarely and mutely. He gave her a slight nod and pressed the number thirteen button.

Kaleigh's hands twisted together as she anxiously tapped her foot and watched the orange light blink to the rising floor numbers. Just six more floors, she thought to herself. Then a cold chill ran the length of her spine as if someone had lightly stroked her. The inside of the elevator became ghostly quiet as the over head lights dimmed to a dark ominous yellow.

Four more floors.

Something was terribly wrong. There was a tiny voice in her head telling her that Mark was in trouble and she needed to run away. She couldn't do that! If Mark was in trouble then he needed her help. Running would be cowardly and couldn't help Mark no matter how loud the voice screamed in her head.

The bellboy turned around and Kaleigh shrank back. His face had turned from his boyish good looks to a twisted, ugly face of a watery dream. His eyes were hollow and black. His mouth was large and opened. His cheeks and jaws were peeling away from his bone as it twirled and twisted like a tornado.

Run Kaleigh!

She wished the voices would stop screaming at her. Mark was in serious trouble!

"Floor thirteen." The bellboy's voice echoed in a deep, hate-filled whispered

Kaleigh closed her eyes and shook her head and then reopened her eyes. The bellboy's face was back to normal and the elevator music was playing and the lights were shining brightly and the voices were gone.

"Ma'am?" His voiced was soft and sweet now. "You're here."

She blew out her breath and rushed outside of the elevator and then stopped when the elevator doors closed to rub her temple and catch her breath. She hadn't experimented with this type of delusion in three years when she was getting felt up in back seat of Randy's BMW. As he was about to slide is hand under her skirt, she saw through the steam of the back window that a demon was watching and waiting for her. Kaleigh pushed Randy away with all her strength and told him to take her home. He didn't understand what he did wrong, but after that incident, he never talked to her again.

Now she was experimenting with them all over again because she decided to open up to Mark tonight. Only she hesitated before did so because she had this dominant voice telling her it was the wrong time. The pure souls and her mother's warning told her not to hesitate with the heart that it could only bring evil. She loved Mark enough to take him inside but didn't trust her heart enough to let him. Why did she even bother to let him inside when she wasn't ready? What had she done?

The room was the last door on the left. As she began to race to the room, the voices returned and they were louder than ever, shouting for her to retreat.

But she kept pushing her feet closer to the door.

Then a flash red caught her attention to the floor. She looked down and her hands flew to her mouth as she gasped. The soft blue, cropped carpet was bleeding outwardly onto the sole's of her high heels.
Run! Run! Run!
"Kaleigh," a deep, soothing voice called to her. "Come to me."
Hypnotized by Mark's rich voice, she gathered her strength and courageously proceeded to meet him. Quick flashes of dark shadows rose to greet her and vanished as quickly as they came. Her head felt heavy, her body hummed to the electricity of Mark mentally caressing her breasts and between her sensitive thighs.
"Open to me Kaleigh and give me everything."
She was at the door now, panting heavily from the heat that suffocated her body, and blocking out all voices as she let Mark touch in a way that had never been done to her before. She had already opened up to him. What was he talking about?
Kaleigh reached to knock on the door when the leader of the pure souls called out to her, "Don't."
The door flew opened and there was Mark.

Kaleigh jerked out of the trance. She didn't want to replay the entire dream again.

"Before I entered, you knew I was standing out there. You told me to come in and I did. As soon as I enter I knew it wasn't you. It was one of them—a guardian hunter. I don't know how it took over your soul, but it did."

Kaleigh stopped and saw the vision of Mark yanking her inside as the door slammed behind her. She blocked it out and began talking fast and in quick short sentences.

"Oh, god, he kissed me and was sucking the life right out of me! I couldn't breathe. The next thing I knew I was thrown in the bathroom. He came after me. I saw in his eyes that you were trying to get him out, but he was so strong and I couldn't help because I felt so helpless. I couldn't move or say anything! I just knew that he was going to kill me. He picked me up and I saw you, I saw your eyes screaming for me to help you. All I could think to do was touch his face. I know that our touch is poisonous to a demon. And then he dropped me and he was gone."

Kaleigh paused only to wipe the tears that were slowly sliding her face and spoke more slowly.

"I knelt down to where you lay. You were dead. Everything inside of me died that night. So I blocked everyone out, even my mother. I didn't want anyone to ever find me again. I didn't want the responsibility anymore. I wanted a normal life like you see on the commercials. No demons, no hell, no heaven. All I wanted was an ordinary life that I can share my soul with someone until we grow old. I knew because of who I was and what I am, I wasn't going to find that. You were dead so what was the point of fulfilling out my responsibility?

"I've dated useless men in hoping that one of them would fill the empty void in me. It never happened. Not until you came back to me and turned my safe-bound world I created into havoc that I can't diffuse. I was going to ignore my duties until they sent me to my death. Then Susan died, the guardian hunters found me, and you found me. Here I am again and I have not a clue what to do."

He knelt besides her, stroking his fingers through her hair and brushed his dry lips against her cheek, kissing away the drying tears.

Kaleigh let him touch her. She needed it. She had to feel him. He was alive. The gentle man she knew as Mark was alive. She destroyed the demon that had plagued his spirit. She turned and wrapped her arms around his waist and held him like it was her last night with him. It felt good to lean against the hard contour of his abdomen and cry. She hadn't cried this bad since the last time he died. She vowed to herself that she would never cry like that again and here she was wrapped only in her cover, spilling her tears on a man who would never pull her away. A man that would never leave her and a man that would die to protect her. It made her feel safe and sturdy and that everything from here on out would be fine.

"Don't they know I won't open up until I have the connection with the pure souls," she said at the last of her tears.

Jack kissed her on top of the head, knowing he was about to lie to her again. "Yes, but they are hoping this time you can find a way."

"All you have to do is open up."

Chapter Ten

The guardian hunter's voice rang in her ears. Jack's hand was in her hair as she pulled him closer in the embrace for the protection she needed against the guardian hunter.

"Ignore him, Kaleigh," Jack said soothingly.

Open up to me.

She felt him touch her cheek. In an instant Jack cradled her between his blue-jean clad thighs and she buried her head in the swelling of his chest. Her heart was beating fast as it beat in unison with his. The guardian hunter was here and for the first time Jack was here to help and protect her against the one demon that could destroy her.

Kaleigh!

"She'll never open up to you. She's mine!"

There was a humble laugh that stirred the hair on the nape of Kaleigh's neck. A cool breeze filtered through the air and the bedroom light shattered them into darkness.

Jack held her close and tightly as the silence filled the room to conundrum of their great venture. He wasn't going to let her go. Not for a second until. This was his second comings with the guardian hunter since he found Kaleigh.

Evil could only overcome a guardian's soul when feeling the weight of the loathsome cries of the humans. He wanted to remember what happened that night and what made him feel so inadequate that his soul was possessed. He never in his life felt that his mission or his life was so worthless that he should give it to a demon. When he was around the worst scum of Houston and felt tired and defeated did he ever not feel that his life had become nothing.

As he pulsed through the lost memories, Kaleigh was shuddering against him. He soothed her with whispering words, caressing her hair, face, and anything else he could touch. The guardian hunter was still in their presence and would not let up until his disillusion was shattered. All demons had a weakness. The guardian hunter was Kaleigh's touch, but she had to have the other pure souls' conformity before she could do so.

Kaleigh's words haunted him like a bad vision of the depths of evil. He shuddered in her arms and felt her tighten.

I touched him and he went away.

For a demon it would be possible and this wasn't a demon in Kaleigh's room.

Dark shadows of the dead rose in her room, circling them, reaching out to them. Their cries of immortal hate blistered their skin as the howling of the wind scorched their flesh. He could feel Kaleigh getting weaker by the moment and her breathing was becoming unstable. She was growing limp in his arms and heavy.

To destroy a pure soul, they blindsided her with the hate of the world and her worst fears, making her feel as if she has no control over her life and all that she accomplished has been worthless. Then it strikes fear into her heart and takes her soul with it

His parents' words taunted his mind as he tried to contemplate on what to do about Kaleigh. She was slowly dying from her fears that were scattered in her room and he was thinking hard on what to do next. But the only thing he could think of was to keep holding Kaleigh, letting her know that he was there for her and he was not going anywhere without her.

If Kaleigh would just open her spirit to him, this could all be over with. Why did she keep herself guarded? Why was she letting them die over a stupid oath? Yes, it was very important oath, but was it worth the sacrifice of an entire race?

Jack still couldn't break into her heart without his control that ricocheted off of her. The only thing he could do was send out signals that harm was coming to her. He found her and he let her in without any hesitation. She was the one for him and he was the one for her. But Jack knew the cost if she opened up to him or anyone. He knew whoever she opened up to, would be their death, which meant him. He foresaw their warning in the end.

All of a sudden a great force shook the floor of Kaleigh's one-bedroom apartment as fierce deep howl swept through the room. Jack and Kaleigh clung to each other as the floor picked up and slammed down hard. They were thrown towards the bed. Jack splayed himself on top to keep Kaleigh from any more destruction.

The guardian hunter was not going to get her to open up. Jack was sent here to stop the others like this one from breaking into her barrier. He was the only one that would be allowed to enter and if Kaleigh stayed strong she would do her part well.

Kaleigh never let go of Jack. She wrapped herself so tightly around his neck that he could scarcely breathe. Then he realized that her breathing was short, shallow, and fast.

"Dear God, Kaleigh, just breathe!" But Kaleigh's eyes were unfocused, dilated to the max as if she was on a powerful drug.

She couldn't understand a word that he was saying. He might as well been speaking Greek.

Loud pounding vibrated off of Kaleigh's bedroom door. Sebastian. He must be feeling the same thing as they were. But Jack wasn't worried about him; he was worried about Kaleigh because she wasn't breathing.

The dead chanted their cries as their master hid their shadows echoing their manipulative words.

"*Open to us. Open to us. Open to us,*" they chanted.

He cupped her face hard and pinched his fingers in the softness of her hair until there was a small gasp foaming from her mouth. She responded to the strictness of the pain. It was the only way to keep her from her insanity. He squeezed harder. A louder gasp.

The pounding door never ceased. The trembling of the floor shook like an earthquake that was meant to split the room in half. Jack steadfastly pinched her head, trying not to cause more pain than what was desired.

It was working, though.

She responded and she was breathing.

However, the hairs on his arms prickled and frost brewed in and out of his mouth as the room turned immeasurably cold to the gushing of the icy, chilled wind that grew fastening with the trembling of the floor.

Jack glanced up and saw the orange darkened curtains flapping with the wind, leaving their shadows across the moonlit room. Jewelry boxes, landscape picture frames, and mirrors shattered on the floor. Clothes spilt, dangling by an inch on the wooden frame of the dresser drawer. This was a nightmare. No. Worse. This was reality. This was as real as Jack getting Kaleigh to breathe on her own.

The dead circled them with their cold, red eyes glimmering into the hollow darkness.

He turned his vision back to Kaleigh who was in near panic. He closed his eyes and pictured them in on a warm, breezy beach. No one was around. The calming of the beach set the music to them holding hands, smiling, and kissing as the walk against the tide. She wore a red, string bikini with a red shawl wrapped around her perfect slim waist. Tendrils of hair flowed around her smiling face as she leaned in and kissed full on the lips, pulling back only to let him know that she desired more, but first wanted to taste, sample and tease before she let him knew the full desire of her hunger.

For once, this despondent, tormented woman was in full bloom and content with her insane world. Jack never saw her better than that. He never saw himself happier at that moment either.

Then he opened his eyes and realized that it was just a fantasy waiting to be fulfilled until the demon was destroyed and abandoned from her life. She would never know this happiness as long she was being tormented and a prisoner to this demon's acts.

Jack heard Sebastian screaming on the other side of the door to let him in and help, but Jack neither had the power nor the courage to leave Kaleigh alone while the guardian hunter was invading.

"Jack," Kaleigh whispered. Her eyes were closed, but it was good sign that she was talking.

"Yes?"

She pulled her hand to his cheek and caressed the hard stumbles of his unshaven cheek. Then before he knew it, her lips were on his. Jack hesitated only for a short second and parted his lips to drink the vinery wine. Her mouth was soft, full and promised only sweets. Her tongue was hot and fierce. He kissed her full and hard, letting her know the wanton desire he so badly needed since he first saw her. His tongue stroked the roof of her mouth, teeth, and tangled with hers like he was making love to her.

Kaleigh's hands circled around his neck and pushed him deeper inside of her mouth. A moan escaped, and he couldn't figure out if it came from him or her. It didn't matter. He was enjoying the pure ecstasy of heaven as the room grew more in death and the guardian hunter witnessing the whole thing. The whole army of hell could not stop him unless Kaleigh had wanted him to stop.

The guardian hunter growled so loud that Jack had to break the kiss and cover his ears. Kaleigh bunched up his T-shirt, dragged him to her mouth, and kissed him hard. Her tongue broke through his sealed lips and there he was again kissing her as if nothing was in the room.

Another powerful growl echoed through the room, but this time Jack did not break the kiss. He let the guardian hunter's growl burst his eardrums as he fortified himself with the sweet taste of Kaleigh.

A cold, chill swept through Jack and the guardian hunter was outraged! The demons screamed for the purity of the kiss to stop and for Kaleigh to give them what they wanted.

And when they didn't stop and when Kaleigh ignored them like a bad piece of furniture, they disappeared, leaving their trails of angry cries.

As Kaleigh and Jack were dancing with the demons, Gina was upstairs, praying on her bed for the banishment of the guardian hunter. She pleaded to the ones up above that Kaleigh would snap some sense into her and do what she had forbidden herself to do. She even breathed Kaleigh words of encouragement to stay strong.

She knew one day this was going to happen to her daughter. A guardian hunter had warned her on the day Kaleigh was born. When everyone had hidden from the worst of the demon kind, she was the only one left to go against the guardian hunter. It nearly cost her life, but it was well worth it.

"The seed you carry in your womb will be an abomination to the guardian saviors. Others will come for the ripeness of your daughter. Once she's ours, we'll destroy them all, including her."

The demon vanished without a whisper and she was left pregnant and alone. She wished Arthur were still alive. She didn't love him, but she had a soft spot for him. He was a good kid and didn't deserve to die over her.

So many regrets that she wish she could change, starting with her daughter. She should have molded her better, prepared her for the guardian hunters. Instead, she kept her daughter locked out of her heart because of what she was told to do.

She was over five hundred years old and had countless of babies and raised them like royal princesses. All except for Kaleigh. She was her last and would be her last. But if Kaleigh had born a warrior or a protector she would have mothered her as she was supposed to. Yet, she was trying to protect her from them, and wound up hiding her from her responsibility for the world.

It was all Kaleigh could think of while she was losing her breath. The guardian hunter whispered his hypnotic words and touched her with hands of seduction like Jack's, and she almost couldn't resist him. She nearly opened up for him until she felt the fast pace of Jack's heart beating against his chest and the anxiety in his eyes. She nearly opened for him, but the rhythm chanting of the undead made her focus only on her responsibility and what was right in front of her, Jack, protecting her with his life and never letting go. He never let go of her. He stayed with her the entire time.
Ignoring the guardian hunter and his circle of friends was the only way out of her nightmare and to escape what the path that she was heading down. She took one look at Jack and kissed him. She was using him and she hated that, but that is what she had to do to get rid of the guardian hunter. It was her only defense against the demon that could make her open up.
When the hunter growled, she thought she had lost Jack to the voice of the guardian hunter and pulled him back to kiss him again. It was her turn to protect him and kissing him was the defense and protection he needed.
Though, kissing him turned out to be better evidence than what she expected. She never expected to see sparks and feel the electricity of heat flowing through their bodies. When she kissed him the guardian hunter and his friends were not around. They could have been on the other side of the world while she was kissing him. He turned her bones into liquid and she nearly lost her breath when their tongues touched. If she had been standing she would have fallen to her knees. If they have been alone this kiss would have gone on all through the night and never stopped.
She loved the feel of his tongue tasting her and she loved that it made her feel alive and not dead. She kissed many men in the last five years and not one of them had kissed her like this. None of them had been the one for her. He was the one for her and always had been.
When she first met him she knew in the deepest part of her soul that Jack was Mark. His familiar words, the way he walked, and now the way he kissed, she knew that Mark/Jack never left her. He had been lost to her just like she was lost to him. But they found each other and nothing was going to tear them away this time. Not unless the guardian hunter had other plans for them. He had a plan for them five years ago and she thought Mark was dead. Could he do the same thing to them again?

Yes. If Kaleigh decided to open he would make sure that Jack was dead this time and she was dead, too. He wasn't going to make another mistake like he did last time.

She wasn't even aware that there was guardian hunter until it was too late. Her mother warned her that there was a powerful demon waiting to catch them when they least expect it, but Kaleigh was blindsided by the death of her roommate, Melissa, and her new happiness with Mark. She didn't have time to think about a new demon. Every day was a new demon and she did her best to make sure they didn't take control.

That was then and this is now. He came for her. He vanished from their last engagement and waited until he found her at her weakest. She still didn't understand how they knew she was connected with Susan. She had been so careful and cool. Someone had found her and now it was up to her to defeat him.

But why her? Why were they waiting around for her when there were six others like her? They had their share of picks, and yet they decided to pick her.

This was becoming so damn confusing! She wanted all the answers right now. That wasn't happening because life wasn't easy. Life had to be hard for and as she kissed Jack he made it so easy for her open up to him. She would open up to him in a heartbeat if she wasn't so damn important to the world.

The pounding of the door broke their kiss and they were both breathing hard and fast. Jack looked into her eyes and there she saw desire, passion, and a grand sum of what life could be with the man that would put his life in danger just to protect hers.

A flicker of the corner of his lips said that he was going to smile and say something but the immediate pounding seized him from speaking anything else besides, "Let's get you dressed."

Jack turned around as she wrapped the covers around her and dug through the pile of ruins that was left in front of her dresser. She found a white Playtex bra she hadn't worn in three years and a pair of white, cotton bikinis that was on its last wear. There she also found a pair of faded, hipster jeans and a light blue Nike athletic T-shirt with the logo printed across the chest, *Just do it.*

She wasn't at all thrilled at what she was wearing; it made her feel like a slob from the norm of her daily attire. Not only that, her hair was thrown everywhere and she was wearing no make-up. On top of that, she had bandages sticking all over her arms and a bruise in the middle of her forehead (which had gone from a dark purplish color to a pee-yellow stain) that didn't make her look all that attractive.

When she turned around, Jack's back was still facing her. She remembered when she wrapped her arms around that back it was all she could not to just touch and squeeze.

She cleared her mind and her throat. "I'm ready."

Jack turned around and she could tell that he had been thinking. His eyes weren't filled with the passion; the hard lust she saw earlier was gone, but filled with perplexity and overdose of mind running. She wanted to wrap her arms around him and feel his warmth, his strength, and how he felt about her. She knew how he felt about her. There was no denying that if the opportunity arose, he would be in her bed at the snap of her fingers. He wanted her just as badly as she wanted him. Not right now, though.

Tonight wasn't the time and she also had some strange man about ready to break down her door if they didn't answer him in the next five seconds.

"What the hell happened in here? It looks like a fucking tornado blew through," yelled the most gorgeous man Kaleigh had ever seen. There was not an ounce of body fat on him. He was an inch or two taller than Jack and twice as thick in the chest, with broader shoulders, leaner in the hips, and profoundly built thighs that pressured against the expensive dark blue slacks he wore. He could play Arnold Schwarzenegger's stunt double, but the face had to go. Arnold's face could not compete with his. He had shoulder-length, honey blonde hair, long curling eye lashes, thick separate eye brows, and one set of gorgeous icy blue eyes. They were round, deep, and it was like looking through the clear deep ocean. He had the straightest, pearly-white teeth with perfect thin lips that any woman would greatly appreciate kissing. He had a strong square jaw, high cheekbones, and short pudgy nose.

Yes, this man was drop-dead gorgeous and he oozed with self-confidence and sex appeal. This was Sebastian; sexy, scary and mean looking.

But Kaleigh didn't have a flicker in her heart for him. He might be all muscles with come-hither, bedroom eyes, but she didn't play his way. Her heart was only for one man and he was standing not even inch from where she stood. Jack was the only man that could make her heart jump through hoops and do somersaults in the air.

"This wasn't from a tornado," Jack said, his voice dry and flat.

Unexpectedly, Sebastian laughed out loud, causing Kaleigh to jump. He patted Jack on the back and said, "You could have fooled me. What the hell? Did every demon in a twenty mile radius come here?"

There was a moment of silence as they looked around at Kaleigh's ruined bedroom. Pictures were shattered everywhere, her bed thrown apart, clothes literally covered the bedroom floor along with the broken glass, and her night stand was knocked over. It did look like a tornado blew through.

Jack was the first to speak up first. "You know about the guardian hunters?"

Sebastian cocked his eyebrow and there was hint of recognition in his eyes. "Yeah," he said gravely. "They're destroying us like a bad trend. Pretty soon we all are going to be wiped out."

Jack nodded as Sebastian blew sighed and bowed his head. "Fuck. What are we going to do? None of us can destroy them, but a god damn pure soul, and where are they at? In hiding! Don't they understand without their help that in a matter of years we could all be obliterated from the world? Of course they do," Sebastian said throwing his hands in the air. "But they don't fucking care!"

"Try to watch your language, Sebastian," Jack said, looking at Kaleigh. "There is a lady present."

Sebastian turned and gave Kaleigh a heated look of disapproval and then shrugged. "So what? Do you really think I give a shit about what she thinks of me?"

Kaleigh saw Jack's jaw hardened his fist clenching at his sides. What was the matter with his friend? Didn't he have any respect for women? Apparently not, otherwise he would have controlled his language.

"Just curve it, okay?" Jack said.

Sebastian rolled his eyes and murmured under his breath, "Whatever."

"So Jack, are you going to tell me what's been going on since the last time I saw you?"

There was another flicker in his eyes that Kaleigh noticed as warning to drop the issue or not talk about the issue in front of her.

Instead, Jack glanced at Kaleigh for an approval. She shrugged her shoulders and noncommittally waved her hand. Sebastian already thought little about her because she one: was a woman. Two: she was getting his friend in a bad situation that no doubt blamed her for all his upcoming troubles. Just wait till he found out that she was a pure soul.

Kaleigh shivered thinking about his reaction. Jack noticed and asked if she was cold. She shook her head and said she was fine.

He swallowed and finally after minutes of silence he spoke. "Remember about five years ago, I met a woman that—"

"This is Kaleigh? The one that almost got you killed?" Sebastian said, burning her with his eyes.

Jack nodded and then cocked his head to Kaleigh. "This is her."

Sebastian's widen and his jaw dropped. Slowly, his eyes narrowed and his lips thinned. "So this is the woman. Do you realize how much damage you caused?

"What?" Kaleigh said, taken back by his unrelenting words.

Jack touched Sebastian shoulders and applied a hardened look to his friend and shook his head. Sebastian snorted and cursed. "She has to know, Jack."

Looking at Kaleigh, Jack face was impassive, but his eyes told her that there was something that he and Sebastian were leaving Kaleigh in the dark about and she wanted to know. She had to know. If she was going to feel guilty (which she had enough on her plate as is was) then she wanted to know what she had to feel guilty about without playing the blame game.

Sebastian's rancorous behavior towards her was enough to make her take fault for everything evil and bad in the world.

"She already knows," Jack said.

Kaleigh wished they would stop talking about her as if she wasn't in the room with them. If they wanted her to leave, all they had to do was ask. They were treating her like a child like she couldn't take the acrid secret with dignity. Did they expect her to stomp her feet and deny it all? If something was her fault, she would take full responsibility, but not until they told her what they were hiding.

"What do I already know?"

Sebastian glared at her and muttered a curse. "She really is *unbelievable*! What a pair we are, Jack. We know how to pick them."

"Can the sarcasm, Sebastian. I asked you for your help, not your insults," Jack continued. "Something very strange is going on. Do you remember how I met Kaleigh?"

"Vaguely. Remember five years ago, Paris wasn't a place to be, Jack, and a lot of shit has happened since then. Refresh my memory," Sebastian said as he folded his arms across his chest.

"Her friend went missing and I helped with the case. Now the same thing is happening all over again. A friend of hers went missing five years ago and five years later another one of her friends went missing."

"Oh yeah," Sebastian said, pointing his right index finger at him. "Melissa right? Did you ever find that woman?"

Kaleigh's head snapped up as well Jack. Both of them looked stunned and dumbfounded. How could they have totally forget about Melissa Gaines? After the night when she killed the demon in Jack, she forgotten about her past life and never looked back. Wasn't she a great friend? How did they manage to forget Melissa? It was like she never existed.

"Jack?" Kaleigh whispered his name. "Did you ever find Melissa?"

Jack turned his back to her and his friend and ran his hand through his hair. He told her that he could remember everything about except for the night he died. Was that what he had come to tell her? That he found Melissa? She remembered Mark/Jack called her early that evening and said he may found Melissa. When he came back he was a different person. He wasn't even a man anymore; a demon trapped his soul and she had to kill him. But she didn't. She never killed the only man she could open her spirit to.

Jack made a startling chuckle. "I can't believe this!"

"What?" Kaleigh and Sebastian said in unison.

Jack turned around with a smile on his face. "I found her."

"What happened?" Kaleigh asked when Jack didn't say anything, keeping her in suspense.

There was a short pause and an explosion lit in his eyes like he found a map to a buried treasure. "I found her, but shoot me down if I can't remember where her body was buried. I remember I found her. I dug up her body. She was buried in the woods in a town that I can't remember. But I was stopped that night."

Kaleigh and Sebastian were quiet. They knew what had stopped him; a demon that was trying to possess his body.

Jack shook his head and ran both hands through his black tousled hair. "Where the hell was she buried? It was somewhere close, out of the city limits. Damn! I was going to tell..." and it all came back to him. Not the place Melissa was buried, but the night in the hotel room.

"I was waiting in the hotel room. You were at a birthday party for your company. I called you up earlier and told you I found the body. You were going to me meet at the morgue to identify the body, but I told you to stay put until further notice." He took his time to remember that long ago night. His eyes were glazed over with exhaustion and the ache to find the lost memories. Then a spark of life hit his eyes and Kaleigh held her breath and so did Sebastian.

"I went to the hotel. I was angry about something." He paused. "I was angry at you," he said diverting his eyes to Kaleigh. "I was so mad at you that I was enraged. Then everything went blank."

Silence gripped the air like a vice as Jack tried to focus on the distorted memory of the past. Why was he mad at Kaleigh? She knew what he said to her right before he kissed her. Why did you hesitate? She had to tell him. She had to tell everything that was said that night.

"I know why you were mad," Kaleigh whispered.

He didn't say anything; he looked at like she was a figment of his imagination. "You said something about me hesitating. You were angry because I hesitated to let you in, to open up to you, but it wasn't you that said it. It was the guardian hunter. When I was at the party I was thinking of you and decided to let you in, but I paused before doing so and you must have felt it.

"I'm sorry Jack. That's why the guardian hunter took over you soul. You felt the hesitation coming from me and I let you die." She turned and ran out of the room, slamming the door behind her. She began to cry when she felt someone touch her shoulders. The tears stopped.

It was Jack. She knew his scent, his warmth, and his touch. Her heart plummeted and she sighed.

"I'm sorry Jack. I never meant to cause you any pain. I don't know why I hesitated, but I did. Then I killed you. What were they thinking giving me you as my protector?"

He wrapped his arms around her waist and pulled her close against the hard plane of his stomach. There Kaleigh found strength, love, and devotion. She leaned her head against his shoulder and ravished in his strength. She could feel the rapid beats of his heart and his warm breath against her ear.

"I wish I could open to you, to let you know how I feel, but I'm scared if I do, they'll find the others and there won't ever be a chance for them to help. Do you understand why I don't open up or let you in?"

She felt an affirmative nod that he did. He tightened his grip around her waist and her knees nearly buckled when he placed a soft, seductive kiss against the nape of her neck.

"Kaleigh," he whispered to her ear. "I'll die protecting you. I was meant to protect you and you were meant to bring them out. That's something that can't be avoided. You need to figure how to defeat them without touching your soul to destroy them because you are the only source we have and you can't keep running from them."

"I know," she said. Then turning around in his arms and wrapping her arms around him. Together they held each other like that night so long ago. Kaleigh felt her heart race and then stop when he ran his hands through her hair and kissed the top of her forehead. His heart was beating fast as hers. She couldn't let him feel her love, but she could show him.

"Jack," she whispered as she tiptoed to meet his mouth.

"Jack," Sebastian said as he entered her living room. Kaleigh stepped down and unlinked her arms around his neck, blushing the entire time and moved slightly away from Jack, not meeting Sebastian eyes.

"What is it?" Jack said. She could sense that he wasn't too thrilled about Sebastian interrupting what might have been, but from the strain of Sebastian voice, it was something important.

"I don't think it's safe to stay here tonight," he said momentary looking around her apartment and then back at Jack. "They haven't left; I can still smell their scent and they'll be coming out of hiding soon if we don't leave now."

As they drove to Jack's apartment in his Jeep, Jack and Kaleigh were filling in Sebastian with the parts of the story he didn't get earlier. Sebastian listened carefully and didn't say a word; he sat the passenger side seat, looking at Jack when he talked and then looking at Kaleigh when she talked as they told their story from beginning to now, finishing each other's sentences and taking turns on their side of the story. Jack was discussing his findings at the mayor's house, concentrating on the road as much as possible when Sebastian said his first words.

"You said you felt like you were being watched?"

Jack nodded his head. "The whole time I was in there it was like I had a hundred eyes following me, but no one was there except for the housekeeper and pretty much most of the time she was near me, though it wasn't her. It was something else. When I went into his office, I was expecting at any moment for someone to hit from behind, but nothing happened."

Sebastian made a grunt sound under his breath and flicked something off the breast of his pocket. He stared back at Jack who was going on with his story and still never taking his eyes off the road.

"You wouldn't believe what I found in his desks. I couldn't believe he left it out so blatantly! Anyone can find it. Anyway, what I found will put the mayor away for a long, long time. I could hardly believe my own eyes at first, but there it was in black and white photos along with documents, addresses, and the victim's names." Jack closed his eyes only briefly. When he opened them back up they narrowed and his muscles tensed as Kaleigh leaned in from the backseat of the Jeep and placed a hand on his shoulders.

"What is it Jack?" Kaleigh asked.

She thought he wasn't going to answer her and then he opened his mouth to speak, when Sebastian screamed.

"Stop!"

The intensity in his voice made Jack not need a reason why. He knew why. He felt the demon's presence as quickly as Sebastian did.

He slammed on his brakes, gripping the steering wheel as the tires squealed down the highway. All three were thrown forward, but Kaleigh was the only one that got damage; she was thrown forward against the back of the driver's side seat. Jack cursed under his breath as he took control of steering wheel, maintaining control of the vehicle as it went to the shoulder of the road.

Sebastian reached for his sword that was wedged between the passenger side door and his seat when the roof of the Jeep slammed downwards. Kaleigh screamed as she covered her head with her arms as Jack yelled, "What the hell is that?"

"What the hell do you think?" Sebastian screamed.

Jack stopped the Jeep on the shoulder of the highway and Sebastian unlocked his seatbelt and was already climbing out with his sword drawn in his hands. Jack grabbed Sebastian's shoulder and slammed him against the seat.

"What is your problem, Jack?" he screamed.

"You can't go out there like that!"

"And why the hell not?" he said heatedly.

There was a brief hesitation from Jack. "Think about it. They," he said pointing his thumb towards the few cars that passed them. "Can't see the demon; only we can. What's it going to look like if you go out there with a sword and attacking something that only we can see? They'll call the cops. Stay inside—"

"And let it bring us to an executioner?"

Jack ran his fingers through his hair and shook his head. "No—" the demon's high pitched growl sent waves of chills up their spines as their eyes widened and hearts pounded against their chests. The creature of the dark began pounding its fist through the hood, shaking the body of the Jeep and tossing them around like wads of trash.

Kaleigh fell to the floor and she heard Jack mumble from the front. She heard the *whoosh* of his seat belt being tossed off as she continued to be thrown around in the back. Why she didn't put her seatbelt on was beyond her. Maybe she thought she would be safe on the twenty minute joy ride or maybe she just thinking think it was important at the time. She should have put it on anyway; it was the law.

Her wrist was shackled by a large hand and another hand wrapped around her waist, picking her up as her limbs hit everything in the car, including Sebastian, who mumbled a curse when her foot slammed into his face. Jack had straddled her over his large, hard thighs and held her with her head facing the back windshield. The pounding was getting deeper and louder and at any moment the creature would be inside if they didn't do anything about it.

"Jack I have to go out there, I have no room in here," Sebastian said as the creature made another deep, hissing growl.

Jack whipped his head to the backseat and looked at the top of his roof and the demon was making progress. He turned back to his friend and shook his head. "No, you can't."

"We're going to fucking die if we don't do something, Jack!" Sebastian screamed.

He threw his hands in the air and gently laid them on Kaleigh's back as she was staring mystified at the back windshield. "Just hang on!"

"We don't have a moment!"

As both were screaming at each other, Kaleigh saw a dark, shadowing figure no more than fifty feet away from the jeep. It had no face or bone structure; it was a black shadow figure with legs, glaring its red eyes at her. Kaleigh couldn't look away. She didn't look away when the demon punched through the hood, and she didn't look away when it reached for her. She continue to stare at the guardian hunter that was waiting expectantly to take her soul, waiting for her to do what she had to do. He knew it and she knew it and there was no way to escape her powers; it was jut like the last night in her bathroom when all she had left had been her powers to save her.

Jack squeezed her closer against his chest as Sebastian threw himself outside with his sword ready to do battle. Kaleigh was the only one that was calm about the situation. She slowly reached out her hand, grabbed the bony, slimy black arm that had fallen through, and squeezed with all her might as she whispered her weapon words and the guardian hunter laughed at her and then disappeared into the thin air of the night.

The demon howled.

Outside Sebastian never had a chance to swing his sword as the demon was struck by a bolt of lightening, screamed in pain, for his skin was melting off his body and shrinking into unknown object.

Kaleigh continued to constrict its arm until it disappeared from her grasp as Jack hurled another lightening bolt from the sky.

Sebastian watched the transformation of the demon's bones constrict and break as grey feathers began to sprout on its back. It was disgusting to watch, but Sebastian found it fascinating. He only knew of the pure souls that could transform a demon into life. They had their good qualities, but they were all still bitches in his dictionary.

As quickly as the demon changed to the pigeon, a bolt of blue lightening shot from the sky, and exploded the bird. Guts and feathers went everywhere. Sebastian quickly stepped back and was saved of bird droppings.

Kaleigh shuddered against Jack and he held her close, so close that he was squeezing all the air out of her lungs.

Sebastian climbed in threw his sword in the back seat. Kaleigh quickly glanced at him; he was shaking his head as he buckled his seat belt back together. "Well, that pigeon was toast. It never got to spread its wings. You have bird guts all over the top of your jeep, Jack."

"It can be washed off," Jack said as he loosened his grip on Kaleigh and pushed against the steering wheel. The horn blasted and all three jumped in their seats.

"Jesus H. Christ! Are you trying to give me a stroke?" Sebastian said rubbing above his right breast.

Jack laughed at his suspense and then focused on Kaleigh who was looking intensely at his face. He cocked a lopsided smile on her and then cupped her face. "Are you all right?" She nodded her head and smiled. "You sure?" he asked again.

"I'm fine, Jack, really," her voice sounded uneven, but Kaleigh did feel fine; she didn't feel like herself.

In the past few days everything that she had vowed never to do again she had done. She was using her powers, getting stronger by doing so, and therefore giving the luxury to her soul for the guardian hunter's use. She had to be careful at what she could do and what she couldn't do and the one thing she knew she couldn't do was opened up.

It was going to be up to her to maintain her control over her own selfish wants and get used to the idea that she couldn't have Jack completely. She had him once before and lost him because of the stupid oath she promised the other pure souls.

Guardians couldn't fall in love, period. If they did, their powers were stripped and their longevity stopped. They have to start living a normal life in the real world where they couldn't see a demon to help the losing battle with the guardian saviors. It was sad really that their souls were the only ones that had a warning label about falling in love.

She had to forget the notion about that and concentrate on the reality that something much worse than falling in love was after them.

Jack was staring at her, hands still holding her face, and looking as if he was going to say something else. She smiled sweetly and touched his hands with hers, "I fine, Jack."

"This place isn't sacred, we need to keep moving before one of those bastards come after us again," Sebastian said looking ahead, and moving his legs uncomfortable on the floor.

Kaleigh realized that she still straddled Jack's thighs, and slowly climbed off his lap, making sure not to hit Sebastian again, and climbed into the back seat. This time she put on her seatbelt. She looked up at the hole in the hood that was just as big as a baby's fist. If something that small could do that much damage, she wonder, what in the world could the guardian hunter do if they took control of a pure soul? Kaleigh shuddered. She didn't want to think about it.

"You all right back there?" Jack asked as he must have seen her shake.

"Yeah, just get us out of here."

Without anymore delays, Jack drove them to his apartment.

Kaleigh was helped out of the Jeep by Jack and got stuck in the middle of the two "giants" and felt rather short in comparison to them.

They reached the elevator, Kaleigh was a little reluctant. She remembered what happened when she went to Susan's apartment. Memories like those don't fade away, and she feared she would always be a little afraid of elevators.

Though when she stepped off the elevator, none of her inner voices commanded her to run and there was no sign of Susan to distract her.

Everything was at peace, and for the first time in days, Kaleigh felt she was safe and contained in her small world. Of course, she was exhausted to the max and didn't have the emotional stamina to stay awake more than she had to, but Jack fought with her for her to go to bed. She grudgingly gave in when her eyes became heavy and her body could no longer stand.

Without protest from her, Jack helped her to his bed, tucked her in and as he was leaving, Kaleigh suddenly came wide awake.

"Where are you going?"

Jack stopped at the opened door and turned to face her. "I need to talk with Sebastian. If you need anything, I'll be either outside your door or in my office, which is right across the hall."

Kaleigh wanted to scream that she needed him now, to hold her and comfort her while she slept. But through the clear message on his face that what he needed to discuss with his friend was important. She nodded her head and once Jack left, she instantly fell asleep.

Chapter Eleven

Jack filled Sebastian in on last five years. He explained what the voices wanted him to do and what they had done to him to make his body weak and on the verge of turning into something he would only do for the world…and Kaleigh. When he explained why Kaleigh couldn't open up, Sebastian seemed a bit more reluctant to treat her like she was the demon.

After awhile, Jack and Sebastian stewed in their own silent turmoil while they sipped on the coffee. They were in the kitchen, sitting at the breakfast table. It was a little after one and both were dog tired; especially Jack. Every minute awake seemed to drain his energy and a take a little piece of his soul.

He hated that they had chose him to do this mission, and he particularly hated what he was going to do to Kaleigh at the end. He wasn't too keen on looking forward to it, considering that he was madly in love with her. Jack would have never let her in if he didn't feel one ounce of affection towards her or anybody for that fact.

Seeing her again let his heart open, and he wasn't strong enough to stop it. He was defenseless against Kaleigh and at the end he would be nothing to her again.

To fill the silence, Jack asked, "What happen to her tonight?"

Sebastian sighed and closed his eyes. "There was so much blood, Jack; I couldn't even begin to imagine where it all came from. She was kneeling in it like it was the sanctity of life right there in the middle of her bathroom floor and looking like she was speaking to someone, but nobody was there. It must have been a guardian hunter speaking to her because I was the only one there, besides the two demons, which I took care of quickly. Then she just fainted. I bandaged her arms and cleaned up the blood and got you."

"What happen to her arms?"

Sebastian took a sip from his steaming cup of coffee and shrugged as he placed the cup down. "I don't know. I wasn't there when it happened. I got there afterwards."

Jack moved the newspaper out of the way and leaned in on the table with his elbows as a thought hit him. "She killed a demon."

"All that blood, though? That's impossible! Since I was twelve, I've killed hundreds of demons and not one of them spilled that much blood! I'm telling you Jack, I was down on my hands and knees for two hours cleaning up the bathroom and there was no way that that much blood could come out of a demon. Not only that, most of them don't bleed, that usually just explode into dust or melt. To tell you the truth, I don't think I've ever seen one that bled."

Jack ran his hands through his hair. He needed a shower and another twenty-three hours of sleep. He felt like shit and he wanted to climb next to Kaleigh's warm body and hold her.

"Before Jack, in the jeep, you were mentioning something about the mayor…what was it?"

He completely forgot about Mr. Chandlery and his hidden obsession and was well interrupted by a demon. That was a good reason to forget something important like that.

"Remember what I said, that it felt like I had a hundred eyes watching me?" Sebastian nodded. "I think Mr. Chandler's is a human servant."

"Holy shit," Sebastian whispered. "Where the hell did you get these?"

"From his office," Jack said, leaning over Sebastian's shoulder as he strolled to the next picture on his computer screen that brought up a woman no older than twenty, foreign, from the Middle East somewhere, and naked except for the white cotton underwear she wore. Her hands and feet were bound by a thick rope as her head propped against a smooth pattern of a black wall and tears were running down her cheek.

"What the hell is he doing to these women?"

He couldn't take the sight of the photos anymore so Jack closed the window. He folded his arms across his chest and leaned against the cool surface of his office. "Torturing them is my guess. What for? Because he has too much money and power with no heart or conscious and feels the need to make someone suffer for his boredom."

"What else did you find out?"

Jack shrugged his shoulders. "It may be something important, but he has something planned for Saturday at Creegan, Texas, at nine p.m. and I'm going to be there to discover it."

"I'll go with you," he said quickly.

"Yes," Jack said quickly. "It'll probably take more of us if there's any trouble—."

The sudden penetration of dizziness hit Jack like a blow to the gut. His head rolled to the side as his body lost control of his strength and nearly dove into Sebastian. "What the hell? Are you all right?" Sebastian said, catching him in him by his shoulders.

Jack rubbed his face. "I need sleep. It's causing me to lose more of myself by the day. I don't how much longer I can control it."

"If you want me to, I can find…"

"No!" Jack quickly said. "Don't do that for me. I couldn't ask you to do that for me, Sebastian. I knew what I was getting into when I agreed and who I'm going to take that should keep me fine until…" Jack couldn't finish the words.

"We'll discuss this further when you have more strength," Sebastian said.

He wanted to tell Sebastian that there wasn't a spare bed in room in his apartment and it would be better to sleep on the floor, but he was already pushing him out of his office.

Jack found Kaleigh curled in a fetal position. Her breathing was slow and soft which meant she wasn't having any bad dreams. He didn't bother with his clothes as he pushed the covers aside and slid next to Kaleigh's warm body. One of her arms was thrown across his chest, knocking the wind out of him. He carefully removed her arm and folded her body into his. He could smell the herbal shampoo she used in her hair and it acted like an aphrodisiac to his body. It awoke his every nerve cell, jolting him out of his sleep-deprived phase and into a crazed, seduction one.

He gritted his teeth together, held her tighter, and let his crazed phase harden his body as he told his mind that it was time for sleep. But how could he sleep with her ass was firmly against the one thing that wouldn't listen and her scent smoldering him?

Apparently no time. As soon as he closed his eyes he fell asleep to the warmth of Kaleigh's body, and her scent that would haunt his dreams.

While Jack was recuperating, Sebastian took it upon himself to do a little searching of his own because something did not add up right with Melissa Gaines.

He was dead tired and could have used a couple of hours of sleep himself, but sleep never came easy to him when every time he shut his eyes, the ghastly visions of his horrendous past came to life. He was lucky to get five hours a sleep a week that weren't interrupted by his nightmares.

Before his years in Paris, he visited Houston quite frequently because Jack was pretty much his only friend. Sebastian was the first to admit that he was a hard person to get a long with. He was temperamental, uncouth, and never had the graceful social skills to simply get along with other people.

Sebastian simply didn't like humans to begin with. He never disliked a group so much as he did the humans. They were conniving, malicious, strenuous, arrogant bunch that all deserved the punishment they would receive when their time came. More than half of them desired to be destroyed because they created more chaos in the world than the demons. The rest could use a slap in the face as a wake-up call to get in touch with reality.

The sorceress that raised him until he was seven taught him that humans were these dumb, innocent creatures that needed to be guarded at all times because they simply could not resist the temptation of the wicked.

He saw that it was all true. He witnessed it every night he went out to hunt. They were the reason why he couldn't sleep at night. Yet, he had to protect them to keep them safe when they never showed him the small amount of thoughtfulness or comfort.

He didn't care. He never cared for anything or anyone except for destroying demons.

Sebastian thought that once he was grown that the nightmares would stop, but they hadn't. They scared him more than any demon could do.

If it weren't for Jack, he may not be able to trust anyone ever again. Luckily, Jack was there for him that night and he didn't make the biggest mistake of his life.

He searched for records on Melissa Gaines that lived around in the Houston area. A few birth and death records came up, but the ages didn't fit.

They were either too young or too old for the person he was looking for. He searched the *Chronicle* online and found nothing about a missing person named Melissa Gaines who was found buried alive, but an article did come up about a body discovered in Chambers County.

He clicked on it and read the headline JANE DOE BURIED ALIVE and then read the article:

Detective Jack Pierce discovered a Jane Doe in her mid thirties, Caucasian, and perhaps a resident of Harris County that had been found buried alive on Saturday, April 16, 2000 at 11:45 p.m. in the Chamber's County woodland area… The unidentified woman was bound by the wrists and ankles and had series of blows to the head…She was DOA…No information has been reported about her captor(s), but Chambers County, Sheriff Michael DeLane and Houston Police Department are searching further for clues…

Sebastian searched more thorough through posted investigation of the Jane Doe. Most of it was about the continued search for her and when the investigation that came to a dead end. He had nearly given up, when he clicked on the next page and quickly clicked the link and read the article. This article was more important than the first one: This article had a picture of Jane Doe when her body was discovered. He clicked the print button and then searched for any record on Kaleigh's other missing friend, Susan Garrett.

A ton of articles came up about the recent marriage of Devin McChandey and Susan Garret and the low-profile divorce that was two years later. He chose the first article and jumped three feet from his chair, shaking his head.

How could the American eye be so blind? Here was their missing Jane Doe, smiling like a blushing bride while holding her husband's hand, and not one of them put the pieces together that only took him one hour to discover. Jane Doe's face was badly bruise and her eyes were closed the entire time, but anyone that had twenty-twenty vision would see clearly that these two women were identical.

He printed out the second picture and decided to catch a few hours of sleep before telling his friend his discovery. He also knew that it would be impossible to wake up Jack and why waste the effort when he could try catch some Z's himself.

If he could…

Jack didn't know what caused him to wake up in panic, but he was awake, full of energy and ready to take on the world. The sun cast shadows on the walls and Jack quickly glanced at the clock and found that it was almost was seven o'clock in the evening. Kaleigh had turned on her stomach and was sleeping soundly. The late morning sun hugged her body and made her honey-blonde hair that was splashed across her face, shine like a poet's song. Jack's heart swelled deep inside of him.

    He reached out and smoothly brushed her from her face to look upon the beauty of her face. The corners of his lips rose as he slowly and softly ran the back of his hand along her cheek. She stirred, and for the first time since Jack had reacquainted himself with her, as her eyes were closed and she stretched her long arms above her head, she smiled deeply and Jack fell in love with her all over again. He thought his heart would burst because of her smile and it nearly did.

    Slowly, her emerald green eyes opened and the smile remained as she shifted her gaze from the white painted wall to the smoky eyes of Jack.

    "Hi," he simply said, not wanting to see that smile fade.

    She licked her lips and Jack's lower half went rigid and hard. "It feels like I've slept a week." She set up and propped her elbow on the pillow and lowered her head on her palm. "What about you?" she asked still smiling.

    He blinked not once, but twice before he answered. He was sealing this memory forever. "It feels the same. How are you feeling?"

    With her free hand, she untangled strands of her hair and shrugged her shoulders. "I'm feeling great. Better than great…I feel like dancing!" She said plopping her head on the pillow and laughed.

    Before Jack knew what he was doing, (he knew what he was doing; he didn't care) he bent his head and kissed her firm and full on the lips.

    Kaleigh didn't have to think when Jack leaned over and bent his head to kiss her. She saw it coming and yet she didn't want to move away. Her brain screamed for her to move, but her heart…well that was a different matter. No matter what her brain function she couldn't push away from him. Not then, not now, or in the future.

    Now in the throes of the battle with the demons and the sun coming to its departure, Jack's warm lips were on hers and there was no interference and she was going to make this last forever.

    The sheer touch of his lips awoke an emotion that had been dormant for five lonely years. After the many useless dates she suffered through, she kissed every lip in hope to find the emotion she desperately seek would come alive, and lying in the middle of the bed, a pair of firm, powerful lips were seducing her, and her entire body was on fire. She never expected to find this again until her protector came back to her.

When his lips touched her, it was like every nerve ending shot to the core of her heart. She parted her lips and felt his tongue, hot and moist and rough, thrust into her mouth, and let him take all that he could from her.

His mouth was fierce, seeking his passion to reduce the hunger that had been building for so long, but it only made him hungrier for more. He tasted of raw male power and it made her weak in the knees.

He pulled her tongue into his mouth, sucking, nibbling, and tasting his way to her heart.

She threw her hands around his neck as he parted her thighs with his knee. A shiver that made tears spring into her eyes ran through her body. She felt the need of his desire burning through his denim onto her sex, and Kaleigh arched up to meet him when he thrust hard. Her loins caught on fire and she moaned.

"Kaleigh," he whispered in a guttural slur when he broke the kiss to move his mouth down her neck.

She ran her hands through his tousled, black hair, and rubbed herself wantonly against his lower half to end the elation that was building within her. He nibbled and kissed her along her neck, down to her shoulders, and finally to her right breast, that was aching for his attention.

Jack pushed her T-shirt up and filled his palm with her full breasts. They weren't exactly small, but enough for her soft flesh to overflow the side of his hands. He stroked his thumbs over and over until they puckered and were so hard they shimmered through the thin fabric of her bra all the while he was looking deeply into her eyes.

His look changed from a cool calm to an untamed looked of a predator that stole her breath and made her heart do a dive. He then pushed the bra to the side, dipped his head, and closed his mouth around her left nipple and sucked. Kaleigh arched to meet his demand. He suckled hard, tasted and kissed as he pressed his stiff cock against the heat of her sex.

"*Jack.*" It was Kaleigh's turned to moan.

He removed his mouth moved from her breast to the other, leaving it glistening with his moist as he nipped and licked at her other nipple. He felt squirm beneath him, seeking for something he knew he could give her. Jack lifted his head and smiled. Her eyes were wild with abandon and it made her the most beautiful woman in the world.

Jack stared at her mouth and almost lost control when she flicked out her tongue and licked her lips. His bottom lip quivered and a whimpered scarcely came out. He wanted to see if the rest of her was just a beautiful as her glowing face. He knew it would be, but memories weren't as accurate as seeing her naked and sprawled underneath in the present.

He grabbed the hem of her blouse and in one quick move had tossed it over her head and thrown it somewhere to the right of him.

She lay with the cups of her Playtex spread to her sides as her breasts gleamed with his wetness. They were full and round as her rosy-tipped nipples were hard as he, standing for his attention. Her arms to her sides, clutching the sheets, her soft belly trembling with excitement, and her legs bent up, waiting for him to return. He was ready to devour her and she was waiting for him as well. Jack wanted to take it slowly as he did the first time with her; he didn't want her to see the wild part of him coming between them.

"You're so beautiful," he said hoarsely.

He lowered his eyes and slowly raised them to meet Kaleigh's. Her eyes widened and her heart turned over as she saw all the emotion flowing into his dilated pupils. Was it love or was it admiration?

It couldn't be love or his powers would be stripped. It had to be admiration. A small part of her wanted him to love her and a big part of her wanted to love him. Sadly, they didn't have that option.

She opened her arms for him and he came into them, settling between her bent thighs, and cupping her face to kiss her madly, and she gave him the same commitment as his kiss.

Together they made love with their tongues. Together their hearts beat wildly and together their breaths were deep and loud as their passion for one another filled the bedroom.

Jack's hand moved to her pumping breast and pinched and squeezed the hard nipple firmly.

Kaleigh gasped. It hurt, but in a good way; the pain brought a more intense pleasure.

She moved her lips over the stumble of his jaw and down his neck where she lightly bit and sucked him. Jack's breath whispered in her hair as he squeezed harder on the peaking breast and rubbed his swollen cock against the sweetness between her thighs. Kaleigh arched to meet his thrust and felt like at any moment, she was going to shatter into millions of pieces.

Her nails dug in his shoulders, her toes curled through the softness of the sheets and she had to clamp her teeth together from screaming.

He bit down softly on the lobe of her ear and with his free hand it came swiftly around to her back and unlatched the clasped of the bra as the straps fell below her shoulders. Without moving his head, Jack tossed the barrier to where Kaleigh's shirt was thrown and lifted his head to see what lay discovered.

Kaleigh looked down at herself and found that both of her nipples were pebbled-hard, ripe, full, and pumping fervidly for his touch. She looked wild, she felt wild, and it made her hotter inside where the disturbing ache was bubbling to pop.

Then Jack bent his head to her left breast and took the swollen nipple in his mouth. Kaleigh's body liquefied inside and arched further up to feel everything he gave her.

The inside of her mouth had gone dry. Her breathing was labored and she knew that Jack could hear the beating of her heart.

One hand was thrust into her hair, tangling it with his fingers as the other moved to the lonely breast and caressed with great delicacy. His lips met hers once again and Kaleigh could feel the dampness that was left on her breast that was pleading for him to come to back. Instead he kissed her quick and hard on the lips, down her neck, through valley of her breasts, to her belly, stopping to lick around her navel.

She was going wild inside and he looked and felt as calm as if he was just sitting there. But Kaleigh thought again when she saw the feral look he gave when his mouth reached to the wetness between her thighs. It was hard and intense and he was going just as crazy as she.

When his mouth bit the rough denim between her spread thighs, she bolted straight up and shouted, "Jack!"

He came up and looked her in the eye and without smiling; his face demanding and tensed. "Let me love you, Kaleigh the way I want to."

He grabbed the inside of her thighs before she could protest further and then ran his hands up, around her hips, and cupped her ass, giving it a tight squeeze.

Then she felt his left hand move and heard the loud snap of her jeans, followed by the zipper. She didn't know the sound of a zipper could be such an aphrodisiac to her senses.

Suddenly, they were being pushed down and she had to lift her hips to remove them completely and they were easily tossed to the side with the rest of her clothes.

Her insides were shaking and she something in the back of her mind told to her call a halt to this, but she couldn't. She wanted him. She desperately needed him now more than ever.

The only thing she wore now was a pair of white panties and he was still fully clothed.

Kaleigh wanted to shout, "Unfair!" She wanted to see and touch his exquisitely made body.

Jack looked down on her and everywhere his eyes roamed, her skin burned and melted. He dipped one finger under the elastic of her panties as he looked hungrily into her eyes, showing her the imperative of his needs, and then smoothly circled the soft surface above the patch of her brown curls. She was swelling and aching to be touched and her arms swiftly came under his shirt to brush her fingers through his chest hair, rubbing his solid chest, urging him on.

He had to grit his teeth not to take her now.

His finger tumbled downwards to the folds of her soft curls, cupping her heat in his large hand. Jack could smell her womanly scent and it made him brazen as he sniffed her scent. She was wet, wetter than the night before and it was going be delicious feeling having his cock sheathed by her velvet home.

With his other hand, he firmly grasped her quivering right thigh, spread it open, and held it into place as his dominant finger slid inside of her panties, separated her sleek folds, and pushed forward.

She was so tight, hot, wet, and ready for him that Jack had to tamper on his control to keep from taking her right now. He wanted to please her over and over again until she begged for mercy and even then he wanted to do it to all over again.

Kaleigh moaned and held tighter to the broad shoulders that were anxious and tight. She arched up to meet the magic of his finger.

"You're tight," he said more as an observation.

And she would be because it'd been five years since she had a man in her bed and didn't want any man in her bed but Jack. He was the only one that could set her soul aflame and make her feel like her body was going to higher and higher to the clouds.

Jack could feel her muscles constricting around him his finger. She was so close to coming that it would be shame if he didn't get to sample her cries in his mouth. Lowering his mouth to her stomach, he pushed his finger deeper inside and then licked around her navel.

"*Oh God,*" she moaned as her fingers dug in his shoulders. She was on the verge of exploding.

"Not yet," he patiently said as he licked down from navel and pushed his middle finger into her.

His fingers were long and rough and made each thrust deeper and deeper to the hilt. His knuckles scraped the inside of her thighs, making Kaleigh sigh and groan.

She was so close. She wanted to end this terrific ache that steadily continued to build.

"Please Jack. I-I don't think I can hold out much longer!" she said with her breathing hard and fast and her head plowing against the pillow, and her body desperately arching to meet each and every thrust of his long, strong fingers.

He pushed his fingers deeper inside of her, as he lowered his head and pulled the bud of her into his mouth and sucked as if he was kissing the inside of mouth.

Kaleigh spread her thighs further, giving him total admittance. He richly laughed as his tongue and finger made her wetter and demanding for her release. And then his hand moved to her breast, cupped, and pinched the tip of her nipple.

"Now come for me," he said

On key, Kaleigh exploded. Her eyes tightly squeezed shut and her body lifted off the bed as Jack continue to make love to her with his fingers. She screamed her glorious cry, shuddered, shook, and fell back onto the bed depleted of all strength, panting like a runner.

Kaleigh opened her eyes at the same time Jack pulled out his dampened fingers from her sex that gleamed in the descending sunlight.

The weight of his body lifted from the bed and Kaleigh shot up, afraid that he was leaving her. What he did to her was the most wondrous experiment, but she wanted to have Jack inside of her when she came.

"Jack, what are you going?" she said.

He grabbed the hem of his shirt and pulled it over his head and was spellbound when she saw his muscles ripple as he lazily stretched out his arms. "You didn't think I was done with you, did you?" he asked wickedly smiling.

"Oh," she said, still flabbergasted by the perfect six-pack abs, broad shoulders, and strong arms. This man was the perfect model she saw in the women magazine she secretly read at work when she had nothing better to do than googgled eye them. Then she the length of his bulge and her mouth fell open. He was so large and thick and she tight—almost virginal that she feared that it was going to hurt.

The sound of his zipper coming down sent waves of excitement through Kaleigh's body, forgetting her fear as the ache began to rebuild. She always had this sinful part in her that wanted to explore her sexuality, but the only one she ever wanted to explore that part of her with was Jack. He was standing there waiting, looking at her to take initiative on her wild side.

Kaleigh really wanted to and she did.

She sat humbly on her knees, boldly reached and flattened her palms on the hard contour of his abs and Jack literally shook. She slowly and sensuously ran her hands up and down his hard stomach and then bent her head and kissed and licked around the flat plane of his stomach as her thumbs reached up and circled his hard, flat nipples.

"*Kaleigh*," he said harshly. He captured her wrists with his strong hands and brought them to his lips and kissed each finger and then lowered her to the bed. "You keep doing that I might as well die right now."

She laughed, but not too long as his hands gripped the hips of his jeans and quickly tugged them down, taking his jockeys with him to his ankles and stepped out.

Kaleigh eyes grew wide with excitement as she saw the reality of his enormous erections pressing almost to his navel. She looked at him and thought how he was going to fit in her, and before her mind could wondered anymore, he lowered himself down on her, Kaleigh really didn't care anymore.

He settled between her thighs and she felt the warm drops of the tip of his penis, gliding through her brown curls of her folds. His mouth was only a space away from hers as he cupped her face between his palms and looked into her eyes. He wasn't smiling, now, but only a hunger of mad passion smolder in his sapphire eyes.

Jack didn't know how much longer he could last, but he was going to make it last to please her and to see that contented look on her face that he gave her.

"You're mine." She opened her mouth to speak, but took the opportunity and crashed his mouth down her hers, filling his hands with her breasts, he plunged deep into her tightness that was so damn tight, wet, slick from her previous climax that he almost completely lost it.

When Jack entered her, everything felt right, completed. It was as if their bodies were made for each other and no other.

Kaleigh wanted to cry from the sheer perfection and ecstasy of their joining. It was too impossible to find words of something that was pure bliss of heaven.

Jack removed her hands from her breast to cup her face and look into her eyes and she knew that he was feeling what she had felt as their body joined and became one. Neither one spoke as this moment was faultless.

Then Jack began to move in her. Slowly at first with deep, long strokes. Kaleigh bit her nails into shoulders and wrapped her legs around his waist as he slid deeper inside of her, filling her all the way to her womb. She cried out loudly from the pleasure of him inside of her. Jack as his body picked up speed, moved faster and deeper within her. Kaleigh held on and arched to be there for his every thrust he gave her.

Sweat gleamed on his forehead as his hands threaded with hers and held them above her head. His muscles straining and bulging as his breath got harder and faster. Kaleigh, near her climax, held on tight and moved with his body. Her legs began to quiver and quake and tremble when she was on the edge.

Jack pulled out and drove into her hard. Kaleigh cried out. He did it two more times and Kaleigh shattered.

"Oh, Jack," she cried as her nails dug in his hands as Jack quickened his strokes until he found his release.

Jack threw his head back, gritted his teeth, and squeezed her name through his lips. He crashed down on her, and buried his head between her neck and shoulder.

When Kaleigh drifted back from the clouds or heaven or whatever she floated to, her first thought was she made a mistake. She shouldn't have made love with him; she knew it was costing her life and among others and she knew the consequences if she did. Well, she had. Now she was facing the aftermath.

His chin prickled her neck as his deep breathing stirred her hair. She didn't know what to say or what to do, but lay there as if nothing had happened. Oh, but something did happen. Something so traumatic and disrupting that Kaleigh couldn't believe she had let it happen. She should have run far, far away from this man and never looked back. Blame it on her curious mind or blame it on stupidity but she chosen her path and now she had to walk down that road that was murky, filled with confusion.

She wasn't going to let him know. She wasn't going to give him a clue or whisper while he was asleep. She was going to keep it all bottled up for her and no other to learn because if he or anyone found out there was sure to be trouble (which she was already in).

As she lay with their hands still clasped together, she couldn't help but think how beautiful they were together. It as pure sublime and everything as she thought it would be like.

And she loved it.

She felt sated. Whole and utterly loved.

Jack unleashed some wild part of her spirit that she never let anyone see before, but him. He gave her one of life's pleasures she thought she never be able to participate in—twice in fact. To have this magical experience with Jack was the greatest feeling she ever had in her life and she wanted more magic in her life with Jack.

Her dreams never created the illusion of this completeness or this crashing wave that made her heart do flips.

The reality was scary and the best thing she would ever get in her life.

But she couldn't fall in love. She couldn't love Jack the way she wanted to. All they could ever be is companions that once had a fling together while he was protecting her.

That was awfully depressing

To keep her mind occupied without Jack, she thought about Susan.

Susan's death was still a mystery and the guardian hunter was always a step a head of her. It was probably looking from the shadows as she and Jack were making love.

Thinking of the guardians, he had let her at peace for several hours now, and didn't try to manipulate its way while they were together. There was no telling when they were coming back for her.

She hated waiting in suspense and mostly she hated knowing that he was hiding and waiting to spring into action when she least expected. Though, Jack was here and had gained all of his energy back. He would protect her and save her from it. He wasn't there in the beginning but she knew that he had sent help.

There was Susan of course; she was always there in voice and in spirit giving her warnings. Then there was Sebastian who slayed the two demon dogs. Kaleigh could have done it herself if she wasn't so damn weak minded and feeling of loss of control. But Sebastian was here and was planning on staying here from what she gathered until Jack told him he was no longer needed.

She could tell Sebastian was a good person, but there was darkness and coldness flowing through his eyes. She saw it when he burst through her door and she saw it when he wasn't looking. Someone had hurt him in the past and deliberately had done it.

What cruel person could be harmful and deceiving to a man as beautiful as he?

A cold-hearted bitch, that's who, Kaleigh thought.

A beautiful creature such as he shouldn't encounter deception or hate; he should only encounter love and trust. But the warrior's souls were known for their tempers and impatient. She also saw that when the demon sprang onto the jeep. He wanted to kill it so badly and not thinking of what might happen if he went out there with a sword in his hand.

Jack was right, no human could see a demon and therefore, if Sebastian had gone outside with his sword, swinging like a barbarian, and he would have been thrown so fast in the loony bin that only more darkness would be filled in those gorgeous sea swept eyes.

Enough about him, though. She had to decide what to do next with Jack, the only man that was worth the price of all the heavens and hells.

Funny, she thought. She wanted him out of her mind, but everything she thought about it went circling back to him.

She unconsciously ran her fingers up his hair and rested them on the back of his scalp as she was thinking what to do next. She wanted to sigh, but giving away any signs of grief might make him suspicious and that was something she didn't want or need at this present time. She gently kissed his forehead that was drying from the sweat and scratched his head.

Jack's head came up and he was smiling. Her heart turned over and she stopped herself before she could fall in love with him.

"I guess you want me to get off you?" he asked lazily.

She pondered the question. He wasn't crushing her. In fact it felt nice that he lay on her, purring like a kitten. She wrapped her arms around his back and snuggled her head against his stubby chin. "No. You can stay a little longer."

He kissed the top of her head and rolled her on the flat on his stomach. "Sorry, it felt like I was crushing you."

She kissed the tip of his chin. "You weren't, but it does feel much better up here." She kissed his mouth, his jaw, and back to mouth again where Jack took advantage by giving her passionate kiss and then held her tight against his beating heart.

"I meant what I said earlier," he said in a whispered. Kaleigh didn't say anything. "You're mine. I'm not going to let anything or anyone ever have you, but me."

She still didn't say anything.

But he continued. "I know you have your reasons for not opening up to me or the others, but I want you to know that when you're ready I'll be here waiting for you. No matter how long it takes." He kissed her quick on the mouth and ran his hands up and down her spine.

She couldn't look him the eye because if she did, he would know the affection she was bottling and keeping well protected.

Protected was the right word to use. The more she stayed with him, the more she was going to fall in love with him, risking her heart, the lives of others, and his life. She didn't want to lose him again. She wouldn't be able to handle losing him again, even though she really never had him in the first place.

Kaleigh made a split second decision while she nestled against his scratchy beard. She was going to spend her time loving him, using him for her comfort. This man just confessed some type of love to her and was willing to wait to the end of time for her and she was about to do the most unabashed, sardonic act to a man that would die a thousands death so she wouldn't have to.

She kissed him lightly on his stubby cheek and tightly wrapped her arms around his neck. He was rough and relaxed. She smoothly caressed his cheek and kissed him tenderly with all the love she had for him. It didn't feel enough to give him, but it was the only way Kaleigh could show him how much she loved him.

She cupped his face with her hands and parted her lips and felt his tongue hot, fierce, and passionate, thrust into hers. His hands flew to the back of her head, pushing her further into the torment of his tongue. Kaleigh moaned. She pushed herself up and straddled Jack, lowering her sex onto his powerful hard shaft. She gripped his shoulders as he stretched her completely.

Slowly, she started to move, looking into his sapphire eyes that overflowing with an intense pain and love.

Kaleigh closed her eyes; she couldn't let her heart be manipulated.

Jack filled his hands with her breasts and kissed the peak of them. Kaleigh moved faster and faster, straining for her release and at the same time, wishing they could stay this way forever. It was a hopeless dream for the simple mind and Kaleigh really wanted to believe in that dream. She wanted to make love to Jack morning, noon, and night. She wanted to marry Jack and have hundred children with him. She wanted to wake up every morning, curled in Jack's warmth. She wanted to go to bed at night, knowing that he was going to be there when she woke up. She wanted Jack for herself and she wanted Jack because she loved him more than anything in the world and she was about to end her dream when she came down from the clouds.

She felt her release coming and knew he was on the verge of his by the way he gripped her hips and thrust deeper inside of her.

"Oh, Jack," she screamed and then kissing him once last time.

Chapter Twelve

Jack knew something was wrong the minute she cried his name. The kiss she gave him was a warning of that she was unhappy and he knew damn well it was because of him. His cock was still plunged in her velvety heat, breathing like she just ran fifty miles, and hanging onto him like she wasn't going to let go. He knew better. She wasn't going to be hanging on much longer.

He kissed the top of her head and held her tighter. He loved her and would never stop loving her. Five years ago, he felt this passion but it was never this fierce or sated. He was gentle with Kaleigh because he thought she was fragile.

Man, was he wrong.

She loved just as primitively as he.

And when he felt her heat, her wetness, coaxing his cock, it was all he could not to blurt out those three little words that have been haunting him since the first time he laid eyes on her. When she stepped into his life, he never felt a powerful, climatic emotion as he let her into his heart.

He was glad they had sent to him to protect her or else he would never feel this great emotion that humans could feel. Someone up there must like him a lot because he was dumbly and madly in love with her. He was willing to die, cheat, kill, for her. Shit, he'd always felt that way for her. As a young boy, he knew that she was going to be the death of him and he didn't care as long as she was happy.

Only for her. He would only turn his life around from a guardian savior to a complete waste of demon to make her happy. He would go against the maker himself to prove that Kaleigh's was worth every risk.

All she had to do was ask and he would become her servant.

Jack knew the pure souls were able to love because that's how Kaleigh was in this predicament. Now if she could just love him back with the same intensity he felt for her.

"I love you," he whispered before he could stop the words from rolling off his tongue.

He felt her tense and then slowly relax. "No, you don't. You can't, Jack. If you love me, then you wouldn't have any powers. It's the sex talking."

It angered Jack that she didn't believe him. The pain in his heart sliced through his spirit and made him fall apart inside. He balled up his fist as emotions swelled in a heated anger. He felt just a little more of him slipping away. Quickly, he squelched his anger before his iris could change color on him. Kaleigh had already seen the change several times, but she never committed on it.

Very easily he said, "It's not the sex."

Kaleigh got off him, and Jack missed the warm. She brought her knees to her chest, wrapping her arms around them, and using the sheet to cover her body. Jack felt his anger rebuilding. "Jack you are not in love with me."

"And how do you know?" he said sitting up next to her. "You can't possibly know what I'm feeling because you are too damn scared to find out."

She threw her arms up in the air. "And you're right. I am. I won't find out what you are feeling because you know the consequences."

"Would it be so bad?"

"Yes," she exclaimed. "Jesus, Jack, do you remember what happened the last time? What if I hesitate again? I can't go through with that again. Ever! I hated what I had to do to you."

"Then you do feel something for me besides lust?"

Kaleigh dropped her head and sighed.

"I wish I could help you." He paused. "I wish that you didn't have to go through with this alone and I wish I could make you love me."

Jack looked at her and saw tears in her eyes. She was trying hard not to let them fall. He then knew she was going to run again and he wasn't going to stop her. He knew where she was going to be at. Even though he wasn't an authentic sorcerer anymore, he would be connected to her and aide her if she needed help. Kaleigh had to stay alive until he died.

The world needed the pure souls and she was the only one that knew where they were hiding. For her he was going to give her time to adjust to his feelings. And for the world, he was going to get her opened up for him. For her, he was going to die.

Jack closed his eyes and abandoned the words that were plaguing his mind and continued. "I wish I could give you a life that didn't consist of this hell and I wish I could make you happy. I want to let you go, but I can't. I can never let you go; I am your protector and will protect you to the end of time."

He unfolded her arms and kissed her softly on the lips. When he let go, he rolled her over and put his clothes on as she buried her head in his pillow and wept. He wanted to put her arms around her and if he did, he would never be able to let go.

"I'm going to leave you alone for a while." He walked out of the room and very gently shut the door behind him.

Chapter Thirteen

Jack opened the door to his office and found Sebastian crashed on the floor. Jack understood why he was sleeping on the floor, he either rolled off the lumpy, pea-green sofa he found at a garage sale or he figured the couch was too small to accommodate of a man of his size.

He nudged him with the tip of his toes. "Sebastian, I need you awake." He didn't move. He nudged him again and talked louder. "Get up, Sebastian." He sounded harsh, because his heart was breaking. On the third try, Sebastian mumbled unchastely words. "Sebastian, I need your ass up now!"

"What the hell, Jack? I'm trying to sleep!" he roared and turned over and pretended to go back to sleep.

This time Jack kicked him in his thigh, hard. Sebastian bolted up so fast that Jack didn't have time to move. Sebastian tackled Jack's legs and brought him crashing down on the floor.

"What the hell do you want!?" he screamed as he hovered over Jack with his fist raised for battle.

He sighed. He knew warriors were temperamental and he knew what would happen to him if he kicked Sebastian the way that he did. Jack needed him awake so they could discuss Susan's death. He needed his mind occupied without thoughts of Kaleigh, which would be damn near impossible, but he had to try.

"I didn't want to wake you because I know how hard is for you to sleep, but the faster we solve Susan's murder the sooner we'll know who's coming after Kaleigh, and the faster she can get the hell out of my life." Sebastian didn't understand, but his fist came down quickly and he got off Jack.

"Is something wrong? What happened?"

Jack stood up and pulled his shirt down. "No. Nothing is wrong. Everything is fucking wrong! Shit! How could she do this? Doesn't she know what the importance of herself? Why in the hell is she making this so goddamn difficult? Why is she doing this to me again?"

Sebastian was silent. He watched Jack's face become a shadow from the darkness as his iris changed from his calm blue to his violent purple. Jack turned around so he couldn't see his transformation.

"Calm down, Jack. I don't need you losing control right now. You know better than to let your emotions get out of control. We need you sane until this whole shit is over with."

A tear slid down his cheek and Jack sucked in his breath and released it slowly. His friend was right. If he lost control now, it would be too late to save what he sacrificed for and he shouldn't have confessed his love to her so early in the game.

"I promise I won't lose control. Just help me, okay?"

"Sure."

One moment Kaleigh was weeping and the next Gina and Mr. Walker were standing next to her.

"What are you guys doing here?" Kaleigh asked.

Mr. Walker looked unabashed about Kaleigh's state of nudity as did Gina. "We need to tell you some things about...well about everything," Gina said in her detached voice. "Why don't you get dress and meet us in the living room.

They vanished from the room and Kaleigh in robotic motions got up and dressed in the clothes she wore to bed. She went to Jack's bathroom, found a comb in the medicine cabinet and ran it through her hair. She didn't bother to look in the mirror because she could guess how appalling she looked. Puffy eyes, red cheeks, and tousled hair were nothing to look at and she didn't care what her mother or boss thought of her appearance either. Let them think what they want to think. Then she splashed some cold water on her face, toweled off, and left the room.

"What's going on, Mother?" Kaleigh asked as she stepped into the living room and found Mr. Walker sitting in the recliner and Gina in the sofa.

"Sit down," Gina said coolly.

Kaleigh sat next to her mother and folded her hands in her laps as Mr. Walker position his body in the chair to look their way.

"I should have told you from the start about Adrian. I was wrong to keep that information hidden from you for so long, but I guess I was trying to protect you in a sense." She sighed and waited for Kaleigh to say something. When she didn't she continued. "In my entire life, I've never encountered a guardian hunter until I got pregnant with you. It was my only experiment and I'll never forget it for as long as I live.

"Most of us sorcerers were in hiding, while shielding the warriors so they could continue to walk the streets to destroy the demons. Sorcerers are more substantial to a demon than warriors because of our unique powers to manipulate demons or humans and we are easier to subdue under a dominant demon such as a guardian hunter. Warriors are just skilled, refined fighters that can kill a demon on contact and their minds are very strong and stubborn. It was more natural for the demons to come after us than the warriors, which is why we went into hiding as the warriors took on a great responsibility of defeating the demons alone.

"Anyway, I was still in hiding, but I had to work to make a living. We don't get substantial bank account; we had to work. I normally worked as a waitress because it's easier to conceal your identity among the humans.

"I was working at a truck stop when I met a man; a human. He came into the truck stop one night and we started talking. He was a drifter that was passing through town in hopes to finding a job. I told him that we needed a night time dishwasher. One thing led to another and we became really good friends. I made a mistake like you did with your friend Susan; I let him inside of my spirit.

"One night after work, I was walking to my car and encounter a guardian hunter for the first time in my life. I wasn't expecting it and he caught me off guard." Gina shuddered.

"It felt like it wrapped its hands around my heart and started squeezing the life out of me. I couldn't breathe. I couldn't move. I knew that I was going to die. But then he was there. Your father. He couldn't see the guardian hunter because he was not one of us. He thought I was having a panic attack. But he managed to stop the hunter for just a short while. He got me to breathe again and then the guardian hunter killed him."

"How come you never told me?" Kaleigh asked callously.

Gina's face became impassive, but Kaleigh could feel her mother's regret. "Because, I was afraid you'll never opened up to anyone. You did, but you hesitated. It's the worst thing for a pure soul to do," she said with grave disappointment. "You take the risk of getting your love one into a deep remorse and mixed feelings of doubt and false illusion that could bring him to the mercy of a demon. Jack knew that you hesitated and it enraged him. That's why it was so easy for the guardian hunter to steal his soul and use him against you."

"Is that what happen to my father? You hesitated?"

Gina shook her head. "No. The guardian hunter killed your father just to make me feel his death. Pure souls are the strongest among us and yet they possess they most obdurate spirits for the fear of destroying the ones they let inside. The truth is, you create the chaos and the destruction of your spirit by not letting yourself open and bringing someone into your soul.

"I know you never asked to be born a pure soul, Kaleigh, but it's something they gave to you because they saw strength in you. You nearly defeated one before, Kaleigh, and you can do it again if you stop running from your fears."

"Mom, you don't understand," she said shaking her head. "If I open up to Jack, we all die. That's what the hunters want from me. They need me to open up to find the other six pure souls, and I can't because as soon as I do, they will find them and destroy us faster than we can blink."

Gina softly touched her daughter's cheek and brought her face to meet hers. "Listen to me, Kaleigh. A guardian hunter will eventually get you to open up whether you want to or not. It will use any force of means to manipulate you. It will seduce, threaten, and use Jack against you. By opening up to Jack, you're saving him, us, and you. You alone have the power to destroy them."

"Not without the other six souls I can't," Kaleigh said sternly.

Gina looked from Kaleigh to Mr. Walker then back to Kaleigh. She ran her tongue over her lips and closed her eyes. "After he killed your father, I didn't know I was pregnant. The guardian hunter was there, laughing at me. I was so weak that all I could do was ask for help, but I couldn't find anyone because they were all closed up so they wouldn't be found. I was left alone, facing one of the most prevailing demons of all time and I had nothing or no one to help me or defeat him.

"It said it was going to use me to get to the others. Therefore, it left me alive, but tortured me daily until the day you would be born. I couldn't leave my house for the fear that it'll be waiting for me on the other side. I wouldn't give in, though. I fought it off everyday until I was so weak that I couldn't breathe to stay alive.

"The day I went into labor, the guardian hunter was there. I knew he had come to take you away. Then there was Adrian with a woman, and another man that looked so dangerous, I feared him more than the guardian hunter. The woman was a pure soul just like you; she was the one that found us because of your connection with them. It was the stranger that had defeated the guardian hunter. I don't know how, but he did."

"Who was he?"

Adrian and Gina looked at each other with wide eyes and then looked at Kaleigh. Adrian was the one that spoke. "A very powerful sorcerer that is old as time and some believe to be the very first-born guardian that had been gifted with the blood of the pure soul. My wife refuses to say who gave him the blood, but she did reveal to me that he's the only guardian that has ever been able to carry a pure soul's blood without dying other than Jack."

"Why them and no one else?" Kaleigh asked. It was something new to her. They never told her that a guardian couldn't take their blood, but Jack had and he lived.

Gina and Adrian eyes clashed with a committal reference of a secret that they were about to reveal.

"Because they were both sanctified by the maker to destroy guardian hunters and protect the pure souls until they are reunited. They are the strongest of the guardians and therefore have the powers that none of us have. No one knows why just those two, but be glad that we have something to stop them rather than nothing."

"Also," Gina continued without missing a beat, "Before the guardian sorcerer defeated the hunter, he said 'The seed you carry will suffer your consequences. You may have destroyed me for now, but others will be back for the ripeness of your daughter. Once she is ours, we'll get them all, including you.' Hours later when you were conceived, the sorcerer pricked your heart with his dagger, tasted your blood, and then whispered your destiny to you. He then said to me that I was never to interfere with your life; it would change the outcome of our future, and I believed him. The only one who was allowed to interfere with your destiny was your protector, Kaleigh, who was the only guardian born by human parents and therefore the maker chose him and made him strong like him so Jack could be connected with you always. He was able to carry the blood of a pure soul so he can protect you or any other pure souls.

"So I never got involved with your life because I didn't want to take the chance of changing your destiny."

Kaleigh was silent. Better yet, she was shell shocked into utter speechlessness. She sat frozen with her lids downcast to her tightly folded hands in her lap and her mouth partly opened as if she was trying to find the right words to come out.

Finally she shut her mouth, licked her lips, and said, "Does Jack know any of this?"

"No," Gina and Adrian said at the same time and then Gina added, "He has the strength to defeat the guardian hunters, but he does not know because all his life he was raised to be your protector."

"And the strength is from my blood?"

Gina nodded.

"Why do I get the feeling that you are not telling me something?" Kaleigh said to Gina and then looking at Adrian for a sign of concealment on his part.

There was a long, deadly stretch of silence as Gina looked to Adrian and then to her daughter. Kaleigh was ready to declare a war herself if they refuse to answer her questions.

After sometime, Gina spoke. "Jack is to die."

"What!" Kaleigh said jumping to her face.

Quickly Gina said, "I don't know why or when, but he is. I saw that in my dreams. You are going to destroy him, Kaleigh."

"That can't be true! You said it yourself, Jack is my protector. Why on Earth would I want to destroy him?"

"The signs are unclear," Gina spoke silencing her daughter.

"Liar!" Kaleigh accused. "You know why, but you refused to tell because you think I'm not strong enough to accept his death. Well, there you are wrong, Mother! I destroyed him once before and managed to get on with my life. What makes you think I can't do it again?"

"Not the way you were supposed to."

"Kaleigh," Adrian said. "Your mother is right. My wife's premonition is strong about this, but the reason of Jack's death is unclear except that you are the one that is to destroy him."

"And who is your wife Mr. Walker? I thought after you slept with the office bimbo that you no longer had a wife! And guardians aren't supposed to fall in love or get married."

Adrian's jaw locked, his mouth quivered, and slowly grinned, downcasting his eyes. He looked ready to kill and his main victim would be Kaleigh.

Kaleigh took a step backwards as Mr. Walker lifted his eyes and met hers. "I never slept with that woman," he said dangerously close to losing his temper. "Rumors are easily spread when a woman is scorned, and falling in love with a pure soul is an unbroken bond with all the benefits of being a human. You become impotent to all others, but you get to keep your powers as you are able to love. How do you think Jack is still gifted to fight?"

"Your wife is a pure soul? But...I thought..." Kaleigh sighed.

"I met her a little over fifty years ago in San Juan. We paired up and fought together. I didn't know she was a pure soul until I broke and fell in love with. I tried hard to fight the temptation, but feared I would lose my powers. When I fell, I fell hard and didn't care that my powers were lost. I was still able to keep my powers. She loves me, but she still won't open up to me until the pure souls are reunited."

That was a shock Kaleigh wasn't ready for. Kaleigh knew that pure souls were the only guardians that could fall in love without the frightful consequences of losing their powers, but she didn't know that other guardians could fall in love with them.

Jack wasn't lying when he said that he loved her, but Kaleigh wasn't allowed to love because they said since the beginning of her life it could mean the fate of the world. Is that why she didn't have a soul?

It couldn't be because every time she was around Jack she felt the stirring of her own emotions beat in her. She didn't feel empty like the other guardians that didn't want to accommodate with the human souls; she didn't behave like Sebastian. Kaleigh behaved as her nerves caused her to.

Why did it have to be her? Why couldn't she fall in love with the only man she had ever had feeling towards? All she wanted in life was to love and be love, and she couldn't have that. Why was she cursed with such a burden in life?

She knew Jack was to die if she dared opened up to him, but she didn't know it was to be her hands. It all made sense to her. Gina's dreams weren't wrong; she was going to destroy Jack in a matter of time because her feelings for him couldn't hold out much longer. Gina was wrong, though. She may not be the one with her hands around his throat, but she was going to play a part in his death and it would all be her fault. Kaleigh knew that all along.

Question was: should she run away or stay? Either way, she was going to lose Jack. She needed some encouragement for guidance.

"Where is your wife, now Mr. Walker? I really would like to talk to her."

Adrian Walker ran his hand through his hair and then threw his hands in the air. "Talking to her would only make matter worse. She told me its safer keeping all the other pure souls separated. But even if she could talk to you, she wouldn't. One of our sons is very sick and she's not leaving his side for a second. A demon infected him with his poison and the only thing that can cure him is lots of rest, but it's hard when the infection burns his insides. My wife has him under a sleep spell to heal him and won't budge an inch until he's completely healed. That's why I look disarrayed."

"I'm sorry, Mr. Walker. I had no idea." Kaleigh's voice was soft and low. She didn't raise her eyes to meet his for the reason that she would have seen his hurt and pain that he was feeling for his sick son.

This is her destiny and she came to terms with it alone. No one could help her and she couldn't run. It was just so easier to run than to face what might become of her and Jack and the rest of the lives that depended upon her. It was something she had to do because they depended on her.

Mr. Walker never cheated on his wife; it was office gossips that made her think the worst about him and it was the gossip that made her keep her distant from him.

Why were lies easier to accept than facing the truth?

They told her a way to defeat the guardian hunter: Jack.

"Mr. Walker, if there is anything I can do to…"

He threw his hands up. "Don't worry about it, Kaleigh," he interrupted with a wave of his hand. "He just needs to sleep off the infection. By the way, from now on call me Adrian, and if you have questions I may be able to help. Radella has told me a lot about the pure souls."

Radella was the nicest one of all the pure souls and had trouble with the grudge just as she did. Radella may have not said so in many words, but when she spoke of resentment towards their maker it was as if she didn't one hundred percent agree to all. As if she was going along because she was told to do so.

"Then do you know why I was born without emotions?"

Adrian laughed. "You were born with emotions just like the rest of the pure souls or else you wouldn't be angry about your responsibilities, your bitterness towards your mother, or your conflicting emotions about Jack. You choose not to feel and that's a big difference than not feeling anything at all, Kaleigh. Have you ever met a guardian that didn't a take human soul in?"

Sebastian came to mind, but she didn't know for sure. "They are the coldest immortals to ever come across. They don't care about anything except for what they hunt because it has been inbred into them since they were conceived. They only thing they can feel is when they have to eat, and only that comes when their hunger is at their strictness."

"Oh," Kaleigh said silently to herself.

"It's very hard to be in the same room with one."

"Why would one refuse to take in a human soul?"

Adrian shrugged his shoulders. "Usually if the guardian had a traumatic experience with a human when he or she was growing up as a child, they usually refuse to bring one in their spirit like a wolf guardian who I know."

"Who is it?" Kaleigh asked out of concern.

Adrian didn't answer her for a long time as he thought the best way to tell her. "It doesn't matter, just be thankful that he's on our side."

Kaleigh let the issue drop as another bugged her about Jack. "How long do I have with Jack?"

"Not long; only a few short days. Spend them wisely," Gina said.

Then Adrian and Gina vanished about the same time a red-faced Sebastian entered Jack's apartment.

After Jack toppled the desk and punched a whole in the wall, Jack found a place to center his anger as Sebastian stayed out of his way. When he was calm, they began silently to spend the next half hour picking up office equipment and papers that had flown from the desk. Sebastian tried to warn Jack that some valuable information about Susan's death was on the desk, but the words didn't come out fast enough when the desk went flying in the air.

Once that was settled, Jack asked Sebastian to check on Kaleigh to see if she needed anything while he searched for the important information about Susan he had lost in his fury. Needless to say, Sebastian didn't want go because he truly hated Kaleigh. If he ever felt anything before, it was nothing compare to the rage he felt towards her. He never physically hurt a woman before, but she would be the first but she would be the first if he the chances of that ever arose.

As he entered Jack's apartment, he saw Kaleigh standing in the middle of the living room, chewing on her thumbnail, and caught the warmth stirring in the air.

Someone had been in the room with her. No. More than one person had been in the room with her and they left as soon as they heard him coming. Smart guardians, Sebastian thought. They knew when to get out of an anger warrior's way.

Kaleigh was about to see how uncultured and nasty he could be.

"What the hell did you say or do to Jack?"

"I don't want to talk about it," she said with much politeness as she could. She didn't look his way as she continued to chew on her nail.

"Well, we're going to talk about it!" he shouted.

Kaleigh turned around and flashed him a dirty look that was a replica of his fuming face. "Well, I don't feel like talking about it and you can't make me!"

"You wanna bet?" he said disdainfully.

Kaleigh bet he could, but she wasn't going to call his bluff. He could scream, threaten her life, and bully her, but she wasn't going to talk about Jack with him of all guardians. He didn't know the first thing about a relationship as complicated as theirs, and she definitely didn't feel like talking to him or anyone else for that fact.

"You can intimidate me all you want, and I'm telling you for the last time I don't want to talk about it," she said calmly while gritting her teeth.

"Jack's a good person. He's the most honest, good-hearted guardian I know and that's saying a lot coming from me. I don't trust anyone with my life except for Jack and he doesn't deserve a snobby little bitch—a pure soul no less—like you."

Kaleigh was floored. Her mouth fell opened. "Excuse me?"

"You heard me loud and clear, lady. You broke his heart and you don't even care. You're standing there as calm as can be, not shedding one god damned tear that you tore Jack up inside."

"How dare you say something like that? You don't know the first thing about me, Sebastian! You don't think I'm hurting? Well, screw you, I am. I'm crying inside! My heart is breaking, too! You don't know how hard it is to want something so much, but never can have? You don't know a damn thing about me!" Tears were flooding her eyes, but she was not going to let them fall. She cried too much tonight over Jack and couldn't get weaker. She couldn't.

It was Sebastian's turned to be shocked—for once anyway. He knew what it was like to want something so badly that you could taste it, but couldn't have it because it was forbidden by all natural things to guardians. He wasn't going to let her know. No one would ever know what he wanted out of his immortal life. Jack didn't even know and he was the one guardian Sebastian allowed to be connected to.

When Sebastian spoke next, it was softer than normal and it surprised him that he could speak like a normal human. It wasn't because of her useless tears; he just wanted to understand her motivation. "Then why are you leading him on?"

"Oh god," Kaleigh chuckled as she wiped the tears away from her eyes. "Are you always this belligerent towards women or is it just me?"

"It's everybody, lady," Sebastian said smugly. "But you just happened to be on top of my shit-list."

"That's lovely," Kaleigh mumbled. "You know Sebastian, you are wrong about me. I never wanted to hurt Jack and I tried my best to keep myself distant, but...I wanted to feel what heaven was like."

"Heaven doesn't exist for people like us," Sebastian said emotionlessly.

"It does to me," Kaleigh said quietly, turning her back to him.

"Then you are a bigger fool than I thought."

Kaleigh realized at Sebastian heartless words that she wasn't the only person that was seeking a heavenly bliss of her own. Sebastian might never admit it, but he was feeling just as lonely as she and probably others like them that get to see every day the kind of love only made for humans they could never have. Why did everything have to be so hard?

She looked over her shoulder and saw that Sebastian's head was lowered and his shoulders slumped. He looked like a man defeated. "Why are you here?"

Sebastian looked up and his commando take-no-prisoner look was back on his grim face. "Jack asked me to check on you. Said you needed some space whatever the hell that means."

"You still think I deliberately hurt him?"

"Hey," Sebastian said with a nod. "If looks like a duck and quacks like a duck, then it must be a duck, right?"

"That is the dumbest thing I've ever heard in my life," she said, and then added. "Do you know why I can't open up, Sebastian?"

"Because the pure souls are a bunch of stubborn bitches that refuse to help us for something that happened almost two thousands years ago."

"In a sense, yes," Kaleigh said glaring. "But if I do before they tell me to, then Jack dies. You die, Sebastian. The guardian dies. The pure souls die...and then the world dies. There won't be anything left to grieve for.

That's why it's important for me not to opened up and reveal the rumbling, two-thousand-year question that's been on everyone's mind. I killed Jack before and frankly I don't want to do it again."

"He didn't die, Kaleigh. He told you he didn't die." Sebastian's tone had changed from ballistic to the gentleness she heard earlier.

"He died to me, Sebastian," she whispered more to herself than to him.

"You know he used to talk about you all the time while he was helping you find your friend. It was always Kaleigh this or Kaleigh that. I got sick hearing about you. He loves you, you know?"

"I know," Kaleigh said.

"That doesn't do anything for you?"

"You have no idea what it's doing to me and not to do anything about it."

There was a brief moment of silence. "I never thought he was going to find you. If it were me, I would have given up a long time ago. He never gave up, though. Not once."

Kaleigh turned around again as Sebastian continued.

"When he woke up in that hotel room he had no idea why or how he was there. He called for me and I went there because I know he would have done the same thing for me. Even though I had my own problems, I couldn't ignore him. He was my friend and he needed my help.

"When I got there, it was like someone had planted him there and marked him as dead." Kaleigh was startled when he laughed. It was the first time she ever heard him laugh. It sounded pleasant, relaxing.

"He wasn't dead, but he sure did look dead. All the color was drained from his face and it looked like he hadn't slept in weeks! I helped him home and the time I was there he kept saying that he forgot something important. I, being concerned about my friend, asked him what he was doing there in the first place. He said he didn't remember and I believe him.

"I asked him if he knew where you were at and he just gave me this confused look like I was crazy and laughed in my face. He said, 'How in the hell should I know where you keep your women' and that's when I knew something went terribly wrong. He would have never forgotten you in a million years and yet he did.

"I took the initiative of tracking you down, but you were no where to be found. I went everywhere looking for you, and came up empty. About two weeks later, I came back to Jack and…he wasn't the same. He had this different look in his eyes; they were cold and angry and black as the ace of spades and in motion to kill. I feared that he would actually kill someone. I tried touching his arm and he freaked out! He started punching and kicking holes in the walls, screaming and yelling about the loss of innocence and the morals of our souls." He paused to take a deep breath.

"I tackled him down and held him there until he stopped fighting me. I may be bigger then him, but Jack can hold his own. I had to take couple of punches and let me tell you, they hurt like hell.

"Once I got him calm, he started whispering. I didn't know if he was talking to me or to himself. I bent down lower to hear what he was saying and he wasn't talking to me or to himself. There was someone else in the room with us and it scared the hell out of me. I've only been scared twice in my life and the second time when he was whispering to the other person in the room.

"I can't remember all what he was saying, but I caught just a little to know that he was talking to a spirit. He was asking for help in controlling the demons that were taunting him; he was weak and couldn't control them much longer. I guess the spirit gave him words of encouragement because his eyes changed from black to blue and all the coldness was gone. I cautiously let him up and he was so weak that he could barely stand on his own two feet. I told him that I was trying to find you, and he suddenly remembered everything. He then said, 'I will find her.'"

"A week later he resigned his position as detective and started his private investigation business. He uses the excuse that the captain was breathing down his neck about secretive informant, which is a bunch of bullshit. They never questioned him once as long as it was legal.

"Apparently, he made the right decision from all the business he's been getting lately. And he seems to be happier working on his own than under men laws.

"But he found you and when I seen that look in his eyes tonight like he did five years ago, I thought he was going to lose it again. That's why I was so pissed at you; I thought he was going to turn again."

Kaleigh didn't know what to say. Turn again?

Like he did five years ago.

Kaleigh suddenly felt sick. She realized every time Jack got angry, his eyes changed color to that creepy violet that made her feel the presence of evil. He had lied to her. He said the demon was no longer living in him anymore, and it was. Sebastian lied to her as well. Why did they want to keep it a secret from her? Yet, how was she able to touch him without destroying him?

No less, she still felt very deeply for him and if she had the opportunity of a lifetime at her fingertips, in a split second she would break open her heart and hand it over to him on a silver platter.

Jack was battling a demon all because of her.

Damn! How did she get herself in these predicaments? Everything seemed hopeless to her. She couldn't have the normal life she wanted. She couldn't have the man she wanted and she couldn't shake the responsibility of the world's fate off her shoulders.

Jack was a demon! It hit her so hard in the stomach that she doubled over and fell to her knees. That's why he wanted her to open up. That's why he talked of love. He didn't love her; he wanted the pure souls.

Oh dear lord! Why didn't she think of this before? He wasn't sent here by the imperious guardian sorcerer. He was sent by the guardian hunters themselves! She was such a fool!

What are you thinking? asked a gentle voice in her head. *Jack could never hurt you!*

Then why did you not tell me he was a demon? Kaleigh asked back to Danette.

Because he's only partially a demon, she said with a funny laugh. *Sebastian was right, you never killed Jack, but the demon has come back to live in his spirit. It's a constant; one that he fights for you because he does love you.*

Why was he sent to me if we could never be together?

"Kaleigh are you all right?" Sebastian asked.

Kaleigh didn't hear Sebastian.

Sometimes, Kaleigh, you have to go through the fires of hell to find what you want.

Does that mean I have to destroy Jack?

There was a short pause as Sebastian repeatedly tried to get her out of her daze.

You already know the answer to your own question.

What am I suppose to do? I'm so lost.

Trust your heart, Kaleigh. Love Jack with everything you have or else you will lose.

Are you telling me to open up? Kaleigh asked confused.

I'm not telling you to do anything, but you don't have much time left. The guardian hunter that is after you is very strong and Jack is the only one to defeat him without jeopardizing our position.

Because he's a demon?

Because he has the power to stop him as you do, and yes, because he's a demon just like the guardian that was able to save your mother. I must leave you for now, Kaleigh; I can't interfere anymore.

The voice was gone from Kaleigh's head and she realized that Sebastian was shaking her shoulder. "Kaleigh are you all right? Speak to me!"

Kaleigh blinked several times before she responded, and then instantly pushed herself away from Sebastian, jumping to her feet. "Well, I discovered your grand secret."

"Oh yeah? And what's that?" Sebastian said as he folded his arms across his chest.

"Jack's a demon."

Chapter Fourteen

"God dammit!" Sebastian shouted. "If you do anything to—"

"Oh, but don't worry, Sebastian. I'm not going to do anything! I'm going to let nature take its course. You see, Jack can defeat a guardian hunter because he has the strength of the pure soul's blood in him—mine. But he doesn't know that I gave him the power to destroy them. We need him very much alive and I'm not going to do anything to endanger the pure souls' existence. So you can bet that I won't be opening up to him, but if Jack loves me as much as he does, then he will destroy the guardian hunter that has been chasing to protect me."

"You are a fucking bitch!" Sebastian roared as he stalked towards her.

Kaleigh threw her right hand up and stopped him with an invisible wall. Sebastian slammed into it and stumbled backwards, cursing the entire time. "No, Sebastian, I'm smart. Jack can destroy the guardian hunters with my help. What do you think I was going to do? Sit back while Jack puts his life in danger?"

"Yes," Sebastian said

"Sebastian, I don't know what woman wronged you in the past, but I wish you stop comparing her to me. I told you I would never hurt Jack and I meant it. But I do need him to help, and you, too, Sebastian, if you are willing."

"What do you want?"

"The guardian hunter needs me because I'm the only one that knows about the pure souls. I can lure him out and Jack can destroy them as you fight the demons he sends for us."

Sebastian looked at her for a long time and then suspiciously asked, "You won't destroy Jack?"

"If he turns on us, I have to. You of all people, should know how demons can be."

"I know," Sebastian whispered. "I wish there was a way for us to change him back to a regular old guardian."

"You and I both, Sebastian. So we have a deal?"

"Yes," Sebastian said. "Just answer me this. If Jack can take your blood and kill the guardian hunters, couldn't we all? Wouldn't that be simpler than waiting for the pure souls to get out of their fix?"

It made sense, but from her understanding, only two guardians could carry the blood of a pure soul. Technically, Jack wasn't a guardian anymore, but their maker must have made some kind of deal with the devil to allow him to take in a toxin that was poison to his system.

"From what my mother said, anyone that takes in our blood will die. They are not strong enough to carry us in their spirit, but Jack and another sorcerer are."

Kaleigh crashed through Sebastian's invisible wall and touched his cheek. "Tell Jack that I'm perfectly fine. Don't tell him anything that I told you, please."

"I won't," Sebastian said in his calm voice. He didn't know why he was cooperating with this pure soul, but for some odd reason, he had to. When she touched him, she made him feel funny inside like his heart was beating for the first time in many, many years, and he hated it. He wanted to feel the emotionless ride of the guardian warrior he grew up to be.

He stepped back from her hand and took a deep breath. "When are you going to tell him?"

"Later."

"Jack, you really need someone to come in here and clean this place from top to bottom," Sebastian said as he frantically tried to find the pictures he printed on Jack's cluttered desk.

"I did," he responded. Jack was sitting in the client's chair when Sebastian walked in. From the way he looked, everything went smoothly between Kaleigh and him.

He was glad. Sebastian wasn't an easy person to get along with and Kaleigh was so fragile that he wouldn't tolerate his friend hurting her more than she already was hurt. "But since I'm not going to be around much longer, what's the point?"

Jack hired a young girl early last week to work as his secretary, but she wanted to finish out her two week recognition before she started working for him. Then with a sudden change in his divine plan to branch out his business, he called her and told her she was no longer needed.

After he flipped the desk over, he must have lost whatever Sebastian had placed there. He should have told him not to set anything on there because it would get lost in seconds. Sebastian had gone through every scrap of paper on his desk twice. "Damn it! Where the hell is it?"

Jack slumped in his chair and folded his hands behind his head. He had no clue what he was searching for, but it was fun watching him look through the disaster; it helped him to forget about Kaleigh for seconds at a time.

When Sebastian came in, Jack didn't want to know what they talked about. Well, he didn't want to ask what they talked about. He wanted Sebastian to bring it up on his own time while he was starving for the pass words that went between them.

"What are you trying to find?"

Sebastian glanced up and gave him a piercing look. "I hope you're finding this amusing because I'm not!"

Jack smiled. "Just tell me what you're trying to find. Maybe I can help you."

He flipped over another document and cursed. "You could have helped by not flipping over the desk. At least you didn't go totally psycho."

Jack stood up quickly. "What the hell does that mean?"

Sebastian dropped the document in his hands and planted them squarely on the desk with his head bent between his arms. "It means you didn't lose control like last time." He looked up and sighed. "Whatever you think it means."

"You thought maybe I was going to turn like the last time?"

He nodded his head. "I was mad at hell. I'm still mad, but I learn to control it."

"That's good, Jack, because I would hate to destroy you. Oh, by the way, I know I shouldn't get involved, but Kaleigh gave me a glimpse of why she won't open up. I guess I can understand from her point of view."

Finally Jack was going to get tidbits of what was spoken between them. He sighed, waiting in anticipation. For thirty minutes, he had been waiting for Sebastian to share something of what Kaleigh said, and now the suspense was killing him!

Then it struck Jack that Sebastian wasn't his normal brooding self. He looked...well relaxed. His muscles weren't corded and his eyes held this peace that he never seen before. It was weird and funny.

"What the hell did she say to you?"

Jack saw Sebastian tense for a second and then relaxed as if he said nothing of importance at all. "Not much, but the usual, 'I'm scared,' bit."

"Of what? I could never hurt her."

Sebastian backed away from the desk and came around and gripped his shoulder. "She knows that. She's not scared of you; she's scared of them. She's afraid if she opens up, you'll end up dead for real this time, and she would rather keep you at arm's length so there won't be any reason for her to open up."

"They are all relying on me to get her to open up, Sebastian. I can't fail this time."

Sebastian gripped both of his shoulders and gave him a hard shake. "Trust me, Jack. She's doing what's best."

Jack shook his head. "Since when have you become Mr. Sensitive? I thought you wanted her to open up as badly as the rest of us?"

"I do, but I understand her reasons for not wanting to, and until then, we just have to keep on doing what the guardians have been doing for last two thousand years."

He let go of Jack's arm and came back to the desk and continued to look for his missing document. "I need to find those pictures." As soon as he said that, he flipped over a legal notebook pad and found what he'd been looking for.

"Found them," he shouted in triumph.

Jack came around to him as Sebastian scooped up the pictures and in both hands he held the two pictures up that he had been looking for. Jack came to abrupt stop when he recognized that both of the pictures were of Susan.

He looked closer and read every detail feature on both of her faces and didn't understand why Sebastian found these pictures meaningful. He looked even closer and studied hard at every word, dot, and line as Sebastian waited patiently with a straight face for his recognition.

Jack then noticed something that was relatively different from one of the pictures than the other and it hit him so hard that Jack stepped back and took in a large gulp of air.

The picture in Sebastian's left showed Susan battered and severely beaten and the picture in his right showed Susan smiling with a sparkle in her eye. Mayor Devin McChandey was involved with both of these women: The left was his mistress and the right was his wife. No one knew that Mr. McChandey had a mistress by the name of Melissa Gaines that later became his wife as Susan McChandey.

The pictures showed the same identical woman. And both were dead.

He was thinking hard now. The flashback came fast and heavy, and it only took him seconds to remember every little detail of the past five years.

The flashbacks showed him from the first time he saw Kaleigh filling out the missing report form, the first time they kissed, the first time they made love, and the first time he encountered the guardian hunter. He remembered being shot at by a human servant. He remembered making love to Kaleigh in the shower and in his kitchen. He remembered the guardian hunter trying to steal her life away. He remembered Devin McChandey standing with a group of men near the bank of Creegan Lake, hauling at least six young ethnic woman that were no older than sixteen from a small fishing boat to a white van with no license plate. His men were heavily armed as he yelled at a dark man about the prices of the girls. The argument got so heated that Mr. McChandey shot the dark man right in the face and left them there.

He remembered following them to a shack deep in the woods in Creegan and that's when he noticed that one of the women he pulled out of the shack was Caucasian, young, and scared beyond her control. He recognized her from the picture that Kaleigh had given him and she was Melissa Gaines, Devin McChandey's mistress. She looked nearly beaten to death as they threw her in a fresh grave and then quickly tossing dirt on her still breathing body. Jack had to wait to intercept for he was one armed man one against seven armed men. There was not a chance that he was coming out of alive or that he would be able to save Melissa Gaines. He called for back-up and crept low to the shack. Someone had noticed him. They started shooting and so did he.

They must have thought that one of their bullets had hit him because they scattered like flies and quickly loaded the young girls up in the unmarked white van and sped out of his sight.

Jack called for back-up again as he quickly tried to get Melissa Gaines's still-breathing body out of the grave. He succeeded, but when back-up finally arrived not one of the officers believed his story. Without any hard evidences and a witness to the crime in a coma, they couldn't arrest Devin McChandey for he had a solid alibi.

Melissa Gaines shortly died before the paramedics arrived.

But here was Susan smiling like a blushing bride on her wedding day with the man that killed her and no one (not even Kaleigh or him) noticed the resemblance of the two women. She was a stranger to them on the streets and they did not know it was Melissa Gaines.

When Jack delivered the news at her company's birthday party, he asked her to meet him in a hotel room for privacy about the case. He felt her open up with hesitation about their relationship and he got very angry that she had doubts about them. That's when everything went blank and he woke to see Sebastian leaning over him like he was dead.

Jack had this dark feeling that everything came down to Melissa/Susan and Mayor Devin McChandey. They were the key to all their problems. The guardian hunter never showed up before in Kaleigh's life until Melissa's disappearances. It didn't show up again until Susan came up missing.

Everything was happening all over again, all because of a very complicated woman wouldn't allow anyone access to her soul to reunite the six pure souls.

Jack remembered the strong sense that he was being watched in his home and it felt like he was always in the presence of a demon. McChandey was not a demon, but a very well disguised human servant and that's how the guardian hunter was able to find Kaleigh both times. He used Melissa/Susan to get vital information on Kaleigh to give to his master, a guardian hunter.

He snatched the pictures out of Sebastian's hands and tossed them on the cluttered desk.

"You saw what I saw, huh?" Sebastian asked.

Jack nodded and sat in his chair that was parked in front of his desk and scratched his two day growth of a beard. He needed to shave, shower, and get something to eat all in that order.

He had to have a plan that would catch Mayor McChandey in the act of exporting these women and find Susan. He had hard evidence staring him right in his face, but nothing pointing to the mayor's way. He needed a confession, witnesses outside of McChandey's illegal faction. Or he could take what was offered to him; a chance to get a soul. If he did, no one would know what a monster the mayor was and Jack sincerely wanted that face spread across the six o'clock news on every major network.

"Mayor McChandey is meeting with some people on Saturday," Jack said as he stared at the blank computer screen. "That gives us three day to come up with a plan and set up surveillance to catch this bastard in action. Susan/Melissa is dead because of this asshole and deserves every mortal fatality coming to him. Meanwhile, I'm going to put a friend of mine to follow his every move." Jack paused as he thought back to Monday when the two thugs invaded Susan's apartment.

"There were two men that were looking for something in her apartment. They said that it was on her night stand, but it wasn't. They were supposed to come back to check the place out." Jack rubbed his chin and went into deep concentration.

Sebastian sat down in the client's chair and crossed his ankles as he studied Jack. "Watcha thinking, Jack?"

He cleared his throat and leaned his elbows on the desk and slumped forward to Sebastian. "I keep thinking why Susan divorced the mayor. In the articles they barely mentioned anything about their separation. Wouldn't that have made front page headlines?"

Sebastian shrugged. "Sure for any regular red-blooded American politician, it would have. But we are not talking about a red-blooded American; we are talking about a human servant working for a guardian hunter, Jack. A human servant that has a lot of influence from the darkness."

"With free reign to manipulate anyone," Jack said.

"Whoever, the mayor's master is, must be very strong to control such a large population. He wasn't expecting the divorce. They were only married a couple of months and it was kept out of the media as much as possible. She also must have signed a prenuptial agreement, which left her with no money. So she had to get a job and where did she go?"

"Walker Security," Jack finished for him. "Kaleigh was working there when I first met her and she hired her because she felt pity for the woman and never once knew who the woman was." Jack paused. He placed an elbow on the desk and rested his chin in his palm.

"I have this theory, so don't take account on my words: I think McChandey found out that Susan reunited with her old friend, Kaleigh because she was connected with her. If McChandey has any ties with Susan that means that he found out what every demon and guardian savior, plus me, has been trying to find: a pure soul. And whoever is McChandey's master is has found his trophy and killed Susan to bring Kaleigh out in the open."

"Sounds like a hell of a theory, Jack, but there's something that contradicts with your theory. What were the two thugs looking for in Susan's apartment? She must have something on him or why else would they have gone there?"

Jack sagged further into his chair and rubbed his chin. "Then Susan must have left some incriminating evidence that would get the mayor in a lot of trouble. Let's go search her apartment and we're not leaving until we find something."

As Jack stood, Sebastian came around the desk to catch his friend's arm. "We have a little problem."

It didn't take a genius to figure that one out. "Kaleigh," Jack said. "Leave her here. My apartment is sacred with my blood and Kaleigh's. They won't get in and I'll know if she's in trouble."

Chapter Fifteen

Jack and Sebastian checked every crack and hole to find the missing object in Susan's apartment and came up empty. The first place Jack looked was all around the night stand where the supposedly missing object was placed. The thugs didn't find it and neither did they.

He entered the kitchen and found Sebastian kneeling on the floor digging underneath the kitchen sink. "Find anything yet?"

"If I did, wouldn't I have said something by now?" If he sounded provoked, Jack couldn't blame him. He was at his wits' end, too, and he, too, wanted to give up searching the small apartment, but he knew it was buried somewhere in this apartment. He couldn't tell how many times he checked under, behind, and in the small drawer of the night stand. He was sure that it was hidden around there somewhere, but it didn't exist on the small wooden furniture.

"Maybe we should take a breather?" Jack asked.

Sebastian shook his head under the sink. "No. It has to be here somewhere. Did they say when their coming back?"

"No, but I can tell they haven't been back yet."

Jack checked his watch. It was a quarter after eight, the sun had gone down, and the sky was blank canvas for the stars. He ran his hands through his hair and settled on a bar stool as Sebastian hastily searched under the sink. He wasn't subtle about it, more like a bull in a china cabinet. He was knocking over household cleaners, throwing old metal, rusted pots on the kitchen floor, and every other minute banging his head on the pipes.

"Shit!"

"Why don't we take a rest? Neither one of us had anything to eat probably since yesterday. I'll order a pizza."

Sebastian came from the under the sink and said a silent prayer. Jack smiled at his frustration. He knew how it felt, but he could control his temper better than Sebastian.

"Fine," he said throwing his hands up.

When both men headed for the door, they froze. Jack had an ominous awareness that wouldn't go away. Sebastian tried to reach for his sword and realized that he left it in Jack's office. Both had a sense of dread about something coming down the hallway and both reacted simultaneously.

Jack moved to the right side of the door as Sebastian moved to the left. Whoever entered, they were going to have Sebastian's fist in his face and Jack's elbow slammed on the back of his or her head.

Silence stilled the apartment as they heard the quiet footsteps of the intruders. Jack could feel his heart pounding against his chest. He was the one never to fight. In junior high when he was a tall, lanky seventh grader, he had to suffer a lot of fights because he was an outcast. Kids called him a devil worshiper because he accused a kid of being of a demon. Not a good choice of words if he wanted to be in the popular crowd, but he couldn't help to hide the fact.

Consequently, after weeks of getting jumped by five or more boys on a daily basis he signed up for the self defense class at Wushu Self Defense School. In a five month period he went from a green belt beginner to a black belt expert. It did help him to that his father was an expert in fighting; he was a warrior and the bullies never picked on him again.

Though, whenever the need to fight arose, he still felt he was back in seventh grade; scared and weak.

The intruder's footsteps stopped an inch away from the door. Jack and Sebastian held their breath as their bodies stiffly leaned against the walls, waiting for them to enter. That's when Jack noticed that the door wasn't locked. He waved his hand in the air and got Sebastian's attention. First he stared at him, amused. Jack mouthed that the door wasn't locked. Sebastian squinted. Jack silently cursed, and then pointed to the door knob. Sebastian registered what Jack had seen and carefully, with quick-quiet speed, turned the thin, metal lock.

They both breathed.

Neither one wanted the intruders to get suspicious about the door being unlocked. The intruders locked the door on their way out and it should be locked when they came back.

One of the intruders jiggled something inside the tiny space for the key and made the lock turn to the right. The door slowly and quietly came open with a large shadow appearing between Jack and Sebastian.

"What the fu—," an intruder said. But that's all he could get out because he was thrown against Jack's hard chest from a mighty blow by Sebastian's fist. Jack grabbed the intruder's shoulders and twisted them around his back and pushed his stomach to the floor. He dug his knees in the intruder's back and when he screamed, Jack pushed harder.

The man underneath Jack's knee looked very much like the man from the club that had dance with Kaleigh. He was nearly as tall as Jack, smaller than Sebastian in the chest, and a lot softer in his gut. Vulgar tattoos of naked women covered his entire left arm as the right arm had articulate drawings of Lucifer in every maniacal pose that would make a nine-year-old girl cry. The other man, who was still in shock at seeing his friend, was Hispanic, short, stout, and couldn't fight to save his life.

Both men smelled of stale cigarettes, cheap beer, and urine as if they just came from a little hole-in-the-wall bar. Jack had to suppress his urge to vomit.

The Hispanic man didn't have time to run or fight; Sebastian grabbed his arm and threw him against the coffee table. The table folded and shattered beneath the man's large weight as his body crashed against the floor. Sebastian slammed the door shut behind him as the Hispanic man stood up and pulled a switchblade from behind his trousers.

"You wanna play rough," he said in a rich, northern accent as he dashed the blade from hand to hand. "Let's play."

He swung the knife in Sebastian's direction and missed terribly. Sebastian jumped back with a smile on his face and the man with the knife charge at him. Sebastian's leg flew up, kicked the knife out of his hands and then he did an uppercut in his stomach. The man dropped to his knees with his hands wrapped around his waist. Sebastian picked up the loose knife that flew towards the destroyed coffee table and grabbed the back of the man's thick, greasy hair and put the knife under the man's chin.

"Who are you?" Sebastian asked in his old menacing voice.

"Fuck you, man," he spat. "I ain't telling you shit!"

Sebastian laughed and tugged harder on the man's hair. "Wrong choice of words for a man that's weaponless and has a knife against his throat. I'll ask you again: who are you?"

The Hispanic man didn't say anything. Sebastian dug the tip of the man's knife under the man's chin; just enough to make him squirm on his knees. The man that Jack held captured didn't move a muscle. A man knew when he was outweighed by two martial arts experts that could take them down in less than two minutes.

"You better answer my friend," Jack said deviously. "He has anger management problems." Sebastian flashed Jack a look that told him he was about to get the same treatment as his newfound friend.

Sebastian's man closed his eyes and sighed. "All right, I'll tell you."

Jack saw before it happened. The Hispanic ran jabbed his thick skull under Sebastian's chin and as Sebastian staggered backward, took a cheap shot by kicking him twice in the ribs. Jack reacted instantly and charged at the loose man. They both went flying down on the couch.

Jack was on top and both struggled for each other's throat. He lost his balanced and fell against the floor with the thug on top of him. With opened palms, Jack slapped both of the man's ears. The Hispanic man grabbed at them and let out a long groan of pain. He fell backwards and screamed as he was holding his reddened ears, "You dick!"

Ducking low, Jack stretched out his right leg and kicked the man in his left knee cap. The man went down with an agonized scream as he saw from the corner of his eyes that Sebastian was wrestling with the other man. He quickly scrambled to his feet and picked the Hispanic man up by his throat and slammed him against a picture of the beach on the wall.

The picture fell halfway down behind the man's back as he tried to grip Jack's arms. But when Jack kneed him in his groin he went down permanently. Jack took off his T-shirt and rapidly tied it around his wrists and knotted it.

Sebastian punched his man a little too hard in the face and he passed out cold at his feet. Jack's man was whining about his groin as his labored breathing filled the tiny spaced living room.

Jack turned to Sebastian. "You okay?"

He shrugged his shoulders, rubbed his chin, and nodded his head. "Never better. Let's get these two talking."

Sebastian grabbed the passed-out man by his upper arm and tossed him on the couch. He then walked into the kitchen as Jack swung the Hispanic man beside his friend. Sebastian came back with a handful of dish towels and began shredded them in half with his hands. He tossed Jack four pieces and began tying his victim by the wrist and ankles. "I suggest you do the same."

Jack did and put back on his shirt with one quick move. Sebastian picked up the knife again and pointed it at the conscious victim. "Let's try this again. First off: why are you two here?"

The victim looked deadly and ready to kill. Sweat beaded off his forehead and his weight caused him to breathe harder and faster than them. He sucked in his breath and spat on Sebastian face. Before Jack could contain Sebastian's temper, his fist slammed in the man's left jaw. The man's head shot sideway. He growled and sang a stream of curse words.

"Don't do that again," Sebastian said venially. "I'm going to ask you again, why are you here?"

The man didn't say anything for he was clearly venting his anger and contemplating what he would do once he was free. The man also showed signs of resistance that he wasn't going to say anything that he wasn't forced to.

Jack knew Sebastian's anger and that his lack of self-control for the wicked would only hold out another minute if this man didn't start answering his questions. Though this man feared for his life from his employer and would not say anything that he wasn't forced to. The man was in for a rude awakening if he tried to lie or short Sebastian on information. Sebastian could sniff out a lie and would bring bigger fear to a man's heart than the devil himself. Jack had witnessed himself what Sebastian would for the truth and it wasn't something that Jack wanted to witness again.

Jack gripped the man's shoulder and leaned to his ear and whispered, "If you want to survive tonight, you better start talking. You don't want to fuck around with this man." He leaned back and saw the raw rage fade away from his eyes to a look of desperation.

The man sagged and lowered his eyes, not wanting them to see his fear. "We here to find a tape," he said crudely.

Sebastian pierced his gaze on the man's fallen head and sighed. "What for?" he asked in evenly tone.

The thug shrugged his shoulders. "I don't know. We got this call in last early Sunday for us to find this tape. He didn't say what for or what was on it. The deal was two thousand to get the tape and then another two thousands once he received it. The woman that lived in this apartment told our employer that she left it on her night stand, but when we got here it wasn't there."

Sebastian cast a sly glance to Jack and turned his attention back to the captive. "What did you tell your employer?"

"Exactly what I told you—it wasn't there. He told us he would increase our payment by another thousand if we found it and if we didn't find it..." the man trailed off. Jack and Sebastian knew what would happen if they didn't retrieve the tape.

"Who's your employer?"

"I don't know. I've never met him. I usually get a call from a man by the name of Mr. Baker, who works for the guy that pays us. He tells us what to do and once we're finished, we give him a call. Then we usually meet at night in a park or alley and we get our pay. I've never really seen him, though. He sits in a tinted car wearing black sunglasses and doesn't say nothing when he gives us our money. He just rolls down his window and hands us our bills and then leaves."

"What color is his skin?" Jack asked.

"He's white."

"Tell us everything," Sebastian said with grim coolness. "Tell us how he wears his hair, what kind of clothes he wears, and the scent of his cologne. I want to know everything you know. And be wise; I can tell when you're lying."

"All right, all right," the man said, obviously believing Sebastian. "Ya'll some kind of cops?"

"We're everything you don't want us to be. Now stop procrastinating!"

The Hispanic man rolled his eyes and quickly opened them as if he discovered the secret of life. "He has black hair and always keeps it slicked back. And he always wears a black suit with a black tie. I don't know what kind of cologne he wears because I've never thought to sniff his neck or ask him about it."

"Stop being a smart-ass," Jack said.

"Look, that's all I know! Okay. If you want to know anything else, you're shit out of luck, because I don't have nothing else to tell you!" The Hispanic man becoming enraged again and Jack stiffly held his shoulders and looked down into the man's black, hatred-filled eyes.

"Thank you, but I have a question. Does Mr. Baker ever refer to his employer?"

The man looked away from Jack and shook his head as he studied the broken table that was in pieces. Jack almost felt sorry for all the hard luck he had in the past, but than had a moment of aloofness that this man was holding something important back. He was lying about his employer's name. Jack knew for certain that he knew who it was, but if Sebastian found out (which he could sense that he already did) than this man was going to be in a lot more trouble than a busted lip if this man didn't tell them, he would never know for sure.

"Are you sure you don't know his name?"

The Hispanic man didn't say anything. He was focused on the broken table.

Jack thrust his chin up like a kid in trouble and asked with a much firmer and colder tone. "Are you sure?"

The thug looked to Sebastian and then at Jack. He sighed heavily and shook his head. "I can't tell you who he is. If I do, then I'm dead."

"You're already dead for the life you chose," Sebastian said wryly.

"Hey, go fuck yourself, man!" he growled. "I don't have to take this shit from you or you," he said pointing his head from Sebastian to Jack.

He struggled to get up, but Sebastian pushed him down—hard, and the man fell against his still unconscious friend. The tattooed man mumbled something and went back to sleep. Sebastian grabbed the strip of cloth that was tied around the Hispanic man's wrists and hauled him up until there was only a half inch of air of space separating them.

"Give me his name," he said with deadly softness.

"Go to hell. If I tell you, you're gonna kill me anyway. So why bother?"

"Because if you tell me, I'll let you and your buddy, go." Jack studied the Hispanic man and saw that he was really considering giving him a name. He just needed more persuasion. "Give me his name."

"I already told you, he'll kill us if I say anything!" The man was weakening. Jack could see that he was scared. He was facing two men that were in better shape, smarter, and more dangerous.

"No he won't because we won't let him. You're going to call Mr. Baker back and tell him you found the tape," the man went to go protest, but Jack held up his hands. "You're going to act like everything is peachy-keen. Do not let him know that you've been caught. When you go meet him, you're going to give him a tape…just not the one he wants. Once you get your money then go back to your car and leave and never show your face around here again. What is his name?"

The Hispanic man sighed and quickly said, "It's the goddamned mayor!"
Jack shot Sebastian look. "What're your and your buddy's, names?"
Without hesitation or protest the man freely gave Jack his and the tattooed man's name. "I'm Carlos and this Howard."

Chapter Sixteen

Sebastian said she would be safe while he and Jack were gone searching in Susan's apartment for what the two men had been looking for on Monday. They been gone for almost two hours, and she started to believe that they got in some kind of trouble. She knew that they could take of themselves, but she couldn't shake the feeling that she should have gone with them or not been left alone.

As she sat in the recliner, the television played to the late night news. She could care less what the middle-aged reporter was talking about; there were bigger problems in her world than the humans that couldn't be ignored. So why were there suddenly chill bumps racing up and down her arms and the back of her neck tingled with an awareness that was cold as ice and she had a sudden urge to look behind her?

Get a grip, she told herself. *Nothing is behind you.*

But there was nothing *behind* her.

A large, black cloud of mist swam above her head with red, beady eyes and a hollow mouth. Gracefully as the wind, it floated from the ceiling and hovered around her head, wrapping it's blackness around her neck.

Kaleigh stiffened and turned her head to look and found nothing. She shivered as the room began to get colder. Something was in the apartment with her and she wasn't going to find out. She wasn't scared, but she had no protection with her and had never been trained to defeat something she couldn't see.

Standing on shaking legs, her teeth chattered as the coldness dropped twenty degrees more. The blackness floated to the ceiling, crawling on its dreamy hands and knees and stretched its head to sniff Kaleigh's hair.

Kaleigh knew there was some form of evil standing behind her, but she wasn't going to be the lead heroine to figure it out. She had to get to Jack, quickly.

She was barely had the other foot out the door when a warmth mingled against her skin. She turned around and discovered Jack, like a warrior preparing to go to battle.

Her knees weakened, her heart slammed into her chest, and she found herself at a loss for words. He was so handsome and strong looking and he was the only person that she could open and give her love to, and he was going to die.

She bravely looked into his sapphire eyes, forgetting about the evil that just interrupted her night, and saw ignited heat flare that made her light headed and her stomach clench. He showed every sign of wanting her and anger that flex in his jaws.

"I'm sorry."

Before she could say anything else, he took one large stride and pulled her against his hard chest and kissed the top of her head. She wrapped her arms around his waist and they held each other like that for what seemed like an eternity.

He smoothed a tendril of hair out of her face and kissed her forehead, her eyes, and on the cheeks. "I accept whatever you're about to say, but please; tell me you are all right," his voice was rough, strained, and yet soothing to hear him.

She held tighter, feeling his racing heart beat against her. "Yes, Jack I'm fine. I think I overreacted because it was taking you two so long to get back."

If Jack was looking at her face, he would have seen the lie that was written on her face n black ink.

He kissed her again and wrapped his arms around her tighter. "I didn't mean to stay gone that long."

Kaleigh braced her hands on his chest and looked up to see him frowning. He looked very sad and at a loss for words, and Kaleigh was feeling guilt again. She wanted to tell him, but his eyes held a flicker of pleasure that she was in his arms and then she knew she would never tell him. For once she had this insane idea to freely open her heart and let Jack in to feel what he was feeling.

She touched his stubble cheek and smiled warmly at him. He lowered his head and tenderly took her mouth with his. She wrapped her arms around his neck and pulled his tongue into her mouth.

At the touch of their tongues, Kaleigh's body melted inside and her loins clenched from the fiery rage. She pulled him closer to her body until her breasts crushed in the thickness of his chest and his cock nestled hungrily against her navel. His heart was beating wildly, uncontrollably, outrageously just as hers. She wanted to feel all of him: her legs wrapped around his body, her hands stroking his back, her mouth touching anything that it could taste.

A soft moan escaped from deep inside of her as his mouth slanted to the corner of her mouth and kissed her. His hands thrust in her hair as he pulled her mere inch away from him. Kaleigh saw desire in his smoldering, blue eyes. His face was hard, tense, and she felt her limbs grow weak to the despair for another kiss.

She gently stroked his cheek and felt her body grow tense as his eyes grew ravenous. Kaleigh pressed herself against the hard plane of his body and the rigid, carnal desire that was burning through his jeans. He savagely gripped her shoulders and pushed her against the door as his mouth brutality crashed on hers. Kaleigh gasped at the sudden raw male need and felt the same savage desire that stirred within her.

She locked her arms around her neck and deepened the kiss as brutality as his. Their tongues clashed, tasting and devouring like the battle for control. He lifted her left leg up and wrapped it around his waist as he planted himself between her thighs, letting her feel his desire that was aching. She arched to meet his thrust and felt him tremble. She did it again and again until his legs were shaking between her and she was driving herself mad.

"While you two are disgracing yourself against that poor door, I would like to call your attention to our little problem in Susan's apartment."

Kaleigh blushed from head to toe at the sound of Sebastian's deep voice. She peeked at Jack and saw she wasn't alone in her embarrassment. His cheeks were flushed as he mumbled a curse under his breath. They both forgot they were in the middle of a hallway, which at any moment, anyone could walk by.

Jack slowly unwrap her leg and released the breath that he was holding. He took a step back and closed his eyes. "I'll be there in a minute," he said waving his hand in the air.

Sebastian snorted as he teleported his body from the hallway and disappeared.

They stood for several seconds before either one of them said anything. Jack ran a nervous hand through his hair and sighed. He flashed a smile that sent Kaleigh's heart on fire and her knees weak. His smile widened as if the problem in Susan's apartment wasn't as significant as theirs. It was great toss-up between Susan and returning to Jack's apartment, but the obvious choice was to a problem they couldn't ignore.

She pushed herself from the door and walked to Jack's side. "What's going on?"

Jack tugged her hand and hugged her to his side. "Feel like your first teleport?"

He didn't wait for her to answer or give her a warning. One moment she was standing outside of Jack's apartment and the next she was outside of Susan's apartment.

"Wow!" Kaleigh said. "That was fast."

"Remember that day in Kaleigh's apartment when those two thugs broke in?" Jack said, breaking her zealous interest in the quick teleport.

Kaleigh nodded her head. "Well, they're in there right now and they may be able to lead us to Susan. What have you decided, Kaleigh?"

She was taken back by his words. A few seconds ago, nothing mattered as long as they were with each other. Now they were in reality and everything mattered.

Did she really want to know? Yes and no, but she found out anyway.

Kaleigh reached for his free hand and cupped it in hers. She smiled up at him and lowered her lashes so he couldn't tell of the deceit she was feeling. "Everything I decided has come back to you, Jack. I can't leave you and yet I can't love you, but it doesn't mean that I don't feel anything for you, because I do, more than I should. But you have to realize Jack, I can't open up. And please don't make me."

He didn't say anything. He squeezed her hands under his strong ones and led her to Susan's door and before he opened the door for her, he stopped her and looked at acutely. "Is there something you're not telling me, Kaleigh? I feel like you are holding something back from me and if you are, I want to know."

She knew she couldn't fool him with her words, he could see deep into her soul without opening up to him. He was a powerful, truthful man and she couldn't deny that his strength was the inner control of her heart. He was of a lesser god, but in all reality of her small part in the world, he was greater than all men she known and that came close to being a god. It was one of those small corners of her heart that she wanted to give fully to him and fall before his feet and be a slave to his heart.

However, the wounding that penetrated his sedated eyes, made her feel deceitful and malicious of a siren's call. She didn't want to hurt him. She didn't want to bring the news of his death when it was so critical to find Susan body and set her free. The distressing news might provoke him to cause more harm to himself or to her.

On the other hand, he may accept it her proposition.

"Kaleigh?"

He was demanding for an answer something she couldn't put in plain words. He had to know what his fate was going to be and it would be unfair to him if she kept it hidden until it was upon him and reacted to a total diverse way then she had planned it for them.

"Kaleigh," he said gripping her shoulders. "What is it?"

She lowered her eyes and sighed. "I'm sorry, Jack. I never knew it would come to this. Tonight my mother and Adrian came to your apartment while you and Sebastian were in your office."

Jack propped himself against the wall next to Susan's door and folded his arms across his chest. How was she going to explain this to him? He as already in his defensive mode, primed for the news for which was about to deliver. If anything, she should have been angry, accusing him of lying to her about what he was.

That troubled her. Back in Sebastian's apartment the truth didn't hit her hard now that she was standing in front of Jack. His eyes were consistently changing color and she wanted to cry. He was going to die because the demon inside of him could only stay dormant for so long until it wanted to release its fury on the world and Jack was fighting hard to control it.

"Why did you lie to me?"

He didn't say anything. He stood there with his jaw locked, his face impassive, and his eyes swiftly changing back and forth from blue to violet.

"Will you say something?" she urged.

He pushed his shoulders from the door, steadily shaking his head. She wanted him to say something anything that would get the mad expression off his face. She hated him to look dangerous; it made her feel she was the thwart in his heart. She wanted to see him in wanton desire and make her feel like she was the only woman that could bare his seed.

After several minutes of silence he spoke, but his expression never changed. "It's my fate, Kaleigh. I can't change it. I admit that I foresaw this coming; I knew all along what was going to happen between us."

"Why does it have to be you?"

Jack rolled his eyes an eerily chuckled. "I swear Kaleigh, can't you ever take anything at face value. Can't you accept the way things are in the world and just let it be? Why do you have to have everything explain to death?"

"Because I want to what's going on!"

"Some things you shouldn't know the 'why' to; it will all come out in the end. I accepted my fate Kaleigh; have you?"

He could have slapped her in the face; it would have gotten the same reaction.

"I know what I'm suppose to do when my time has come, and Sebastian will, too, when his fate comes, but I want to know if you will?" he asked as he swung Susan's door open, leaving her alone.

So he wanted to hurt her because he was hurting so much inside. She found out the truth that he was leaving the world for good this time—without his Kaleigh. She was going to be alone—again, facing the cruel world and her instability of being happy.

He hated knowing that he was going to die, but what was he to do? He'd known for the past several days that he was to be sacrifice and yet, hearing it from her mouth was a painful blow to the gut. The demon's soul was half-way to molding with his and he couldn't change what fate brought him. All he could do was come to terms with it and wish Kaleigh all the happiness in the world.

Sure, he was mad as hell that he had to be the sacrifice so Kaleigh would never be deceived as the pure soul that died for her forbidden love. He was mad that his only love was going to be the end of him. How could he not be mad? Angry?

When he first met Kaleigh, it was the first time he ever felt weak and out of control at the same time. With the humans emotions it was neutral, but with Kaleigh it was explosive! He knew that his downfall would be her, and he knew she had the one emotion that made his parents fall fatefully in love.

He had been looking for what they had and be damned losing his powers and immorality. But he never did when he fell. Jack never lost any of his abilities that gave him the powers to save humans from the demons. He didn't understand then, but now he knew why.

Then everything went to shit when that treacherous night happened.

Jack looked at the two men who were whispering to Sebastian and stopped when they noticed his presence. They noticed his playing "good cop" attitude was gone and they both tensed up as Sebastian cocked his brow up and noticed the sudden change in the atmosphere.

"What's the word?" Sebastian studied Jack under x-ray vision. He knew something had gone terribly wrong from the time he walked out and walked back in the apartment. He sent that looked twice tonight and it was the cause of woman that could only get Jack into his demon mode. He prayed that he wasn't going to beat the shit out of these jackals.

"Never mind that, what happened? Where's Kaleigh?" he asked in soft tone that would not further anger Jack.

As soon as the words left his mouth, Kaleigh came through and Jack heard her gasp. He turned around to and stared at her coldly. He shifted his glance to his friend and he knew not to ask any more questions about Kaleigh.

"What's going on?" she asked, walking past Jack to the two strangers. She knelt next to Howard, the man she danced with at The Temptation, as both of the thugs heads lowered, ashamed that they chose of life of crime. "What happened?" she asked Sebastian.

Jack couldn't blame the woman if she didn't want to speak to him. He did insult her earlier and it wasn't one of his proud moments. Still, it pissed him off that she didn't have the nerve to ask him when he was standing behind her.

Sebastian cleared his throat. "Don't worry; head wounds bleed a lot. But they decided to help us find Susan, didn't you boys?"

They didn't say anything. Their heads still lowered in shame for this woman they would normally not give an ounce of respect to.

Jack felt pity for them. The first time he saw Kaleigh he wanted to lower his head to until he discovered that she was his. And he still would after death. Nothing could change that. No god or demon could take that pleasure out of him. Death would be the only thing that could separate him from her, but only physically.

"How?" she asked, asking once again to Sebastian.

It was really starting to piss Jack off. He wanted to grab her and shake her senseless and then make love to her until neither one of them could muster the strength to move.

"They are going to bring us to their employer. And in return they going to live another day."

Kaleigh turned her attention to the two thugs and calmly asked, "Did you find what you were looking for?"

"The tape?" Howard asked. Kaleigh nodded her head. "No."

"We looked all over for it. It's not here," Jack spoke up from behind Kaleigh and startled her. She wouldn't turn around and face him. She straightened her back and lifted her chin.

"It has to be here somewhere," she said.

"Well, it's not. Sebastian and I tore this place apart as you can see, and haven't found shit yet." This time she turned to him and gave him a vicious, cold glare.

Jack's blood began pumping as she turned around. She was heating his loins and making his heart slam against his chest. He wanted to find the closest bed and have her legs wrapped around him so tight that it made him pump harder into her.

He ran his hand through his hair and tousled it at the front. He had a hard-on bigger than life and burning a hole through his jeans and he was mad as hell at her! He needed some control before he threw her over his shoulders and dragged her out like a caveman, like his father.

"When are we meeting them?" This question was directed to Sebastian.

"Thursday night at eight." He told him the meeting place which was behind an alley that Jack thought twice before he agreed to it.

"Well let's get these men on their merry way," Jack said.

Jack picked up Howard as Sebastian pulled out a switch blade and cut the towels that bound their wrists and ankles. When they were released, they rubbed their wrists and staggered as if they were drunk.

"You two behave." That was Sebastian signal for them to leave.

They left and didn't glance at Kaleigh, Jack, or Sebastian as the door slammed behind them.

"So what the hell is going on?" Sebastian asked.

Jack sat on the couch were the Howard had sat moments before and waved a hand at Kaleigh. "Ask her, she knows all the answers," he said sarcastically and vengeful.

"Go to hell Jack!" she said and then raced out of the door.

"Shit!" Jack went after her.

When he ran outside, the two thugs just entered the elevator. Kaleigh was pacing outside the apartment, her fist balled to her side, and angry lines were forming around her mouth. Jack was just glad that she didn't run.

He grabbed her elbow and she turned around so fast that Jack didn't have time to react to the exploding slap. Jack winced as his head shot to the right and he lost his grip on her. He reached for her again. Her hands shot up and pushed him against his chest. He didn't budge. He wrapped his hand around her wrists and steadfastly pulled her to his chest. She struggled against him and finally relaxed her head in the dip of his chest.

"Kaleigh, I'm sorry." He saw the tears and his heart clenched. He was a damn fool for hurting her. "I'm sorry."

"I don't understand, Jack," she whispered, effortlessly trying to push him away. "I'm trying. I really am."

He wrapped his arms around her waist, and said quickly, "I know."

"Did you ever stop and think what this is doing to me? Did ever think what the cost of losing you will do to me? I've lost you once before and it nearly killed me! I can't possibly go through that again, and I don't want to. I can't bear the thought that you're no longer going to be with me, to hold me, and to love me. I'm going to be alone in the world again and all I have are a few memories of us. I hate knowing that I'm going to be the one responsible for your death. Could you live with that Jack? Could you live knowing that you had to kill me?"

All of Jack's anger fled as her words bounced over and over again through his mind. He never stopped once to think what it was doing to Kaleigh. If he were in her shoes, he would be tearing up the city to find that miserable bastard so she wouldn't have to die by his hands. He was a complete bastard.

She wasn't fighting him anymore, but the tears broke his heart and he pulled her against his chest and held her as her tears soaked his shirt. "I'm sorry, Kaleigh," he whispered in her ear.

"You really hurt me, Jack," she breathed.

He held her tighter and rocked her. "I know and I'm sorry. And it hurts me more see you cry by me than by someone else. I won't hurt you ever again." He promised and then hugged her tenderly and kissed the top of her head. "I love you, Kaleigh, and I thought we were going to be together forever, but I guess forever is turning out sooner than I planned."

"Then we should make the best of it." He could feel her smile.

He lifted her chin and kissed her gently on her soft lips. "Are you hungry?"

She laughed and nodded.

The three of them found an all-night diner and binged on greasy hamburgers and french fries. They ate like it was their last meal and savored every bite to the fullest. They talked of old times together as Sebastian made a few adult humor jokes and had Kaleigh cramping at her sides. They were living in the past and present and not thinking of the future. None of them spoke of the guardian hunter or the continued search for Susan. This moment was for keepsakes that would live long in their lives.

They finished eating and left. Kaleigh had this nagging feeling since she left with Jack on Saturday like she forgotten something at her apartment. She didn't know what she could have possibly forgotten that was so important, but the voice in her head repeatedly told it was. Before they left the diner, Kaleigh mentioned that she needed to go back to her apartment.

Jack set his drink on the ring of water and cocked a brow. "What for?"

"I don't know," Kaleigh said. "I keep telling myself that I left something extremely important there."

"Do you think that's a wise decision?" Sebastian said.

Kaleigh shrugged. "Not really, but I have to see what I left. I promise I won't stay any longer than I have to. I'll be in and out."

The two men gave her an unwilling nod.

"I never got to tell you what I found at the mayor's house and Sebastian and I discovered that's really going to knock your socks off," Jack said as they rode to Kaleigh's apartment.

He told her of the pictures he found and what Sebastian discovered while they were sleeping.

"You mean Melissa and Susan were the same person? Like with you and Mark?" Kaleigh asked, almost disbelieving. "This is unbelievable! Why would they block out your and her faces?"

"Because they wanted you to get it right this time. Melissa—as your memory recalls her name—was dating McChandey before they came after you the first time. Susan—same person—married McChandey after she died the first time."

"Melissa never told me the man she was dating while living with me. I never even met the guy face to face, but I always had this feeling from Melissa told me about him that he wasn't exactly a good person. I now know who he is.

"The first time he tried to kill her he found that I was linked to her. I never let Melissa in, but they found her by pure luck," she said. "I connected with Susan and she was the only person who knew where I was at. How could I've been so blind? How could I have not seen that they were the same person?"

"Just like you couldn't recognize me," Jack said. "They wanted to make sure you could destroy a guardian hunter without giving away their existence."

They entered Kaleigh's apartment. It was dark and very cold. "They're still waiting for me. I can feel them here."

Kaleigh walked from her living room, down the hall, to her bedroom. She turned the light switch on and looked around. Something was out of order. She pinched her eyebrows together and frowned. She studied her bed and memories of her and Jack struggling together came back in a flash. She looked around everything and couldn't spot anything out of the ordinary, but something was definitely out of place.

Kaleigh bit down on thumb and studied hard and still found nothing wrong. It was as she was leaving her bedroom that she noticed something slightly amiss at her night stand. She remembered before she left that it got pushed away from the wall when her room got turned into wreck but the guardian hunter that was after them.

Now it was back to its original position. She never touched the night stand when she with Jack. She stared at it for a moment before she called to him.

Just as she was thinking about him and the night stand, Jack came into her bedroom and stood behind her. "What is it?"

"Wasn't my night stand pushed away from the wall?"

Jack cocked his head and studied the night stand. "Yes, it was. How did it get back like that?" Kaleigh shrugged her shoulders and walked over to the night stand. All her premonitions told her it was safe and a key that would help them find Susan.

She dropped to her knees and opened the small drawer and nothing was out of place. Her calendar/date organizer, a bottle of aspirin, a few pens, and a spy novel she was reading were all there. She looked inside the small cubby hole under the small drawer and found nothing that would cause her eyes to do a double take.

Jack came around to stand by her side as Kaleigh grabbed the back of the night stand to pull it away from the wall. "Here let me," and then pulled night stand from the wall with hand. Looking down behind the night stand, he chuckled.

"What?" Kaleigh asked amused.

"I think I found what they were looking for." Without kneeling, he reached behind and pulled out a small, black cassette tape. He tossed it from one hand to the other and handed it to Kaleigh. "Do you have a tape player?"

A gust of icy air ran through her body, making her shiver.

"Jack I don't want to stay here any longer. I keep getting these chills that are making me edgy. Let's listen to it at your place or on the way."

He grabbed her hand and led her out of her bedroom, and then told Sebastian, who was sitting down on her couch, that they found the tape and it was time to go.

"Why is the tape at your house?" Sebastian asked as he climbed into the Jeep.

"I don't know." It was her only answer.

Susan never visited Kaleigh's apartment and knew the answer now. But how in the hell did it get into her apartment if Susan never stepped a foot in there? Kaleigh shrugged to herself and thought some things are better left unknown.

"Well let's pop it in," Sebastian suggested.

Jack did.

A high-pierced screeched exploded from the speakers like a nail scrapping across a chalkboard. All three jumped. The tape went silent for two minutes. Another high-pitched screech came from the tape. Even though they were prepared, they jumped again as the goose bumps grew on top of each other. There was more silence. Then a deep, hoarse voice came into place. It was Mayor Devin McChandey.

"When are they expected?"

Another voice spoke. His was mellow, smooth and had an accent from the Middle East. "Two weeks from this Saturday at Creegan Lake. You'll recognize my boat by the naked mermaid painted on it. Then once the exchange is made, you'll have seven beautiful virgins you can fuck each night of the week"

"Your money has already been posted to your account as we speak, but only half. You'll get the other half when they are safely in my care."

"Good to do business with you Mr. McChandey or is it still Mayor McChandey?"

"Still Mayor McChandey. I plan to be that way for a long time. These idiots have no idea who they elected."

"I hope I never see you in the president seat."

"Why not?"

"Who else conducts good business as well as you?"

One last screech ended and the tape shot out from the player. Kaleigh yelped as she saw the tape flying to her chest. She ducked and the tape landed behind her.

"Are you all right?" Jack asked, turning quickly, and examining her.

They would have found this strange if they were normal beings walking the Earth, but they weren't, so therefore, it like it was a normal, everyday occurrence.

"Yes," Kaleigh said rubbing her chest. "They said everything except for the time."

"Well, I already know where everything is taking place and until then Sebastian and I are going to put a man to follow him until catch the bastard in action."

Kaleigh wanted to argue how unsafe that was, but she remembered she was sitting with a temperamental male that could crush Hercules in a fight and another man that was controlled and could make himself invincible. They were well taken care of, but while they are out playing detectives what was her part? Was she just to sit back and wait for the guardian hunter? What if he came to her while she wasn't with them? She prayed that it wouldn't have to come to that.

"You two just be careful."

"Don't worry, we will," Jack said.

Chapter Seventeen

It was after one in the morning when they reached Jack's apartment, and they were wide awake. They slept the previous day and had been awake for five or six hours. They needed their strength for the "just in case." Sebastian switched on the television and watched CNN in the recliner (where he was also going to sleep tonight) as Jack and Kaleigh headed for the bedroom. There was no denying where she was sleeping when Jack led her to his room, pulled her into his arms and kissed her breathlessly.

Their tongues came together like long lost lovers as they stripped away each other's clothes in a fury. He filled the palm of his hands with her breasts. They hardened instantly. He stroked and pinched them as she ran her hand up and down his spine. His cock nestled against her navel and it was hot, huge, and swollen for the desire to be between her thighs.

Jack deepened the kiss and made love to her mouth with such exquisite experience that it made Kaleigh wondered how many women Jack had kissed. Kaleigh felt a pain of jealously; a new emotion to her, and didn't like it. She pushed that obtrusive annoyance away. Jack was with her and no other.

Kaleigh felt daring and courageous and ran her hands up his back, stroked him down his spine and then circled them around to the hard plane of his chest. Her nails scraped over his nipples that grew hard from her touch. He sucked in his breath and kissed her harder. She lowered her hands in the brownish curls of his chest and slowly dipped it lower. She ran her finger down the patch of black crisp hair that arrowed down to the great length of him.

Jack didn't stop her exploration of his body and Kaleigh was excited. This was her chance to her learn his body. She wanted to explore every inch of him.

Taking a small step back, her gaze roamed from his heated blue eyes that were storming with passion and drifted down to his hard pectorals, lingered at his brown nipples that were hard. Her gaze went further down to his flat abdomen to his navel and the enormous length of his hard-on. Kaleigh's eyes flew up to meet his and parted her lips with a sigh. He was truly a magnificent man. She couldn't restrain herself another minute. She had to touch him or die.

Feeling braver and more wanton than ever in her life, she erased the space between them. She placed her palms flatly on his chest and ran her fingers through his brownish chest hair. Slowly, she ran a hand down his flat, hard stomach as she fearlessly gazed into Jack's eyes. Her fingers came into contact with the base of his cock, scraping the tip with her fingernail. Jack sucked in his breath and closed his eyes.

Kaleigh wanted to feel all of him. She circled him with her hand and stroked the long length of him from the base of his cock to his tightened balls. Kaleigh realized that Jack was holding his breath. Every muscle had tightened, bulged, and strained for the loss of control. Yet he didn't do anything but let her explore. He was staring at her like he wanted to throw her down on the floor where they stood.

With her free hand, she circled Jack's neck and kissed him like he had been kissing her before as her hand surrounding Jack's swollen cock stroked it up and down, testing him to see how long before she brought him to his knees. But as Kaleigh stroked him, she found pleasure in giving him pleasure. She wanted to do so much more for him. She wanted to learn every inch of his body and explore where she never explored before.

She kissed his stubby cheek, feathery kissing him on his jaw and down his chest. She dipped her head and kissed one of his pebble-hard nipples. She heard him suck in his breath and didn't release it until she was slowly going down on her knees, kissing him the whole way down.

Kaleigh licked around his navel. Jack groaned and then drove his hands into her hair. He fisted her hair around his fingers, straining for control of his body. She flicked out her tongue and tasted him. He was warm, vibrant, salty, and smelled of pure man power. She circled her tongue on the tip and felt the warm liquid moistening her lips. She nipped him on the inside of his thigh and Jack shudder.

"Do you like this?" she asked as her tongue came up and licked him to the base of his cock.

"You know damn well, I do," he said through clench teeth.

She fully took him in her mouth, swollen and harder than a brink wall, and suckled and licked him from the hilt to the top of his cock, and made love to him until he moaned her name. He gripped her head, setting her at the pace he wanted her to go. Kaleigh sucked with each thrust as she cupped his balls in the palm of her hand and squeezed. Jack let out a guttural groan.

Before she knew, she was being pulled away by strong hands bruising her shoulders and then being tossed on the bed like a rag doll. Hot raging desire burned in Jack's eyes. Kaleigh briefly fantasized that she was in a meadow with the dire need to make him chase her. But she was in the bedroom, there was nowhere to run, and she laid flat on her back, submitting to him as he came between her already parted thighs.

He knelt between her and licked the inside of her thighs. It was the most thrilling experience Kaleigh could remember. He sucked and nipped and pushed her parted her thighs further for his entry. He kissed her between her silky, wet folds and Kaleigh arched up, wrapping her legs around him, feeling his heat. He pulled the bud that was covered by her black curls into his mouth, and kissed it as if were her mouth. She arched up further, screaming his name, digging her fingers into his scalp, begging for him to end the torment.

Jack caressed her breasts and pinched the nipples until they were as hard as his cock. Kaleigh moaned out loud.

Every second that went by, she was coming closer to exploding. She wanted him inside of her, hot, swollen, hard, and making love to her like it was their last night together. She wanted him making love to her like a man who was going to die and not like a man who had the rest of his life to make love to her. She wanted him now.

"Jack I want you inside me!" She couldn't believe the words came out and there was no way to take them back because they were true. She wanted him to grab the back of her head and pound into her. She wanted nothing to be held back.

Jack stopped what he was doing, and as if he read her mind, grabbed the back of her hair and tangled it around his long fingers. He settled between her thighs that were shaking on ecstasy.

He was on top of her now, his chest crashing down on hers. His silky chest hairs scraped across her breasts, enticing them further.

He was going to love her like she wanted to be loved. "Is this what you want?" He plunged into her tight, wetness. Kaleigh arched and moaned and screamed, "Yes," as her nails dug into his shoulders.

The only time Jack could ever really control his demon was when he was touching Kaleigh, kissing her, or buried deep inside of her. It was the only time the demon did not want to come out and join him in this pure bliss of heaven.

He felt sane, relaxed, and then so out of control that he couldn't believe she belonged to him.

None of the guardian hunters were ever going to touch her. He was one of them and he had to protect her. She belonged to him. Always had and always would. Nothing could ever compare.

Taking Kaleigh this wild and savagely, and to feel her hot velvet surrounding the length of him was more than he could stomach.

He shouldn't be doing this to her because he was no more a guardian and she was the one that would destroy him in the end.

Yet, if this demon inside of him could feel, it would know what good felt like. It would know what love could do to a man and it would know why evil never won.

"Spread your thighs further for me," he demanded as he began slow, deep strokes.

And she did.

Anything Jack asked for, Kaleigh would lovingly obliged it for him. He may have a demon living inside of him, but this was her Jack. *Hers.* Nor heaven or hell could take this forbidden love away from her. It was hers to keep.

Kaleigh felt Jack throbbing and hard all the way to her womb as she grinded her hips against his cock. She wanted him all the way inside of her, touching her soul, feeling him as if they were one.

Then she did the unthinkable. As he was deeply thrusting in her, Kaleigh titled her head back and then bit down on his shoulder. Jack stopped as the rush of her sting took over his body and made a part of the demon come out.

He could feel the demon storming through his veins as if it was commanding his troops into battle.

He couldn't believe she did that! He never asked that or her and would never ask her to do that! She would feel what he was feeling right now as the demon beckoned to come and play.

All he wanted from her was to accept her fate and love him like he loved her.

An organism so powerful and forceful shot through the core of her heart; Kaleigh screamed and clenched her thighs around Jack's waist as his blood entered through her spirit. She was connected with him and felt his every emotion beating within him.

Jack had to control the demon before Kaleigh could feel what it was like inside of him.

For a second a dark, deadly, dangerous emotion swept through Kaleigh and she pushed at Jack's chest to get away. He hugged around her waist and squeezed her. "Don't leave me, Kaleigh. Just give me a minute to control it."

She looked up Jack and saw his eyes were tightly shut and a vein pulsating at the temple of his head. Now she knew what he was feeling every time his eyes changed colors. How awful to feel such a noxious emotion.

Jack let out a gush of cold air against Kaleigh's throat. It made her breath an icy mist as she felt the ominous touch of the demon. He was fighting it hard and Kaleigh felt as if she should do something.

She reached up cupped his cheek and feather softly kissed his lips. Jack felt the demon silently burying itself deep inside of him. The demon couldn't fight the purity of Kaleigh's touch.

He could breathe again. He looked into Kaleigh's eyes and saw the warmth that was touching his heart.

"Thank you," he whispered against her mouth and than gave her the sweetest kiss she had ever felt in her life as his body regained to his normal self.

Kaleigh still wanted him more than ever. This proved she had control over Jack and proved that she had the power to defeat his demon.

"Make love to me, Jack. Make love to me as you were before."

Jack snapped, but not from the demon; it was his love that broke.

He gripped the headboard and began pounding into her savagely, roughly, as Kaleigh held on tight and met his every thrust.

"Oh, Jack," she whispered in his ears as her arms circled his neck and her legs tightly wrapped him. She arched to each hard thrust, pushing him further in her body, wanting to feel him all.

"I love you," she whispered louder as her body was trembling on the verge of her release.

Jack lost control of his body from her words and pounded into her until Kaleigh exploded with his name on her lips and Jack felt his release.

He sank between her neck and shoulder and cuddled her against his chest. He was breathing hard and sweating profusely. Kaleigh could feel his sweat drip through her hair onto her neck where it cascaded down her back.

Their breathing was the only thing that filled the void of the silence. Jack held her tight and then pushed her hair away from her neck and planted a soft, tender kiss.

"You didn't have to that, Kaleigh."

She felt the rhythm of his heart beating inside of her. She felt his soul and all the love he carried for her beat inside of her veins. She did the unexpected without thinking about it. She had connected with him without opening to him and it was the best she could offer him.

Kaleigh turned into his arms and was nose to nose with him. "I love you, Jack. If you're going to be leaving me, I'd rather feel you're lost than not feel you at all. Hold me, Jack," she whispered.

She placed her hands in his hands and fell asleep to the soft music and the beating of Jack's heart.

Chapter Eighteen

He didn't remember walking into the pit of hell. He didn't remember the demons being here a minute ago. He didn't remember the shadows of the darkness taunted him for his soul. The last thing he remembered was lying in a cold hotel room with the feeling that he was missing something.

Jack Pierce watched the demons circle his feet, begging for his soul and blood.

What was he doing earlier? Why was he at the hotel room? He had been coming here a lot lately to find the missing attribute of his life. He had been visiting here for the past two weeks after he woke up to find what was missing.

He didn't know what he was looking for. He did know, though, it was very important. It was a part of his life and something he couldn't live without.

What was it?

A small demon that was no older than a child, latched onto his boots and clawed at his legs.

"I want your soul," she cried.

He closed his eyes and kicked the little girl away from him. Another was there at his feet. "Give us your soul and we'll show you a life of power."

Jack was about to kick the boy back when his beeper went off and all the demons scurried away from him and covered their ears. He checked the number. 911 from the captain at the precinct. He needed to go, but what to do with all these demons? They couldn't be here when he left. What if someone walked in here and saw all these children, manipulated them into thinking they were starving and homeless. He had to get rid of them before they were found.

Just then, one jumped from the pile that had cowered in a corner and attacked him. He went down as the claws ripped through his chest. "Give me your soul," it cried.

"You'll never take my soul!"

"Oh, I will if you don't tell us where the pure soul is. Where is she?"

"I don't know," he shouted back at the demon.

The demon sunk its claw deeper into Jack's flesh, but he didn't give it the satisfaction of screaming for his life. Never had a demon attacked him. Never before he was taken down by one and yet here he was dying.

"Leave him," a new voice entered. "He's mine." The demon crawled off Jack and slithered back to the pile of demon children who were all bowing before the voice.

Then Jack was picked up. He didn't remember being touched or handled, but he was hanging in mid air waiting for the voice to take control of his soul.

"Jack," the voice ripped through his mind and he could only obey to listen to the seductive voice. "Where's our Kaleigh?"

"I don't know who you are talking about." Jack was slammed against a wall. He, the presence of the voice, climbed on top of him, breathing all over him.

"Don't play games with me, Jack. Where is she?"

"I don't know who you're talking about. Even if I did, I wouldn't tell you a fucking thing!" he spat.

Jack was thrown from one wall to another. He bounced in the air like a rag doll as the blood from his wounds splattered against everything he hit. The demon children were laughing at him, begging for their master to give him a painful death.

"Let us drink his blood," said the demon girl he kicked earlier.

As Jack was hanging in suspense, his beeper went off again. The children hollered and vanished from the corner they were hiding. But not the seductive voice; it was still here with Jack. He could still feel its breathing on his skin and the cold chill that ran through his blood.

"Tell me where's she's at, Jack, and I promise you, I'll spare you."

"Go to hell!" he screamed.

"Been there," he said as he laughed. "Tell me where's she at."

"I keep telling you, I don't know!" Jack dropped from the air and landed on his hands and knees.

The voice hovered over him and clamped down on Jack's head. "I'll find her myself." Jack felt the voice sucking everything out of his system. Memories of his parents, grandparents, Sebastian, and the only woman he ever loved. They were all gone from his memory as he sucked for information he didn't have.

The voice howled and Jack was thrown through the wall that connected to the bathroom. He shattered against the mirror and fell helplessly to the cold floor. He was lying on his stomach, wishing the pain would disappear and he could die. The guardian hunter had taken everything from his life and had no reason to live anymore.

He breathed in and out, waiting for death to arrive. He felt the cold chill of the voice enter the bathroom with him. "You're a worthless piece of guardian! You blocked her on purpose, didn't you?"

Jack gathered all of his last strength and shot him the finger. The voice laughed and kicked Jack on his back. "You'll pay for this," he whispered.

He saw the darkness descend upon him and held open arms for its embrace. But it never came. The darkness went away and he was left lying alone in a cold hotel room. Then why was Sebastian standing next to him, looking at him like he gone crazy?

He saw that the blood was gone from his body and he was whole, built like a new man.

Something disturbed Jack from the inside. Jack felt powerful, malicious, and like a god. It was his turn to rule the world and get rid of those who plan to suffer his mission. And here was his first victim; a warrior's soul. But Jack knew this man; he had been friends with for years. He couldn't attack him. But the voice in his head shouted for him to end this man's soul.

His friend reached out to touch him and Jack attacked like a corner dog. "You have lost your innocence and the morality of your soul will be judged by me!"

"This isn't me!" Jack shouted over the voice. "What has happened to me? The darkness; it has taken over my soul. I embraced it and it's here in me. I need help. Someone help me. My friend, help me! Someone in the good heavens, help me."

A flash of white light filled the small capacity of his room as he struggled to feign off his friend. A woman of beauty and grace appeared at his side and touched his face like he was child. Jack stilled and looked into the beauty of the blue eyes that held him captivated.

"You must remember that you have a soul to save, Jack. She's out there waiting for your return."

"I need help," he whispered. "It's in me."

She smiled. "Then you must control it for it is your destiny."

Jack awoke, catching his breath. It was still dark outside and sometime during the night, Kaleigh had crawled on top of him. It was like the first time they spent tonight in each other's arms.

He breathed in and out and lay back on his pillow. He gathered Kaleigh's tired body and hugged her tightly as he focused back on the dream. He hadn't had that dream for a while now. Why was he having it now?

Because he knew, he was getting closer to his death. He had to stay strong and focus on what the world would be like if he let the guardian hunter take over the world. There would be nothing but a vast endless darkness; a wasteland for dead souls and a world that once was.

The guardian hunter would not win. It hadn't won yet and it would not succeed.

It almost seems pointless going to their destination tonight. They had all they information they needed since they found the real tape. He could give it to two thugs and let them sort their own problem out.

No.

Sebastian and he made a promise to them by letting them go unharmed. It would very unwise to go back on their word. He was just going to have to convince Sebastian to make sure the fake tape got in Mr. Baker hands and the two thugs were as far away as possible.

Not only that, he had to stay here for Kaleigh. He was here to protect her just in case it should show up without him being here for her.

Kaleigh stirred in his arms and mumbled something in her sleep. He smiled to himself and held her tighter. If only they were in another life and he wouldn't have to worry what would become of Kaleigh once he'd gone.

Don't think about that right now. Think about the woman who's in your arms, sleeping peacefully as the morning sun is rising. Think about her blonde hair and the feel of its softness spread across your chest. Think about how rich, smooth her skin is. Think about her beautiful emerald eyes. Think about the way she smiles. And think about the way she laughs.

If Jack was glowing, he had every right. This was his woman, his fate, and he loved her more by the passing seconds.

He kissed the top of her head and then wrapped his arms tighter around her body.

Today was a new day and he wanted a million new days with her. He wanted to wake every day for the rest of his life like this and not wonder what the future held.

Last night he planted his seed in her womb and knew from the moment of his release that it took. She was with child and he would never know if it was going to be a boy or a girl or if it was going to be a sorcerer or a pure soul.

Whatever it may be, he hoped that it had her mother's eyes and smile.

Suddenly, a hand fisted around his heart as a splintering pain stabbed his brain. He carefully rolled away from Kaleigh. The pain hit him again, knocking him completely off the bed. His back hit the floor with a hard thump. His head bounced up and slammed down with such a force that it felt his bottom teeth jammed to the roof of his mouth. He sucked in his breath and strained his muscles to the full tautness of a stretch out string from the pain that affronted his body like ice needles pricking his skin.

Another series of sharp pains penetrated his body. Corded veins bunched down his throat, his back arched, his arms bent to the middle of his chest as his fingers—slightly curled—locked, and the heel of feet dug in the carpet. His eyes rolled backward. To keep from shouting his pain, he bit down on his tongue. Blood rushed down his throat, gagging him.

The macabre whispering voices began chanting at him. *Tell us of her soul. Tell us of her soul. Where are they hiding? Where are they hiding? Help Jack. Help us take the pure souls. Tell us where are they at. Tell us of her soul. Where are they hiding?*

Jack shook his head from side-to-side. Their haunting voices ripped through his mind, tearing at his inner soul, breaking the barriers of his conscious thoughts, and making him surrender to their calls. He wasn't going to give in to them. He rebuilt the barrier and just as quickly they tore it to pieces.

He wasn't going to give them what they wanted.

Darkness folded around him and a hundred red, beady eyes and black, crippling bodies with jagged, sharp fangs surrounded his vision. He tightly closed his eyes and they were there, too. Their slimy, grueling claws seductively caressed his skin. Jack sucked in his breath, concentrating only on the hellacious pain that was killing him. No thoughts of Kaleigh could enter his mind.

Tell us of her soul. We need them. Give us what we want. Your pain will die. Join us, Jack and feel the power that will fortified your strength.

Jack's mind raced. Images of Kaleigh's beautiful face, his parents' horrid death, and Sebastian sword flashed before him.

Sebastian. Help me.

The guardian hunter wasn't among the demons, but Jack could feel it controlling the demons. If it were, he would be calling Kaleigh to wake and perform her fate.

Jack heard the bedroom door crash against the wall and he sighed with relief. Never before had he been rendered this immobile by demons. He could fight them off, but with the contradicting elements that his mind possessed, he could easily open them to Kaleigh. And he was using the rest of his powers to shield Kaleigh from them.

The demons turned with a hiss of the new intruder as Jack lifted his head to see his friend under the threshold of the door, ready for battle. Their eyes glowed brightly, sending a mirage of red light streaming across the room and landing on Sebastian's tall frame. Sebastian smiled wickedly and gave them a quick nod.

The demons moved liquidly from Jack and crowded Sebastian, the tallest one reaching mid-level to the navel of his abdomen. Jack threw his head back and rapidly filled his lungs back with air. He was slowly gaining his strength back, slowly surfacing away from the demonic change to his norm. He breathed a quiet prayer and then weakly stretched his arms to the bed and hauled himself to his feet. His head was pounding, his body bending like a newborn baby deer.

Jack rubbed his face and then looked at Kaleigh. She was peacefully sleeping on her stomach. Her arms were bunched underneath her. The sheet wrapped around her waist, concealing her tender backside.

Good, he thought. She was safe. He turned, feeling his strength come back ten fold, and looked at his friend that was slicing and dicing the demons. Body parts flew in the air and quickly burst into dust.

Jack, feeling it was safe to use his powers, raised his right arm, spread his fingers wide, and threw a blue bolt of lightening at the throng of demons. About ten screamed, puncturing the eardrums of the two fighters, rattling the window, and then burst into the dust.

About fifty remained. Half of them turned towards Jack, flicked out their razor sharp claws and hissed. The voices were coming back. Jack blocked them out as much as he could while he concentrated on destroying the demons.

One jumped at him and his thoughts transferred to throwing the demon against the wall. It did, holding him place, and then Jack sucked the air from its body. It exploded as his other hand, throwing the lightening bolts raised the ceiling, calling the energized powers of lightening to the palm of his hand. A neon blue light balled in his hands and threw at the remaining demons. They shot backwards, howled, and exploded.

Sebastian had about five remaining. With one quick motion, his sword ran through the lot of them, cutting their heads from their bodies. Finally the room was free of demons.

Jack sank to his knees and buried his head in his hands. He felt Sebastian kneel beside him, not touching, just breathing and thinking the same thing as he.

"It won't be long," Jack whispered. "We don't have that much time. We need to find Susan's body and get this over with before I completely turn."

Sebastian was quite for a moment. "Yeah, I know. Are you going to tell Kaleigh?"

Jack shook his head. "I can't. I may only have a few days left with her. I don't want her to be afraid of me."

He helped Jack to his feet and sat him on the mattress. Kaleigh's body rolled slightly towards him. Sebastian stood in front of Jack and folded his arms cross his chest. The room was dark; therefore, Jack couldn't see his friend's expression.

"Why didn't she wake up?"

"There was no guardian hunter here, and so there was no point in waking her; I was shielding her. I have to keep her safe until I completely turn."

"Maybe you should go ahead and give in."

"No," Jack said shaking his head. "I can't."

He didn't know how much more his body or his mind could take the abuse conflicting sides pulling him back and forth.

"Get some sleep," Sebastian said, nudging him down the mattress. "You need rest."

Jack was out before he could band his arms around Kaleigh.

Kaleigh had this sudden, internal feeling that Jack was in trouble. She had to help him.

Her eyes opened and she was alone in the bed and very, very cold. Where was Jack and why was it so cold? She could see her breath fogging in the dark shadows of the night. The imprint of Jack's body was warm and smelled of him. As she closed her eyes she inhaled his scent and released it to the open room. Her eyes were still closed when something brush her hair. It whipped over her shoulders and landed over her breasts. The sheet she was holding to her chin fell to the bed and exposed her pink-tips to whoever was in the room. It wasn't darkness and it wasn't Jack.

The room got colder as the presence was determined to make Kaleigh feel like she was needed.

Moist, pruning hands swept over her slumped shoulders and slithered down her back and then back up to cup her face.

Kaleigh couldn't speak nor open her eyes. The sizzling effects of the woman's hands scorched her body like fire and ice. She rose slightly and the woman's hands covered Kaleigh's eyes and brushed her bosom against her back. Kaleigh stiffened and stopped breathing.

"Open you eyes, Kaleigh, and I'll show you a world were my body lies, waiting for you."

Kaleigh obeyed.

She opened her eyes and she wasn't in Jack's bedroom or in his apartment. She was in a dark, extremely cold bedroom that had once belonged to Susan. It smelled of lilies galore and it nearly gagged her to breathe. Kaleigh couldn't see anything, not even her breath that foamed before her. The sheet had come with her and she wrapped it around her like an oversize bath towel. She was still cold, shaking with chills, her teeth chattering, and her body numb from the cold.

Kaleigh took a step forward and the door burst open. Three men all dressed in black ski masks, sweaters, and pants, came rushing forward to Susan's sleeping body. She didn't cry out or struggle. She accepted it as it was and came willing with them. They didn't see Kaleigh's standing silhouette to Susan's bed. They treated her like she was a painting on the wall and didn't give her once-over.

They carried out her body and slammed the door behind them. Kaleigh closed her eyes and reopened them to find her standing outside a small wooden, white shack. The painting had been chipped in various placed and cracks were the foundation of the small shack. Overgrown trees of vast numbers surrounded the little shack with a pier connected from the rear to a lake. Next to the shack was a plain, white van that was dingy and covered with dirt and no markings. It belonged to the three masked men who abducted Susan.

Kaleigh froze when a scream pierced through the night and she was taken inside of the shack. Susan's body was strapped to a chair. Her hands were tied behind her back and legs tied around the legs of the wooden chair. She was completely naked, bleeding from her face and bruises discolored her skin.

Once again, Kaleigh was unnoticed as one of the three masked men beat her with his fists. Kaleigh's hands flew to her mouth. She wanted to call out for help, but remembered this was Susan's last memories of her tortured death and calling out for help would be ineffective.

Susan's head fell forward; her mass of hair covered her face, and the tears that shed behind it. She was crying silently to herself as the three masked men tortured her body, punching her, biting her, and molesting her.

They were asking her question she couldn't answer. *Where is she? What do you know?* A slap when she refused to answer. *Tell us where she's at? Tell us what you know?* One of the men kicked at her chair and she flew down, her face smashing against the cold, hard floor. Susan breathed in and out. In and out. *Where is the fucking tape?!* They screamed at her as the shortest of the three men came around and kicked her in the ribs. She cried out and still wouldn't answer their questions.

The tallest of the three knelt beside her and grabbed the back of her head and yanked her hair around his fist, bringing more tears to her face. With his free hand he cupped her breast and dug his dirty, blacken fingers nails deep into her tip. *Where's the tape? You think you can blackmail him and not get away from it?* He pulled harder on her hair until she screamed out from the pain. Kaleigh closed her eyes and heard another scream. She didn't want to open her eyes and be a witness to her death.

Susan's dead body was standing beside her, cocking her eyes at Kaleigh. "I'm sorry," Kaleigh whispered. "I'm so sorry." The short man kicked her in her ribs again.

The shack door flew open and in walked the Mayor of Houston. He was dressed in a full-length trench coat and a three-piece black suit underneath. Kaleigh could smell the expensive cologne, but it couldn't cover up his demonic soul. He was smiling, his bushy eyebrows lowered as he looked at his men. *Anything, yet?* He said in a cold, deep voice. The three men shook their heads and came to stand by their employer. Mayor Devin McChandey made a tsking sound and walked to his ex-wife. He knelt before her and kissed her tenderly on her brow. *Tell me where she's at, love. Tell me where the tape is at.* He asked in a calm voice.

Susan closed her eyes and then spat on his face. He pulled a handkerchief from the breast of his pocket and wiped the spit from his face. He turned his head to his men and Kaleigh got a good look at the mayor. He was handsome; he had the classy beauty of a movie star, and had an athletic build. Any woman would be happy to have him by her side, if he were a man and not a demon that exploited helpless young women.

Mayor Devin McChandey pulled out a small switchblade from his pants pocket and cut the rope from her wrists and legs. *Does that feel better, love?* She didn't answer him or move. She lay like a helpless animal, waiting to die. *I'm giving you one last chance. Where is she and where is the tape? I have a special coffin made just for you. You don't want to die, do you?* Susan sat up, her hands pushing the ground. She came to eye level with her ex-husband and sighed. *Forgive me Kaleigh.*

She spoke softly as the three men hauled her outside. Kaleigh blinked and she was with them. She noticed next to the white van was a parked black Mercedes. It was brand new. No dirt or dust settled upon it. It could only belong to one person.

All three men raped and beat her as the Mayor watched, with his hands folded and smiling, loving every minute of it. *This will all be over if you just tell me what I want to know.*

The middle man was the last to take his free ride and when he was through he zipped up his pants as the Mayor nudged her nearly-lifeless body. She slowly, grabbed his legs and rested her head against the bony part of his knees. She began to speak, but it was slow, spaced out, and inaudible. *The tape...is in my...night stand.* She told Mayor McChandey where Kaleigh lived and where she worked. Kaleigh for a brief moment felt betrayed and used. But they had beaten her, raped her, tortured her until her sanity ran out and giving them what they wanted was her only means to defend herself. Under the circumstances she wondered if she would have done the same thing. Though, Kaleigh had an advantaged that Susan didn't possess; she had the power to call upon others when she was in dire need of help. Susan didn't realize she had that option till it was too late.

Her head fell to his fine, leather Italian shoes. He kicked her off and she rolled to the box coffin he had made especially for her. The three men grabbed their guns from their holsters and pointed at her just in case she decided to jump at the last minute. Didn't they see clearly that this woman was beyond jumping to save her life? She couldn't even breathe properly and they expected her to attack them?

See what greed gets you? Cover her up boys and make sure that not a goddamned soul finds her! He grabbed his cell phone from his trench coat and pressed a button as he walked to the trees. *Mr. Baker, call Carlos and Howard...*

The three masked men dropped the lid of the coffin on Susan's slowly dying body. They grabbed shovels that were leaned against a large, rounded oak tree, and began dropping shovel loads of dirt on the homemade wooden coffin.

Kaleigh's eyes switched from the three masked men to the one man that would pay dearly for his crimes. He was talking low. *April 15 at nine p.m. at Creegan Lake and don't be fucking late. I need you there.*

Chapter Nineteen

Kaleigh closed her eyes and woke up in Jack's bedroom. It was early in the morning and she was alone. The imprint of his body was freshly made and then the connecting door of the bedroom opened and Jack walked out with a towel wrapped around his lean waist. Kaleigh felt her heart leap in her throat at the sight of his nude, wet body. She started growing warm between her thighs and quickly shook her head. This was no time to be thinking about sex. They had people to protect tonight and she just found the biggest piece to their missing puzzle.

Water beaded off his black, shiny hair, and his lips curved to a half-moon smile. He looked like a sex god standing in front of her and all she wanted to do was rip that towel off his body and make passionate love to him for hours.

She shook her head again. Did he know about her dream? Or was it even a dream last night?

"Where were you last night?"

He looked at her strangely like she had completely lost her mind. "I was here all night, Kaleigh. I just got up a few minutes ago to take a shower. You all right?"

She shook her head. "I know how Susan died. I know what they did to her."

He sat on the bed, shifting the mattress under her. "I know what they wanted from her and I know why."

"Tell me," he said as he touched her shoulder for support.

"I woke up last night and you weren't with me. The room was so dark and it was cold. I was so cold that I thought I froze. Then Susan was here with me and she told me to close my eyes and I did. I was at her apartment. It smelled of lilies and was a lot colder in her bedroom than yours. They came in and took her body. Then I was at this little shack in the woods. There was a body of water behind it with a short pier. I can't remember much of else because I was totally focused on what they were doing with Susan.

"I watched them as they brutally beat and raped her for information she withheld from them. It was so horrible. She was so much in pain and I couldn't do anything about it. All I could do was stand and watched as they beat her to death. I wanted to help, yell, do something, but I was totally oblivious to them. Then Mayor McChandey came in and took her outside and dumped her next to this giant hole that had a coffin built inside of it. All three of the men raped her, and I couldn't stop them.

"When the last one stopped, she told them where the tape was and where I lived. McChandey then called Mr. Baker, Carlos and Howard's employer, and told him to find the tape."

Jack rubbed his freshly shaven face and shook his head. "How do you know this?"

Kaleigh looked at him and bit her lower lip. "Don't you dream what I dream?" He nodded his head, but she noticed that he was holding back. "Then you should know."

"Kaleigh, you didn't dream that last night or else I would have known. I was here with you all night. I think I would have known if Susan had come into this room."

Kaleigh stiffened and moved away from him. "Are you saying that I'm lying?" She was furious.

"No!" he said defensively. "I'm not saying that at all. I just don't understand how it happened to you! I was with you the whole time, Kaleigh and if you didn't dream it than it must..." he trailed off lost in thoughts.

Kaleigh studied his face as if went pale. He looked as if he were trying to find words that would come out right. As he looked into her eyes he looked apologetic and worried, but not for himself...for her. He cupped her hands in his and closed on the empty the space that Kaleigh had made for them.

"What?" she whispered.

He shook his head. "Kaleigh what she did last night was inappropriate."

Kaleigh shook her head. "W—what," she stammered.

"She brought you in her world. You weren't supposed to go with her, Kaleigh. She tricked you."

She launched off the bed, the sheet wrapped tightly around her. "What the hell do you mean Jack? None of this makes sense!" she said waving her hands in the air.

He came off the bed, his towel slipping by the inches, but he didn't touch her. "She made you walk in the gates of her hell!"

"She wanted me to find her!"

"She wanted to use you!" He took a step closer to her. His voice wasn't screaming anymore, but Kaleigh detective a little anxiety. "She brought you into her world. You've overstep the boundaries of reality, Kaleigh. Do you realize what you have done? You crossed another dimension; the guardian hunter could have found you and taken your soul without a backward glance. She knew you wouldn't resist because after all, you were a good friend to her and you were looking for her. She used that against you. She was trying to bring you to them, while I was fighting my own demons."

"You were what?"

"But they thought I was too weak to protect you and that's why you are still here."

"What the hell are you talking about, Jack? You're speaking in riddles!"

Jack ran his hands through his wet hair. He gripped her under her shoulders and pulled her to stand in front of him. "Last night as you were sleeping, the demons came for me this time, but I didn't give in. They were using the demons to distract me, weaken me, while Susan pulled you into her world to give her the pure souls. But they didn't distract me; I used all my strength to protect you. They couldn't get what they wanted."

Kaleigh gasped. She blindly stumbled to the bed and slumped. She couldn't believe that her only friend before Jack would try to hurt her. She loved Susan like a sister and she betrayed their friendship for whatever reasons she had.

She rubbed her eyes and folded her hands in her lap to keep from biting her nails. "Why would Susan want to do this? I've never sensed anything ugly in her soul. It was because of her that I got to feel something beside the emptiness.

"Why would she do this to me?"

"I don't know. Maybe a guardian hunter offered her a deal to get vengeance and is using her against you. It's the only thing that makes sense. You did say they tortured her mercilessly. Vengeance is my only guess is to why she would betray your friendship."

Jack knelt next to her and pulled her hands into his. He tilted her chin up, making her look into his eyes. Kaleigh didn't want to, but with Jack, it was a losing battle. "We will find out the whole truth before it's over with, Kaleigh. We won't let those men go unpunished. In the end they will get their penitence and it will because of us. We will find Susan's body."

Kaleigh slid to the floor next to Jack. He cradled her head to his chest and rocked her as he rubbed her arms up and down. She really needed to be held and the only arms she wanted around her were his. He spoke the truth from his heart and made Kaleigh believe that everything in the end would be like her childhood dreams of a normal life. But nothing would ever be normal in her life and nothing would ever be complete without Jack.

They were quiet for a long time, caressing each other, and thinking of only each other. They felt each other's spirit and the worrisome died and grew only their love. It would be a short love, but a love that would last an eternity. Kaleigh thought of Jack's dying face and felt the pressure of the tears coming.

"Don't think about," Jack whispered.

"Jack, I'm scared."

He kissed her forehead and rubbed his hands up and down her arms. "Don't be. Everything is going to be fine."

"I don't want to lose you, Jack. I don't want to be alone anymore. I've been alone for so long that I made myself out to be this viscious, heartless person and I didn't like her. With you, I feel like that girl doesn't exist. I feel alive and…happy."

She heard Jack breathed in as he pulled her closer to his body. "Just remember, Kaleigh, I'll always be with you in life or death. We'll never part." She breathed in his soapy smell and relaxed against his body. "I love you, Kaleigh. Always have and always will."

They held each other for so long that Jack's hair completely dried and early afternoon sun broke through the mini blinds. Finally, Jack sat up, raising Kaleigh with him. He kissed her mouth and smiled into her eyes. "Go take a shower, get dressed, and I'll make us some breakfast. You'll feel better if you do."

Kaleigh did. She showered until the water turned cold. She fixed her hair, putting it in a black banana clip, and applied her make-up. Jack was right: she was feeling half-way better about herself. She dressed in a pair of hipster jeans and a sleeveless, midnight blue tank top. She tucked the shirt in her jeans and grabbed a black belt from her suitcase and looped it through and buckled it. She put on some white socks and a pair of black, narrow boots. Luckily she had skinny feet and they could endure the narrow tips of the boots. She was getting closer to feeling like herself.

The next two days passed quickly. Kaleigh and Jack learned a lot about each other's wants, likes, dislikes, and annoying habits. Kaleigh learned that Jack's private investigation business was prosperous, and he had hired a young girl straight out of high school to do his clerical work while he was away from his office, and that he was thinking about taking a partner because his workload was too much for him do his first responsibility to the world and his job, too, but things change

Kaleigh told him about her harsh childhood and how growing up with Gina was worse than fighting with the demons when she was alone in her room as a child.

"My mother used to ignore me for days," Kaleigh said as she snuggled up Jack late Wednesday night. "Sometimes, it would be a week before she spoke a word to me and it wasn't anything special. It was more like 'You're being too loud' or 'What day is it?'."

"I was so glad when I finally graduated high school and got the hell out of there. My first time away from home was paradise compared to her. I just wish she would have told me why she was ignoring me than treating me like some stranger living in her home. At least I know now, but the hurt is still there."

Jack kissed her on the forward and snuggled her closer to his heat. Kaleigh relaxed and Jack began telling her how sorcerers and warriors hunt the night to find demons.

"Because there are so few sorcerers in the world many of them stay blocked from the rest of the guardian saviors and connect with one warrior. At night they hunt together. They use the demons scent in the air to track their location, much like teleporting. We find the scent in the air that we need.

"Anyway, sometimes the demon scent is very weak and you would never know that you were passing a demon. Then sometimes the smell is so atrocious that you can barely breathe.

"When they find the demon and if it hasn't taken over the human yet, then the warrior destroys it. But if it has taken over the human body, then it is up to the sorcerer to pull the demon from the body so it can be destroyed. We try not to kill any humans that can be saved, but if they are too far gone with the demon's soul then the humans have to be destroyed."

"How can it be justified to kill them when it was the demon that put them in situation to begin with?" Kaleigh asked.

"The demon will use any means to capture a human soul for its strength, and they usually find humans that are totally set on the act of pure hatred. Then it's very easy for it to the let the demon inside. The humans we destroy are the ones murdering children and serial killers that the police can't catch. The humans that fight the demon inside of them are the ones that end up locked in a padded room."

Kaleigh ran her hand through the black crisp of Jack's chest hair and sighed. There were many deviant essences in the world, and it was easy to blame the demons for the responsibility of mankind's destruction on life. It was just hard to accept that the humans had no control over their own emotions. The guardians had plenty of control because they were born without any emotions. They had to gain their conscience through a human to feel anything, and if that human lacked the convictions to reside with normal human behavior then the guardian would disconnect with that human.

Jack told her earlier he'd connected with many humans to have the emotions of one. Kaleigh had only been connected to one and it was an experiment that forever lived in her heart. But, being connected with Jack, feeling his gentle spirit was the most wonderful thing that had ever happened to her.

What must he feeling from her?

Kaleigh felt the steady heartbeat pounding against her hand and more in her heart. He wasn't feeling any remorse for taking the lives of the defective humans. He felt serene and so did she, but only because she could feel it from him.

"What's troubling you?" Jack asked softly as he stroked her cheek with his knuckles.

"What do you feel from me, Jack?"

"Everything," he said with a small grin.

Kaleigh folded her hands under her chin and looked into Jack's eyes. In them she saw that he only spoke the truth. She reached up and cupped his face in the palm of her hands and kissed him softly on his chin. Jack wrapped his arms around her, pulled her to his mouth, and kissed her with all the love had for her. She kissed him back with the same devotion of their beating hearts.

Sebastian lounged in the recliner pretty much most of the Wednesday and Thursday, watching CNN or ESPN while Kaleigh and Jack spent their time alone. It was early in the afternoon when they came home from doing some grocery shopping and Sebastian was still flipping between CNN and ESPN. He did actually move to go take a shower and wore a pair of baggy jeans and a hunter green T-shirt that belonged to Jack. The clothes were very snug on him and the jeans (even though they were made to be baggy) appeared to be cutting off his circulation. He still wore his black loafers. Kaleigh wondered if he wearing Jack's underwear, too.

"Don't laugh. It was all I can find that will fit."

Jack dumped the groceries on the kitchen table. "You look like Joan Rivers's worst nightmare. Why didn't you come with us? I would have stopped by your hotel to pick up stuff."

"And miss this?" he said as he pointed the remote control to an elderly man of sixty with balding hair, and a wart so big on the left side of his nose that it literally covered his left nostril. He was talking about the decline of employment rates of the last ten years. But it was quickly switched to a black man talking about the latest gossip in the sports world.

"You're pathetic. I hope you're not wearing my underwear, too," Jack said as pulled out a loaf of bread from the brown paper bag.

Sebastian didn't answer. He cleared his throat and rolled his eyes to the television. "You're disgusting, Sebastian. When you're done with them, burn them. I don't want them back."

The rest of the day went by quickly. Sebastian continued to watch the two same channels over and over as Kaleigh and Jack acted like two teenagers in love. They kissed or touched each other whenever they passed. They made two stops in Jack's bedroom, leaving poor Sebastian to listen to their lovemaking. One time they heard something hit the bedroom wall and realized afterwards, Sebastian threw one of his loafers at the wall.

While Jack was taken his second shower for the day, Kaleigh sat on the sofa and began chatting to Sebastian.

"So what do you do for a living, Sebastian?"

"I'm a gigolo," he said with pride.

Kaleigh gasped. "What?"

Sebastian sighed. "You know, a male prostitute."

That was ironic. A man who despised woman was making a living giving them pleasure or…was it the other way around? Maybe he didn't make his living with woman, maybe it was with men.

It didn't matter. Sebastian sold his body for money, which in Kaleigh's book was degrading for a man or woman. But she wasn't going to be judgmental; she was going to understand why a man as intelligent as he was selling himself short.

"What did you think I was?"

"I don't know? A bounty hunter?"

Sebastian laughed. "Don't think I don't like what I do. I love it and it pays a hell of a lot more than catching idiot humans on the run. Besides, I'm very good at what I do," he said slanting his eyes at her.

Kaleigh glared at him. "Like I wanted to hear that."

"Hey," Sebastian said lifting his shoulders with a condescending smile. "I was just leaving it out there."

Her mouth dropped open and quickly looked away. What kind of friend was he to imply that he would sleep with his friend's lover?

Sebastian knew what he was doing and hopefully it worked. He wanted her to leave him the hell alone while he had this little time for himself. Sebastian had no interest in her whatsoever, but Jack would be gone soon…

He could never do that to Jack. What the hell was he thinking! Kaleigh was beautiful woman, but he hated everything about her because of what she was and had to do. It wasn't her fault; he understood that. Yet, he couldn't shake the feeling that Kaleigh adapted her fate to Jack's and that's why he hated her.

"How can you say that to me?"

"Just leave me alone, okay?"

Kaleigh nodded her head, understanding why he had told her that. He wasn't much of a conversationalist and didn't want to talk about himself. Sebastian was a door full of information but locked it so no one else could enter. What would happen if he did find that soul that could strip his guards and render him to his knees? Would he walk away from her or would he let his powers die for the devotion to be united with a love so grand it could kill him?

Knowing Sebastian these couple of days, she believed he wouldn't have to think about his morals if he came to that crossroad. He would choose the first one without any hesitation. Too afraid to let anyone get close to him because of his haunting past.

She didn't have to be a rocket scientist to figure out why Sebastian lashed out before anyone could get close to him. He was hurt and still hurting.

Though, it gave him no reason to treat her as if Jack was already dead. They had to come to an understanding for the sake of Jack.

"What do you do on your free time?"

Sebastian sighed and turned down the volume to the newscaster and was quoted a basketball players line of the day. "What did you ask?"

"I asked what did on your free time."

"Oh," he said. "I hunt demons."

Kaleigh shook her head. "That's not what I meant. Do you have any hobbies like read or build model airplanes?"

"What? This is what I do on my free time, when I have it. During the day, I'm all business and at night, I'm a demon slayer. What else is there in life?"

Kaleigh shrugged. "I don't know. Companionship?"

Sebastian laughed in her face. "Lady, that's a life for a dreamer. I'm a realistic and don't believe in fairy tales. I don't pine all day waiting for my Rapunzel to let down her hair."

"I wasn't talking about that. I was thinking more like friends to hang out with."

For a brief moment, coldness flickered in his eyes and his jaw tense. Kaleigh could hear his teeth grinding and it sent chills up her spine. He snapped his teeth together and turned the volume up. That was her cue to leave him alone. And she did. So much for trying to get mutual respect. Wasn't there anything that didn't set this man off?

She wanted to know who this woman was that had hurt this man so badly that it made him distrust women and left the sadness in his eyes. He was a very attractive man, smart, and had a sense of humor, but there was no kindness to him. He did everything because he had to, not because he wanted to and not because he cared. He had spent most of his life doing what he had to do for survival. There had been love shown for him and he never showed towards another person. The woman that betrayed him scarred his heart for life and it was a question if he ever would find his soul mate.

For such a strong, bountiful man he was sure was a lonely man in desperate need of attention. But a dog could only take so many kicks before he attacked. Sebastian spent his life being isolated from others because he was scared of being attacked by those that got close to him.

Not Jack. That was one person Sebastian could trust and hold on to.

She didn't mean to analyze him, but that was a weakness of hers. Every person she met she had to dissect their brains and find out what kind person he or she was.

Funny, she thought. She never tried to dissect Susan or Melissa. It was like she already knew her and didn't have to judge.

Kaleigh went into the kitchen and started making dinner. She pulled a large, black pot from the lower cabinets of the kitchen and filled it with water and placed it on the stove to boil. She heard Jack getting out of the shower as she grabbed the spaghetti from the pantry. She smiled to herself at the thought that he was clean, shaved, and hers.

Her heart turned over when he wrapped his strong arms around her waist. He kissed her on the cheek and whispered love words in her ears. Kaleigh laughed and slapped his hands away. They water began to boil and she tossed the noodles in and stirred.

Jack left the kitchen to join Sebastian. She overheard them talking about tonight. They had two hours before they left to meet this Mr. Baker. Kaleigh eavesdropped as she continued to the stir the noodles. Jack was telling him what he had told her earlier about her coming with him. She knew Sebastian was going to reject the idea, but if Jack thought it was necessary then he wouldn't reject the idea.

She opened the can of spaghetti sauce and dumped it into another smaller pot and listen as Sebastian tried to rationalize the danger of Kaleigh going. Jack reminded him that Kaleigh couldn't be by herself due to the fact that he was a target for the guardian hunter and all three needed to be together at all times. She heard Sebastian sigh and finally give in. He knew it was the best for them.

Jack was right about the guardian hunter: he could come at any minute and take his soul, and if all three weren't together than that meant the guardian hunter was a loose target for destruction.

He came into the kitchen and dipped his finger into the sauce. "Taste just the way mama used to make it," he said giving her the thumbs up that everything was set for tonight.

Chapter Twenty

"Sorry about the delay, Mr. Baker," Carlos said. "It wasn't where the bitch said it would be."

"Pity," Mr. Baker said more to himself than the two thugs, who were sweating for their futures.

Carlos and Tony were right about the Mr. Baker, he was a man to be feared. Jack got cold vibes by the relentless behavior of Mr. Baker immoral soul. He could smell hate and greed lusting from the breath that disturbed the warm, peaceful night.

They were parked twenty feet from where Mr. Baker and his employees were parked on a vacant street with only the shadows of the trees protecting their existence.

"He's a demon," he whispered to Sebastian.

"Yeah, I can see through his shades that his eyes are red and the stench in the air."

"We need to hurry up and get those boys out of there before they end of up dead."

"Do you think he'll kill them?" Kaleigh spoke from the backseat.

"If it doesn't suspect anything is foul, then it'll let them go, but one false move, then I fear for them."

Kaleigh threw her hands up. "I don't want to know anymore," she whispered.

Jack pressed the small earpiece deeper inside of his ear and listened as the two thugs and the demon discussed their bargain. It was Jack's idea to let Carlos wear a wire; he had the excess weight to steal away an extra package.

"I hope there wasn't any trouble finding it," Mr. Baker's smoothly said, "because if there was, I hope you took care of the problem."

Jack saw both of the men shake their heads. "There wasn't no problem, Mr. Baker. It just took us a little longer to find it—that's all," Carlos said, shrugging his shoulders.

Mr. Baker rubbed his hands together and folded them in his lap. He smiled and when he did, Sebastian gasped.

"Oh, sh...er...crap," Sebastian gasped. "Just what we need, a freaking bloodsucking vampire. Let's get those boys out of there now, Jack." Sebastian reached for his sword that was sitting next to Kaleigh. "I don't think he's going to let them go."

"Stay in the car, Kaleigh. If were not back in twenty minutes, call Captain John Foster, my ex-captain and give him the tape and tell him everything. Got it?"

Kaleigh shook her head. "No! You think there's a possibility you won't be coming back?"

Jack laughed. "Oh, we'll be back, but I'm saying just in case."

Then he and Sebastian jumped out of the car and slammed the door behind him. Jack opened the passenger back door, grabbed Kaleigh's upper arms, crushed her against his chest, and kissed her hard on the mouth and was gone before she knew it.

They walked silently to the car, not making any sounds with their shoes. They walked like two deadly lions spotting their prey. Jack walked to the left as Sebastian rounded to the right. Jack could hear from his earpiece that Mr. Baker was becoming thirsty for blood, and quickened his pace.

"Good," Mr. Baker said. "Because if there was, I'd have to kill you." He paused "But I think I will anyway for making me wait almost a goddamn week!" The thugs stepped back, but not quick enough.

The demon reached for Carlos's throat and ripped it completely out. Veins and skin dangled from his hands. Howard was too frozen to scream or move. He stood entranced by the gruesome scene he just witnessed.

Carlos body dropped to the ground as the demon exploded from the car and dropped on his feet on the ground like a graceful feline. He bared his fangs and threw off the black shades, crushing them under his booted foot as he charged for Howard

"Run!" Sebastian screamed to Howard, who was still paralyzed with fear. The demon looked back and laughed.

Jack and Sebastian stopped dead in their tracks, no more than five feet from the demon.

The demon shrugged off his black, leather jacket and exposed his pulsating veins that etched in his liquid skin. The demon's eyes grew redder as his fangs grew longer. "What do we have here? Guardians?" He laughed. "I will enjoy sucking the strength of your blood!"

He charged at them as Jack pulled out his gun from his waist and Sebastian drew his sword like a warrior ready for final battle.

Jack's gun exploded and the demon jumped over them in one bounce. They turned around and it wasn't in sight. But they both knew it was still here. They could smell its scent in the air and feel his presence as if it were standing next to them.

As Jack and Sebastian waited for the demon to return, Kaleigh watched spellbound the ominous vision that infiltrated her mind. She covered her mouth with her hand and closed her eyes when Carlos's throat was ripped out. She never saw a more horrific death than the one that plagued her tonight.

A cold, frightened expression was painted on Carlos face the moment the demon claws sanctioned his throat. She felt endless hope for him and wished she could have been there to comfort his death.

Her mind whirled with blood lost and the enemy that lusted after her. She feared that she wouldn't have the strength to destroy Jack when the final time came. She feared she would fail and compromise her mission to the ones that live to torment their souls.

She wished she had the faith Jack did. She wished she didn't lack her faith in the world and to her maker. She wanted to have the faith, but it seemed impossible when the fate of the world lay in her hands! She was never a strong person. She never had the faith like the other guardian saviors.

Kaleigh would have to think about giving her life to save the world; unlike Jack took it like a command from his general; ask no question and do what you're told. Kaleigh would have a billion questions to ask because she couldn't judge her fate by just one person.

She wasn't going to fail. She was going to do what she had to do and when this whole mess is over she was going to make her own destiny in this world.

She was going to move far away from this city (possibly country) and live alone to be alone, while doing her duty for mankind. She was going to have her own life that didn't consist of killing the love of her life.

With their weapons drawn, they breathed and search all around the perimeter of the small, dampen alley. Jack could use his elemental force to destroy the demon, but he was saving most of his strength for Saturday. He knew he would need it. For now he was going to his guns, their bullets were blessed by his blood and were poison to any demon., including bloodsucking ones.

God, Jack hated vampires. They were harder to control than most demons because they had an ego the size of Texas. It was hard to bend them to a guardian's will and that's why most protectors brought a weapon with them blessed by their blood just in case they encountered a vampire.

Jack felt his hair stand up on the back of his neck and quickly turned around and pulled the trigger of the gun. They demon laughed as he took three more bullets to the chest. He wiped the blood that trickled running from on the bullet holes. "Your weapon is pathetic. It's a pity you didn't bring that luscious woman with you. She's a real beauty. I think after I kill you, I might fancy myself in showing her what a real man is like." He laughed again, but he didn't see what Jack saw.

Jack smiled. "I think you're not her type."

The demon shrugged his shoulders. "Oh, I'm every woman's type."

A gush of blood came spurted out of the demon's mouth. Mr. Baker clutched the sword that was pierced through his heart and pulled it forward as he kicked his leg back at Sebastian. Sebastian fell backwards, taking his sword with him, and dropping the sword as he fell. The sword was quickly replaced in his hands, but wasn't quick enough to get up. The demon kicked his ribs two times and flew in the air like a bat into the night and came rushing towards them with his fist leading him down. The pavement split under his fist. Sebastian was already on his feet.

Jack used the rest of his bullets, shooting him everywhere he aimed at. He dropped the empty clip, reloaded and started shooting again as Sebastian thrust his mighty sword through the middle of his chest, twisted it in the demon's heart, and quickly removed it.

The demon lay still. He didn't explode or liquefy and that meant it was still alive.

With caution, they walked to the demon and hovered over him, looking down at him. Jack had his gun pointed at the middle of its forehead as the tip of Sebastian sword was held under its chin.

The demon was covered in blood. His clothes were literally shredded off of him, and his breathing had stopped. He looked dead, but looks could be deceiving. They waited another minute.

The demon's arm shot up.

Jack shot him where he aimed as Sebastian sword punctured his throat, literally decapitating it. The demon screamed and evaporated into a puddle of gooey substance.

The two men sighed and looked at each other in silence. Sebastian was the first to speak. "It was pretty strong."

"Let's head back. I don't want to leave Kaleigh alone any longer than I have to."

They rushed back to the jeep and realized that Howard must have hightailed out of there for he was nowhere in sight. They stopped next to Carlos's nearly decapitated head and winced.

"Shit. We can't just leave out here, Sebastian. What the hell are we going to do with him?"

Sebastian reached down and picked up the demon's leather, black jacket and covered Carlos. "What do you suggest? That we load him up in the car and drive him to the morgue?"

"Hell, no! But we can't leave him here!"

"I hear sirens; the cops will be here any minute. Let them deal with. Right now we need to the get the hell out of here."

Sebastian was right. Jack was feeling guilty because they weren't there in time to save him. He quickly pushed back the guilt. He didn't need any self-loathing that would jeopardize their mission. He had to stay strong for Kaleigh, Susan, and Sebastian. They needed him and he needed them. It would pointless to mourn about a thug whose life was only known to street crime and had a reckless history of violence. But, Jack could scarcely shake off the feeling that he came here to protect him from being endangered. He felt as if he failed.

He felt the darkness drifted towards him. The high-powered shadows circled his body and began taking their claim on his soul. Jack felt small, useless, and totally in the demand of the shadows.

NO! He screamed to himself. He couldn't let Kaleigh know yet.

He ran his hand through his hair and heard the sirens coming closer as they paid their last respects for Carlos. "Come on let's go."

As they were driving down the road, Jack and Sebastian didn't say much. They were sweaty, smelled of the outside air and musky deodorant. They appeared calm as a drifting feather, but inside they were anything but calm. The tension was so strong it could have been cut with a knife. Their inner souls were feeble and lost, trying to rebuild their inner tranquility to a place where darkness could not hold them.

Kaleigh unbuckled her seatbelt and kissed Jack softly on his cheek and whispered her love in his ear. All the darkness was gone for now. She touched Sebastian's shoulder and gave him a warm smile of affection.

The tension was obliterated and their souls rapidly began to build to high self-esteem. It wasn't their time to come across the guardian hunter. They weren't ready and she wasn't ready. They had to find Susan and expose the mayor for what he was.

She clicked her seatbelt back and listened to the hum of the engine and quiet breathing of the two men that were relaxed. They were safe.

Kaleigh opened her eyes with a fright. Jack was having a nightmare about his run with a guardian hunter five years ago. It was gruesome and painful to watch.

Since she had connected with him, she had felt every emotion he put towards her and his task, and every hunger pain, love pain, and emotional pain he felt. Together they were one person, one heart. Together they shared dreams and awakening fears. Together they lived and breathed for the future of their fate and together they made harmonious bliss.

Kaleigh sprawled her hands over his chest and listened to his heart beating. It was soft and slow. She ran her fingers through the dark patch of his hair and snuggled closer to him. He smelled like soap, minty toothpaste, and arousal. She lowered her hands down to his flat abdomen and kissed his chin as her left leg overlapped his right. She kissed higher on his chin till her mouth reached his and planted a soft butterfly kiss on his lips.

Her hands dipped lower and found him fully aroused and ready. She circled her hands around his engorged shaft and stroked the length of him. She heard him moan and captured his opened mouth with hers. She cupped his face and kissed him lovingly and with every unbelievable emotion that was making her heart beat faster and her soul soar higher through the clouds.

His arms came around her, stroking her back like a cat. He then cupped her bottom, rose her, settling her on his cock. Kaleigh moaned and kissed him even harder. He moved her hips back and forth, giving her the rhythm he wanted. She arched up and ran her hands on his inner thighs until she had his sac firmly in her hand. She heard him catch his breath and completely stop breathing. She fondled more provokingly, filling her hand as she continued to move in her slow, seductive dance.

He reached up and captured her breasts in his hands and squeezed them, twirling her nipples between his forefinger and thumb. They were already hard, but the aching increased. He dipped his head and took one nipple in his mouth and suckled, nipped, and kissed.

Kaleigh was crying out at the pure ecstasy that was throbbing between her thighs. She parted her thighs further and pushed him deeper inside of her, filling her to her womb. She lowered herself to his mouth, taking him, drinking him as if she couldn't get enough of him.

Then her world exploded, followed by his release.

Much later, she lay on his chest, playing with his chest hair, thinking how she would love to have his babe. She knew she was carrying; she felt it the other night when their lovemaking was frantic, wild, and unlike anything she ever felt before. She blushed a deep red when she remembered the words she spoke to him. Never before had she ever used such foul language in her life. But her climax was demanding hard, pounding sex and wouldn't settle for anything less. But the after-effect got her pregnant and she had been glowing ever since.

She knew Jack knew, but he hadn't mentioned it to her yet. If she could feel everything about his body than he could feel that she was carrying his babe.

She kissed his chest and cleared her throat. "You know, don't you, Jack?"

He tightened his grip around her waist and pulled her to his face. He kissed the tip of her nose and smiled. "Of course I know. I love you, Kaleigh." He kissed her sweetly and closed his eyes.

"I love you too," she whispered and then closed her eyes and instantly fell asleep.

Chapter Twenty-One

Kaleigh went into the kitchen and Jack had a plate of buttermilk pancakes waiting for her. Sebastian was at the head of the kitchen table as well, with Jack sitting in the middle. They were both chomping down on the pancakes, like they hadn't eaten in a week. Jack was wearing another black T-shirt and another pair of jeans. He wore the same Nike tennis shoes. His hair was tousled in front like it was suppose to be combed that way, but it only made Kaleigh's heart swell more.

Sebastian was wearing some more of Jack's clothes: another pair of baggy jeans and a very blue Hawaiian shirt that had parrots and palm trees plastered everywhere. The Hawaiian shirt was tight under his armpits and it lifted whenever he took a bite of his breakfast. He still wore his loafers. He looked like a Don Johnson replica from Miami Vice. All he needed was the shades and to be sockless. She wanted to laugh.

She took her seat at the other of the table before she poured herself a cup of coffee. She noticed that Jack had been reading *The Chronicle* and on the front cover was Mayor McChandey's bright smile. The headline was something about a new proposal of construction for Houston.

Kaleigh forked a bite and asked after she swallowed. "So what are we going to do for tomorrow night?"

Jack pushed his plate away from him. "We're," as referring to Sebastian and him, "going to be waiting for the Mayor exactly where he said he's going to be at."

"You don't think Susan set the whole thing up to confuse us, do you?" Kaleigh asked.

Jack shook his head. "No, he's going to be there. Everything she showed you was the truth, but just in case I have a man watching every step he takes."

"Who?"

"A warrior that Jack knows," Sebastian said after he swallowed a mouthful of pancakes.

Kaleigh watched Sebastian fork in another mouthful of pancakes and completely lost her appetite. How can someone with such moral duty to the world eat like a pig?

"Didn't your mother teach you any kinds of manners? It's rude to eat with your mouth full." Kaleigh said shielding her eyes from eat habits.

After they finished their breakfast, Sebastian returned back to his CNN and ESPN as Kaleigh and Jack remained each other's shadows.

In the middle of the afternoon, Jack's cell phone rang for the first time in almost a week. He used his cell phone primarily as his business phone, and hesitated to answer it at first. When he saw the number flashing on the screen, he knew he had to take the phone call.

"Hello," he said in hoarse voice.

"Mr. Pierce, you should get better security."

Jack gripped the phone so tight that his knuckles showed white. "What the hell did you do?" Sebastian and Kaleigh stalked next to him.

"Let's just say your friend is resting with Mr. Baker. You killed one of my men—a very close and dear friend—and I killed one of yours. So now we're even."

"You asshole!"

"Let's not swear, Mr. Pierce, it's so unbecoming of your behavior. Besides you don't want to do anything stupid do you? What'll happen to that pretty lady if you weren't thinking of your actions?"

Jack deeply sighed. He knew what would happen if he let his emotions get out of control. He shook his head feverishly and said a stream of curse words instead of lashing out on the poor furniture.

"Mr. Pierce, I'm disappointed in you! From my understanding, you're the All-American Boy Scout, and you don't want me to get the wrong impression of you."

"You can go to hell."

"Been there, done that. I'm free to wander and I happen to like it here. Your kind are so weak and foolish that I can probably take over this country in a matter of months."

"That's not going to happen!"

"I think it will happen. Actually, I'm counting on it, and there's no way you can stop me."

"Oh, I can stop you."

"No, Mr. Pierce, there's where you're wrong. I have all the power to stop you and you have nothing, but a pure soul scared of her shadow an overzealous bully that will probably die before he can help. Come tomorrow night if you think you can stop me! Come and let me see you grow weak before me. I want to see you groveling before the hands of my master! Come, Mr. Pierce, if you think you have an ounce of strength to stop me—to stop us. You know the time and the place. Oh, before I let you, if I see one sign of police all the women will die. Good day." The phone went dead on the other end.

"Shit! Shit, shit, shit!" Jack yelled as he threw the phone across the room, but it didn't break; only cracked it a bit.

"What the hell was that all about, Jack?" Sebastian protested.

Jack ran his hands through his hair. "The mayor; he's the guardian hunter that has been taunting us. He knows we're coming tomorrow night. He killed the warrior I had watching him. Shit."

"Calm down, Jack. You're starting to act like me, and that's not a good sign. All we need to do is come up with a plan and take him off guard. Do you still know anybody on the force that will help us?"

Jack nodded his head. "But what good is it going to do? If he thinks the cops are on to him, he's going to kill all the women. And he will. At least he can't kill us. No, I'm going to bring the cops into this until everything is over with."

Sebastian laughed. "That's easy for you to say, Jack. He can't kill you or Kaleigh without a struggle, but he sure as hell can kill me without a backward glance."

Jack cursed under his breath. Sebastian was right: All the demons in the world could kill Sebastian without a glance. They, however, could not kill him or Kaleigh. They were to be kept alive for the guardian hunter. Jack realized this was they what they wanted from the start, even five years ago when Kaleigh and he first met. Melissa/Susan and McChandey were to bring them together to complete the finalist of the guardian hunter conquest of the world.

It was perfectly laid out and they fell in the trap like blind men.

Though, if they came up with a half-way decent plan, they could save the young girls and destroy McChandey at the same time, and only have to deal with it. Dealing with the guardian hunter would be easy, but dealing with McChandey (and considering how many men he had with him) it would a great interference. Jack had a remedy to fix that problem.

His main plan was to get the girls to safety and take out McChandey and his business partner, who still remained nameless.

But they were going to Creegan Lake, a place where McChandey's business partner could dock and carry on business transactions without getting the coastal guards involved or any other higher authorities' brows raised.

It was the perfect place to sell and buy illegal immigrants without getting caught.

Damn him!

They needed a plan: A good, fast plan.

They spent the rest of the day and most of Saturday coming up with a good enough plan to take down the mayor and his goons. Finally around seven at night, everything was set up and hopefully everything would go as planned.

Kaleigh baked frozen lasagna, but none of them really had the appetite to eat. Kaleigh picked at her food as Jack and Sebastian only ate about half on their plate. She cleaned up as Jack and Sebastian gathered all of the gadgets and equipment in the living room. She was in the bedroom, just looking around, for she knew tonight would be the last night that she and Jack would spend together.

The guardian hunter was going to be there with them tonight and it was all Kaleigh could do to keep her depression from escalating in the opening.

She lay half-way on the bed, with her bottom slightly off the mattress. She made the bed earlier and couldn't fathom the reason why she even bothered. Jack would never be coming back here again and it was pointless task, but something Kaleigh enjoyed doing for him. He was still a bachelor at heart and needed someone to pick up after him

She sighed and embraced his scent of the sheets. They smelled of laundry soap and Jack's masculine smell. She rolled over to her stomach and reached for his pillow. She hugged it with all her strength and decided that this one piece of furniture that was coming with her, whether or not she had to break in his house to get it.

Her mind drifted to the past days. Jack and she really got to know each other's body, habits, and mood swings. They discuss little of each other's past for it was about the same for both of them. The growing pains and the differences between their lives and the normality of the other children's was a topic best left for a journal. They didn't discuss ex-boyfriends or girlfriends or lovers. They were in tune to each other and only thought of the present.

She also noticed that since she connected with Jack that the guardian hunter had not visited her. It was like it disappeared from the world and let them alone for their comfort. But she knew that wasn't what it was thinking. It let them alone for a very good and selfish reason. For when the time came it was going to use all their weaknesses to confuse, manipulate, and destroy them until one of them gave up and he won.

She heard Jack's footfalls behind her. She stayed as she was.

"You look beautiful like that. Too bad I don't have a camera; you're in a nice pose."

She threw the pillow at him and he came after her. She shot up and leaped to the middle of the bed. He jumped beside her and pulled her underneath him. He captured her wrists and brought them above her head. He dipped his head and captured her mouth. "I love you so much, Kaleigh." He kissed her again and then began stripping her clothes off one by one. "I love you, love you, love, love you." He kissed her deeply, wildly, and passionately.

This was their last night together and they only had forty minutes to spare, but they were going to expand it to an eternity. They were going to savor the ecstasy and the wanton desire of each other's ache. They were going to explore every inch of their bodies and make tonight's memories last until death and cherish this small piece of heaven and forget about what was to become of the night. This hour was theirs and theirs alone. They were going to use as their pleasure demanded it.

When they were both dressed, it was time to go. Jack and Sebastian loaded everything up in his jeep as Kaleigh took one last look in the apartment and mentally blew a kiss for the memories that would be forever saved in her mind. She shut the door behind her and followed Jack and Sebastian to the jeep.

Tonight would end the worst fate of evil and tomorrow the day would be safer. To Kaleigh it was going to be lonelier and colder, but at least she wouldn't have to live in fear anymore. She could begin her duties to the world without fear.

Trust your fate, Kaleigh. The voice of the pure soul appeared in thin air. Kaleigh listened and finally understood what her fate, Jack's fate, and Sebastian's fate, meant to the world. It was up to them to stop the evil from uprising and to balance the world.

Well they were going to make sure evil did not take over. The fate of the world relied on them and only them: The Pure Soul. The Sorcerer's Soul. The Warrior's Soul.

For the first time in days, clouds had moved in and a 20-mile-per-hour wind pushed through from the north. The forecast say the front wouldn't be coming in till next Wednesday. Well, it came earlier and from the looks of the dark grey clouds, it was going to be a mother of a storm.

Drops of rain sprinkled on them as they drove out of Houston. The trio was quiet on their ride, like so many other rides. Jack steadfastly looked in this rearview mirror to take quick peeks at Kaleigh. She noticed, and would flash him a smile, letting him know that she was going to do what she had to do to bring down Mayor McChandey and the guardian hunter.

Each smile expressed more undying love and more faith in her and in him.

Sebastian was trembling with fervor to take down the ones who rein evil on the world. He constantly checked the side mirrors, behind him. He chewed on his thumbnail and played with his bottom lip. He was riding on the edge and the closer they got to their destination, the more he became uncontrolled. He was lashing out on Jack's speed limit, his braking technique, and the control of his jeep. Jack had enough and asked if he wanted to drive. Sebastian shut up and pretty much kept quiet. He continued to fidget with his thumbnail and bottom lip, but at least he wasn't criticizing Jack's driving ability anymore.

It was late in the evening and the temperature had dropped a good twenty degrees from the warm mid-eighties, bringing a cool wind and dark, gray clouds.

Jack drove into the night in silence. Kaleigh looked out the back passenger window, watching over the highway watching the chopping waves bounce up and down to the coarse wind. When they got too high, the waves appeared stilled and very far away. She wanted to stand over the edge and just let her mind drift with the coasting waters, the swinging branches of the distant woods, and to feel that her life held no importance to the world.

But if felt like the closer they got to the destination, the more the atmosphere became moot. The wind picked up resistance, the night flyers scattered from the high branches, the crescent moon darkened and hung low, and as the thickening clouds dimmed the twinkling stars. Kaleigh shivered.

They were waiting for them. And would they be prepared when the final act was upon them? Would Jack sacrifice his soul for the guardian hunter and their entire species of the guardian saviors to protect seven pure souls (that refused to lift a finger) that could end this chaos of their destruction in a blink of an eye?

They had to because no other would be able to do it. They could keep on running, but what would the point? They would eventually find them.

Why couldn't the other pure souls put aside their difference and aide the guardian saviors? Why hold a grudge when their species was dying? Why were they allowing this to happen?

When this was all over, Kaleigh promised to get answer.

Kaleigh looked away and caught Jack looking at her from the rearview mirror. He flashed her comforting smile and Kaleigh returned it half-way.

Demons of the night would be waiting for them. And she would be ready.

As they passed through forgotten small towns, the air outside became unbearably putrid. They could barely breathe in the small jeep and they had to roll down their windows. The air smelled of sulfur.

"Man, this shit stinks," Sebastian said cringing.

They exited the ramp of Beaumont, made a U-turn under the overpass, drove on the feeder, and entered the ramp leading to Creegan, getting another blast of malodorous order. Jack entered the small town and the first they saw was a short, brick monument welcoming them to the town of Creegan. The powerful essence of demons hit them like a cold bucket of water. They all drew their heads back and gasped.

"There must be hordes of them," Sebastian said as he cupped his hand over his mouth and nose.

"Try not to breathe so much in," Jack suggested to them. "The potency of their stench is liable to knock us on our asses!"

There was no argument with that. Kaleigh had tears brewing in her eyes. She copied Sebastian's swell idea by covering her mouth and nose with her hand. She breathed in short, shallow dips of air enough to keep her from passing out. But the effect left her dizzy. Kaleigh tried to keep her mind off by looking to the right of the dark scenery. There were so many trees that reminded of her last nightmare. She shivered thinking about the future that was soon going to take place in less than an hour.

Suddenly, the jeep jerked, spurting out of control. The headlights vanished. The radio blared and then quickly fizzled out to nothingness. A loud piercing scream erupted in the small confines of the jeep and shattered the rearview mirror. Glass sprayed everywhere. Jack maintained control of the vehicle and pulled to the right-hand shoulder.

Kaleigh was shaking from head to toe. Her heart beat wildly against her chest; she was suffocating from the odorous stench and fear. As much as she didn't want to, she had to gulp in the grotesque air. The acrid scent burned her lungs, watered her eyes, and dizzied her mind. She closed her eyes and shook the unwanted feelings away.

"You okay back there?" Jack asked.

She opened her eyes and saw Jack was looking over his shoulder with his hands plastered so tight on the steering wheel that his knuckles turned white and the tips of his fingers were swollen red.

Kaleigh gave him a faint smile. "I think so," and then added when she realized that they had stopped before a deserted road that looked it led to nothing good, "where are we at?"

Jack looked out of the driver side and said, "Dunno, but this has to be the place where they are conducting their business. They know that we are close to them and they are going to do everything that they can to reel us back. But they don't realize that we are not going to turn tail and run."

He put the car back into drive and turned down the street. The wind picked up sped, blowing Kaleigh's hair in all directions. She knew she should have put her hair in a clip, but it was too late for should haves. The stench grew stronger and stronger with each passing mile as to the left and right of them were red, beady eyes flashing in the nighttime woods.

Kaleigh said a silent prayer.

The road curved sharply to the left, leading them further from city lights and civilization. Jack had to slow down to keep from tipping them over. Kaleigh expected at any moment to see inbred hillbillies stalking the night with their banjos.

Jack drove for another minute and then pulled into a small entrance that led only God knows where with a rusted and chipped, white gate swinging aimlessly with the wind. He drove past the gate and advanced into the woods until they could no longer see the road behind them. He finally came to a stop and they all sat in silence.

They were near a creek and somewhere out here was their future that would change their lives forever.

Sebastian was the first to open his door. He stepped out and stretched his legs. Jack followed his lead and opened the back driver's side door for Kaleigh. Sebastian came around to them and the three of them stood in silence, waiting for the signal.

They were all dressed in black from head to toe. Sebastian was wearing black motorcycle boots, leather pants, black T-shirt, and his favorite black leather jacket. Jack and Kaleigh wore the same matching black, denim jeans, plain black turtle necks, and black sneakers. Kaleigh resembled a harmless cat burglar as the two men resembled every man's worst nightmare and every woman's fantasy. Tall, dark, and dangerous they were, and just the aura of their presence could send a man hiding in the darkest corner.

"When will the signal come?" Sebastian asked, breaking the silence.

Jack walked to the back of the jeep and opened the trunk. He pulled out the binoculars from the large, army duffel bag that was packed with various odd gadgets. He adjusted the vision of the lenses, and then looked out for several seconds before saying anything.

"Now," he finally said.

Chapter Twenty-Two

No sooner did the word leave his mouth did a gush of hard wind sweep by and a blinding, white light spread across the darken sky and targeted over their bodies. Simultaneously they all looked up, shielding their eyes with their hands propped on their forehead.

"Jesus," mumbled Sebastian. "How many came?"

Jack looked to his friend and, dropping his hand to his side. "As many as I could get to come." Then he looked at Kaleigh with a smile spread across his face. He loved her so much that it hurt to think about leaving her for eternity. It was going to wound her more once she saw what he had to pay his life for to save mankind. That was the terrible misery of it all—seeing the wounded look in her eyes from his betrayal for what he had to sacrifice for. But it had to be done. He promised the maker that he lay his life down for the fate of the world; to become a merciless guardian hunter so Kaleigh would have the strength to defeat, and not become like Lucia. She might not have opened up to him, giving him everything that love could bring, but she kept the pure souls well guarded.

When they moved away from his jeep, the change would happen and there no was stopping it, but to embrace it. Kaleigh was going to be the only one that would destroy him.

And if he didn't kiss Kaleigh now, he was going to die a very sad man.

Jack pulled her to his side, cupped her face with his large hand, titled her head to meet his lips, and kissed her hard. "I love you."

Before either one could say another word, one-by-one, large bulbs of light scattered throughout the woods until the glow in the sky disappeared. For the first time in centuries, sorcerers and warriors were going to fight side-by-side. A battle of good versus evil; the same ole cliché from the beginning of time, was going to be fought in this nowhere city to placate souls that knew nothing about them. They weren't meant to know anything about them. If a human did then it could be remedied easily by a simple mind control.

Jack felt something wet hit the back of his neck. He looked to the side with Kaleigh still by his side and saw the first drops of rain.

Tonight was going to make history in the books of the guardian saviors.

"Let's go," Jack ordered.

Sebastian vanished in an instant. Jack hugged Kaleigh's hand and whispered in her. "You ready?" She gave him a weak nod and then teleported. They went from the thicket of the woods to more woods that were thickly scattered across the deserted road. The three stood by another wrecked gate. Sebastian pushed it opened and it gave a loud shriek.

Lightening clashed, thunder rolled, and the wind became the velocity of a tornado. The moon blanked out by the thick clouds. Darkness descended upon them so fast that when the cold, hard rain came crashing down on them and they could barely see what was standing in front of them.

"Stay close together," Jack yelled over the roaring of the rain.

They stepped through the gates, walked for about fifty feet, and soon came the dim lights of the lake. Jack could make out several men rushing around a large sail boat cruiser, trying to fasten the boat to the pier. Parked near the men was an unmarked, white van with its headlight beaming on the boat, providing extra light for them.

The wind howled as lightening crashed and thunder vibrating under their feet.

"They're about a half a mile up the lake," Jack said, feeling the change become him. "We'll split up. Sebastian you go to the left of them as I will go right. Kaleigh—"

She threw her hand up and quickly said, "I know what to do. Just stand here and looked pretty and if any demon comes my way destroy them."

Jack pulled her to his chest and kissed her again. "That's my girl."

"I'm really yours," she stated. "I love you. Please be careful."

He hugged her tightly, stroking her back. "I will." Jack paused as pulled away from her, but held her hands. "Promise me you'll tell our child everything about me."

"Oh Jack, don't think like that. We can control it," she cried.

Jack pulled her to meet his eyes and saw the tears falling from her lashes. He shut his eyes and said a curse under his breath. It felt like a fist wrapped around his heart and squeezed. He hugged her one last time and kissed her with all the love that was left in his soul. They tongues met and loved.

The change was becoming demanding and he couldn't ignore it anymore. It was painful and unbearable. Jack did not want Kaleigh to see him go through the transformation. He broke the kiss and quickly pushed away from her. As soon as he did, a jagged throb hit him square in the chest. He nearly buckled to his knees, but fought against the weakness. He had to keep walking. He had to keep on going before it was too late.

Jack took one more look over his shoulder and cringed when he couldn't spot Kaleigh in the cascade of the horrendous storm.

Then the demons came out of hiding.

Kaleigh could see the lake through the storm. There were about ten to twelve other boats parked at their piers that were miles away from them. If anyone were on that boat, no one would hear them scream. If gunshots were to be fired, they would hear it as a firecracker going off in the middle of the woods. More than likely they wouldn't hear a damn thing from the thunder and the loudness of rain.

Kaleigh leaned against a rounded, thick tree and hugged her arms as she watched walk away and then saw him look over his shoulder. Something was different about his eyes. Even though it was dark as hell out here, she could see everything as if she were looking through a pane of glass. But something was ominously different with his eyes. They were no longer the deep pools when he kissed her. They almost appeared to be a dark shade of violet.

Then Kaleigh felt Jack's guardian blood rip from her body, his emotions thrown in the dirt as the blackness that haunted his soul unleashed and became him.

Jack wasn't gone two seconds from her before he succumbed to his demon. He was a guardian hunter.

"Oh, Jack. Why so soon?"

She sank to her knees and pushed back the tears that were threatening to pour. *You must strong too, Kaleigh.*

I will, she promised.

The snapping of a twig broke the voice in her head. Her ears perked. Forgetting about Jack for just a minute, she turned around to the disturbing sound and gasped.

Surrounding her was at least twenty Susans as the day she died: naked, bruised, bleeding, and covered from head to toe in dirt.

Along the way, Jack sensed he was being followed. And why wouldn't he be? He just turned from one of the greatest responsibility of the world to a guardian hunter. His priorities were still lodged in the back of his mind somewhere, but the demonic scent of his essence was sure to provoke the saviors. He wouldn't hurt them. Even though he had the urge to destroy them, he had a small ounce of good left in his spirit from destroying them.

Jack stopped in his tracks and turned to the scent of a warrior. A large wolf growling on all fours sprang from the trees and threw himself on top of Jack, toppling him over to the ground. He wasn't just any regular wolf, but a black wolf with a gold crucifix hanging round his neck. He knew immediately who it was, but his scent meant nothing to Mace.

"Mace!" Jack yelled as he blocked his throat. "It's me, Jack."

The wolf paused for a second and shook his head. "Yes it is. I can prove it."

Jack raised his hands and threw a force ball at the wolf's chest, throwing him in the slippery of the mud. Jack hated to do that, but it was the only way to make a wolf or any animal of the guardian warriors to surrender to his command.

Hastily Jack stood and stopped Mace with an invisible wall. Mace couldn't change to human form while Jack held in this position. He had to make his warrior friend see the reasoning behind his betrayal of his brethren.

He looked directly into Mace's yellow eyes and showed him everything of his destiny. Mace whimpered and bowed his head to Jack, giving him a truce.

"I need a distraction," Jack said to Mace. "But I need you to stay in your wolf form."

As Mace knew what he was talking about, he gave Jack a nod with his furry head.

They stood behind some trees that hid him from the boats and watched an Arab snap open a suitcase and smile. He shut it and shook hands with a tall, blonde-headed man. It was a Mayor Devin McChandey.

Jack felt his blood boil with the urge to fly over there and suck the life out of the deceptive mayor; Jack bent down to the wolf's ears and whispered, "Stop them." The wolf wagged its tail. "Get 'em."

They wolf took off like a rocket, running his full speed through the trees, kicking dried up leaves, loose sticks, and air at Jack's chest. Jack remained behind him, pacing himself for a reason. He wanted them to be off guard and unconscious of the space he occupied.

"What the hell is that?" Jack heard one of the armed men cry.

The wolf was growling wildly and foaming out of the mouth. If these men had any sense (and Jack figure they wouldn't) they would stand were they were at. But did they do that? No. One tried to reach down and pet it and Mace reacted like what a rabid dog would: he attacked, snapping at the man's finger tips.

"God damn it!" the man cried, holding his hands to this chest. "Shoot the bastard!"

The other three armed men raised their guns and aimed, but didn't fire. "You stupid assholes!" McChandey yelled, yanking the gun out of the wounded hands. "We're trying to keep a low profile, go find a stick or something and knock him out!"

One of the men turned very unhurriedly, trying not to make any sudden movements with a vicious, rabid wolf on their heels, and that's when the first shot rang out. The bullet hit one of the thug's shoulders, sending him down to his knees and dropping his gun in the process.

Jack quickly hid behind another tree as the rest of the men ran around frantically trying to find who the shooter was. He could have sworn he heard McChandey whisper his name and wanted to laugh.

Before Jack fired the first shot, Sebastian was on a mission to get the women to safety. He heard the shot ring out and responded. As the criminals went mad, searching for the shooter, which was Jack, he raced to the only boat with the naked mermaid painted on it. He searched promptly to find the seven girls that were bought and sold for the simple purpose of being destroyed.

He frantically searched the top deck and when he came across nothing, he went below deck and found seven, beautiful, dark women with tangled, black hair, huddled together on a naked, full size mattress. On his way over here, he spotted an unmarked white van. It was large enough to carry two adult and eight or nine children in the back, but seven teenaged girls plus the men that were going to send them away to their destiny was almost as bad as these girls cramped in their small holding area.

They girls were filthy that even one bath would not get all the grime and dirt off them; it was going to take two. They smelled like the dead and weren't far from looking like them, too.

Sebastian's eyes and nostrils burned from the days-old bodily fluids and the unwanted smell of the thick perspiration that was stifling in the small bunker. They all were wearing the same long-sleeved, ratty, brown dressed that covered their entire body.

The woman took quick glances his way and tightened their huddle as they saw him as a threat. He didn't want to scare these women any more than they were already scared in this boat. Lord, only knows how long they been down here and it made him mad as hell that these beautiful creatures were abducted from their homes and deported to a world they didn't know, and didn't know what would become of them.

He clenched his fist at his side and relaxed his face. He wanted to make sure that these women knew that he was here for their escape and rescue.

In a calm, soothing voice he spoke, gesturing that he was one of the good guys. "It's all right," he spoke slowly and softly. He wasn't sure if these women knew any English, (he only knew English, French, Spanish, and a little Italian) but if he presented himself that he was here to help then maybe they would rely on his trust to get them out of here. "I'm here to help."

He reached out a steady hand and one of the girls squealed like he had already touched them. He threw his hands up and waved them in front of him. "No. No, no, no. I'm here to help you." He didn't know how to get them out of here without threatening them. Jack should have been the one to rescue them; he knew their language and was a lot more patient than him. Then a thought struck him.

He tapped on the door in the ceiling and pointed for them to come up. The girls watched in disbelief, but Sebastian saw one believed him. He waved at them to come forward and to be quiet. They didn't budge. He ran his hand through his hair and exhaled slowly. His patience was running thin and shouting was not going to help with this situation. These girls were scared beyond belief and all he had to help them was his strength. No soothing voice. No polite gesture to ensure that they would be safe. All he had was proof of his muscles.

But time was a-wasting and he had to hurry up and get these girls of this god damned boat. He charily grabbed one girl's wrist and hoisted her to the ladder. He signaled for her to go up, but the girl remained on the first step, crying and shaking uncontrollably.

He was at a loss. His clenched his fist at his sides terribly frightened them. "Get up there now!" he shouted at the top of his lungs.

The girl nearly lost her balance and Sebastian was there to steady her and then he forcibly pushed her up the small, metal ladder. He turned to the other girls, furiously shaking a finger at them. "All of you get there now!" The girls jumped at his voice, but soon enough they obeyed and followed the first girl out to the top deck.

Sebastian was the last one to come and saw all the girls huddled together like they were on the mattress. If he had a gun he knew for sure they would obey every command in his unknown language without any hesitation. But he didn't have a gun and had no use for a gun. He had his sword that was blessed with the righteousness of the purity.

He put his index finger to his lips and motioned for them to be quiet. He then pointed that same finger to the man that sold them. They saw what he saw: McChandey having their master in a choke hold.

Sebastian led them to the edge of the boat where it was tied to the pier and one-by-one, helped them off the boat. He gathered them in the woods and motioned them to follow him. On his way up to the boats he found a perfect hiding spot that would keep the girls safe for the time being. It was near the edge of the woods and close to the water. It was a small abandon shack that may have used to store boating equipment.

Three sorcerers and two warriors that he had never seen before were waiting for him when he arrived with the girls.

A pretty redhead with blue eyes smiled at them. She spoke to young victims in a language that Sebastian could decipher as their cultural language. The girls slowly calmed and then dropped to their knees, praising them all for their rescue. The pretty redhead blushed from head to toe and slanted her eyes to Sebastian. "Who are you?"

Her voice dripped with honey and seduction.

"Sebastian Ames."

"It's good that we finally meet," she said. "You must go now. They are here."

"I know," Sebastian whispered.

He telepathically sent a message to Jack that the girls were safe.

Down by the lake men spread out to find the person who started shooting. The only one's left on the field were McChandey and his Arab friend (with his men) that looked righteously pissed! He grabbed handfuls of the mayor's trench coat and began yelling, "What the hell is going on? Is this some kind of set up? Are the authorities involved?"

McChandey snatched the man's arms and wrapped his arms around his neck and squeezed so fast that he didn't have time to react. His men began pointed their guns at McChandey to avenge his betrayal and protect their leader. McChandey laughed and twisted his hands tighter around the Arab's neck. His men moved in closer.

"Your weapons are useless to me! Go ahead and shoot me if you please, but by the time you pulled the trigger you all will be dead!"

They should believe his words.

By the time one of the men shot through McChandey's head, the Arab's head snapped completely around. McChandey grabbed the pistol of the man that shot him and quickly yanked the gun out of his hands and used it to shoot the other two, putting a bullet in each of their heads, before they could pull their triggers.

Mace seemed to be frozen in spot and thought, shit. Of all his luck, he ran straight into a fucking a guardian hunter.

Then the mayor grabbed the last man standing and sent his palm straight up through his nose. His man that was shot earlier was pleading for his help. He had one bullet left in the gun and used it directly for the dying man's heart.

He picked up the brief case and swiftly kicked Mace in the head. He gave a loud yelp and found that he could move. He race to the woods to inform the others that a guardian hunter was in their company.

Mayor McChandey swung the briefcase over his shoulders. "Come out, Mr. Pierce. Play time is over."

The three McChandey men were covering every inch of the woods, trying to track down the lone shooter. Already there were five men killed on the battlefield and any more might cause suspicious that would be pointing the mayor's way. They needed to find this man before their employer was thrown in jail and they were out of a job.

One of the thugs heard a snapping of a stick behind him. He turned quickly with his gun pointed out and found nothing but more trees. When he turned back, a giant man was standing in front of him with a large sword pointed at his chest. "Move and I'll fucking kill you."

The man began to shake and yet, found the courage to back talk the giant. "I have a gun, you have a knife. Who do you think is gonna win?" He cocked his Beretta and Sebastian quickly swung around, slicing the man's trigger hand off. It hit the dirt as the man's mouth dropped open and he screamed like a woman.

Sebastian crouched and swung his left leg out, kicking the man to the ground. He quickly knelt beside him. He eased the sword in front of his victim's eyes and laughed. "Not so much a knife anymore, is it?"

The man was grabbing his handless hand, begging Sebastian to spare his life while the whole time crying. "Please don't kill me! Please. I have kids, a wife, and a home. I'm not worth killing!"

"You're right about that. Change careers or you'll be seeing me real soon!" He stood up and wiped his blade on the man's cheap leather jacket. "How many more are out here?"

The man was crying harder and Sebastian rolled his eyes. "How many more?"

"Two, I believe."

"Thank you."

He picked up his feet and ran with the shadows.

Jack heard McChandey entering the woods. He saw a flash of body movement from the corner of his eyes and quickly pointed his gun at the moving target. He found the target on the thug's body and pulled the trigger at the man's left shoulder. The man went down with a loud agonizing scream. Jack ran to him and pulled his gun from his hands and put it in the back of his jeans. He raced to another shadow of trees, waiting for McChandey's arrival.

Jack never killed anyone before, unless it was a demon. But for the petty thugs and people he raided, he merely wounded so they could pay for their crimes behind bars.

He was slightly glad that these men hadn't committed their mortal souls to the ways of the wicked. They hadn't killed, raped, or abused anyone yet. They were petty thugs that were looking for an easier life and fast money. He hoped this experience would have a brighter outcome for them when their standing behind bars for smuggling in illegal immigrants.

He knew the Arab and his men were dead. He witnessed it and could only feel shame for them. He hoped Mace was all right, but then again, felt no guilt for sending Mace out there alone. He needed a distraction while Sebastian rescued the girls.

His lingered to Kaleigh's connection and breathed cursed. "God damn, Kaleigh!" Why did she have to block herself? She was failing—again. Why couldn't the maker show her what it showed him? If they really wanted the pure souls to involve themselves in the world again, they needed to guide her.

Chapter Twenty-Three

Deep into the woods, the guardian saviors as humans and animals fought bravely against the demons. The protectors fought with the ability of their elements. They shot lightening down from the sky struck the demons. They drove the water from the lake and drowned their sorrow cries. They used their force control and threw them against hard bark of the trees as the warriors slashed and diced until they exploded into dust.

Sebastian and Mace joined the chaos and fought side-by-side in the huddle of worst, gruesome demons. They pretended to be children, using their childlike voice to plea for their help. As if they were going to buy that act! How stupid did they think they were?

Slashing a raging sword in the heart of pretend child was quite unsettling, but had to be done. They closed their eyes to the cruel images as they saved the world.

Kaleigh gasped and wanted to run, but stood frozen. All the Susans merged together and became one. Susan reached out and snatched Kaleigh's wrists. With the heel of her shoes, she kicked Susan's foot and it went right through her. Susan laughed eerily and sent shivers down Kaleigh's spine.

Kaleigh tried to pull away and push Susan's dead body off her at the same time, but failed. Susan had the paradox of warrior's strength! This woman would not budge.

"Kaleigh, don't fight me. It's useless!" She laughed again, sending another set of cold chills down her spine.

Then her eyes turned from stone blue to coal black. Kaleigh's eyes widened, her mouth dropped, all the while trying to pull her grip from Susan's cold, damp hands. She fought feverishly, trying to break Susan's grip, but no amount of exertion she gave served any purpose. Susan was stuck to her like she was a part of her body. If she could only maneuver her wrist just a tad bit to wrap her hands around hers. If she had control over Susan then she could stop.

Susan yanked Kaleigh against her chest and fell through. Kaleigh stumbled and hit the ground. Her chin smashed into dirt and leaves as her hands and knees made an imprint on the soil. She quickly turned to look and found Susan gone.

She had vanished, but she was still close by.

Kaleigh closed her eyes and awoke in her office. She was sitting in her executive chair like every other day at the office, flipping through resumes and applications. For some reason, her office was extremely dim and a bit chillier today. She grabbed her black cashmere sweater from the back of the chair and dropped it over her shoulders. She read through more applications and then glanced at her wall clock. It was ten minutes till five; almost time for her to go home.

She stacked the papers in the middle of her desk and put her glass, kitten paperweight on top of them. Tomorrow she would finish the rest and start calling for interviews. She already knew who she was going to call and who she wasn't going to waste doing a second glance over. Nope. She knew who was going to work hard for their money and she knew who had the experience and honesty of an employee for Walker Security's.

While grabbing her purse, she thought she heard someone call her name. She swung the purse over her shoulder and opened the door to her office. It was bit noisy. The employees were wrapping it up for the day and getting ready to go to home.

Kaleigh...

She turned around, but nobody was there. She shrugged her shoulders and thought perhaps she was working too much. She sighed. She only had about month until she was on vacation. She was going to enjoy it relaxing on the beach, away from everyone.

Kaleigh...

She closed the door behind her and locked it. She walked past all the cubicles to the elevator. She pressed the down button and waited a minute. The doors came open and her and her best friend Susan stepped inside.

"What are you doing tonight?" Kaleigh asked while pulling her car keys out and not paying attention to her friend.

"Oh, this and that. Probably go to the Temptation tonight."

The elevator stopped and Kaleigh assumed the door was going to open and it never happened. She glanced at her friend Susan and a grin plastered was across her face. Kaleigh glanced at the button that was glowing orange. Then for some reason her friend hit the stop button. She took a cautious step towards her. "What are you doing?"

"Taking your soul," she said like she was giving her advice on what to wear.

Kaleigh shrank back. "What?"

"Your soul must die!" Kaleigh gripped her purse not knowing what else to do.

"Susan, what the hell are you talking about?"

Susan took a step forward as Kaleigh took a step back and came against the cold metal of the elevator wall. "Kaleigh, I need your soul. He has to pay!"

"Who has to pay?"

She turned her back to Kaleigh and ran her fingers down all the elevator buttons without pressing any buttons. "I chose this place for a reason, Kaleigh," she said with a smile. "It's safe from him."

Kaleigh shook her head. "Please. Tell me what you're talking about, Susan."

"You saw what he made them do to me. They beat me, raped me, and murder me all because of you!" She said turning around, her eyes once again black.

Kaleigh snapped at what she was saying. Just a few minutes ago she was fighting with this woman. She had to go back. She had to be there when Jack came for her. She had to destroy the guardian hunter.

"Look, Susan, I know what they did to you and I'm so sorry. If I could have taken your place I would have. I have to get back Susan! They need me!"

"You're not going back, Kaleigh. He's going to pay for what he did to me!"

Kaleigh only assumed she was talking about her ex-husband, Mayor Devin McChandey. She had to talk some reasoning in this woman or else it would be too late.

"Susan, Jack is going to take care of Devin. You don't have to worry about him anymore. I promise you." Susan was dead, but sometime the dead still believe they are alive. And she was going to say anything to bring her back to the woods.

"I shouldn't have tried to blackmail him, but I needed the money, Kaleigh. I was in debt to my eyeballs and had no other way to get the money. I tried asking for it, but he just shoved me out the door. So I decided to use what I knew about him. Most people don't know about his activities outside the office. He's a perversion of a new kind. Buying virgins and then raping and killing them. I found out before we were married and he tried to kill me, but I survived. He found me and made me become his wife. He said if I stayed with him and kept my mouth shut about his personal life that I would never have to worry about money and I could have all the freedom I wanted.

"I couldn't resist and fell for his trap. The whole time I was married to him, he beat and raped me; tortured me endlessly. I believe I was starting to go a little crazy while I was married to him. I started looking forward to the beatings and the rapes.

"Then I saw an ad in the job section of the newspaper for a mail clerk at Walker Security's. I knew that you worked there, and thought it was one chance to get the hell away from him and live my own life.

"I packed my things that morning and called a divorce lawyer out of the yellow pages. I lived in one hotel from and another, hoping he wouldn't find me. I don't know why he signed the papers, setting me free from him, but he did and I was totally free. I was on my last dollar when you hired me. I knew that you wouldn't remember me because Devin said he made sure that you wouldn't. So I took my chances and you hired me. I was never so grateful to a person than I was to you for what you did to me. But when I started to get more into debt with my new life, I needed money. I was afraid to come to you because I thought you might think less of me. So I went to him. And that's how this how mess started. I told him everything from the time I left until I met you again and he knew what you were.

"I'm sorry, Kaleigh, I never meant to harm you or scare you, but I can't let you back."

"Why?"

"I did something extremely horrible, Kaleigh, and I don't know if you're going to forgive me," she said with her eyes filling with tears. "While I was lying in that damn box, a voice came to me out of nowhere. He said he would let me have my revenge against Devin if I could help him get to you. And while you're dying anything sounds sane.

"I asked him what he needed you for and he told me that you were the abomination of the world. You were going to be the one to destroy the world if you should prevent his death. I didn't know I was making a deal with the devil. I just kept thinking if I were alive that I could kill that sonuvabitch myself! But, that voice sucked the rest of the life out of me and turned me into one of his creatures. I couldn't quite believe it at first, but the only thing on my mind was revenge. So I took the tape from my night stand and placed in your apartment to get you involve, but you got involved anyway because you cared about me."

"Why are you keeping me away from there? We need to go back, Susan," Kaleigh stressed.

"I made a deal with him. If I keep you here—"

"Then I'll be out of his way when he tries to destroy Jack." It struck Kaleigh light a bolt of lightening. Why couldn't she see it before? Jack was still protecting her even though he was a demon. He was doing his part just as he said he would. That's why he turned. A guardian hunter could destroy other demons, and the mayor meant to destroy Jack to get him out of the way, while he came after her.

Jack said being in Susan's world would weaken her and tried to avoid it all cost. But she was here and had no idea how to get back. Susan brought her back the last time and she wasn't planning on bringing her back now. She was going to be stuck here while Jack's body gets consumed by the worst possible demon.

She couldn't let that happen.

"I'm so sorry, Kaleigh. He promised me if I kept you here, he'll let me have my revenge on Devin. It was too much to pass up," Susan whispered.

Kaleigh shook back her anger and was going to reason with this woman until she was blue in the face. "Susan, listen to me. If you don't let me back, he will destroy everything that's good in the world, leaving only the evil." She wasn't seeing the reasoning. Kaleigh tried harder. "Don't you see, Susan? Once he takes over there will be nothing left! He tricked you. Devin is the voice you heard. You're not going to have your revenge. You won't get your revenge—ever. He will take over everything and everybody will be a slave to him. He used you. He lied to you. He tricked you, Susan. Help me get back and I'll promise you'll get your revenge, and make sure that everybody knows what he did to you!"

Silence came from Susan. She looked angry and upset. Her eyes flickered back from blue to black. Her skin changed from pure white to the dirt, covered filth she was buried in.

"Help me, Susan, and I'll make sure they know. I'll make sure they all know."

Susan closed her eyes and sighed.

Sebastian stalked silently through the trees. Most the demons had been destroyed or had vanished in their terror. He began following the last of McChandey men, oblivious to them in the dark rain; just the way he wanted it. Catch them totally by surprise and they won't know which way to run.

He wondered how Jack was doing. He knew that he turned the moment he left Kaleigh's side. The love that crossed between them was something he never seen or felt before and for a brief moment he wanted to have that. But guardian saviors aren't supposed to feel anything unless they take a human being into their spirits. At the moment he didn't have anyone inside. What happened to him in Paris was enough for him to stay away from everyone for a lifetime.

He thought about seeking Carly out, the Ames's real daughter, the only one that ever showed him kindness, but thought he didn't need her emotions to feel. He was doing quite fine without them. All he had to do in his life was to destroy demons; not get distracted by emotions.

But for some strange reason, he wanted to see her. He wanted to know if she was happy. God knows why, but he did. Maybe after this whole fiasco was settled, he would go home to Caledonia, Montana, and pay her a visit, not his adoptive parents. As far as he was concern they were dead to him.

Sebastian saw a wounded man dripping with blood, trying to crawl away from the battle zone on his hands and knees. If this man had half of brain cell he would find cover and stay put till it was safe for him to leave. So Sebastian decided to help him.

The wound wasn't severe; he was going to live. He quickly tore the man's shirt off and ripped it three pieces. One piece was for his wrists, the other for his ankles, and the last to gag his mouth so he wouldn't scream. He hogged tied him and left him behind a tree, safe from McChandey, but not quite safe from the police who would come.

He found the last man a few feet in front of him. His feet didn't touch ground as he walked in silence behind him. The man was dressed like the others in black attire and a gun. He was more heavyset than the others, but smaller than Howard. He decided to go easy on this guy because McChandey must have hired the most dim-witted criminal he could find.

He was right behind him when the thug stopped in his tracks. Sebastian could hear his heavy breathing and smell the infectious body order pouring from his glands. He shrank back just a little to keep his nose out of the cross fire of his odor.

The man looked to his left and then his right, but never once glanced back. Sebastian tapped his right shoulder. The man turned around and jumped as his face sprinted to a shocked expression that Sebastian wanted to laugh.

He didn't give the man much time to ask anything. He quickly uppercut him in his jelly gut and when he went down, Sebastian took advantage of his poor fighting skills and smashed the right side of his face. Then the man completely fell on his face as Sebastian grabbed his loose gun and walked off to find Jack.

Jack had his eyes on McChandey the whole time he was searching the woods. McChandey came close several times to exposing Jack's hiding space. Jack wouldn't let that happen. He was a lot smarter than McChandey and a lot quicker.

The whole time he was keeping an eye for McChandey, he was trying to connect with Kaleigh again. She had fell victim to Susan's cruel powers and was lost in another world that he couldn't pull her out.

If Susan wouldn't let her back then all would be lost.

"Come on, Mr. Pierce. Let's not make this any more difficult than it is. I'm not here to kill you."

Yeah and the moon is purple.

"I'm here to help you out. I'm here to make it easier for you." Jack didn't reply. He knew what he had in mind. Jack had the powerful knowledge of the pure souls.

Late Friday night, Radella, Adrian's wife, visited him, and sent him of their existence, and the only way for the guardian hunter to earn that great knowledge is by killing him. Jack refused to let that happen. His strength outnumbered the hunter's because he was a sorcerer with the powers of a guardian hunter.

The urge to kill was getting extremely hard to avoid and the refusal of taking a soul was making him weak. He had to destroy McChandey before his body loss its senses.

"Come on, Mr. Pierce. I don't have all night."

Jack was going to have to take his chances and come out of the shadows. He was tired of playing this cat and mouse game with him and it was becoming a bore watching him going in circles.

He stepped out and found McChandey's back to him. He cleared his throat and saw him shiver. He turned around and smiled wickedly. "It's about time, Mr. Pierce. I was wondering when you were going to grow some balls and face me."

Jack shrugged his shoulders. "I was having too much fun watching you make a fool out of yourself."

The demon chuckled and clasped his hands together. "You're going to pay for that," he said wryly. "It's going to be fun taking your soul." The demon took a giant leap to Jack, but Jack already had his gun drawn and quickly pulled the trigger before he made it over there to him.

The demon shot back and flipped back on his feet. He dusted off the dirt and leaves from his trench coat and laughed. "Is that the best you got?"

Jack used the rest of the rounds through his chest and one in head. His bullets were purified by his blood, but they were acting like annoying mosquitoes to the dark demon. The bullets zipped through him like air as his skin resurfaced back together. He laughed the whole time Jack fired and it was beginning to piss him off.

"Come on, Mr. Pierce. I'm getting bored."

Before Jack could retort, the demon jumped in the air and threw his entire weight on top of him. Jack grabbed around his waist and tossed him over his head. For an instant they were head to head on the ground, and quickly rejoined their feet on the ground. The demon looked mad as hell as well as shocked. His eyes were drawn together and his nose flared as his breathing wheezed.

"What's the matter? Tired?" Jack said, provokingly.

McChandey pointed his finger up in the air and Jack felt the rain stop. He looked up and saw that the clouds rushing together. The wind picked up great speed as a bolt of lightening lit up the sky and roll of thunder echoed the great sky. Rain shattered on the Earth again and Jack was impressed.

Jack turned his attention to the demon and met his cold, black eyes. The demon winked at him and smiled his wicked smile again. "Face facts, Jack;

you're fucked. You can't win against me. You're a useless demon with no powers and no way to defend yourself. Give it up. Admit that you've lost."

It was Jack's turned to smile. He was drenched from head to toe and walked to the demon like he was dry as a bone. The demon's smile faded to a mere smirk. "What do you have planned Mr. Pierce? Going to fight me?"

Jack shook his head and then charged full speed to the demon. The last thing Jack saw before he knocked the demon on his back was his black eyes spread open and the dropping of his mouth. They both fell hard against the ground and tumbled down the short slope and splashed into the cold, creek water.

They fought in the water like two warriors battling for conquer of the world.

They were battling for control of the world!

Jack lost his balance and was being dragged under the water by the force of the demon's hands and felt his lungs clenching for air. He couldn't breathe and slowly felt the darkness coming closing in on him. He saw Kaleigh's beautiful face and her extraordinary green eyes and thought to himself, he wasn't supposed to die like this. He had to be there for her. For Kaleigh and her future. For Kaleigh and her freedom of the guardian hunters. For Kaleigh and life.

He shot straight up like a rocket and bashed the top of his head into the demon's nose. He sucked all the air that surrounded him and quickly ran back to land as the demon scrambled to surface behind him.

Jack reached land and felt a powerful force hit against his back and fell flat on his face. The demon was behind and he turned over to find the demon, dripping wet with a winning smile smeared on his face. In the palm of his hand he held a fireball.

The demon licked his wet lips. "Prepare for my master!"

He chanted the words of the ritual of ancient death of taking a guardian soul and threw the fireball at him. Jack rapidly brought forth the water, surged it in the palm of his hand, and threw it at the fireball as he cast a protecting spell to his spirit. The two elements collided and dispersed in smoke. The demon growled and charged at Jack again.

This time, Jack was prepared. He grabbed the demon's wrists with one hand as the other burst through the barrier of his chest and grabbed its beating heart. Jack repeated the ancient guardian hunter curse and squeezed the heart of the demon.

KALEIGH'S PROTECTOR

Jack felt the demon's soul slipping from his body and entering his. He could feel all the malice and evil in the world spring alive in his spirit, coursing through his veins, hitting the target of his heart, and feeding him delusions of murder and rape of all the young women he taken souls from. Jack slipped his hand from the demon's chest and released its wrists.

Now it was time to summon the pure souls for the takeover of the world.

No! He had to find Kaleigh. She was to destroy him.

But his mind played back and forth to the conquering of the world and saving it.

Then he heard the sweetest voice ever known to mankind and he wanted to squish it! The ripeness of the voice sent a revolt of revulsion down his throat that it made him sick to his stomach.

He was going to kill that bitch and take her soul. Kaleigh was going to be the first. She wasn't going to tempt him any more with her body, voice, or beauty. His purpose was to gain the seven souls and serve them to his demon master!

Jack shook his head.

Kaleigh, where are you?

There were sorcerers and warriors here waiting for the taken. He breathed in the rain and stopped it with his powerful mind. Instantly the clouds vanished, the wind stopped, and the moon showed beautifully high in the sky surrounding by the sparkling stars. He smelled the guardians' souls and captured them all.

But he fought not to take their souls. He held them frozen in time. Not yet. He didn't need them right this moment. All his concentration needed to be focused on the pure soul.

"Jack!"

The voice was richer than wine and sweeter than divinity. He was going to love stealing that bitch's soul!

"Jack!"

Jack turned around and saw a frightened Kaleigh dragging an even more frightened Susan behind her. Sebastian popped before them with his sword drawn. Jack stopped the warrior as he did with the other saviors. Sebastian knees buckled, fell, and then hit the dirt. He flicked out his hands and captured Susan's soul. "You belong to me!"

Kaleigh screamed as she watched Susan's ghostly body, slim to a fine thin smoke and pierced through Jack's heart.

"Kaleigh," Jack said scathingly, feeling energized and ready to conquer the world. "I've been waiting for you come. Where have you been?"

Chapter Twenty-Four

Kaleigh locked her feet to the ground and gasped. Jack had greatly paled, his eyes were wickedly red, and veins corded around his neck. But that wasn't what had her hand heart slamming against her chest and her breath suspended in her throat. It was the enormous shadow that flapped behind Jack's back. With great black wings stretching twenty feet on either side of Jack's side, standing thirty feet in the air with blazing, hypnotic red eyes.

Jack's tattoo came to life in a form of the most legendary, repugnant, vicious creature ever known to man and Kaleigh didn't know whether to run for her life or just hand her soul over to Jack right now and pay for the sins of her losing faith.

No! She couldn't and wouldn't do that. She had come to give up now!

Kaleigh sucked in her breath, looked away from the dragon to Jack's face. She was no more than twenty feet away from him and it painfully hurt her not to move her feet. In her insane mind, she wanted to rush into his arms and make love to him right here in the woods. This wasn't her Jack though, it was his body.

Closing her eyes, she blocked out the sadistic look from his face and his shadow, and thought about the last time they were alone together. It was beautiful. They only had a few minutes alone to enjoy in each others arms.

His love embraced her heart, deep down into her very soul, and her world. He was changed everything about her. He gave her strength and her faith, and she wasn't about to lose it all in one second because she was afraid of the sacrifice Jack had to make for the world.

It hurt to see him like this and it hurt even more to think that he wasn't going to be a part of her world after tonight.

"What's the matter Kaleigh?" Jack said with a cruel laugh. "Afraid of me?"

"I'm not afraid of anything," she said with her eyes still closed.

He laughed, sending chills up her spine. "Then why are your eyes closed? Mmm?"

She didn't answer him back because she wasn't going to fall into his trap of taunting words. He wanted her weak and she wasn't going to show any weakness to this demon.

"I'm going to summon them to their deaths, Kaleigh, but first I want yours."

"No," Kaleigh whispered. "I'm not going to let you destroy anybody! You won't have them and you won't have me!"

"Oh, I've already had you, Kaleigh and I would like to point out that I have had so much better in bed," he said with a laugh.

Kaleigh opened her eyes and glared at him. It was the demon talking, not Jack. She wasn't going to listen to his lies. He may anger her, but he was not going to reduce her stability of her moral conviction to the world.

"Come on, Kaleigh." She wished he would stop saying her name. "We had so much fun and I shall never forget the first pure soul I've fucked."

She wasn't going to let his words hurt her. She had to think of something that would get her close enough to touch him. All she needed to do was touch him and he would be destroyed, but his cryptic shadow and Jack's overpowering strength made her feel inadequate about her own physique.

"Damn you, Jack," she spat. "What are you supposed to be doing?"

"Not anymore, darling. Not anymore," he said twirling his hand in the air. "I'm no longer interested in being destroyed. I happened to like these new-found powers and won't give them up for anything in the world."

Kaleigh took a small step forward. "Not even for your child?"

Jack laughed. "Not even for that bastard that will be born into the world."

She knew his words didn't mean anything, but it still felt like he punched her in the gut. Ignoring the pain, she took another step and then another step.

"Feeling brave, Kaleigh? You've never been brave in your life! Why start now? How about you join me and we can dominate this world together?"

"Why would I do that when I have all the powers in the world?" she said mockingly.

"You truly are a stupid bitch, aren't you? Where did you get the notion that you can defeat me?"

There was no way for Kaleigh to walk up to Jack and let her capture him. He was strong and wouldn't allow her to come closer than the space that already separated them. Then she remembered the dream. She remembered running away from him. She remembered tumbling down to the ground. She remembered the way his body crushed her. And she remembered the way he kissed her.

The pure souls' words finally held their purpose in this cruel game of their fates. She knew what she had to do to bring the pure souls together. It was all a ploy in the maker's sick little, twisted game. They had to make her fall in love with a guardian hunter and be sure to destroy him like Lucia was unable to do.

Run, Kaleigh!

She took a step back and heard the demon laughing. "What's the matter, Kaleigh? Afraid?"

Kaleigh nodded. "Very afraid."

Then she turned around and sped away for her life.

The late night sky and the hidden moon almost made it impossible to see where she was going! The trees steadily popped out in front of her, smacking her in the face with their loose branches. At least it stopped raining, but the slippery mud was hard to run through.

Her feet were tired as if they had been running hundred-mile marathon and she still had a hundred miles to go. She wanted to stop and take a breather, but he was after her. He wasn't that far away and if Kaleigh's feet could keep their balance and avoid those ghastly tree roots she might outrun him.

"Kaleigh! Kaleigh!"

Jack screamed her name from behind, but it sounded like he was calling her from the entire perimeter of the woods. Her name echoed off the water, bounced off the ground, and sang with the breeze. He confused her sounding so tender. She wanted to stop and run to him instead of running away from him. She promised that she would never run away from him, but she wasn't running away from Jack. Kaleigh was running away from the guardian hunter.

Just like in the B-rated horror movies, Kaleigh stumbled over a thick tree root and quickly regained her balance. He was getting closer to her. Her breathing was tired and sweat poured over her face like she was caught in an unexpected summer storm, which she was.

The dragon roared, too, after Jack's demented screams, sending her heart beating frantically.

Another tree branches whacked her in the face and this time the greenery scratched her eyes and she was blinded by the stinging tears. She was totally blinded by the night and her tears and she had no idea where she was going. She just knew that she had to run. He had to come after her. He had to kiss her. And she was going to keep on running for her dear life until he caught her.

"Kaleigh!" Jack screamed her again. His voice was louder, not so tender when he called her name, and so much closer than before. He was coming up close and any minute the guardian hunter was going to tackle her down and kill her with all the force and strength he had left.

That wasn't going to happen. She led him to believe that because it was her best defense.

Then he was in front of her and the dragon was right behind him, breathing flame. She turned around and he was there again. Everywhere she turned there he was, waiting with that damn smug grin of his!

She had to touch him. She needed to bring him to her. He was in front of her, but he was keeping distant because he knew the power she held over him. He was going to wait for her to make the first move.

"Come on, Jack," she said cajoling him in her sweetest voice. "Don't you want me anymore?"

His smile broadened as a bolt of lightening exploded the earth between them. Neither one move.

"You can do better than that, I hope," she teased again. "I'm not wasting my time here, am I?"

His dragon roared, his grin faded, and everything in the woods became darker.

Then she knew what would really get him in a temper. Demons hated to be on the reverse end of the taunts. She turned around, and laughed and said, "You can't destroy me, Jack. You don't have the powers to do it."

In a flash she was tumbling down on the center of the earth. She clawed, kicked, and screamed for the mercy of her life. Jack tackled her back, sending her flying headfirst into a puddle of mud. She choked to breathe and then was quickly turned around.

She fought him weakly with all her strength. Let him believe that he was winning.

Her arms were above her head, pinned down on the dewy grass. Her thighs were trapped underneath him. She couldn't move a muscle. Before her, death chanted.

She wanted to close her eyes. She didn't want to see Jack this way!

"You belong to me, Kaleigh."

She opened her mouth to scream, he played right into her trap. He took possession of her mouth and Kaleigh opened up to Jack as she called for the pure souls before it was too late. She would not fail where Lucia did!

Ab cor, evenire castimonia, she said in her mind as she called for the six pure souls.

They were connected with her in an instant, circling her heart, clasping their spirits with her hers, and giving Kaleigh the strength she needed to destroy the guardian hunter as they chanted the ancient language over and over with her. If she defeated him, her mission would end, and her life would be much easier to live, but so empty without Jack.

Kaleigh kissed Jack back with all the love she had for him, with all the love of their child, and with all the love of the goodness in the world. She let him feel her happiness of their memories. She let him feel her heart beating for him. She let him feel the babe's heart beating for him.

Jack froze and dropped her hands. Kaleigh wrapped her hands around his wrists, squeezed with all her might, and destroyed the only man she could ever love. He crushed her with his dead weight.

Kaleigh lay there breathing hard with tears streaming down her face. Absently, she kissed the top of Jack's head and wrapped her arms around him. "I love you," she whispered. "Always and forever. You gave me a moment of happiness and your child will know what a great man you were. I hope whatever gives you a special place in its kingdom."

Jack's body rose from hers and a blue light shot from the core of his body. Kaleigh closed her eyes. She didn't want to witness the destruction of his body. She curled into a fetal position and let out the most sobbing cries that filled the woods with her anguished defeat. She cried for so long they turned into silent sobs and hiccups.

Strong arms wrapped around her thighs and under her back. She was being lifted in the air and then pressed against a powerful chest. She was to too tired to fight and too weak to do so.

Instead, she wrapped her arms around the man's neck and buried her head in his neck. The expensive cologne hit her hard and she started crying all over again.

"Shh," Sebastian cooed. "I'm going to take you home, Kaleigh."

Chapter Twenty-Five

"We are not going through with this again, Crset. Jack made a great sacrifice for our world and we are not going to stand here and let you manipulate the outcome."

Crset folded his fat arms his chest and sighed deeply. This pure soul was driving him insane! He couldn't get a moment's peace with her crowding his every move! He had to make her and the rest understand. "Jack knew the consequences of his sacrifices!"

"How can a god be so cruel?" Salene shouted, flipping her black hair over her shoulders. She was dressed in red, low-cut dress, exposing her small, ripe bosoms, hoping to divert him from his decisions.

And it was working a little to well.

Crset looked from her breasts and caught the glare of her blue eyes. He cleared his throat. "That's where you're wrong, Salene I am no god. I just am. I can do whatever I want to."

"You sound like a spoiled little boy, Crset! If I were your mama, I'll be spanking that fat butt of yours!"

"Salene!" he roared. "Don't talk to me like that! I can send you away just as quickly as I can wipe this entire planet of their existence."

"Oooh," Salene cooed, waving her hands in the air. "I'm so scared."

"You should be," he snarled. "Without me, you don't exist."

"And without us, you don't exist, Crset. It's not the worshipping that keeps your ancient butt here; it's the power of the mankind's existence. Without them and without us, you'll have nothing to control but an empty wasteland. Now am I right?"

"Like always, Salene. Maybe I should keep you around as my bride."

Crset had always liked Salene. It could because she was the only one he associated with except for his servants and they were a great bore. No one knew about him but his servants, and that's the way he wanted. He didn't come to this tiny planet for worship or devotion. He came here because of other problems of other existence.

Salene was the first guardian he created and one of his biggest accidents. How was he to know destroying her would cause so much chaos?

Well he fixed the problem and that damn woman still found him.

He might also like her because she unconsciously found ways to arouse his dead heart. He thoroughly enjoyed fighting with her whenever she made him a visit. Sometimes, he summoned her to his kingdom just to pick a fight with her.

He loved seeing her all rallied up and frustrated.

Salene snorted. "I don't think so, Crset. I'm not your type."

"You mean you're not easy?" Crset slapped his forehead. "What was I thinking? From your attire and previous chosen profession I for surely thought you were one hot firecracker that everyone gets a chance to pop."

She tapped her foot on the marble floor and squared her shoulders. She glared at him and folded her arms under her breasts. "Crset, don't make me hate you."

Crset couldn't understand why Salene turned him on so badly. When he came to this planet, he was utterly alone (besides his three servants he brought with him) and decided to create someone especially for him. That all shot to hell as they say in America.

Salene was beautiful—then again—all his little angels were beautiful. He didn't want to create repulsive creatures that would disgust him.

He was vain and very proud of it.

But Salene stirred his blood like no other could before and it was faith that kept him away from her. She didn't want him. So to ease his suffering, he would find a broken down human woman and make her feel special. Then he would give her a good life and leave as quickly as he came.

Though with Salene, he knew once spread underneath him wouldn't be enough. Would it be worth it to be dipped once into heaven? Crset looked her up and down and nodded. Just once he would like to feel alive again. That's all he wanted. Curse his gods for their betrayal!

Crset wanted Salene for several reasons and if he could barter with her, maybe. Then maybe he could feel like his old god-like self.

"What are you smiling about?" Salene asked with her eyes pinched together.

"A deal," he said before could slap his hand over his mouth. He didn't mean to blurt it out like some idiotic nine year old boy. Though, the way she made his body stir, he was acting like a little boy.

Salene's eyes pinched her eyes together. "What kind of deal?"

Crset looked over her shoulder and signalled for his servants to leave him. He turned his attention back to Salene when they left and then smiled. "You want something and I want something. I think we can compromise."

Salene wrinkled her nose and eyed him suspiciously. "What is it that you want?"

"You."

"I'm not a whore, Crset," she screamed, throwing her hands in the hair.

"Not anymore," he said unsympathetically to her words, while inside he was cringing. He hated to hurt the one and only person he ever wanted in his life, but cruel life made him defensive towards others, for it was the only way to make himself feel superior. "But still I want you. Give me one night of your body and I will give Jack back to Kaleigh. Fair?"

Salene was appalled by his idea of fairness. Obviously he didn't look in the mirror too often or else he would have seen how unfair his proposal was! Compared to her ethereal beauty, he was a giant toad. Crset was short and fat with a greasy face and bulging cow eyes! She didn't that touching her body. He was by far the ugliest thing she'd ever encountered in her life! And it wasn't just his appearance either; his personality was of equal attraction.

But with closed eyes, she could bear…what? Four or five minutes of his sweat pouring over her body?

Then a sly little thought ricochet off her brain. This man wanted her. She could see it in his pants. If she could up the cost of her body for an exchange of a greater purpose then she could get whatever guardian had been wanting for hundreds of years.

"What's going through that little brain of yours?"

It was her turn to smile and Crset didn't like the looks of that. "I'll give you something better if you choose it."

"I'm listening," Crset said keenly.

"I'll be yours forever under one condition."

Crset didn't miss that cringe crinkling around her face. She didn't want him. That was as plain as day on her face. What was she thinking to let him have her any time he wanted? Just the thought made him hard and throbbing. He'd always wanted her—had her at one time and since then couldn't live without—and this would be his chance to rebuild what was ruined so long ago. Would it be worth it?

"What is that you want?"

What was it that Jack had said? All men think with their dicks? Yes that was him all right; thinking with his lower head instead of the one on top. And right now he'll probably agree to anything.

"Give Jack back to Kaleigh and let the guardians keep their powers and immorality if they fall in love."

"Impossible!" Crset screamed as he jumped from his throne. "That, my dear lady, is never going to happen! You see how corrupt humans can get when they fall in love. Just think if a jealous warrior falls in love! Think about his powers in a jealous rage!"

"If you bonded the two souls, there wouldn't be a problem."

"Bonding? What kind of foolishness is that?"

Salene lifted her shoulders and turned around. "Good-bye, Crset."

She started walking to the door, swaying her hips, making Crset burn even more. He wanted her. He could already feel her underneath him. "Wait!"

She did. Salene peeked over her shoulders and fluttered her eyes lashes. "What?" she asked seductively.

"Fine. I let them have this moronic notion about bonding, but I need to time to convince the Gods to allow this."

"And you'll give Jack back to Kaleigh?"

"Yes, yes, yes," he said angrily, cursing his own lust. "I will give Jack back to Kaleigh as good as new with his powers intact."

"I'm extremely happy!" she said purring. "But when you give them make sure they are totally, to die for in love with each other."

He didn't want to discuss this anymore. She was going to let him fuck her anytime he wanted and now they were wasting valuable time.

"I have to convince the gods first, which I'm sure they won't decline. Right now go to my chambers and wait for me in my bed."

"Uh, Crset, if the gods do happen to decline, you'll only have me when you let go of Jack."

"I know, Salene."

She started to leave again and then stopped, turned around and frowned at him. "Why are you so eager to agree? I thought you wanted your guardians emotionless."

He did, but it was getting quite boring watching them all turned into humans, and leaving his army unfilled. He needed more guardians now than ever and if they were human they couldn't breed anymore. And he was longer responsible destroying the guardian hunters anymore and that left a ton of time on his hands. What better way to fill his free time with the woman he always wanted while getting involved with his guardians' lives.

It was going to be quite fun until he got bored again. Then what?

Crset didn't care at the moment. He had one thing on his mind and she was standing ten feet away from him.

"Let's just say, it'll be an adventure together."

When Salene left, Crset waited until she was down to Earth and then turned towards the marble stairs. They were useless to him, but he loved the appearance of the hard granite. He flashed himself outside of Jack's room and entered without knocking.

Jack stirred when he felt the warmth touch his skin. His eyes came open and saw the tallest and the most powerfully built man he ever seen in his life standing over him with a blank face. He made Sebastian look like Mr. Blanchard, but the strict opposite of Mr. Blanchard. Jack had to say this man was darkly handsome.

The room was decorated in navy blue and black and about as large as Jack's entire apartment. There were no windows or doors that he could see pass the stranger and a soft melody music filter through the room. It made him relax about being in the unknown. Not something one would expect to see in the afterlife of heaven or hell.

"I see that you are finally awake. My condolences for not waking you sooner, I know how badly you want to get back, but I was in a very important business deal that couldn't wait any longer. How are you feeling?"

"Who are you?" Jack asked, ignoring his question because the stranger was more important than his well-being and found his voice scratchy.

The man above him laughed. "My name is Crset. I'm awfully glad, Jack, that you succeeded in your mission."

Kaleigh, his voice screamed like a siren.

"Kaleigh passed her mission with flying colors and is doing fine. Saddened by your sudden loss, but she can physically continue with life and Sebastian is doing splendidly as well. Oh, before you ask, you are not dead. It's rare when I give out apologies, but please accept mine that I didn't mean to destroy you."

"What?" If Jack had the strength he would have shot up from the bed. But his body felt like he was thrown into a brick wall and then stomped on by a large animal.

"What is it with you guardians that I have to constantly repeat myself? I said I never meant to destroy you, but some things got out of control. I quickly saved your soul before Death could take it." Crset rolled his eyes. "Talking about a struggle there."

"You mean I was never to—"

"Die? No! I know I sent you the visions of dying, but I would never intentionally kill one of my guardians! They are too important to the world to be sacrificing them. There aren't many of them left as it is. And yes you can go back to Kaleigh."

"Will you stop doing that and let me speak? What the hell are you," Jack asked before Crset could read his mind.

"First and foremost, I am not a god. I'm just a wandering entity that got stuck here and is doing my best to help balance the world with the other gods."

Jack was silent for a moment as his mind ran blank. "You are our maker?"

"I'm the maker of the guardians and do not ask anymore questions about me because they will not be answered. Of course by the time you leave here, you will never remember meeting me and so I guess it doesn't really make a difference what you ask about me."

"When can I see Kaleigh?"

Before Jack knew it, he was standing on his own two feet, dressed in the same clothes he wore battling the guardian hunter, standing in an opulent room with a pure white marble floor and rich silk drapes blowing aimlessly by the unseen force.

"Where are we," Jack whispered as he realized that his strength was back in his spirit.

Crset was standing beside him, silently brooding to himself. Jack got the distinct impression that it had nothing to do with him, but about the man's own personal problems.

"A room that leads you to Kaleigh," Crset said as he touched Jack's shoulder and seriously, "Click your heels three times and say there is no place like home."

Jack unexpectedly laughed. "Does that really work?"

"No, I just wanted to see if you were really going to do it. I guess you're not a fool. Just close your eyes and think about where you want to be."

Jack closed his eyes.

Crset entered his chambers and found Salene sprawled on her stomach underneath his silk coverlet. He smiled greedily to himself and admired her in a peace he hadn't felt in centuries.

"Are you ready?" he asked in his ancient voice.

Salene jerked up and gasped. "Where's Crset?"

His smiled broadened as he stretched out his arms and presented himself. "This is me; I'm in my true body."

Her eyes widened and sparkled with carnal lust and then Crset strolled to the bed.

Kaleigh was just leaving for the day when Adrian knocked on her office door. "Come in," she said.

It had been over a month since the chaos of the woods. Mayor Devin McChandey's secret pastime was exposed, his men were sent to prison, and Susan's body was found buried underneath where she lay as Jack left her life. Susan's burial was very nice from what she heard. Kaleigh was too depressed to leave her apartment, but when she had to get over her depression and take proper care of Jack's baby growing inside of her womb, the first place she visited was Susan's grave site.

She hadn't spoken to anyone about Jack's death and had hardly talked to anyone since then. Adrian let her have as much time she needed to grieve, but after the first week of blindly living from day to day, she was ready to go back to work. She hadn't spoken to her mother since their last departure or talked to Sebastian since he left her lying in her cold, lonely bed. He called once, leaving a message on her answering machine about her state of grieving.

She didn't call him back.

When she came back to work, she functioned normally, like the rest of the employees, but detached herself away from everyone. She connected with the pure souls as they traveled the world defeating the guardian hunters. She would, too, as soon as they said it was her time.

Adrian was really the only one that she associated with, and that was mindless conversation about his son's recovery or when they passed each other in the hall or rode the elevator together.

It was a few days after Jack's death when Salene, the leader of the pure souls paid her visit one night as she was crying herself to sleep. Kaleigh's met her several times before and always had the same fixation on her beauty. She was the most beautiful woman she'd ever seen in her life and was still mesmerized when Salene sat next to her and held their hands together.

"We are proud of you, Kaleigh. I know you may hate us for what we made you do, but there was no other option. We had to make sure that you had every innovation to defeat a guardian hunter. They are very powerful and now you see why it takes all seven of us to defeat just one."

"I know," Kaleigh said through her sobs. "I just never thought it was going to be this hard without him."

"Jack was a wonderful guardian," Salene said sympathetically. "We chose him because his parents loved each other so dearly, that we wanted him to have that chance to feel what his parents had."

"Yes, but he had to die for it!"

Salene cupped her face and erased the tears spreading down her face as she smiled down into Kaleigh's eyes. "Sometimes, love can be funny. To achieve it, you have to do things you wouldn't normally do for others. You opened your heart to Jack, which you were forbidden to do, and he died for you so we can all be safe."

"I understand, but why does love have to hurt so much? I was never allowed to see his death to prepare for this kind of emotion."

"What did you say?" Salene asked very slowly as she tilted her head up to meet her eyes. "What are you talking about?"

"I…I thought you knew that I can see anyone's death if they are connected with me."

"That isn't possible," Salene said as she pushed away from Kaleigh. "I've never heard such a thing in my life."

"Do you think it may have been from my father?" Kaleigh asked.

Salene shook their heads. "No. Your father was a human and no human carries that kind of supremacy. I don't know how you are able to see the humans' death, but it will be something that will need to be asked to our maker."

"And who is that?" Kaleigh asked. "No one knows who he or she is."

Salene was silent for a long time, thinking as to object the pure soul's comment. "A very powerful being that you are not allowed to associate with."

Kaleigh pushed herself against the headboard of her bed and folded her arms under her breasts. "You've met him?"

Again, Salene was silent for a long time that Kaleigh thought she was in a trance and then she forgot what they were talking about. Kaleigh shook her head and for the life of her she couldn't remember anything after they spoken about her strange powers. "Salene?"

"We will find out why you can see these deaths. It does raise some questions about who your real father is."

Kaleigh's thoughts broke when Adrian stepped through her office and shut the door behind him. "Are you about to leave?"

"Yes. Why?"

"I need you to have this employee I just hired today fill out his papers so he can begin working for me tomorrow morning," Adrian said.

"It's almost five o'clock. Can't you tell him to fill out his papers in the morning? I have to go home," she said as she stuffed documents into her briefcase.

"It will only take a few minutes. I would wait myself, but I'm pressed for time. Radella has some dinner guest arriving and I promised her I would be on time."

Kaleigh dropped her briefcase on her desk and slumped in her seat. "Let him come in," she said with weariness.

As Adrian left her office, she plopped her elbows on the desk and rested her chin in the palms of her hands. She was so damn tired that she could fall asleep right here. It sounded like an excellent—

"You're not going to sleep on me, are you? After all, I just got here. I would hate not to see your eyes."

Kaleigh's head snapped up so fast that she almost fell out of her chair. All the air left her body and her heart slammed against her chest. Her knees went weak and her brain was incapable of making any coherent sentences.

She just stared at Jack with her mouth gaped opened. How? He was dead! This isn't happening all over again. This couldn't…

"Kaleigh, what are you thinking about?"

She could sense now that her powers were fully intact, that Jack wasn't a demon. He was her protector, her sorcerer, and her Jack in the flesh. He was still all-powerful looking and so handsome that it was hard for her to breathe.

"Why…are you here?" she stammered.

He smiled and Kaleigh's heart melted away. She had to hold onto the desk to keep from falling or fainting.

She had missed him so much over the past month. Why did they send him back? They weren't playing some cruel joke on her just to see him for only a minute were they? If they did, they were going to have one scorned lady on their hands.

"I'm here because they let me come back to you."

"Who?"

"The pure souls," he said with another smile. "They said you haven't been too happy and you needed me. If you don't believe, you can ask them."

"I believe you," she said quickly. "I just thought…"

"The power of our maker exceeds all. No more will I have to make sacrifices as I had to do for the fate of the world."

"You've met…it?" she asked slowly.

"No, but a pure soul gave me some enlightenment that's going to help rebuild our—," his words were cut off as Kaleigh threw her arms around his neck and kissed his face all over.

Kaleigh couldn't take it anymore standing so far away from him. She had to make sure he was for real. She had to be in his arms or she was going to die.

"It took you long enough," Jack laughed, and then capturing her mouth and kissed her.

"Oh, Jack," Kaleigh cried. "I was so alone. I don't care how you got back or why they let you come back as long as you are here with me!"

Jack wrapped one arm around her waist and slid the after to her stomach. "They sent me back for you and for our child," he whispered in her ears. "And I promise you, Kaleigh, I'll spend the rest of my life making you and our family happy."

"All you have to do is love me."

"And I do, Kaleigh," Jack said. "I do."

Epilogue

He laid his hand over her smooth belly and grinned. Soon, Jack thought as the waves of the warm splashing beach water sprayed over their bare feet. Soon her belly would be swollen with his child and they—together—could have that dream that was always out of reach for them.

They lay under the sunset of the dying day, wrapped in each other's arms as it was always meant to be. Kaleigh's rested on Jack's shoulder with her fingers stroking through his wet hair and beaming with such happiness that she hoped it never faded.

When Jack arrived in her office, they spent the next week in bed, loving each other with their hearts and their souls, joining in a bond that was unbreakable as the devotion of the guardians' reverent faith to destroy demons. It was rapture only few guardians in five thousands years have felt and they were among those few. Soon, soon they, too, would start to feel the inexplicable feeling of a bonding love that would have them weakened in the knees and willing to die desperately to feel the wanton passion that their mate would bring them.

Then they would all know what it would feel like to be a sacrifice for the only person they could ever love.

Kaleigh couldn't wait until the soul mate rituals began and could scarcely contain the little secret that only she, Jack, and Salene held dear to their hearts. She smiled.

"Is that smile for me?" Jack asked.

She sighed against his flesh and then kissed his shoulders. They took their little vacation away from the world at Richardson Beach in Hawaii when the rituals were completed. It felt so good to get away from everyone that it was a shame they had to go back in a few days. Jack would continue his private investigation business along with his new partner—Sebastian Ames, and she would continue her employment at Walker's Security as they would stalk the night destroying demons.

"Yes," she said rising to her elbows, planting a soft butterfly kiss on his lips and his arms came around her, pulling her completely on top of him. He ran his hands down her spine and brought them back and cupped her face to kiss her more deeply.

"I love you," he whispered against her lips. "I love you so much it hurts."

Her smile was huge as tears glistened in her eyes. "I want to tell you something."

"Yeah," Jack said.

Kaleigh licked her lips and Jack's body hardened. He wanted to take her right here on the beach as he did yesterday morning when no one was around. A few people were still coasting along and so he had to wait until it was private for the two of them.

"Well, do you want to know?"

"Now who's talking in riddles?"

"If it's a boy or a girl?" Kaleigh said with a laugh.

Jack already knew from the energy he was getting from her womb and every time they made love. He didn't want to spoil her moment. "Sure, tell me."

"I'm having a girl and guess what."

"What?"

"It's going to be a pure soul."

That he didn't know. He stood up quickly, bringing Kaleigh in his arms and twirling her in the sand, kissing her with all the love his heart and soul.

"My god! This is incredible!" He shouted with pure delight.

"I know. But there's more," she said with a frown.

Jack stopped and put her back on her feet, taking in a deep breath from the bad news. "More?" He could barely get the words out.

"She's not going to be alone."

He took a step back. What was she trying to say to him? Was this good news or bad news? Then her face broadened with a beautiful smile as tears began to slide on her face. Jack reached for her and held her in his arms. She wasn't going to be alone. His daughter wasn't going to be alone! They were having twins! Both pure souls! How could they be so blessed?

Kaleigh curled her fingers in his shoulders and kissed his neck. "She's going to be a twin and he's going to look just like you."

Jack choked. "He?"

"Yes and they are both going to be pure souls."

His emotions burst. The good news was overwhelming and for the first time in Jack's life, he knelt to his knees, wrapped his hands around her waist, and wept.

Printed in the United States
91988LV00009B/131/A